At Large by E. W. Hornung

Ernest William Hornung was born in Middlesbrough, England on 7th June 1866, the third son and youngest of eight children.

Although spending most of his life in England and France he spent two years in Australia from 1884 and that experience was to colour and influence much of his written works.

His most famous character A. J. Raffles, 'the gentleman thief', was published first in Cassell's Magazine during 1898 and was to make him famous across the world as the new century dawned.

Hornung also wrote several stage plays and was a gifted poet.

Spending time with the troops in WWI he published Notes of a Camp-Follower on the Western Front during 1919, a detailed account of his time there. This was especially close to his heart as his son, and only child, was killed at the Second Battle of Ypres on 6th July 1915.

Ernest William Hornung died in Saint-Jean-de-Luz, in the south of France on 22nd March 1921.

Index of Contents

CHAPTER I

A NUCLEUS OF FORTUNE

A hooded wagon was creeping across a depressing desert in the middle of Australia; layers of boxes under the hood, and of brass-handled, mahogany drawers below the boxes, revealed the licensed hawker of the bush. Now, the hawker out there is a very extensive development of his prototype here at home; he is Westbourne Grove on wheels, with the prices of Piccadilly, W. But these particular providers were neither so universal nor so exorbitant as the generality of their class. There were but two of them; they drove but two horses; and sat shoulder to shoulder on the box.

The afternoon was late; all day the horses had been crawling, for the track was unusually heavy. There had been recent rains; red mud clogged the wheels at every yard, and clung to them in sticky tires. Little pools had formed all over the plain; and westward, on the off-side of the wagon, these pools caught the glow of the setting sun, and filled with flame. Far over the horses' ears a long low line of trees was visible; otherwise the plain was unbroken; you might ride all day on these plains and descry no other horse nor man.

The pair upon the box were partners. Their names were Flint and Edmonstone. Flint was enjoying a senior partner's prerogative, and lolling back wreathed in smoke. His thick bare arms were idly folded. He was a stout, brown, bearded man, who at thirty looked many years older; indolence, contentment, and goodwill were written upon his face.

The junior partner was driving, and taking some pains about it—keeping clear of the deep ruts, and pushing the pace only where the track was good. He looked twenty years Flint's junior, and was, in fact, just of age. He was strongly built and five-feet-ten, with honest gray eyes, fair hair, and an inelastic mouth.

Both of these men wore flannel shirts, buff cord trousers, gray felt wideawakes; both were public-school men, drawn together in the first instance by that mutually surprising fact, and for the rest as different as friends could be. Flint had been ten years in the Colonies, Edmonstone not quite ten weeks. Flint had tried everything, and failed; Edmonstone had everything before him, and did not mean to fail. Flint was experienced, Edmonstone sanguine; things surprised Edmonstone, nothing surprised Flint. Edmonstone had dreams of the future, and golden dreams; Flint troubled only about the present, and that very little. In fine, while Edmonstone saw licensed hawking leading them both by a short cut to fortune, and earnestly intended that it should, Flint said they would be lucky if their second trip was as successful as their first, now all but come to an end.

The shadow of horses and wagon wavered upon the undulating plain as they drove. The shadows grew longer and longer; there was a noticeable change in them whenever young Edmonstone bent forward to gaze at the sun away to the right, and then across at the eastern sky already tinged with purple; and that was every five minutes.

"It will be dark in less than an hour," the lad exclaimed at last, in his quick, anxious way; "dark just as we reach the scrub; we shall have no moon until eleven or so, and very likely not strike the river to-night."

The sentences were punctuated with sharp cracks of the whip. An answer came from Edmonstone's left, in the mild falsetto that contrasted so queerly with the bodily bulk of Mr. John Flint, and startled all who heard him speak for the first time.

"My good fellow, I implore you again to spare the horseflesh and the whipcord—both important items— and take it easy like me."

"Jack," replied Edmonstone warmly, "you know well enough why I want to get to the Murrumbidgee to-night. No? Well, at all events, you own that we should lose no time about getting to some bank or other?"

"Yes, on the whole. But I don't see the good of hurrying on now to reach the township at an unearthly hour, when all the time we might camp in comfort anywhere here. To my mind, a few hours, or even a night or two, more or less—"

"Are neither here nor there? Exactly!" broke in Edmonstone, with increasing warmth. "Jack, Jack! the days those very words cost us! Add them up—subtract them from the time we've been on the roads— and we'd have been back a week ago at least. I shall have no peace of mind until I step out of the bank, and that's the truth of it." As he spoke, the fingers of Edmonstone's right hand rested for a moment, with a curious, involuntary movement, upon his right breast.

"I can see that," returned Flint, serenely. "The burden of riches, you see—and young blood! When you've been out here as long as I have, you'll take things easier, my son."

"You don't understand my position," said Edmonstone. "You laugh when I tell you I came out here to make money: all the same, I mean to do it. I own I had rotten ideas about Australia—all new chums have. But if I can't peg out my claim and pick up nuggets, I'm going to do the next best thing. It may be hawking and it may not. I mean to see. But we must give the thing a chance, and not run unnecessary risks with the gross proceeds of our very first trip. A hundred and thirty pounds isn't a fortune; but it may be the nucleus of one; and it's all we've got between us in this world meanwhile."

"My dear old boy, I'm fully alive to it. I only don't see the point of finishing the trip at a gallop."

"The point is that our little all is concealed about my person," said Edmonstone, grimly.

"And my point is that it and we are absolutely safe. How many more times am I to tell you so?" And there was a squeak of impatience in the absurd falsetto voice, followed by clouds of smoke from the bearded lips.

Edmonstone drove some distance without a word.

"Yet only last week," he remarked at length, "a store was stuck up on the Darling!"

"What of that?"

"The storekeeper was robbed of every cent he had."

"I know."

"Yet they shot him dead in the end."

"And they'll swing for it."

"Meanwhile they've shown clean heels, and nobody knows where they are—or are not."

"Consequently you expect to find them waiting for us in the next clump, eh?"

"No, I don't. I only deny that we are absolutely safe."

Flint knocked out his pipe with sudden energy.

"My dear boy," cried he, "have I or have I not been as many years out here as you've been weeks? I tell you I was in the mounted police, down in Vic, all through the Kelly business; joined in the hunt myself; and back myself to know a real bushranger when I see him or read about him. This fellow who has the cheek to call himself Sundown is not a bushranger at all; he and his mates are mere robbers and murderers. Ned Kelly didn't go shooting miserable storekeepers; and he was the last of the bushrangers, and is likely to remain the last. Besides, these chaps will streak up-country, not down; but, if it's any comfort to you, see here," and Flint pocketed his pipe, made a long arm overhead and reached a Colt's revolver from a hook just inside the hood of the wagon, "let this little plaything reassure you. What, didn't you know I was a dead shot with this? My dear chap, I wasn't in the mounted police for nothing. Why, I could pick out your front teeth at thirty yards and paint my name on your waistcoat at twenty!"

Flint stroked the glittering barrel caressingly, and restored the pistol to its hook: there was a cartridge in every chamber.

The other said nothing for a time, but was more in earnest than ever when he did speak.

"Jack," said he, "I can only tell you this: if we were to lose our money straight away at the outset I should be a lost man. How could we go on without it—hawking with an empty wagon? How could I push, push, push—as I've got to—after losing all to start with? A hundred pounds! It isn't much, but it is everything to me—everything. Let me only keep it a bit and it shall grow under my eyes. Take it away from me and I am done for—completely done for."

He forgot that he was using the first person singular instead of plural; it had become natural to him to think out the business and its possibilities in this way, and it was no less in Flint's nature to see no selfishness in his friend's speech. Flint only said solemnly:

"You shouldn't think so much about money, old chap."

"Money and home!" exclaimed Dick Edmonstone in a low, excited tone. "Home and money! It's almost all I do think about."

Jack Flint leaned forward, and narrowly scanned the face of his friend; then lay back again, with a light laugh of forced cheerfulness.

"Why, Dick, you speak as though you had been exiled for years, and it's not three months since you landed."

Dick started. It already seemed years to him.

"Besides," continued the elder man, "I protest against any man growing morbid who can show a balance-sheet like ours. As to home-sickness, wait until you have been out here ten years; wait until you have tried digging, selecting, farming, droving; wait until you have worn a trooper's uniform and a counter jumper's apron, and ridden the boundaries at a pound a week, and tutored Young Australia for your rations. When you have tried all these things—and done no good at any of 'em, mark you—then, if you like, turn home-sick."

The other did not answer. Leaning forward, he whipped up the horses, and gazed once more towards the setting sun. His companion could not see his face; but trouble and anxiety were in that long, steady, westward gaze. He was very young, this lad Edmonstone—young even for his years. Unlike his mate, his thoughts were all of the past and of the future; both presented happy pictures; so happy that his mind would fly from the one to the other without touching the present. And so he thought now, gazing westward, of home, and of something sweeter than home itself; and he blended that which had gone before with that which was yet to come; and so wonderful was the harmony between these two that to-day was entirely forgotten. Then the sun swung half-way below the dark line of the horizon; a golden pathway shone across the sandy track right to the wheels of the wagon; the dark line of scrub, now close at hand, looked shadowy and mysterious; the sunset colours declared themselves finally in orange and pink and gray, before the spreading purple caught and swallowed them. The dreamer's face grew indistinct, but his golden dreams were more vivid than before.

A deadly stillness enveloped the plain, making all sounds staccato: the rhythmical footfall of the horses, the hoarse notes of crows wheeling through the twilight like uncanny heralds of night, the croaking of crickets in the scrub ahead.

Dick was recalled to the antipodes by a mild query from his mate.

"Are you asleep, driver?"

"No."

"You haven't noticed any one ahead of us this afternoon on horseback?"

"No; why?"

"Because here are some one's tracks," said Flint, pointing to a fresh horse-trail on the side of the road.

Edmonstone stretched across to look. It was difficult in the dusk to distinguish the trail, which was the simple one of a horse walking.

"I saw no one," he said; "but during the last hour it would have been impossible to see any one, as close to the scrub as we are now. Whoever it is, he must have struck the track hereabouts somewhere, or we should have seen his trail before sundown."

"Whoever it is," said Flint, "we shall see him in a minute. Don't you hear him? He is still at a walk."

Edmonstone listened, and the measured beat of hoofs grew upon his ear; another moment and a horseman's back was looming through the dusk—very broad and round, with only the crown of a wideawake showing above the shoulders. As the wagon drew abreast his horse was wheeled to one side, and a hearty voice hailed the hawkers:

"Got a match, mateys? I've used my last, and I'm just weakening for a smoke."

"Here's my box," said Dick, pulling up. "Take as many as you like."

And he dropped his match-box into a great fat hand with a wrist like a ship's cable, and strong stumpy fingers: it was not returned until a loaded pipe was satisfactorily alight; and as the tobacco glowed in the bowl the man's face glowed in company. It was huge like himself, and bearded to the eyes, which were singularly small and bright, and set very close together.

"I don't like that face," said Dick when the fellow had thanked him with redoubled heartiness, and ridden on.

"It looked good-natured."

"It was and it wasn't. I don't want to see it again; but I shall know it if ever I do. I had as good a look at him as he had at us."

Flint made no reply; they entered the forest of low-sized malee and pine in silence.

"Jack," gasped Edmonstone, very suddenly, after half-an-hour, "there's some one galloping in the scrub somewhere—can't you hear?"

"Eh?" said Flint, waking from a doze.

"Some one's galloping in the scrub—can't you hear the branches breaking? Listen."

"I hear nothing."

"Listen again."

Flint listened intently.

"Yes—no. I thought for an instant—but no, there is no sound now."

He was right: there was no sound then, and he was somewhat ruffled.

"What are you giving us, Dick? If you will push on, why, let's do it; only we do one thing or the other."

Dick whipped up the horses without a word. For five minutes they trotted on gamely; then, without warning, they leaped to one side with a shy that half-overturned the wagon.

Side by side, and motionless in the starlight, sat two shadowy forms on horseback, armed with rifles, and masked to the chin.

"Hands up," cried one of them, "or we plug."

CHAPTER II

SUNDOWN

There was no time for thought, much less for action, beyond that taken promptly by Flint, who shot his own hands above his head without a moment's hesitation, and whispered to Dick to do the same. Any other movement would have been tantamount to suicide. Yet it was with his eyes open and his head cool that Flint gave the sign of submission.

The horsemen sat dark and motionless as the trees of the sleeping forest around them. They were contemplating the completeness of their triumph, grinning behind their masks.

Flint saw his chance. Slowly, very slowly, his left arm, reared rigidly above his head, swayed backward; his body moved gently with his arm; his eyes never left the two mysterious mounted men.

He felt his middle finger crowned by a cool ring. It was the muzzle of his precious Colt. One grasp, and at least he would be armed.

He turned his wrist for the snatch, gazing steadily all the while at the two vague shadows of men. Another second—and a barrel winked in the starlight, to gleam steadily as it covered Flint's broad chest. He who had called upon them to throw up their hands spoke again; his voice seemed to come from the muzzle of the levelled rifle.

"Stretch an inch more, you on the near-side, and you're the last dead man."

Flint shrugged his shoulders. The game was lost. There was no more need to lose his head than if the game had been won. There was no need at all to lose his life.

"I give you best," said he, without the least emotion in his extraordinary voice.

"Fold your arms and come down," said the man with the rifle, his finger on the trigger.

Flint did as he was ordered.

"The same—you with the reins."

Edmonstone's only answer was a stupefied stare.

"Jump down, my friend, unless you want helping with this."

Dick obeyed apathetically; he was literally dazed. At a sign from the man with the rifle he took his stand beside Flint; three paces in front of the luckless pair shone the short barrel of the Winchester repeater. The other robber had dismounted, and was standing at the horses' heads.

In this position, a moment's silence fell upon the four men, to be broken by the coarse, grating laughter of a fifth. Edmonstone turned his head, saw another horseman issuing from the trees, and at once recognised the burly figure of the traveller who had borrowed his match-box less than an hour before. At that moment, and not until then, Dick Edmonstone realised the situation. It was desperate; all was lost! The lad's brain spun like a top: reason fled from it; his hand clutched nervously at the pocket where the money was, and he swore in his heart that if that went, his life might go with it.

In another instant the hairy ruffian had ridden his horse close up to Edmonstone, whipped his foot from the stirrup, and kicked the youngster playfully in the chest—on that very spot which his thoughtless gesture had betrayed.

At this the other bushrangers set up a laugh—a short one.

With a spring like a young leopard, Dick Edmonstone had the big horseman by the beard, and down they came to the ground together. There, in the sand, they rolled over each other, locked in mortal combat—writhing, leaping, twisting, shifting—so that the leader of the band, though he pointed his rifle at the struggling men, dared not fire, for fear of hitting the wrong one. But there came a moment when the struggling ceased, when Flint sprang forward with a hoarse cry on his lips and Sundown took careless aim with the Winchester.

Dick Edmonstone was lying on his back with white, upturned face. Two crushing weights pinned down each arm below the shoulder; his adversary was kneeling on him with grinding teeth and a frightful face, and one hand busy at his belt. His hand flew up with a gleam. It was at that moment that the man with the rifle raised it and fired.

The bearded ruffian shook his hand as though hit, and the haft of a knife slipped from it; the bullet had carried away the blade. With a curse he felt for his revolver.

"Don't be a fool, Jem Pound," said the marksman quietly, lowering his smoking piece. "Before you bring the lot of us to the gallows, I'll put a bullet through your own fat head. Get up, you big fool! Cut the mokes adrift, and turn everything out of the wagon."

The man Pound rose sulkily, with a curious last look at the young Englishman's throat, and hell-fire in his little eyes.

"Ben, watch this cove," the chief went on, pointing to Flint, "and watch him with the shooter. I'll see to the youngster myself. Come here, my friend."

The speaker was plainly no other than the rascal who called himself Sundown; the hawkers heard the sobriquet on the lips of the other masked man, and their glances met. He was wrapped in a cloak that hid him from head to heels, stooped as he walked, and was amply masked. What struck Flint—who was sufficiently cool to remain an attentive observer—was the absence of vulgar bluster about this fellow; he addressed confederates and captives alike in the same quiet, decisive tones, without either raising his voice to a shout or filling the air with oaths. It appeared that Ned Kelly had not been the last of the real bushrangers, after all.

"You come along with me," said he, quietly; and drew Dick aside, pointing at him the rifle, which he grasped across the breech, with a finger still upon the trigger.

"Now," continued Sundown, when they had withdrawn a few yards into the scrub, "turn out that pocket." He tapped Edmonstone on the chest with the muzzle of the rifle.

Dick folded his arms and took a short step backward.

"Shoot me!" he exclaimed, looking the robber full in the face. "Why did you save me a minute ago? I prefer to die. Shoot me, and have done with it."

"Open your coat," said the bushranger.

Edmonstone tore open not only his coat, but his shirt as well, thus baring his chest.

"There. Shoot!" he repeated hoarsely.

Sundown stared at the boy with a moment's curiosity, but paid no heed to his words.

"Empty that pocket."

Dick took out the pocket-book that contained all the funds of the firm.

"Open it."

Dick obeyed.

"How much is in it?"

"A hundred and thirty pounds."

"Good! Cheques!"

"More notes."

The robber laughed consumedly.

"Take them, if you are going to," said Dick, drawing a deep breath.

Sundown did take them—pocket-book and all—still covering his man with the rifle. The moon was rising. In the pale light the young fellow's face was ghastly to look upon; it had the damp pallor of death itself. The bushranger eyed it closely, and half-dropped the bushranger's manner.

"New chum, I take it!"

"What of that?" returned Dick bitterly.

"And not long set up shop?"

Dick made no answer. Sundown stepped forward and gripped his shoulder.

"Say, mate, is this hundred and odd quid so very much to you?"

Still no answer.

"On oath, now: is it so very much?"

Dick looked up wildly.

"Much? It is everything. You have robbed me of all I have! You have saved my life when I'd as soon lose it with my money. Yes, it's all I have in the world, since you want to know! Do you want to madden me, you cur? Shoot me—shoot, I tell you. If you don't I'll make you!" And the young madman clenched his fist as he spoke.

That instant he felt himself seized by the neck and pushed forward, with a ring of cold steel pressing below his ear.

"Here you—Jem Pound—have your revenge and bind this cub. Bind tight, but fair, for I'm watching you."

In five minutes the blood would scarcely circulate in a dozen different parts of Edmonstone's body; he was bound as tightly as vindictive villain could bind him, to the off hind-wheel of his own wagon. Sundown stood by with the rifle, and saw it done.

Flint had already been bound to the near hind-wheel, so that the partners were lashed back to back—both able to watch their property looted at the rear of the wagon, but unable to exchange glances.

Sundown strolled about during the operation, which his subordinates conducted with deepening disgust, till he returned and asked what they had got.

"Precious little," was the answer. "Stock sold out—boxes mostly empty."

Nevertheless some few varieties of bush merchandise strewed the ground, and hats, boots, and pipes were quickly selected by Jem Pound and the man addressed as Ben; though as for Sundown, he seemed content with a supply of smoking materials, and, indeed, to be more or less preoccupied while the plunder went forward. At length, at a word from him, the other men mounted their horses, while their leader walked round to where Flint was spread-eagled against the wheel.

"Is there anything you want before we go?" the bushranger inquired, as civilly as you please.

"Yes," said Flint; "I want you to fill my pipe, stick it in my mouth, and put a match to it, if you will be so good."

The other laughed, but complied with the full request before turning his attention to young Edmonstone.

"As for you," he said, "here's your pocket-book. I couldn't take such a treasure from you. Better keep it in memory of the fortune (the immense fortune of a hundred and thirty pounds) it once contained. Not that I have quite emptied it, though; I may be a devil, but I never clean a man out quite; so you'll find enough left to get you a night's lodging and some tucker. And—and don't forget old Sundown altogether; you may be able to put in a good word for him some day!"

These last words, though spoken after a pause, were thrown off lightly enough; yet somehow they were unlike the rest that had gone before. Before their sound had died away Sundown was in his saddle, and the sound of horses galloping through the scrub was growing faint and far away.

Flint was the first to free himself. It took him hours. His teeth ached, his fingers bled, before the last knot that bound his hands was undone. His knife quickly did the rest.

He went straight to Edmonstone, who had not spoken since the gang decamped. Flint found him pale and cold, with a very hard expression upon his face. Dick allowed himself to be set free without a word—without so much as an intelligent glance.

The horses could be heard munching bits of bushes close at hand. They were easily caught. Nor was it a difficult task to a ready-handed fellow like Flint to splice the traces, which the bushrangers had cut.

The crestfallen partners were on the point of reentering the wagon, when Flint saw the pocket-book lying where it had been dropped.

"Better take it," said Flint sorrowfully.

In utter apathy Dick picked it up.

"Wouldn't you see if they've cleaned it entirely?" suggested Flint.

With listless fingers Edmonstone withdrew the elastic and opened the pocket-book.

By this time the moon had mounted high in the clear southern sky; by her pure white rays they might have read small print. Flint's heart smote him; it was by his doing they had carried so many notes, through a fad of his about opening their banking account with hard cash; at cheques the bushrangers might easily have turned up their noses, as bushrangers had done before. But now, as it was—poor, poor young devil!

A cry broke the silence, and rang out loud and wild upon the still night air. It came from Flint's side. He turned to find his companion tottering and trembling.

Dick Edmonstone had dropped the pocket-book, and was nervously counting a roll of crisp, crackling papers.

"They are all here!—all! all!" he whispered in a strange, broken voice.

"Never!"

"Yes, all—all! Only think of it; our fortune is not lost, after all—it's made—the key to it is in my hand again! Jack, the fellow had pity on me. No, I mean on us. I don't mean to be selfish, Jack; it's share and share alike, between you and me, and always will be. But if you knew—if you knew! Jack, I'll put in that good word for him—I'll make it more than words, if ever I get the chance! For I do owe him something," said the poor fellow, carried away by reaction and excitement, so that his breaking voice trembled between sobs and laughter. "I do owe that Sundown something. God bless him—that's all I say."

But Flint said nothing at all; he was much too amazed for words.

CHAPTER III

AFTER FOUR YEARS

One chilly night in June, 1886, the ship Hesper, bound from Melbourne to London, sailed into the Channel. She carried the usual wool cargo and twenty saloon passengers besides. When the Lizard light was sighted, the excitement—which had increased hourly since the Western Islands were left astern—knew no reasonable bounds. For the Hesper was a hundred and eight days out; and among her passengers were grizzled Colonists, to whom this light was the first glimmer of England for thirty years; men who had found in the Colonial Exhibition at South Kensington an excuse to intrust vast flocks and herds to the hands of overseers, and to consummate that darling scheme of every prosperous Colonial, which they render by their phrase "a trip home." Sweepstakes on the date of sighting England, got up in the tropics, were now promptly settled; quarrels begun in the Southern Ocean were made up in the magic element of British waters; discontent was in irons, and joy held the ship. Far into the middle-watch festive souls perambulated the quarter-deck with noisy expressions of mirth, though with the conviction that the vessel was behaving badly; whereas the vessel was a good deal more innocent of that charge than the gentlemen who preferred it. But even when the last of these roysterers retired there was still one passenger left on the poop.

A young man leaned with folded arms upon the port rail, staring out into the night. It seemed as though his eye penetrated the darkness, and found something bright beyond, so wistful was its gaze. One bell rang out from the forecastle, two bells followed half an hour later at one o'clock, but the figure of this dreamer remained motionless. For an hour he did not stir; but, as his imagination became more vivid, the expression of his eyes grew softer, until their yearning melted into a thin, thin film, and the firm lines of the mouth relaxed, and facial creases carved by a few hard years were smoothed away. He was only a few hours ahead of the Hesper after all: she was off the Cornish coast, and he (in fancy) far up the Thames.

Three-bells aroused the dreamer. He stood upright with a start. He passed his hand quickly across his forehead, as if to rid his brain of weak thoughts. He began tramping the deck rapidly. Now the whole man was changed: his step was brisk, his frame instinct with nervous animation, his chest swelled proudly, his eyes sparkled with triumph. He had hung over the rail like any sentimental home-comer; he marched the deck like a conquering hero.

Yet this was one of the youngest men on board, and his years of absence from England were but a tithe of some of his fellow-passengers. During a long voyage the best and the worst of a man's character come out; but this man's display had been less complete than any one else's, and he was probably the better liked on board in consequence. Though reserved and quiet, he had, indeed without being conscious of it, become very popular. Perhaps one factor in this was the accidental discovery, half-way through the voyage, that he could draw uncommonly well; for it opened up a source of unexpected entertainment at a time when the stock amusements of the high seas had begun to flag. But there was one thing about him which, had his fellow-passengers suspected it, in all probability would have interfered considerably with his popularity: this was the astounding fact that at the age of twenty-five he had already made his fortune.

One scene from the bush life of this exceedingly lucky young gentleman has already been set forth. It will be sufficient to briefly glance at the remainder of his Colonial career, since details of unbroken success are voted a bore by common consent.

The firm of Flint and Edmonstone did well out of licensed hawking. Perhaps their honesty—which was as transparent as it was original in that line of business—had much to do with their success; for although squatters were at first sceptical of the new firm, their eyes were at once opened to the iniquitous prices of the Jews, who had hitherto enjoyed a monopoly of their custom. The newcomers thus gained experimental patronage, which they retained on their merits. After a year they advanced a step in the mercantile scale of the Colony: they set up a general store at a rising settlement on the Darling. The store had not been opened six months when the senior partner's chequered life in the Colonies was terminated in a manner utterly unforeseen. Word came that he had inherited, through an accommodating series of deaths, money and property in Ireland. It was no brilliant heritage, but it held out advantages greater on the whole than back-block storekeeping could be expected to afford. Withdrawing a temperate share of the profits, Mr. John Flint kicked the dust of the Riverina from his long boots, and finally disappeared from the face of the desert, and Edmonstone was left sole proprietor of a most promising "concern."

The luck that had hitherto attended him was soon to be enhanced; for, gold being discovered close to the little township on the Darling, a "rush" from all parts of Australia followed. As in most similar cases of late years, expectations were by no means realised on the new diggings. Still, people came, and the storekeeper was a made man.

A colonist of less than three years' standing, he joined three congenial spirits in the enterprise of stocking a station in the new Kimberley district of Western Australia. Here a huge success seemed certain in process of time; when, in the full tide of prosperity, with all he touched turning to gold beneath his fingers, with the lust of wealth upon him, there came a sudden revulsion of feeling. He realised that he had already amassed a fortune—small enough as fortunes go, but beyond his wildest hopes when quitting England. He saw that to go farther was to pursue wealth for wealth's sake—which was a rather lofty view of it; and that luck might not last for ever—which was shrewd; and that, with the sufficiency he had won, a rather better kind of existence was within reach. In short, he sickened of money-grubbing in a single night, and turned desperately home-sick instead; and, as it was not a game of cards, he was able, without incurring anything worse than compassion, to rise a winner. He determined to go home, invest his "pile," live on the interest, and—devote himself to art! He journeyed forthwith to Melbourne, and there succeeded in disposing of his share in the Kimberley station for a sum little short of five figures.

Dick Edmonstone was opposed to sensational methods, or he would have taken the first mail-steamer and dropped like a thunderbolt among his people in England, with his money in his pocket. Besides, an exceptional amount of experience crammed into four years had robbed him, among other things, of nearly (though not quite) all his boyish impetuosity. So he merely wrote two letters by the first mail to his mother and to a certain Colonel Bristo. Thereafter he took his passage by the clipper Hesper, then loading at Williamstown, and prepared for a period of reflection, anticipation, and well-earned rest.

Dick Edmonstone had altered a good deal during his four years in Australia. In the first place, the big boy had become a man, and a man who held up his head among other men; a man who had made his way by his own indomitable perseverance, and who thereby commanded your respect; a man of all-round ability in the opinion of his friends (and they were right); a man of the world in his own (and he was wrong). And all at twenty-five! The old tremendous enthusiasm had given place to a thoroughly sanguine temperament of lusty, reliant manhood. He was cooler now, no doubt, but his heart was still warm and his head still hot. Strangers took him for thirty. His manner was always independent, could be authoritative, and was in danger of becoming arrogant. This much, successful money-hunting had naturally brought about. But a generous disposition had saved him from downright selfishness through it all, and the talisman of a loyal, honest, ardent love had led him blameless through a wild and worldly life. And he was still young—young in many ways. His hopes and beliefs were still boundless; they had all come true so far. He had not found the world a fraud yet. On the contrary, he liked the world, which was natural; and thought he knew it, which did not follow because he happened to know some rough corners of it.

One curious characteristic of young Edmonstone as a public schoolman and a modern young Englishman was the entire absence in him of false pride. Though transported pretty directly from Cambridge to Australia, he had taken to retail trade (of a humble kind at that) with philosophical sang-froid. On leaving England he had asked himself, What was his chief object in going out? And he had answered, To make money and return. Did it matter how he made it, once out there? No. No manual toil need degrade him, no honest business put him to shame. In England it is different; but in her democratic Colonies her younger sons—whether from Poplar or from Eton—must take the work that offers, as they covet success. Dick Edmonstone jumped at his first opening; that it chanced to be in the licensed hawking line cost him hardly a pang.

Indeed, he looked back lovingly in his success on those early days, when all he possessed in the world was invested in that daring venture. He thought of the anxiety that consumed him at the time, and of Jack Flint's cooling influence; and whenever he thought of those days one episode rose paramount in his brain, obliterating other memories. That episode was the "sticking-up" of the wagon on the first trip by Sundown and his men, which must have meant his ruin but for the extraordinary behaviour of the bushranger with regard to the pocket-book and its contents. He did not forget that the bushranger had preserved his life as well as restored his money. And that hundred pounds actually turned out to be the nucleus of a fortune! Sundown—poor fellow—was captured; perhaps by this time hanged, or imprisoned for life. Just before the Hesper sailed, word of the outlaw's arrest in a remote district of Queensland was telegraphed from Brisbane. He had been heard of from time to time during the preceding years, but on the whole his gang had done less mischief and shed less blood than some of their predecessors. As for Dick, when he read of the capture he was downright sorry. It may be a passive order of kindness that refrains from robbing a man; yet Dick was so peculiarly constituted as to feel in secret more than a passing regret at the news.

But as the Hesper drew towards the Channel he thought less and less of the life he had left behind, and more and more of the life before him. He longed all day to feel the springy turf of England under foot once more; to have the scent of English flowers in his nostrils; to listen to English larks carolling out of sight in the fleecy clouds of an English sky. How green the fields would seem! How solid the houses, how venerable the villages, how historic the rivers of the Old World! And then how he longed to plunge into the trio he styled "his people"—his mother the widow, his brother the City clerk, his sister the saint! Yet what were these yearnings beside one other! What the dearest kin beside her who must yet be nearer and dearer still!—the young girl from whom he had fled to seek his fortune—for whom he had found it. In her his honest yearning centred, in her his high hopes culminated. Of her he thought all day, gazing out over the sun-spangled waves, and all night, tossing in his berth. A thousand times he cursed his folly in choosing canvas before steam; the time was so long—and seemed longer; the brightest days were interminable ages; favouring gales were lighter than zephyrs.

He allowed no doubts to interfere with the pleasures of anticipation; no fears, no anxieties. If he thought of what might have happened at home during the last four or five months since he had received news, the catalogue of calamities was endless. He did not believe disappointment possible through any sort of a calamity. If those he loved still lived—as he knew they did five or six months ago—then he was sure of his reception; he was sure of hearts and hands; he was sure of his reception from every one—yes, from every one.

The future seemed so splendid and so near! Yet it was giving the future hardly a fair chance to expect as much of it as young Edmonstone expected during the last days of his homeward voyage.

CHAPTER IV

HOW DICK CAME HOME

A crowd of the usual dock order had gathered on the quay at Blackwall by the time the Hesper made her appearance, towed by two Channel tugs. Some time, however, passed before the vessel swung near enough to the quay for recognitions to begin; and by then the dingy line of dock loafers and watermen was enhanced by a second rank of silk hats and a slight leaven of bonnets. With intolerable sloth the big ship swung closer and closer, broadside on; greetings were excitedly exchanged, and at length the gangway was thrown across and held by a dozen eager hands.

Dick Edmonstone, at the break of the poop, bent forward to search among the faces on the quay, apparently without finding any he knew. But presently, as his eye glanced rapidly up and down the line, he became conscious of one gaze fixed steadily upon him; twice he overlooked this face; the third time, a mutual stare, a quick smile of delight, a bound across the gangway, and Dick was grasping his brother's hand.

"Dick!"

"Maurice!"

Then they seemed to gasp in the same breath:

"Never should have known you!" "Nor I you—from Adam!"

And then they were silent for a whole minute, scrutinising one another from head to heels; until Maurice said simply that he had got away from the bank and needn't go back, and fell to asking about the voyage, and the weather, and the passengers, and had the cabin been comfortable? and what a stunning ship! To all of which Dick replied coherently; and for five minutes they talked as though they had parted last week. Only for such trifles could they find ready words; so much was inexpressible just at first.

They went into Dick's cabin; and there their tongues loosened a little. All were well at home, and happy, and comfortable; the news was good all round, as Dick phrased it, with thankfulness in his heart. That was the first delicious fact to be realised. After that, words flew with marvellous rapidity; the brothers were soon like two competitive human looms, turning them out one against the other. Fortunately the pace was too quick to last; in ten minutes both were breathless. Then they fastened upon stewards and Customs officials, and, by dint of some bullying and a little bribing, managed finally to get clear of the ship with Dick's luggage.

Dick was in tremendous spirits. He was back in old England at last, and testified his appreciation of the fact every minute.

Between Blackwall and Fenchurch Street he made odious comparisons touching Colonial travelling; in the four-wheeler across to Waterloo he revelled in the rattle and roar of the traffic; along the loop-line his eyes feasted on the verdant fields that had haunted his dreams in the wilderness.

The Edmonstones lived in a plain little house in a road at Teddington, in which all the houses were little, plain, and uniformly alike. They called their house "The Pill Box"; but that was a mere nickname, since all the houses in that plain little road were fearfully and wonderfully christened, and theirs no exception to the rule. Its name—blazoned on the little wooden gate—was Iris Lodge; and being sane people, and sufficiently familiar with suburban ideas, the Edmonstones had never attempted to discover the putative point of the appellation. They were satisfied to dub the house "The Pill Box," with malicious candour, among themselves. For the Edmonstones did not take kindly (much less at first) to road or house. And naturally, since five years ago, before Mr. Edmonstone's death, they had lived in a great, square, charming villa, with a garden-wall running a quarter of a mile along the towing-path, within sight of Kingston Bridge. But then Richard Edmonstone senior had dropped dead, at the height of his reputed success on the Stock Exchange and of his undoubted popularity in the clubs. To the surprise of all but those who knew him most intimately, he had left next to nothing behind him; the house by the river had been hurriedly sold, young Richard had as promptly emigrated, and the rest of them had bundled into as small a house as they could find in the neighbourhood.

But squat, snug, bourgeois as it was, Dick felt that the plain little house was nevertheless home, as the cab rattled over the railway bridge and along the road to the left, and so on towards "The Pill Box." It was raining (that June was not an ideal month), and the vehicle was the detestable kind of victoria so much affected by the honest cabmen of the Thames valley; still, Dick insisted on having the hood down to sniff the air of his native heath. Yet, though in sufficiently good spirits, his heart was beating quickly within him. These homecomings are no small things, unless the rover be old or loveless, and Dick was neither.

After all, the meeting was got over, as such meetings have been got over before, with a few tears and fewer words and melting looks and warm embraces. And so Dick Edmonstone was given back to the bosom of his family.

When the first and worst of it was over, he could not rest in a chair and talk to them, but must needs roam about the room, examining everybody and everything as he answered their questions. How well his mother was looking! and how her dark eyes beamed upon him!—the more brightly, perhaps, from their slight moisture. Her hand was as smooth and white as ever, and her hair whiter; how well it suited her to wear no cap, and have the silver mass pushed back like that! He had declared to himself he had never seen so pretty a woman over five-and-thirty—and his mother was fifty, and looking every year of it. And Fanny—well, she, perhaps, was as far from beauty as ever; but her wavy chestnut hair was matchless still, and as for expression, had there ever been one so sweet and gentle in the world before? It was Maurice who had all the good looks, though. But Maurice was pale and slim and rather round-shouldered; and instantly the image of the lad bending all day over the desk rose in Dick's mind and made him sad. What a different man the bush would make of Maurice! Then he looked round at the old familiar objects; the Landseer engravings and Fanny's water-colour sketches; the cottage piano, the writing-table, old pieces of odd ware which he remembered from his cradle, the fancy ormolu clock, which he had hated from his earliest days of discernment. He looked no further—a telegram was stuck up in front of the clock, and flaunted in his face:

"Edmonstone, Iris Lodge, Teddington,—Ship Hesper signalled Start Point ten this morning.—Bone and Phillips."

He read it curiously.

"Why, that's three days old!" he said, laughing. "Do you mean to say you have been staring at that bit of paper ever since—a sort of deputy-me, eh?"

"It was the first we heard," said the mother simply; and a subtle something brought back her tears. "I half think I'll frame it!" she added, smiling at her own weakness.

"I found out your other signallings," said Maurice. "I was in Bone's office half-a-dozen times yesterday."

Dick continued his survey of the room.

"Well, I think I recognise everything," he said presently; "but, I say, Fanny, I've got a thing or two for you to arrange in your high-art fashion; some odds and ends you haven't seen the like of before, I expect."

"No!" said Fanny.

"Oh, but I have, though; and some of 'em expressly for you."

"No!—really?—then what?"

"Aha, you'll see," said Dick. "Maurice, we'll unpack them now—if that brute of a Customs functionary has left a whole thing in the box." And the two left the room.

"To think," said Fanny musingly, "that our Dick is back! Really back, and never going out again; and been through all kinds of fearful adventures; and sailed round the world, and been away four years and a half—one can scarcely realise any of it. But above all, to think that he has made his fortune!"

Mrs. Edmonstone started.

"Oh, Fanny," cried she, "I had forgotten that! He never once spoke of it, and I didn't think of it. Oh, my boy, my boy!" She burst fairly into sobs. Her joy had been too great to bear before she was reminded of this overwhelming fact; it had brought the tears again and again to her eyes; now it became akin to pain.

Yet she did nothing but smile after her sons returned, laden with treasures and curios which they laid out all over the room. There was a famous rug of Tasmanian opossum skins, a dozen emu eggs, the tail of a lyre-bird, the skin of an immense carpet-snake, a deadly collection of boomerangs and spears, and a necklace of quandong stones mounted with silver. Mrs. Edmonstone beheld in silent wonder. As for Fanny, she was in ecstasies ("It is as good as the Exhibition," she said). So the time slipped away, and before half the quaint things had been examined and described it was dinner-time. They were all so happy together that first afternoon!

Few and simple were the courses at Iris Lodge, but at dessert Maurice produced some particular old Benedictine (which had been in the family as long as he had), and Dick's health was drunk with unspeakable enthusiasm. Dick blushed; for it made what he burned to say more awkward; but at last he blurted out, apparently appealing to the mildewed Benedictine bottle:

"I say—will you all think me an awful brute if I clear out for an hour or two? Mother, will you? You know what I have still to do—whom to see—to complete my first day in old England."

"Why, of course!" from the younger ones; and Mrs. Edmonstone simply pronounced the question: "Graysbrooke?"

"Yes," said Dick. "I must go and see them, you know. You know why, too," he added simply.

No one said anything. There was a rather awkward pause, which it fell to Fanny to break.

"By the bye," she said tentatively, "they have a visitor there."

She was prepared to add further information, but Dick looked at her blankly, and clearly was not listening. They rose from the table, and almost directly the three who went into the drawing-room heard the front door open and shut.

Dick was thankful to be out in the cool and the twilight, and alone. The day had been showery and dull, but late in the afternoon the clouds had broken up, and now they floated serenely in the still air, just touched with a pale pink rim to westward. The gravelly ground was wet enough to sound crisply underfoot—nothing more. Drip-drip fell the drops from the laburnums in the gardens all down the road; drip-drip all round, from tree, shrub, and flower; every leaf distilling perfume every minute. Dick appreciated the evidence of his nostrils with the relish of a man who has smelt nothing but brine for four months, nothing like this for four years. Nevertheless, he walked on briskly, down into the London road, that here lies parallel with the river, then down a curve to the left, as the highroad bends away from the river to form the High Street of Teddington; then to a full stop at a corner opposite the old churchyard. He had intended to walk along the lower road towards Kingston, straight to the gates of Graysbrooke, which fronted the river. But now the thought occurred to him (prompted by the sweetness of the evening, and backed up by the fact that it was as yet rather early to drop in casually for the evening anywhere—even at the house of one's sweetheart whom one hadn't seen for over four years). How about hiring a boat and rowing to Graysbrooke? It was no distance; and then, only to be afloat again on the dear old Thames! Dick did not hesitate at the corner long, but turned sharp down to the left, and hired his shallop at the ferry landing.

Down with the stream a hundred yards, and he was level with the lock; a few strong strokes against the stream, and the way already on the boat, and her nose grounded on the rollers; a minute's exertion, a minute's fumbling for coppers, and he floated out into the narrow reach beyond the lock. He paddled slowly along, bestowing friendly glances on the banks. The cottages on the left, close to the lock, he remembered just as he saw them; but the poplars on the island, inverted in the glassy water—he felt convinced they had grown. With each stroke of the oars the voice of the weir grew louder; it seemed to be roaring its rough welcome to him, just as yonder alders, right across the stream, through the danger-posts, were bowing theirs. How glorious it was, this first row on the Thames!

But now the house was almost in sight, and he could think no longer of the river. Slowly, as he sculled on, Graysbrooke discovered itself: a gray, stone, turreted building, set in leafy trees. There were battlements along the coping, which might have looked venerable but for the slates that peeped between them; yet the stone was mellowed by time; and altogether there was nothing either offensively new or unwholesomely ancient in the appearance of the house. Dick saw it all in his mind even before he stopped rowing to satisfy the cravings of his hungry eyes. Still twilight, and the river here a mirror without flaw, every stone had its duplicate in the clear depths below; that parallelogram of ruddy light that fastened Dick's attention showed with especial sharpness in the reflection. The light was in the drawing-room. They had finished dinner. He could storm them now—at once.

A little inlet entered one end of the lawn; in here he sculled and moored his boat. Then he sprang upon the close-cropped grass and stood transfixed.

The light in the dining-room was turned low; but that in the room to the right of the hall-door—the room with the French window—was shining brightly. And through the open window there burst, as Dick's feet touched the grass, the sound of a girl's song. The voice was low and clear, and full of youth and tenderness; it rose, and fell, and trembled, for the singer possessed feeling; it hastened here and lingered there, and abused none of these tricks, for she sang with what is rarer than feeling—taste. Dick trembled violently; he wanted to rush into the room then and there, but he was thrilled, and rooted to the ground; and after a bar or two the voice soothed him and set his spirit at rest, like the touch of a true friend's hand in the hour of pain. Then he stood quite humbly, hoping it would never, never end. What the song was he didn't know, and never thought of finding out afterwards; he might have heard it a hundred times or never before; he knew nothing during these few transported minutes—nothing, except that he was listening to her voice.

As the last low note was borne out upon the air, and voices within the room murmured the conventional grace after song, Dick stepped forward, meaning to boldly enter. Two yards from the window, however, he silently halted; it was so dark that he could see into the room without himself being seen from within. The temptation to avail himself of so obvious an advantage was too strong to be resisted.

There were three persons in the room, but for the eyes of Dick only one—the two men made no immediate impression on his physical perception. It was a supreme moment in his life. He had left England for the sake of a young girl, to make his way in the world so that he might return and proudly claim her: for he had won her heart. And now he had made his way through toil and privation to a small fortune, and had come back to woo her hand. She was here—this girl for whom he had given his early manhood's strength, his brain's essence, the best drops of his life's blood; this girl whose image had beckoned him onward when he grew faint, and urged him still further in the hour of success; whose name had risen to his lips in despair and in peril, inspiring new courage—here, within ten feet of him; he striving to realise it, and to grow cool before going into her presence, yet yearning to fling himself at her feet.

It was good that she was ignorant of his approach, for it showed her to him in a fair light straight away—completely natural and unconscious of herself. She had seated herself after her song at a low table, and was making an indolent attack on some trifling work with her scissors. The lamplight, from under its crimson shade, fell upon her hair and face and neck with marvellous results, for it made her beautiful. She was not at all beautiful. She had a peerless complexion, a good nose, matchless teeth; otherwise her features were of no account. But she was exceedingly pretty; and as she sat there with the warm lamplight changing her ordinary light-coloured hair into a ruddy gold fit for any goddess, a much less prejudiced person than Dick Edmonstone might have been pardoned the notion that she was lovely, though she was not.

When at last he managed to raise his eyes from her they rested upon a face that was entirely strange. A tall, massive man, in evening dress, leaned with an elbow on the chimneypiece, his head lightly resting on his hand, one foot on the edge of the fender. There could be no two opinions as to the beauty of this face—it was handsome and striking to the last degree. Burnt, like Dick's, to the colour of brick-dust, it was framed in dark curly hair, with beard and whiskers of a fairer hue, while the mouth was hidden by a still fairer, almost golden, moustache. The effect was leonine. Dick caught his profile, and saw that the steady, downward gaze was bent upon the dainty little head that glowed in the lamplight. From his vantage-post outside the window he glanced from observer to observed. They were a sufficiently good-looking pair, yet he overrated the one and underrated the other. He was by no means attracted to this unknown exquisite; there was an ease about his pose which bespoke freedom also; and his scrutiny of the unconscious girl was of a kind that would at least have irritated any man in Dick's position.

Dick allowed his attention to rest but briefly upon the third occupant of the room—a man with snowy hair and whiskers, who was apparently dropping off to sleep in a big armchair. Somehow or other, the sight of the men—but particularly of the stranger—acted on his heart like a shower-bath on a man's head; his pulse slackened, he regained with interest the self-possession with which he had first approached the window. He took three steps forward, and stood in the middle of the room.

A startled cry escaped the old man and the girl. The man by the fireplace dropped his forearm and turned his head three inches.

Dick strode forward and grasped an outstretched hand.

"Colonel Bristo!"

"Dick Edmonstone!—is it really Dick?" a well-remembered voice repeated a dozen times. "We knew you were on your way home, but—bless my soul! bless my soul!"

The old soldier could think of nothing else to say; nor did it matter, for Dick's salute was over and his back turned; he was already clasping the hand of the fair young girl, who had risen, flushed and breathless, to greet him.

He was speechless. He tried to say "Alice," but the sound was inarticulate. Their eyes met.

A clatter in the fender. The tall man's heel had come down heavily among the fire-irons.

"Let me introduce you," said Colonel Bristo to this man and Dick. "You will like to know each other, since you both come from the same country: Mr. Edmonstone, from Australia; Mr. Miles, from Australia! Mr. Miles was born and bred there, Dick, and has never been in England before. So you will be able to compare notes."

The two men stared at each other and shook hands.

CHAPTER V

THE FIRST EVENING AT GRAYSBROOKE

"Sit down, boy, sit down," said Colonel Bristo, "and let us have a look at you. Mind, we don't know yet that you're not an impostor. You should have brought proofs."

"Here are five-foot-ten of them," said Dick, laughing.

"To believe that, we must put you through examination—and cross-examination," the Colonel added with a glance at his daughter; "although I half believe you really are the man you profess to be. What do you say, Alice?"

"I have a strong case—" Dick was beginning, but he was cut short.

"It is Dick," said the oracle sweetly.

"You take his word for it?" asked her father.

"No, I identify him," Alice answered with a quiet smile; "and he hasn't altered so very much, when one looks at him."

Dick turned his head and met her eyes; they were serene and friendly. "Thank you," he said to her, with gratitude in his voice. And, indeed, he felt grateful to them all; to the Colonel for his ponderous pleasantry, to Alice for her unembarrassed manner, to Mr. Miles for the good taste he showed in minding his own business. (He had strolled over to the window.)

"And when did you land?" inquired the Colonel.

"This morning."

"Only this morning!" exclaimed Alice; "then I think it was too good of you to come and see us so soon; don't you, papa?"

Very kind of him indeed, papa thought. Dick was pleased; but he thought they might have understood his eagerness. Alice, at any rate, should not have been surprised—and probably was not. "I couldn't put it off," he said, frankly.

There was a slight pause; then the Colonel spoke:

"That's kindly said, my boy; and if your mother knew how it does us good to see you here, she would scarcely grudge us an hour or two this evening—though grudge it you may depend she does. As for ourselves, Dick, we can hardly realise that you are back among us."

"I can't realise it at all," murmured Dick, aloud but to himself.

"I won't worry you by asking point-blank how you like Australia," the Colonel went on, "for that's a daily nuisance in store for you for the next six months. But I may tell you we expect some tough yarns of you; our taste has been tickled by Miles, who has some miraculous—why, where is Miles?"

Miles had vanished.

"What made him go, I wonder?" asked Alice, with the slightest perceptible annoyance. Dick did not perceive it, but he thought the question odd. To disappear seemed to him the only thing a stranger, who was also a gentleman, could have done; he was scarcely impartial on the point, however.

Alice took up the theme which her father had dropped.

"Oh, Mr. Miles has some wonderful stories," said she; "he has had some tremendous adventures."

"The deuce he has!" thought Dick, but he only said: "You should take travellers' tales with a grain of salt."

"Thanks," Alice instantly retorted; "I shall remember that when you tell yours."

They laughed over the retort. All three began to feel quite at ease.

"So you kept up your sketching out there, and drew bush scenes for our illustrated papers?" said the Colonel.

"Two or three times; more often for the Colonial papers."

"We saw them all," said Alice, graciously—"I mean the English ones. We cut them out and kept them." (She should have said that she did.)

"Did you, though?" said Dick, delighted.

"Yes," said Alice, "and I have a crow to pick with you about them. That 'Week in the Sandwich Islands'—it was yours, wasn't it?"

Dick admitted that it was.

"Oh, and pray when were you in the Sandwich Islands?"

He confessed that he had never seen them.

"So you not only cheated a popular journal—a nice thing to do!—but deceived the British public, which is a far more serious matter. What explanation have you to offer? What apology to 'One who was Deceived'—as I shall sign my 'Times' letter, when I write it?"

"Alice, you are an inquisitor," said Colonel Bristo. But Alice replied with such a mischievous, interested smile that Dick immediately ceased to feel ashamed of himself.

"The fact is," he owned, "your popular journal doesn't care a fig whether one has been to a place so long as one's sketches of it are attractive. I did them a thing once of a bullock-dray stuck up in the mud; and how did it appear? 'The War at the Cape: Difficulties in Reaching the Front.' And they had altered the horns of my bullocks, if you please, to make 'em into South African cattle! You see, just then Africa was of more interest to your British public than Australia. Surely you won't be so hard on me now? You see you have made me divulge professional secrets by your calumnies."

Alice said she forgave him, if all that was true; but she added, slyly: "One must take travellers' tales with a pinch of salt, you know!"

"Come, Alice," said her father, "if you insist on pitching into our artist, he shall have his fling at our photographer. Dick, she's taken to photography—it's lately become the fashion. Look on that table, under the lamp; you'll find some there that she was trimming, or something, when you dropped in our midst."

"May I look at them?" Dick asked, moving over to Alice.

"Certainly; but they're very bad, I'm afraid; and since you artists scorn photography—as so inartistic, you know—I suppose you will be a severe critic."

"Not when this is the subject," said Dick, in a low voice, picking up a print; "how did you manage to take yourself?"

He was sitting beside her at the little table, with the lamp between them and the Colonel; he instinctively lowered his voice, and a grain of the feeling he had so far successfully repressed escaped into his tone.

"Someone took off the cap for me."

"Oh. Who?"

"Who? Oh, I get anybody to take the cap off when I am so vain as to take myself—anybody who is handy."

"Mr. Miles, for instance?" It was a stray question, suggested by no particular train of thought, and spoken carelessly; there was no trace of jealousy in the tone—it was too early for that; but Alice looked up, quick to suspect, and answered shortly:

"Yes, if you like."

Dick was genuinely interested, and noticed in her tone nothing amiss. Several of the photographs turned out to be of Alice, and they charmed him.

"Did Mr. Miles take all these?" he asked, lightly; he was forced to speak so before her father: the restraint was natural, though he marvelled afterwards that he had been able to maintain it so long.

Alice, however, read him wrong. She was prepared for pique in her old lover, and imagined it before it existed. She answered with marked coldness:

"A good many of them."

This time Dick detected the unpleasant ring in her words—he could not help but detect it. A pang shot to his heart. His first (and only) impression of Miles, which had fled from his mind (with all other impressions) while talking to her, swiftly returned. He had used the man's name, a minute ago, without its conveying anything to his mind; he used it now with a bitterness at heart which crept into his voice.

"And don't you return the compliment? I see no photographs of Mr. Miles here; and he would look so well in one."

"He has never been taken in his life—and never means to be. Now, Dick, you have seen them all," she added quite softly, her heart smiting her; and with that she rolled all the prints into one little cylinder. Dick was in that nervous state in which a kind word wipes out unkindness the moment it is spoken, and the cloud lifted at once from his face. They were silent for more than a minute. Colonel Bristo quietly left the room.

Then a strange change came over Dick. While others had been in the room, composure had sat naturally upon him; but now that they were alone together, and the dream of his exile so far realised, that armour fell from him, and left his heart bare. He gazed at his darling with unutterable emotion; he yearned to clasp her in his arms, yet dared not to profane her with his touch. There had been vows between them when they parted—vows out of number, and kisses and tears; but no betrothal, and never a letter. He could but gaze at her now—his soul in that gaze—and tremble; his lips moved, but until he had conquered his weakness no words came. As for Alice, her eyes were downcast, and neither did she speak. At length, and timidly, he took her hand. She suffered this, but drew ever so slightly away from him.

"Alice," he faltered, "this is the sweetest moment of my life. It is what I have dreamt of, Alice, but feared it might never come. I cannot speak; forgive me, dear."

She answered him cunningly:

"It is very nice to have you back again, Dick."

He continued without seeming to hear her, and his voice shook with tenderness: "Here—this moment—I can't believe these years have been; I think we have never been separated—"

"It certainly doesn't seem four years," said Alice sympathetically, but coolly.

Dick said nothing for a minute; his eyes hung on her downcast lids, waiting for an answering beam of love, but one never came.

"You remember," he said at last, in a calmer voice, "you remember the old days? and our promises? and how we parted?" He was going on, but Alice interrupted him by withdrawing her hand from his and rising from her chair.

"Dick," said she, kindly enough, "don't speak of them, especially not now—but don't speak of them at all. We can't have childhood over again; and I was a child then—of seventeen. I am grown up now, and altered; and you—of course you have altered too."

"Oh Alice!"—the turning of the door handle made him break off short, and add in a quick whisper, "I may speak to you to-morrow?"

"Very well," she answered indifferently, as there entered upon them a little old lady in rustling silk and jingling beads—an old lady with a sallow face and a piercing black eye, who welcomed Dick with a degree of fussy effusiveness, combined with a look and tone which discounted her words.

"Delighted to see you back, Mr. Richard—a pleasure I have often looked forward to. We don't welcome conquering heroes every day," were in themselves sufficiently kindly words, but they were accompanied by a flash of the beady eyes from Dick to Alice, and a scrutiny of the young fellow's appearance as searching as it was unsympathetic; and when a smile followed, overspreading her loose, leathery, wrinkled skin, the effect was full of uncanny suggestion.

"Yes, it is jolly to be back, and thanks very much," said Dick civilly; "and it is charming to find you still here, Mrs. Parish."

"Of course I am still here," said the leathery little lady brusquely: as if Colonel Bristo could live without his faithful domestic despot, as if Graysbrooke could stand without its immemorial housekeeper! This Mrs. Parish was ugly, vain, and old, and had appeared as old and as vain and as ugly when, more than twenty years ago, she first entered the Colonel's service. She had her good points, however, and a sense of duty according to her lights. Though it be no extravagant praise, she was a better person at heart than on the surface.

She now inquired with some condescension about Dick's Australian life, and how he liked it, and where he had been, and how he should like living altogether out there. She congratulated him on his success (she called it "luck"), which she declared was in the mouths of everybody. On that he felt annoyed, and wondered if she knew any details, and what figure she would bid for some—of, say, his first year—in the local gossip market.

"Of course you will go back," said the old woman with conviction; "all lucky Colonists do. You will find England far too dull and slow for you." At this point Colonel Bristo and Mr. Miles came back, chatting. "I was saying," Mrs. Parish repeated for their benefit, "that of course Mr. Richard will soon return to Australia; he will tire of England in six weeks; it is always the way. Mr. Miles is the happy exception!" with a smile upon that gentleman which strove to be arch—with doubtful success.

"I never said I meant to make 'Home' my home," said the Australian, with the drawl of his race, but in tones mellow and musical. His long frame sank with graceful freedom into a chair beside Mrs. Parish, and his clear blue eyes beamed upon them all—all except Dick, whom he forgot to notice just then.

"I don't think Dick means to go back," said the Colonel cheerily. "That would be treating us all abominably; in fact, we could never allow it—eh, Dick?"

Dick looked gravely at the carpet.

"I mean to settle down in England now," said he; and he could not refrain from a sly glance at Alice. Her eyes, bent thoughtfully upon him, instantly filled with mischief.

"You mean to stay at home, yet sketch the ends of the earth; is that it?" Her tone changed swiftly to one of extreme kindness. "Well, it would be dreadful if you didn't stop at home now. Whatever you do" (he changed colour; she added calmly), "think of Mrs. Edmonstone and Fanny!"

A little later, Alice and her father told Dick all the news of themselves that they could think of—how they had been in Italy last year, and in Scotland the year before, and how they had taken a shooting-box in Yorkshire for this year. And Alice's manner was very courteous and kindly, for she was beginning to reproach herself for having been cruel to him on this his first evening, and to wonder how she could have had the heart. She asked him if he had forgotten how to dance, and said he must begin learning over again at once, in order to dance at her ball—her very own party—on the second of July.

Poor Dick's spirits once more rose high, though this time an uneasy sediment remained deep in his heart. Without the least intention in the world, Alice was beginning a very pretty game of coquetry with her sweetheart—alas! her quondam sweetheart. While they talked, Mr. Miles, at the other side of the room, kept up an entertaining conversation with Mrs. Parish. At the same time he observed Dick Edmonstone very narrowly—perhaps more anxiously than he need have regarded an old friend of his friends'; though perhaps with no more than a social lion's innate suspicion of his kind. At last Dick rose to go.

Colonel Bristo went out with him, and thrust his arm affectionately through the young man's as they crossed the lawn.

"Dick," said he, very kindly, "I thought I would wait till I saw you alone to congratulate you most heartily on having made your way so splendidly. Nay, don't interrupt me; your way in the world is already made, and nobly made. I think you showed your sense—and more—in stopping short, and coming home to follow up the career you love. That was the intention expressed in your letter, I think?"

"Yes, sir. And that letter?" said Dick anxiously. He had felt misgivings about it ever since the heat of triumph in which it was written and posted in Melbourne.

"I liked it," said the Colonel simply; "it was manly and frank, and to the point. You shall have my answer now; and I, too, will be frank. Four years ago, more or less, I was forced to answer in a certain way a certain question—there was no alternative. Dick, think seriously—you are both four years older; are you, for one, still of the same mind?"

"I am; indeed I am," said Dick, earnestly.

"Then take your chance!" said Colonel Bristo. "I cannot say more; I don't understand women; I find it bitter to say this much, I that am to lose her. But you deserve her; come here as often as you will; you will be very welcome. And if you both wish now—both, mind!—what you both wished then, when for obvious reasons I could not hear of it—"

"You were right enough, sir," Dick murmured sadly.

"Then," continued the Colonel, "I frankly tell you, I shall like it. That's all; good-night!"

Dick looked up from the dewy grass, and his lips formed a grateful sentence, though no words could express his feeling just then. He looked up, but the honest, simple-hearted soldier was gone. He who had faced the Russian shot and shell had retreated cowardly before honest English thanks!

The young man stepped into his boat, undid the painter, and floated out upon the broad moonlit river. Ah, how kind of Colonel Bristo! But only to think what those words would have been to them four years ago! Yes, to them; for then Alice besought the consent that had just been given; besought it as wildly as himself. And now did she even desire it? He had found her so passionless, so different from all he had fancied, or hoped, or feared. Once she had been cruel, but anon so kind; and then she had ridiculed him in pure friendliness. Alas, fatal friendliness! Had she but been awkward or shown him downright coldness—anything but that. As to this Miles, no need to think about him yet. The question was whether Alice Bristo still loved Dick Edmonstone, not whether there was another man in the case; time enough for that afterwards. Yet a few short hours ago the question—faced so calmly now—would have stunned or maddened this ardent lover.

Down with the stream came peace and hope, with the soft, soothing touch of the moonbeams; they stole into the heart of Dick Edmonstone; they held it for one brief moment. For a sound broke on his ears which made him stare and tremble, and drove out the sweet influences almost before their presence was felt. Yet the sound of itself was sweet; the very same sound had thrilled poor Dick as he leapt ashore; it was the voice of Alice—singing to Mr. Miles!

CHAPTER VI

SISYPHUS

Dick Edmonstone slept badly, his first night in England; and no wonder, since already a sense of grievous disappointment weighed him down. When he reached home and his own room, this feeling grew upon him; it distracted him, it denied him rest. Where his faith had been surest, disillusion came slowly home to him; in the purest spot of the vision the reality was dim and blurred. What a fool he had been to make sure of anything! Above all, to build his peace of mind on the shifting sand of a woman's love; to imagine—simply because his love for Alice had never wavered—that Alice's love for him must perforce remain equally unchanged. And all that night her voice, as he had last heard it, rang cruelly in his ear, and a light remark, about what she had called her "childhood," lay like lead at his heart.

At breakfast he could not quite conceal his trouble; he looked somewhat haggard. He knew that he was expected to be in high spirits, and did his best to feign them, but his mirth was perfunctory. This was obvious to his sister, and not unnoticed by Mrs. Edmonstone. They spoke about it afterwards, for they knew something of the circumstances at Graysbrooke, and had their own opinion of the guest there.

Dick fidgeted all the morning, and passed some of the time in unpacking his belongings. In the afternoon he left the house full of conflicting emotions. As he walked up the drive, Dick could not tell how he had waited until the afternoon, such a wild elation took possession of him at the thought of again seeing his beloved. Miss Bristo was in the garden, the butler told him—yes, alone; and Dick walked through the house and on to the top of the shaven lawn that sloped to the river.

He found her deep in a magazine and in the stern sheets of the boat, which was moored in the inlet. She was all in white, for the day was sunny; and she smiled sweetly from under the broad brim of her straw hat as Dick stepped gravely into the boat, and sat down on the thwart facing her.

She looked so careless and so bright that he could not find it in his heart to vex her straight away; so they talked lightly of this and that for a full quarter of an hour, while Dick basked recklessly in her smiles, and almost persuaded himself that this was happiness. But at last came a pause; and then he nerved himself to speak.

"Alice," he began gravely, "you know our few words last night? You said I might speak to you today."

"Well," said Alice, carelessly.

"You know very well what I want to speak about," rather warmly.

Alice turned down her leaf, shut up her magazine, leant back, and surveyed him calmly.

"I wish I didn't, Dick," she answered, half in annoyance, half in pity. But her look added: "Say on; let us have it out—and over."

"Last night," said Dick smoothly, "I asked you if you remembered old days, and what there was between us, and so on. You said you didn't want to remember them, and talked about your 'childhood.' You said you were altered, and that, of course, I must be altered." He paused.

So far he had been cool and fluent; but he had rehearsed all this. His next words came hot from the heart, and fell unsteadily from the lips.

"Oh, Alice," cried he, "did you mean that? Say that you didn't! I have never changed, never can. Oh, say that you are the same. Say that you only meant to tease me, or try me, or anything you like—anything but that you meant all that about our being altered, and forgetting the past—" his voice was piteous in its appeal; "say that you didn't mean it!" he repeated in a whisper.

"I did mean it," Alice replied; not harshly or coldly, but with due deliberation.

Dick turned pale. He grasped the gunwale nervously with each hand, and leaned forward.

"Then I—no longer—have your love?" he asked in a hollow voice.

Alice looked at him reproachfully; there was even indignation in her glance.

"How can you force such things from me? Have you no pride?" He winced. "But, since you press for an explanation, you shall have one. Before you went away I knew no one. I was a child; I had always been fond of you; my head was full of nonsense; and, when you asked me, I said I loved you. It was true, too, in a childish way."

"Go on," said Dick, in a low voice.

Alice was flushed, and her eyes sparkled, but her self-possession was complete.

"Well, you come back after four years, and, it seems, expect to find me still a child. Instead of that, I am a woman—a sensible woman," with a good humoured twinkle of the eyes, "disinclined to go on with the old nonsense just where it left off—you must admit that that would be absurd? But for the rest, I am as fond of you, Dick, as I was then—only without the childish nonsense. No one is more delighted to see you back, and welcome you, than I am; no one is more your friend. Dear Dick," she added in a tone of earnest entreaty, "cannot we be friends still?"

"No!" exclaimed Dick, hoarsely.

The flush died away from the girl's face, to return two-fold.

"No!" he repeated. "You give me your love, and then, after years of separation, you offer me your friendship instead. What is that to me? How can I make that do—a lamp instead of the sun? It is too much to ask of any man: you know it. Who has taught you to play with men's hearts like this?"

"I have been too kind," said Alice, coldly. She had stifled her humiliation, and was preparing to leave the boat.

"Say rather too cruel!" returned Dick very bitterly. "Nay, not on my account. I will save you the trouble of going."

He sprang from the boat as he spoke. One moment he stood on the bank with a blight on his brave eyes; the next, he raised his hat proudly, turned on his heel and was gone.

No sooner had he disappeared than the young lady produced a little lace handkerchief, and rained her tears upon its wholly inadequate area. She sobbed for nearly five minutes; and, after that, dipped her pink fingers in the water, and made assiduous efforts to expunge the most tell-tale symptoms. Then she took up the magazine and tried to revive her interest in the story she had been reading, but she could remember nothing about it. Finally she was about to quit the boat in despair, when, looking up, whom should she see but Dick Edmonstone towering above her on the bank, hat in hand.

"I want you to forgive me," he said very humbly. She affected not to understand him, and intimated as much by raising her eyebrows.

"For what I said just now" (rapidly)—"for everything I have said since I saw you first, last night. And I want to say—if you will still have it—let us be—friends."

Her face instantly brightened; every trace of affectation vanished; she smiled gratefully upon him.

"Ah, that is sense!" said she.

"But," said Dick, still more earnestly, "there are two questions I do think I may ask, though whether you will answer them—"

"I will," the girl exclaimed rashly.

"Well, then, the first is, have you taken a dislike to me—a new one? Don't laugh," he said, colouring; "I mean it. It is so possible, you know. I have led a rough life; you might easily be ashamed of the things I had to do, to make my way at first; you might easily think me less polished, less gentlemanly: if it is that, I implore you to say so."

She could scarcely keep grave; even he might have smiled, but for the question he had still to ask.

"No, it is not that; to my mind you are just the same."

Dick drew a deep breath of relief.

"The second question may offend you; if it does—well, it can't be helped. I think my old footing—even though you were a child then—is sufficient excuse for it. It is, then—and, indeed, you must grant me an honest answer—do you love another man?"

"And it is not that," said Alice shortly, nevertheless looking him full in the face.

A great load was removed from his heart.

"Then it is only," he said eagerly—"only that you wish to cancel the past? really only that?"

"Really only that," she repeated with a smile.

"Then," added Dick, hope rekindling in his heart, "may I never—that is, won't you hold out to me the least faint spark?"

"I think you had better leave well alone," said Alice; and she stepped lightly from the boat as she spoke. "Now I must go in. Will you come, too?"

"No; I must say good-bye."

"Really? Then good-bye, Dick." Another sweet smile as she stretched out her hand. "And come as often as ever you can; you will always be welcome."

He watched her slim form tripping daintily across the grass.

"Ay, I will come!" he muttered between his teeth; "and I shall win you yet, Miss Caprice, though I have to begin all over again. To start afresh! How could I have borne the thought yesterday? Yet to-day it must be faced. This minute I give up looking back, and begin to look forward. And it may be better so; for when I win you, as win you I shall, you will be all the dearer to me. I might not have valued you as I ought—who knows? You do not deny me hope; I shan't deny it to myself. You shall be mine, never fear. For the present, have your wish—we are only friends."

His resolution taken, Dick Edmonstone threw up vain regrets; "friendly relations" with Alice were duly established, and at first the plan worked tolerably well. They had one or two common interests, fortunately. Alice dabbled in water-colours; in which Dick could help her, and did. In return, Alice took a lively interest in his sketches; and they would sometimes talk of the career to which he was to devote himself. Then there was the river; they were both good oars, and, with Alice, rowing was a passion.

Beyond these things there was little enough to bring them together. In everything else Mr. Miles either stepped in or enjoyed a previous pre-eminence. At first Dick tried hard to hate this man for his own sake, without being jealous of him; but under the circumstances it was impossible for jealousy not to creep in. He certainly distrusted Miles; the man struck him from the first as an adventurer, who had wormed himself by mysterious means into the friendship of the guileless, single-hearted Colonel Bristo; and observation deepened this impression. On the other hand, the pair saw very little of each other. Dick naturally avoided Miles, and Miles—for some good reason of his own—shunned Dick. In fact, the jealous feeling did not arise from anything he saw or heard: the flame was promoted and fed, as it were, at second-hand.

Deep in his heart, poor Dick had counted on being something of a lion (it was only human) on his return from Australia, at least on one hearth besides his own; and lo! a lion occupied that hearth before him—a lion, moreover, of the very same type. The Bristos didn't want to hear Australian experiences, because they had already heard such as could never be surpassed, from the lips of Miles; their palate for bush yarns was destroyed. Dick found himself cut out, in his own line, by Miles. His friends were very hospitable and very kind, but they had no wish to learn his adventures. And those adventures! How he had hoarded them in his mind! how he had dreamed in his vanity of enthralling the Colonel and thrilling Alice! He had hoped at least to interest them; and even in that he failed. Each little reminiscence yawned over, each comparison or allusion ignored—these were slight things with sharp edges. With Alice, it more than once happened that when he touched on his strange experiences she forgot to listen, which wounded him; or if she made him repeat it, it was to cite some far more wonderful story of Mr. Miles—which sowed salt in the wound. Of course vanity was its own cure, and he dropped the subject of Australia altogether; but he was very full of his romantic life, and this took him a day or two, and cost him some moments of bitterness.

So Dick's first fortnight in England passed, and on the whole he believed he had made some sort of progress with Alice. Moreover, he began rather to like wooing her on his merits. On consideration, it was more satisfactory, perhaps, than reviving the old boy-and-girl sentiment as if there had been no four years' hiatus; more satisfactory, because he never doubted that he would win her in the end. It is to be noted that his ideas about one or two things changed in a remarkable degree during those first days.

One morning, when they chanced to be particularly confidential together, Dick said suddenly:

"By the bye, how did you come to know this—Mr. Miles?" He had almost said "this fellow Miles."

"Has papa never told you?" Alice asked in surprise.

"No, never."

"Nor Mr. Miles himself? Ah, no: he would be the last person to speak of it. But I will tell you. Well, then, it was when we were down in Sussex. Papa was bathing (though I had forbidden it), when he was seized with cramp, out of his depth. He must certainly have been drowned; but a great handsome fellow, dressed like a fisherman, saw his distress, rushed into the sea, swam out, and rescued him with the help of a boat. Poor papa, when he came to himself, at once offered the man money; and here came the surprise. The man laughed, refused the money, dived his hand into his own pocket, and threw a sovereign to the boatman who had helped!"

Dick's interest was thoroughly aroused, and he showed it; but he thought to himself: "That was unnecessary. Why couldn't the fellow keep to the part he was playing?"

And Alice continued: "Then papa found out that he was a gentleman in disguise—a Mr. Miles, from Sydney! He had been over some months, and was seeing England in thorough fashion. Indeed, he seemed a regular boatman, with his hands all hard and seamed with tar."

"And your father made friends with him?"

"Naturally; he brought him up to the hotel, where I heard all about the affair. You may imagine the state I was in! After that we saw a good deal of him down there, and papa got to like him very much, and asked him to come and stay with us when he grew tired of that kind of life and returned to London. And that's all."

"How long did you say it is since he saved your father's life?" Dick asked, after a short pause.

"Let me see, it's—yes, not quite a month ago."

Dick gave vent to a scarcely audible whistle.

"And he has no other friends in England?"

"Not that I know of."

"And writes no letters nor receives any?" (He was speaking from his own observation.)

"Not that I know of. But how should I know? or what does it matter?"

"In fact, he is a friendless adventurer, whom you don't know a thing about beyond what you have told me?"

Alice suddenly recoiled, and a dangerous light gleamed in her eyes.

"What do you mean? I don't understand you. Why all these questions?"

Dick regarded her unflinchingly. He knew what an honest answer would cost him, yet he was resolved to speak out.

"Because," said he, impressively and slowly, "because I don't believe Mr. Miles is what he makes himself out to be."

He knew that he had made some advance in her esteem, he knew that these words would lose him all that he had gained, and he was right. A flash of contempt lit up the girl's eyes and pierced to his soul. "Noble rival!" said she; and without another word swept haughtily past him—from the garden where they had been walking—into the house.

CHAPTER VII

SOUTH KENSINGTON

The first act of every Australian who landed in England that summer was, very naturally, to visit the Exhibition—their Exhibition—at South Kensington.

Dick was not an Australian, and it therefore did not consume him to put off South Kensington until he had been a week or so quietly at home. Nevertheless he was sufficiently eager to inspect the choice products of a land that he regarded with gratitude as indeed his alma mater; and still more eager to expatiate on all that was to be seen to insular friends, who believed that New Zealand was an inland colony, and who asked if Victoria was not the capital of Sydney. On that very first evening he had made a sort of offer to escort Colonel Bristo and Alice; but there he was too late; and he experienced the first of a series of petty mortifications—already mentioned—which originated from a common cause. Mr. Miles had already been with the Bristos to the Exhibition, and had proved a most entertaining showman. He had promised to accompany them again in a week or two; would not Dick join the party? For three visits would be more than impartial persons, such as the Colonel and his daughter, were likely to care about—even with so splendid a cicerone as Mr. Miles.

Of course, Dick was not going to play second fiddle to the Australian deliberately and with his eyes open. He made his excuses, and never alluded to the matter again. But one day, after a morning's business in the City, he went alone.

When he was once in the vast place, and had found his way to the Australian section, his interest speedily rose to a high pitch. It is one thing to go to an exhibition to be instructed, or to wonder what on earth half the things are; it is something quite different to find yourself among familiar objects and signs which are not Greek to you, to thread corridors lined with curios which you hail as the household gods of your exile. Instead of the bored outsider, with his shallow appreciation of everything, you become at once a discriminate observer and intelligent critic, and sightseeing for once loses its tedium. Dick wandered from aisle to aisle, from stand to stand, in rapt attention. At every turn he found something of peculiar interest to him: here it was a view of some township whose every stick he knew by heart; there a sample of wood bearing on the printed label under the glass the name of a sheep station where he had stayed time out of number.

The golden arch at the entrance to the Victorian Court arrested him, as it arrested all the world; but even more fascinating in his eyes was the case of model nuggets close at hand. He heard a small boy asking his mamma if they were all real, and he heard mamma reply with bated breath that she supposed so; then the small boy smacked his lips, and uttered awed (though slangy) ejaculations, and the enlightened parent led him on to wonders new. But Dick still gazed at the nuggets; he was wondering— if he could have it all over again—whether he would rather pick up one of these fellows than win again their equivalent through toil and enterprise, step by step, when a smart slap on the back caused him to turn sharp round with an exclamation.

A short, stout, red-faced man stood at his elbow with arms akimbo, and grinned familiarly in his face. Dick looked him up and down with a stare of indignation; he could not for the life of him recognise the fellow; yet there he stood, his red-stubbled chin thrust forward, and a broad, good-humoured grin on his apish face, and dressed gorgeously. He wore a high white hat tilted backward, a snowy waistcoat, a dazzling tie, and a black frock-coat, with an enormous red rose in the button hole. His legs, which now formed two sides of an equilateral triangle with the floor for its base, were encased in startling checks, and his feet, which were small, in the glossiest patent leather. His left hand rested gloved upon his hip, and four fingers of his ungloved right hand were thrust into his waistcoat pocket, leaving the little one in the cold with a diamond of magnitude flashing from its lowest joint.

"Euchred?" this gentleman simply asked, in a nasal tone of immense mirth.

"If you mean do I know you, I don't," said Dick, only a degree less haughtily than if he had come straight from Oxford instead of from the bush.

"What! you don't remember me?" exclaimed the man more explicitly, his fingers itching to leap from the waistcoat-pocket.

Dick stared an uncompromising denial.

The diamond flashed in his eyes, and a small piece of pasteboard was held in front of him, on which were engraved these words:

"The Hon. Stephen Biggs."

Dick repressed an insane impulse to explode with laughter.

"What! of Marshall's Creek?"

"The same."

Dick stretched out his hand.

"A thousand pardons, my dear fellow; but how could I expect to see you here? And—the Honourable?"

"Ah!" said Mr. Biggs, with legitimate pride, "that knocks you, old man! It was only the Legislative Assembly when you and me was mates; it's the Legislative Council now. I'm in the Upper 'Ouse, my son!"

"I'm sure I congratulate you," said Dick.

"But 'ang the 'andle," continued the senator magnanimously; "call me Steve just the same."

"Well, it's like the whiff of the gum leaves to see you again, Steve. When did you arrive?"

"Last week. You see," confidentially, "I'm in my noo rig out—the best your London can do; though, after all, this Colony'll do as good any day in the week. I can't see where it is you do things better than we do. However, come and have a drink, old man."

In vain Dick protested that he was not thirsty; Mr. Biggs was. Besides, bushmen are not to be denied or trifled with on such points. The little man seized Dick's arm, marched him to the nearest bar, and called for beer.

"Ah!" sighed Mr. Biggs, setting down his tankard, "this is the one point where the Old Country licks us. This Colony can't come within a cooee of you with the beer, and I'm the first to own it! We kep' nothing like this at my place on the Murray, now did we?"

Dick was forced to shake his head, for, in fact, the Honourable Stephen had formerly kept a flourishing "hotel" on the Murray, where the Colonial beer had been no better than—other Colonial beer—a brew with a bad name. Dick observed an odd habit Mr. Biggs had of referring to his native heath as though he were still on it, speaking of his country as he would have spoken of it out there—as "this Colony."

The Honourable Steve now insisted on tacking himself on to Dick, and they roamed the Exhibition together. Biggs talked volubly of his impressions of England and the English (he had crowded a great deal into his first few days, and had already "done" half London), of the Exhibition, of being fêted by the flower of Britain and fed on the fat of the land; and though his English was scarcely impeccable a vein of shrewd common sense ran through his observations which was as admirable in the man (he had risen very rapidly even for Australia) as it was characteristic of his class.

"By-the-bye," said Mr. Biggs, after they had freely criticised the romantic group of blacks and fauna in the South Australian Court, "have you seen the Hut?"

"No," said Dick.

"Then come on; it's the best thing in the whole show; and," dropping his voice mysteriously, "there's the rummest go there you ever saw in your life."

Everybody remembers the Settler's Hut. It was a most realistic property, with its strips of bark and its bench and wash-basin, though some bushmen were heard to deny below their breath the existence of any hut so spick and span "where they come from."

"Good!" said Dick, as soon as he saw the Hut. "That's the real thing, if you like."

"Half a shake," said Mr. Biggs, "and I'll show you something realler." He drew Dick to the window of the hut. "Look there!" he whispered, pointing within.

Three or four persons were inspecting the interior, and debating aloud as to how they personally should care to live in such a place; and each, as he surveyed the rude walls, the huge fireplace, the primitive cooking utensils, reserved his most inquisitive scrutiny for an oddly-dressed man who sat motionless and silent on the low bank, as though the Hut belonged to him. A more colourable inference would have been that the man belonged to the Hut; and in that case he must have been admitted the most picturesque exhibit in the Colonial Courts, as he looked the most genuine; for the man was dressed in the simple mode of an Australian stockman, and looked the part from the thin soles of his plain side-spring boots to the crown of his cabbage-tree hat. From under the broad brim of the latter a pair of quick, dark eyes played restlessly among the people who passed in and out, or thronged the door of the hut. His shoulders were bent, and his head habitually thrust forward, so that it was impossible, in the half-light, to clearly make out the features; but long, iron-gray locks fell over the collar of his coarse tweed coat, and a bushy, pepper-and-salt beard hid the throat and the upper portion of the chest. Old though the man undoubtedly was, his massive frame suggested muscularity that must once have been enormous, and must still be considerable.

"Now, what do you think of that cove?" inquired the Hon. Stephen Biggs in a stage whisper.

"Why," said Dick, who was frowning in a puzzled manner, "he looks the real thing too. I suppose that's what he's there for. Now, I wonder where—"

"Ah, but it ain't that," broke in Biggs, "I've been here every day, almost, and when I see him here every day, too, I soon found out he don't belong to the place. No; he's an ordinary customer, who pays his bob every morning when the show opens, and stays till closing-time. He's to be seen all over the Exhibition, but generally at the Hut—most always about the Hut."

"Well, if he isn't paid for it, what on earth is his object?" said Dick, as they moved away.

"Ah," said Mr. Biggs darkly, "I have a notion of my own about that, though some of the people that belong to this here place share it with me."

"And?" said Dick.

"And," said Mr. Biggs with emphasis, "in my opinion the fellow's the dead spit of a detective; what's more, you may take your Colonial oath he is one!"

"Well," said Dick coolly, "I've seen him before, though I can't tell where. I remember his bulk and shape better than his face."

"Yes? By Jove, my boy, you may be the very man he's after!"

Mr. Biggs burst into a loud guffaw; then turned grave in a moment, and repeated impressively: "A detective—my oath!"

"But he looks a genuine Australian, if ever I saw one," objected Dick.

"Well, maybe he's what he looks."

"Then do you think he's come over on purpose? It must be a big job."

"I think he has. It must."

"Ah," said Dick, "then I have seen him out there somewhere; probably in Melbourne."

"Quite likely," said Mr. Biggs. "There are plenty of his sort in this Colony, and as sharp as you'll find anywhere else, my word!"

A little later they left the Exhibition, and spent the evening together.

CHAPTER VIII

THE ADMIRABLE MILES

If Mr. Miles was systematically "spoilt" by the Bristos, he was more or less entitled to the treatment, since it is not every guest who has had the privilege of saving his host from drowning. But Mr. Miles was in other ways an exceptional visitor. He contrived to create entertainment instead of requiring it. He was no anxiety to anybody; he upset no household routine; he might have remained for months, and not outstayed his welcome; from the first he made himself at home in the most agreeable fashion. In a word, he was a very charming man.

Moreover, he was unlike other men: he was far more independent, and far less conventional. It was impossible to measure him by a commonplace standard. He had little peculiarities which would not have recommended other men, but which in his case were considered virtues: he was quite artless in matters of etiquette. Indeed, he was a splendid specimen of free, ingenuous manhood—an ideal Australian, according to the notions of the old country.

The least breath against their guest on conventional grounds would have been indignantly resented by the Graysbrooke people. They put upon his peculiarities an interpretation which in Mrs. Parish's case resolved itself into a formula:

"They are so free-and-easy out there; they despise conventionality; they are natural. Oh that we were all Australians!" (Mr. Miles was the one Australian of her acquaintance.)

Thus when he swore unmistakably at a clumsy oarsman while piloting the ladies through a crowded lock, the offence was hushed up with a formula; and so were other offences, since formulas will cover anything.

One day Mrs. Parish, going into the drawing-room, paused on the threshold with an angry sniff.

"Smoke—in here! It is the very first time in all these years," severely to Alice, "that I have ever known your papa—"

"It was not papa, it was Mr. Miles," said Alice quietly. "He walked in with his pipe, and I really did not like to tell him. I believe he has gone for more tobacco."

"Why, how stupid of me! Of course, with Mr. Miles it is quite different." (Mrs. Parish assumed an indulgent tone.) "He is not used to such restraints. You were quite right to say nothing about it. He shall smoke where he likes."

Again the little old lady came to Alice, and said very gravely:

"My dear, did you notice the way our visitor refused the hock this evening? Of course they do not drink such stuff in the bush, and he must have what he is accustomed to. I will arrange with Tomlin to have the whisky decanter placed quietly in front of him for the future."

Alice, for her part, not only permitted but abetted this system of indulgence; for she agreed with Mrs. Parish that the guest was a noble creature, for whose personal comfort it was impossible to show too much solicitude—which, indeed, was the least they could do. He had saved her father's life.

That incident—which she had related to Dick with a wonderful absence of feminine exaggeration—had been in itself enough to plant in her heart a very real regard for Mr. Miles. That was but natural; but one or two other things which came to her knowledge furthered this regard.

One Saturday morning in Kingston market-place Alice met a bosom friend, who informed her that she had seen the Graysbrooke pleasure-boat being towed up-stream by a tall gentleman—("So handsome, my dear; who is he?")—while a miserable, half-starved wretch sat luxuriously in the stern-sheets. Rallied with this, the Australian's brick-dust complexion became a shade deeper. Then he made a clean breast of the affair, in his usual quiet tone, but with a nearer approach to diffidence than he had yet shown them. He had gone out for a solitary pull, and had no sooner started than a cadaverous creature with a tow-rope pestered him for a job. Miles had refused the man; doubted his strength to tow a flea with a silk thread; and observed that he, Miles, was more fit to tow the other, if it came to that. At this, Miles, being sworn at for making game of a starving man, had promptly landed, forced the man, speechless with amazement, into the boat, towed him to Kingston, and left him to a good dinner, with some wholesome advice touching immediate emigration.

A few days later, at dusk on a wet afternoon, Mrs. Parish, from her bedroom window, saw Mr. Miles walk quickly up the drive in his shirt-sleeves. It transpired that he had given his coat to a ragged, shivering tramp on the London road—plus the address of the Emigration Office.

"You see," he said, on both these occasions, "I never saw anything half so bad in my own country. If you aren't used to it, it knocks a man's heart to see a poor devil so far gone as all that."

In short, Mr. Miles exhibited to the Bristos, on several occasions, a propensity to odd and impulsive generosity; and the point told considerably in their general regard for the man, which day by day grew more profound.

Among other peculiarities, so excellently appreciated, Mr. Miles had a singular manner of speaking. It was an eminently calm manner; but for the ring of quiet audacity in every tone, it might have been called a subdued manner. He never raised his voice; he never spoke with heat. When he said to Colonel Bristo, clinging to him in the sea, "If you hang on like that I must fell you," his tone was as smooth as when he afterwards apologised for the threat. When he paid Alice his first compliment he did so without the smallest hesitation, and in his ordinary tone; and his compliments were of the most direct order. They once heard him threaten to thrash a bargee for ill-treating a horse, and they were amazed when the man sulkily desisted; the threat was so gently and dispassionately uttered. As for his adventures, they were told with so much of detail and gravity that the manner carried conviction where the matter was most fantastic. Miles was the best of "good company." Apart from the supreme service rendered to him, Colonel Bristo was fully persuaded that he was entertaining the best fellow in the world. Add to this that Mrs. Parish adored the handsome Australian, while Alice meekly revered him, and it will be easily seen that a hostile opinion of their hero was well calculated to recoil on its advocate.

During the short period in which the hero was also the stranger, he spent all his time in the Colonel's society. Apparently the two men found many subjects of mutual interest. Once, when Alice interrupted them in the study, Mr. Miles seemed to be eloquently enumerating the resources and capabilities of some remote district of the Antipodes; for though she spent some minutes getting a book, he took no notice of her presence in the room. On another occasion Alice saw her father examining a kind of map or plan, while Mr. Miles bent over him in explanation. She afterwards learnt that this was a plan of the Queensland station of which Mr. Miles was part owner.

After the first day or two it seemed evident that Mr. Miles disliked the society of ladies.

On the third evening, however, the men patronised the drawing-room for half-an-hour, and the Colonel asked Alice to sing something. She sang, and Mr. Miles listened. When she had finished, Mr. Miles coolly asked her to sing again. The following night he extracted three songs from her. Then Mr. Miles began to spend less time in his host's sanctum. He cultivated Alice; he interested himself in her amusements—photography for one; he got her to sing to him in the daytime. He was civil to Mrs. Parish.

When the young lady sat down to the piano, this sun-burned Apollo did not hang over her, as other men did (when they got the chance); nor did he turn over a bar too soon or too late—like the others. He made no pretence of polite assistance, not he. But he flung himself in a chair, threw back his head, and drank in every note. At first it was generally with his back to the piano, and always with closed eyes. Then he found another chair—one a little further away, but so placed that the girl's profile was stamped like a silhouette on the sunlit window, directly in his line of vision. And he no longer listened with closed eyelids.

Mrs. Parish, a keen observer, hovered about during these performances, and noted these things. She had perceived at the time the impression Alice's first song made upon Mr. Miles: she saw that he had regarded the girl from that moment with a newly awakened interest. Thenceforth he had made himself agreeable to both ladies, whereas before he had ignored them both. Now, although she knew well enough that Miles's attentions, so far as she was concerned, could be but politic, yet such was the inveterate vanity of this elderly duenna that she derived therefrom no small personal gratification. An impudent compliment thrilled her as it might have thrilled a schoolgirl. But this did not prevent her seeing what was really going on, nor secretly rejoicing at what she saw.

She watched the pair together from the first. She watched the girl innocently betray her veneration for the man who had saved her father's life. She knew that it is perilous for a man to see that a girl thinks him a hero, and she awaited results. She soon fancied that she saw some. She thought that Miles's habitual insouciance was a trifle less apparent when he conversed with Alice; certainly his eyes began to follow her and rest upon her; for Mr. Miles did such things openly. But she detected no corresponding symptoms in Alice; so one day she told her bluntly: "Mr. Miles is falling in love with you, child."

Alice was startled, and coloured with simple annoyance.

"What nonsense!" she said indignantly.

Immediately she thought of the absent Dick, and her blush deepened—because she thought of him so seldom. Mrs. Parish replied that it was not nonsense, but, instead of urging proofs in support of her statement, contented herself with cataloguing Mr. Miles's kingly attributes. Here Alice could not contradict her. The old lady even spoke of the station in Queensland and the house at Sydney. Encouraged by the girl's silence, however, she overshot the mark with a parallel reference—and not a kind one—to Dick Edmonstone. She saw her mistake at once, but too late; without a word Alice turned coldly from her, and they barely exchanged civilities during the rest of that day.

From that moment Miss Bristo's manner towards Mr. Miles was changed. Mrs. Parish had put into her head a thought that had never once occurred to her. An innocent pleasure was poisoned for her. She did not quite give up the songs, and the rest, but she became self-conscious, and developed a sudden preference for that society which is said to be no company at all.

At this juncture the ship Hesper entered the Channel, and was duly reported in the newspapers. Alice saw the announcement, and knew that in two or three days she should see her lover. These days she spent in thought.

At seventeen she had been madly in love with young Edmonstone—what is called a "romantic" or "school-girl" affair—chiefly sentimental on her side, terribly earnest on his. At eighteen—parted many months from a sweetheart from whom she never heard, and beginning to think of him daily instead of hourly—she asked herself whether this was really love. At nineteen, it was possible to get through a day—days, even—without devoting sentimental minutes to the absent one. Alice was at least madly in love no longer. There remained a very real regard for Dick, a constant prayer for his welfare, a doubt as to whether he would ever come home again, a wondering (if he did) whether she could ever be the same to him again, or he to her; nothing more.

Mrs. Parish was in a great measure responsible for all this. That excellent woman had predicted from the first that Dick would never make his fortune (it was not done nowadays), and that he would never come back. Another factor was the ripening of her understanding, aided by a modicum of worldly experience which came to her at first-hand. Alice was honoured with two proposals of marriage, and in each case the rejected (both were wife-hunting) consoled himself elsewhere within three months. To this groundwork Mrs. Parish added some judicious facts from her own experience; and this old lady happened to be the girl's only confidante and adviser. Alice gathered that, though man's honour might be a steadfast rock, his love was but a shifting sand. Thus there were such things as men marrying where they had ceased to love; thus Dick might return and profess love for her which was no longer sincere.

In the end Miss Bristo was left, like many other young ladies, with an imperfect knowledge of her own mind, and attempted, unlike most young ladies, to mould her doubts into a definite and logical form. She did arrive at a conclusion—when she learned that Dick was nearly home. This conclusion was, that, whatever happened, there must be no immediate engagement: she did not know whether Dick loved her still—she was not absolutely sure that she still loved him.

We have seen how she communicated her decision to Dick. His manifest agony when he heard it sent a thrill through her heart—a thrill that recalled the old romance. The manly way in which he afterwards accepted his fate touched her still more. She began to think that she might after all have mistaken herself of late; and this notion would probably have become a conviction but for one circumstance—the presence of Mr. Miles.

Dick was jealous: she saw it, or thought she saw it, from the first. This vexed her, and she had not bargained to be vexed by Dick. It made her more than half-inclined to give him something to be jealous of. Accordingly she was once or twice so malicious as to throw Mr. Miles in his teeth in their conversations, and watch the effect. And the effect did not please her.

On the other hand, about Mr. Miles there was no particle of jealousy (one thing more to his credit). Why, he had asked with the greatest interest all about Dick, after he had gone that first evening; and her answers had been most circumspect: she had let him suppose that Dick was a squatter during his whole term in Australia. After that Mr. Miles had asked no more. But Dick had never asked one word about Mr. Miles until he had been in England a fortnight, and then he offended her deeply. Up to that point her interest in Dick had been gradually growing more tender; she felt him to be true and brave, and honoured him; and contrasted her own fickleness with his honest worth. Once or twice she felt a longing to make him happy. Even as she felt herself irresistibly bowed down before him her idol fell. From this man, whom she was learning to truly love, came a mean, unmanly suggestion. To further his progress with her he stooped to slander the man whom he was pleased to consider his rival, and that rival the noblest, the most generous of men.

She could not easily forgive this; she could never forget it, and never think quite the same of Dick afterwards. And then the conduct of the other one was so different! Her manner instinctively warmed towards Mr. Miles: she should be his champion through thick and thin. As for Dick, after that little scene, he did not come near Graysbrooke for a week.

Now, during that week, the words that had offended her recurred many times to Alice. The pale, earnest, honest face with which Dick had uttered them also rose in her mind. Was it possible that his suspicion could be absolutely groundless? Was it not credible that he might have reasons for speaking— mistaken ones, of course—which he could not reveal to her? In any case, his words rankled; and so much sting is seldom left by words which we have already dismissed, once and for all, as utterly and entirely false.

During that week, moreover, there occurred a frivolous incident, of which Alice would have thought nothing before the expression of Dick's suspicions but which now puzzled her sorely. One brilliant afternoon she found herself completely indolent. She wandered idly into the garden, and presently came upon a rather droll sight: her father and Mr. Miles, sound asleep, side by side, in a couple of basket-chairs under the shade of a weeping willow. The girl conceived a happy roguery: what a subject for a photograph! She stole into the house for her camera. When she returned, her father was gone. She was disappointed, hesitated a few moments, and then coolly photographed the still unconscious Mr. Miles. An hour later she greeted him with the negative—an excellent one.

"You said you had never been taken," said she mischievously. "Well, here is your first portrait. It will be capital."

He asked to look at it, in his quiet way. Alice handed him the dripping glass. He had no sooner held it up to the light than it slipped through his fingers, and broke into a dozen fragments upon the gravel path.

Mr. Miles apologised coldly, and proceeded to pick up the pieces with a provoking smile. Alice was irate, and accused him of breaking her negative purposely. Mr. Miles replied with charming candour that he had never been photographed in his life, and never meant to be. Already blaming herself for having yielded to a silly impulse, and one which was even open to wrong construction, Alice said no more; and presently, when the Australian gravely begged her forgiveness, it was granted with equal gravity. Nevertheless she was puzzled. Why should Mr. Miles so dread a photograph of himself? What had he to fear? Would Dick add this to his little list of suspicious circumstances? If he did, it would be the first item not utterly absurd. What if she were to tell him, and see!

As it happened, Dick called the very next day, a Wednesday, and the last day in June. Alice received him coldly. There was a natural restraint on both sides, but she thawed before he went. As he was saying good-bye, she asked him (casually) if he would come on Friday afternoon—the day of her dance—and help with the floor and things. She really wished him to come very much, for she foresaw an opportunity for explanation, without which the evening would be a misery to her; besides, they could talk over Mr. Miles fairly and confidentially. Dick jumped at it, poor fellow, brightened up at once, and walked home a happier man.

The following day Alice accompanied her father to town, on pleasure bent. The little jaunt had been long arranged, and Mr. Miles was their efficient escort.

That was on Thursday, July 1st.

Unfortunately for Mr. Biggs, M.L.C., he could not spend all his days at the Exhibition, so that a certain little drama, not widely differing from that astute legislator's preconception, was at last played to an altogether unappreciative house. The facts are these:

About four in the afternoon, an old gentleman, with snowy whiskers and hair, and with a very charming girl upon his arm, looked into the Settler's Hut. They did not remain within above ten seconds; but during those ten seconds the genus loci—who was in his customary place on the bunk—heard a voice without which caused him to start, pull the brim of his cabbage-tree hat further over his eyes, and draw a long breath through his teeth.

"I won't come in," said this voice, which was low and unconcerned; "I've seen it before; besides, I know the kind of thing rather too well."

The shadows of the old gentleman and the girl had hardly disappeared from the threshold when the man in the cabbage-tree hat and side-spring boots rose swiftly, and peered stealthily after them. What he saw caused him to smile with malignant triumph. A tall, well-dressed man walked beside the old gentleman and his daughter.

The watcher allowed them to pass almost out of sight, then followed warily. He followed them all the afternoon, keeping so far behind, and dodging so cleverly, that they never saw him. When the trio at length quitted the building and took a cab, this man followed through the streets at a double. He followed them to Waterloo. He got into the same train with them. They got out at a station on the loop line; he got out also, paid his fare to the ticket collector, and once more dogged his quarry. An hour later the cabbage-tree hat was attracting attention on that same suburban platform; later still the occupants of a third-class smoking carriage in an up train thought that they had never before seen such an evil expression as that which the broad brim of the cabbage-tree hat only partially concealed.

This also was on the 1st of July.

CHAPTER IX

A DANCING LESSON AND ITS CONSEQUENCES

To enter a cricket-field in mid-winter and a ballroom at midday are analogous trials, and serious ones to enthusiasts in either arena; but the former is a less depressing sight in January than in December, while there is something even inspiriting about a ballroom the day before the dance.

When, quite early in the afternoon, Alice slipped unobserved into the cool and empty dining-room, her cheeks glowed, her eyes sparkled, and the hard boards yielded like air beneath her airy feet. She shut the door quietly, though with an elbow; her hands were full. She carried two long wax candles that knew no flame, two gleaming dinner-knives, and a pair of scissors. These were deposited on a chair—provisionally—while the young lady inspected the floor with critical gaze.

She frowned—the floor was far from perfect. She slid out one small foot, as if trying dubious ice—yes, most imperfect. The other foot followed; it would be impossible to dance on a floor like this. Next instant the lie was given to this verdict by the judge herself, for Miss Bristo was skimming like a swallow round the room.

Would you see a graceful maiden at her best? Then watch her dancing. Would you behold her most sweet? Then catch her unawares—if you can. Most graceful and most sweet, then—I admit that the combination is a rare one, but she should be dancing all alone; for, alas! the ballroom has its mask, and the dual dance its trammels.

In this instance it was only that Alice desired to try the floor, and to assure herself that her feet had lost none of their cunning; and only once round. No, twice; for, after all, the floor was not so very bad, while the practice was very good, and—the sensation was delicious. Yet a third round—a last one—with quickened breath and heightened colour, and supple curves and feet more nimble, and a summer gown like a silver cloud, now floating in the wake of the pliant form, now clinging tenderly as she swiftly turned. And none to see her!

What, none?

As Alice came to an abrupt pause in front of her cutlery and candles, a deep soft voice said, "Bravo!"

She looked quickly up, and the base of a narrow open window at the end of the room was filled by a pair of broad shoulders; and well set up on the shoulders was a handsome, leonine face, with a blond beard and a pair of bold, smiling eyes.

"Bravo, Miss Bristo!"

"Well, really, Mr. Miles—"

"Now don't be angry—you can't be so unreasonable. I was out here; I saw something white and dazzling pass the window twice; and the third time I thought I'd see what it was. I came and looked, and thought it was an angel turned deserter, and dancing for joy to be on earth again! There was no harm in that, was there?"

"There is a great deal of harm in compliments," said Alice severely; "especially when they are wicked as well as rude."

Mr. Miles smiled up at her through the window, completely unabashed.

"I forgot. Of course it was rude to liken you to gods I never saw, and never hope to see. Forgive me!"

But Alice was thinking that her freak required a word of explanation.

"I was only just trying the floor," she said. "I never dreamt that anyone would be so mean as to watch me."

"Unfortunately one can't learn from merely watching," Mr. Miles replied, quietly raising himself upon the sill. "You surely haven't forgotten the lesson you promised to give me?"—swinging his legs into the room—"I claim that lesson now." He towered above her, a column of gray tweed, his arms folded lightly across his massive chest.

The window by which Miles entered was five feet above the river lawn, and one of three at that end of the room—the other walls had none. Standing with one's back to these windows, the door was on the right hand side, and, facing it, a double door communicating with the conservatory. Before this double door, which was ajar, hung a heavy curtain, awaiting adjustment for the evening.

"I did not ask you in," remarked Alice with some indignation. It was just like Mr. Miles, this; and for once he really was not wanted.

"Unfortunately, no; you forced me to ask myself. But about the lesson? You know I never danced in my life; am I to disgrace my country to-night?"

"You should have come to me this morning."

"You were—cooking, I believe."

"Thank you, Mr. Miles! Then yesterday."

"We were all in town. Now do be the angel you looked a minute since, Miss Bristo, and show me the ropes. It won't take you ten minutes; I assure you I'm a quick learner. Why, if it's time you grudge, we have wasted ten minutes already, talking about it."

Impudence could no higher climb; but Mr. Miles was not as other men are—at least, not in this house. There was nothing for it but to give in, show him the rudiments, and get rid of them as quickly as possible; for Dick might arrive at any moment.

"Ten minutes is all I shall give you, then. Attention! One, two, three; one, two, three; so! Can you do it?"

Of course he could not, after a niggardly example of half-a-dozen steps: he did not try; he insisted on her waltzing once right round the room very slowly.

"Then it is your last chance," exclaimed Alice. "Now watch: you begin so: one—a long one, remember— then two, three—little quick ones. Now try. No, you needn't lift your feet; you are not stamping for an encore, Mr. Miles. It is all done by sliding, like this. Now, try again."

Miles bent his six feet three into five feet nothing, and slid gravely round with an anxious watch upon his feet.

"Why, you are bent double," cried Miss Bristo, sharply; "and, let me tell you, you will never learn while you look at your feet."

Miles stopped short.

"Then how am I to learn?" he asked, gazing helplessly at his instructress.

Alice burst out laughing.

"You had better lock yourself in your room and practise hard until evening. The ten minutes are up; but you have exactly six hours and twenty-nine minutes before you, if you make haste."

"Well, you shall suffer if I cut a poor figure to-night, Miss Bristo, and it will serve you right, for I intend to have my share of your dances."

"That remains to be seen," said Alice tritely.

"Stay, though," said Miles, drawing himself up to the last of his seventy-five inches, and speaking in that smooth, matter-of-fact tone that ushered in his most astounding audacities, "suppose we two try—in double harness—now?"

"Mr. Miles!"

"Miss Bristo, I am sure I should get on a thousand times better. Is it so very much to ask?" he added humbly—for him.

The inner Alice echoed the question: Was it so very much to ask—or to grant? The answer came at once: To anyone else, yes; to Mr. Miles, no; grave, heroic, middle-aged Mr. Miles! With a mighty show of condescension, Miss Bristo agreed to one round, and not a step more. She would not have been called prude for the world; but unluckily, prudery and prudence so often go hand in hand.

The two went whirling round the empty room. Before they were half-way round, Alice exclaimed:

"You have cheated; never danced, indeed!"

He murmured that it was so many years ago, he thought he had forgotten. Having thus discovered that she could teach her pupil nothing, it was Alice's plain duty to stop; but this she forgot to do. Mr. Miles, for his part, said not a word, but held her firmly. He, in fact, waltzed better than any man she had ever danced with. Two rounds—three—six—without a word.

Even if they had not been dancing they might have failed to hear a buoyant footstep that entered the conservatory at this time; for the worst of an india-rubber sole is the catlike tread that it gives the most artless wearer. But it was an unfortunate circumstance that they did just then happen to be dancing.

There is no excuse for Miss Bristo, that I know of. Pleas of faulty training or simplicity within her years would, one feels, be futile. Without doubt she behaved as the girl of this period is not intended to behave; let her be blamed accordingly. She did not go unpunished.

After waltzing for no less a space than five minutes—in a ballroom bare as a crypt, in broad daylight, and in silence—Alice, happening to look up, saw a look on her partner's face which made her tremble. She had never seen a similar expression.

It was pale and resolute—stern, terrible. She disengaged herself with little ado, and sank quietly into a chair by the window.

"A fine 'one round'!" she said demurely; "but it shall be deducted from your allowance this evening."

She could not see him; he was behind her. His eyes were devouring the shapely little head dipped in the gold of the afternoon sun. Her face he could not see—only the tips of two dainty ears and they were pink. But a single lock of hair—a wilful lock that had got astray in the dance, and lay on her shoulder like a wisp of sunlit hay—attracted his attention, and held it. When he managed to release his eyes, they roved swiftly round the room, and finally rested upon another chair within his reach, on which lay two wax-candles, two dinner-knives, and a pair of scissors.

A click of steel an inch from her ear caused Alice to start from her chair and turn round. Mr. Miles—pale, but otherwise undisturbed—stood holding the scissors in his right hand, and in his left was a lock of her hair. For one moment Miss Bristo was dumb with indignation. Then her lips parted; but before she could say a word the door-handle turned, Mr. Miles dropped the scissors upon the chair and put his left hand in his pocket, and the head and shoulders of Colonel Bristo were thrust into the room.

"Ah, I have found you at last!" the old gentleman cried with an indulgent smile. "If you are at liberty, and Alice don't mind, we will speak of—that matter—in my study."

"My lesson is just over," said Miles, bowing to Alice. He moved towards the door; with his fingers upon the handle, he turned, and for an instant regarded Alice with a calm, insolent, yet tender gaze; then the door closed, and Alice was alone.

She heard the footsteps echo down the passage; she heard another door open and shut. The next sound that reached her ears was at the other side of the room in which she sat. She glanced quickly toward the curtained door: a man stood between it and her. It was Dick.

Alice recoiled in her chair. She saw before her a face pale with passion; for the first time in her life she encountered the eyes of an angry man. She quailed; a strange thrill crept through her frame; she could only look and listen. It seemed an age before Dick spoke. When he did speak, it was in a voice far calmer than she expected. She did not know that the calm was forced, and therefore the more ominous.

"I have only one thing to ask," he began hurriedly, in a low tone: "was this a plot? If it was, do say so, and so far as I am concerned its effect shall be quick enough: I will go at once. Only I want to know the worst, to begin with."

Alice sat like a stone. She gave no sign that she had so much as heard him. Poor girl, the irony of Fate seemed directed against her! She had invited Dick on purpose to consult him about Mr. Miles, and now—and now—

"You don't speak," pursued Dick, less steadily; "but you must. I mean to have my answer before either of us leaves this room. I mean to know all there is to know. There shall be an end to this fooling between us two!"

"What right have you to speak to me like this?"

"The right of a true lover—hopeless of late, yet still that! Answer me: had you planned this?"

"You know that is absurd."

How coldly, how evenly she spoke! Was her heart of ice? But Dick—there was little of the "true lover" in his looks, and much of the true hater. Yet even now, one gentle word, one tender look from him, and tears of pity and penitence might still have flowed. His next words froze them.

"No conspiracy, then! Merely artless, honest, downright love-making; dancing—alone—and giving locks of hair and (though only by coincidence!) the man you loved once and enslaved for ever—this man of all others asked by you to come at this very hour, and, in fact, turning up in the middle of it! And this was chance. I am glad to hear it!"

Men have been called hard names for speaking to women less harshly than this—even on greater provocation; but let it be remembered that he had loved her long years better than his life; that he had wrenched himself from England and from her—for her sake; that during all that time her image had been graven on his soul. And, further, that he had led a rough life in rough places, where men lose their shallower refinements, and whence only the stout spirits emerge at all.

When recrimination becomes insult a woman is no longer defenceless; right or wrong in the beginning, she is right now; she needs no more than the consciousness of this to quicken her wit and whet her tongue.

"I do not understand you," exclaimed Alice, looking him splendidly in the face. "Have the goodness to explain yourself before I say the last word that shall ever pass between you and me."

"Yes, I will explain," cried Dick, beside himself—"I will explain your treatment of me! While you knew I was on my way to you—while I was on the very sea—you took away your love from me, and gave it to another man. Since then see how you have treated me! Well, that man—the man you flatter, and pet, and coquette with; the man who kennels here like a tame dog—is a rogue: a rogue and a villain, mark my words!"

In the midst of passion that gathered before his eyes a marble statue, pure and cold, seemed to rise out of the ground in front of him.

"One word," said Alice Bristo, in the kind of voice that might come from marble: "the last one. You spoke of putting an end to something existing between us—'fooling' was the word you used. Well, there was something between us long ago, though you might have found a prettier word for it; but it also ended long ago; and you have known that some weeks. There has since been friendship; yes, you shall have an end put to that too, though you might have asked it differently. Stay, I have not finished. You spoke of Mr. Miles; most of what you said was beneath notice; indeed, you have so far lost self-control that I think you cannot know now what you said a minute ago. But you spoke of Mr. Miles in a cruel, wicked way. You have said behind his back what you dare not say to his face. He at least is generous and good; he at least never forgets that he is a gentleman; but then, you see, he is so infinitely nobler, and truer, and greater than you—this man you dare to call a villain!"

"You love him!" cried Dick fiercely.

Instead of answering, Alice lowered her eyes. Stung to the quick—sick and sore at heart—revenge came within her reach in too sweet a form to be resisted.

Never was lie better acted. Dick was staggered. He approached her unsteadily.

"It is a villain that you love!" he gasped. "I know it—a villain and an impostor! But I will unmask him with my own hands—so help me God!"

He raised his pale face upward as he spoke, smiting his palms together with a dull dead thud. Next moment he had vaulted through the open window by which Miles had entered so short a time before—and was gone.

Meanwhile an interview of a very different character took place in Colonel Bristo's sanctum. It ended thus:

"Then you are quite sure that this hundred will be enough for you to go on with?"

"More than enough; fifty would have done. Another Queensland mail is due a month hence; and they can never fail me twice running."

"But you say you are so far up country that you do not send down to meet every mail. Your partner may not have thought you likely to run short."

"I wired him some weeks ago that I had miscalculated damages. I should have had my draft by this mail but for the floods. I feel confident they have prevented him sending down in time; there has been mention of these floods several times in the papers."

"Well, my dear Miles, if you want more, there is more where this came from. I cashed the cheque myself this morning, by the way; I happened to be in the bank, and I thought you would like it better. Here they are—ten tens."

"Colonel Bristo, I can never express—"

"Don't try, sir. You saved my life."

CHAPTER X

AN OLD FRIEND AND AN OLD MEMORY

When Dick Edmonstone opened the garden gate of Iris Lodge he was no longer excited. The storm that had so lately shaken his frame and lashed his spirit had spent its frenzy; no such traces as heaving breast or quickened pulse remained to tell of it. The man was calm—despair had calmed him; the stillness of settled gloom had entered his soul. His step was firm but heavy; the eye was vacant; lips like blanched iron; the whole face pale and rigid.

These are hall-marks graven by misery on the face of man; they are universal and obvious enough, though not always at the first glance. For instance, if prepared with a pleasant surprise for another, one is naturally slow to detect his dismal mood. Thus, no sooner had Dick set foot upon the garden path than the front door was flung open, and there stood Fanny, beaming with good-humour, good news on the tip of her tongue. It was like sunrise facing a leaden bank of western clouds.

"Oh, Dick, there is someone waiting to see you! You will never guess; it is a bush friend of yours. Such an amusing creature!" she added sotto voce.

Dick stood still on the path and groaned. "Biggs!" he muttered in despair.

Nothing directs attention to the face so surely as the voice. There was such utter weariness in this one word that Fanny glanced keenly at her brother, saw the dulness of his eyes, read for apathy agony, and knew that instant that there had been a cruel crisis in his affair with Alice Bristo.

Instead of betraying her insight, she went quickly to him with a bright smile, laid her hand on his arm, and said:

"His name is not Biggs, Dick dear. It is—but you will be very glad to see him! Come in at once."

A flash of interest lit up Dick's clouded face; he followed Fanny into the hall, and there, darkening the nearest doorway, stood a burly figure. The light of the room being behind this man, Dick could not at once distinguish his features. While he hesitated, a well-remembered falsetto asked if he had forgotten his old mate. Then Dick sprang forward with outstretched hand.

"Dear old Jack, as I live!"

"Dear old humbug! Let me tell you you've done your level best to miss me. An hour and a half have I been here, a nuisance to these ladies—"

"No, no, Dick; Mr. Flint has done nothing but entertain us," put in Mrs. Edmonstone.

"A charitable version," said Flint, bowing clumsily. "But I tell you, my boy, in half-an-hour my train goes."

"Don't delude yourself," said Dick; "you won't get off so easily to-night, let alone half-an-hour."

"Must, sir," Jack Flint replied. "Leave Dover by to-night's boat—holiday. If you'd only come in sooner! I wonder now where he's been?" Flint added, with a comic expression on his good-natured face.

"No place that I wouldn't have left for an hour or two with you, old chap," said Dick in a strange tone; "nowhere very pleasant."

Nothing better could have happened to Dick just then than seeing the chum from whom he had parted nearly three years ago. It was as though his good angel had stored up for him a sovereign simple, and administered it at the moment it was most needed. In the presence of Flint he had escaped for a few minutes from the full sense of his anguish. But now, by an unlucky remark, Jack had undone his good work as unconsciously as he had effected it. Dick remembered bitterly that long ago he had told his friend all about his love—as it then stood.

"Mr. Flint has been telling us some of your adventures, which it seems we should never have heard from you," observed Fanny, reproachfully.

This was quite true. Once snubbed at Graysbrooke, his system of silence on that subject had been extended to Iris Lodge. One set of people had voted his experiences tiresome; that was enough for him. This was doubtless unfair to his family, but it was not unnatural in Dick. He was almost morbid on the point.

"Indeed!" he replied; "but suppose he gives us some of his Irish adventures instead? How many times have they tried to pot you, my unjust landlord? You must know, mother, that this is not only my ex-partner in an honourable commercial enterprise—not only 'our Mr. Flint' that used to be—but John Flint, Esq., J.P., of Castle Flint, county Kerry; certainly a landholder, and of course—it goes without saying—a tyrant."

"Really?" said Mrs. Edmonstone. "He did not tell us that."

"It's the unhappy fact," said Flint, gloomily. "A few hundred acres of hills and heather, and a barn called by courtesy 'Castle'; those are my feudal possessions. The scenery is gorgeous, but the land—is a caution!"

"Barren?" asked Dick.

"As Riverina in a drought."

"And the tenants?"

"Oh, as to the tenants, we hit it off pretty well. It's in North Kerry they're lively. I'm in the south, you see, and there they're peaceable enough. Laziness is their worst crime. I do all I can for 'em, but I don't see how I can hold on much longer."

"Evict?"

"No," said Flint, warmly; "I'd rather emigrate, and take the whole boiling of them with me; take up new country, and let them select on it. Dick, you savage, don't laugh; I'm not joking. I've thought about it often."

"Would you really like to go back to Australia, Mr. Flint?" Mrs. Edmonstone asked, glancing at the same time rather anxiously at her son.

"Shouldn't mind, madam," returned Flint.

"No more should I!" broke in Dick, in a harsh voice.

Flint looked anxiously at his friend, and made a mental note that Dick had not found all things quite as he expected. For a minute no one spoke; then Fanny took the opportunity of returning to her former charge.

"We have heard some of your adventures which you seemed determined to keep to yourself. I think it was very mean of you, and so does mamma. Oh, Dick, why—why did you never tell us about the bush-ranger?"

Mrs. Edmonstone gazed fondly at her son—and shivered.

"Has he told you that?" Dick asked quickly. "Jack, old chap"—rather reproachfully—"it was a thing I never spoke of."

"Nonsense, my dear fellow!"

"No, it's a fact. I never cared to talk about it, I felt it so strongly."

"Too strongly," said Flint; "I said so at the time."

For a little while Dick was silent; then he said:

"Since he has told you, it doesn't matter. I can only say it nearly drove me out of my mind; it was the bitterest hour of my life!"

A little earlier that day this would have been true.

His mother's eyes filled with tears. "I can understand your feeling, dear Dick," she murmured; "yet I wish you had told us—though, indeed, it would have made me miserable if you had written it. But now Mr. Flint has given us a graphic account of the whole incident. Thank Heaven you were spared, my boy!"

"Thank Sundown," said Dick dryly.

"Oh, yes!" cried Fanny. "Noble fellow! Poor, wicked, generous man! I didn't think such robbers existed; I thought they went out with wigs and patches, a hundred years ago."

"So they did," muttered Flint. "They're extinct as the dodo. I never could make this one out—a deep dog."

"Oh, sir," exclaimed Mrs. Edmonstone, "do you think there is no spark of goodness in the worst natures? of truth in the falsest? of generosity in the most selfish?"

Jack Flint looked quaintly solemn; his face was in shadow, luckily.

"Yes," said Dick, gravely, "my mother is right; there was a good impulse left in that poor fellow, and if you find gold in an outlaw and a thief, you may look for it anywhere. But in my opinion there was more than a remnant of good in that man. Think of it. He saved me from being knifed, to begin with; well, it was to his own interest to do that. But after that he took pity, and left us our money. That needed more than a good impulse; it needed a force of character which few honest men have. Try and realise his position—a price upon him, his hand against the world and the world's hand against him, a villain by profession, not credited with a single virtue except courage, not bound by a single law of God or man; a man you would have thought incapable of compassion; and yet—well, you know what he did."

There was a manly fervour in his voice which went straight to the hearts of his mother and sister. They could not speak. Even Flint forgot to look sceptical.

"If it had not meant so much to me, that hundred pounds," Dick continued, as though arguing with himself, "it is possible that I might think less of the fellow. I don't know, but I doubt it, for we had no notion then what that hundred would turn to. As it is, I have thought of it very often. You remember, Jack, how much more that hundred seemed to me at that time than it really was, and how much less to you?"

"It was a hundred and thirty," said Flint; "I remember that you didn't forget the odd thirty then."

"Dick," Fanny presently exclaimed, out of a brown study, "what do you think you would do if—you ever met that bushranger again. I mean, if he was at your mercy, you know?"

Flint sighed, and prepared his spirit for heroics.

"No use thinking," Dick answered. "By this time he's a life—if they didn't hang him."

Flint became suddenly animated.

"What?" he cried, sharply.

"Why, the last I heard of him—the day I sailed from Melbourne—was, that he was captured somewhere up in Queensland."

"If you had sailed a day later you would have heard more."

"What?" asked Dick, in his turn.

"He escaped."

"Escaped?"

"The same night. He got clean away from the police-barracks at Mount Clarence—that was the little Queensland township. They never caught him. They believe he managed to clear out of the country—to America, probably."

"By Jove, I'm not sorry!" exclaimed Dick.

"Here are some newspaper cuttings about him," continued Flint, taking the scraps from his pocketbook and handing them to Dick. "Read them afterwards; they will interest you. He was taken along with another fellow, but the other fellow was taken dead—shot through the heart. That must have been the one he called Ben; for the big brute who tried to knife you had disappeared some time before. When they were taken they were known to have a lot of gold somewhere—I mean, Sundown was—for they had just stuck up the Mount Clarence bank."

"Yes, I heard that when I heard of the capture."

"Well, it was believed that Sundown feared an attack from the police, and planted the swag, went back to it after his escape, and got clear away with the lot. But nothing is known; for neither Sundown nor the gold was ever seen again."

"Mamma, aren't you glad he escaped," cried Fanny, with glowing cheeks. "It may be wicked, but I know I am! Now, what would you do, Dick?"

"What's the good of talking about it?" said Dick.

"Then I'll tell you what I'd do; I'd hide this poor Sundown from justice; I'd give him a chance of trying honesty, for a change—that's what I should do! And if I were you, I should long and long and long to do it!"

Flint could not help smiling. Dick's sentiment on the subject was sufficiently exaggerated; but this young lady! Did this absurd romanticism run in the family? If so, was it the father, or the grandfather, or the great-grandfather that died in a madhouse?

But Dick gazed earnestly at his sister. Her eyes shone like living coals in the twilight of the shaded room. She was imaginative; and the story of Dick and the bushranger appealed at once to her sensibilities and her sympathy. She could see the night attack in the silent forest, and a face of wild, picturesque beauty—the ideal highwayman—was painted in vivid colour on the canvas of her brain.

"Fanny, I half think I might be tempted to do something like that," said Dick gently. "I have precious few maxims, but one is that he who does me a good turn gets paid with interest—though I have a parallel one for the man who works me a mischief."

"So it is a good turn not to rob a man whom you've already assaulted!" observed Flint ironically.

"It is a good turn to save a man's life."

"True; but you seem to think more of your money than your life!"

"I believe I did four years ago," said Dick, smiling, but he checked his smile when Flint looked at his watch and hastily rose.

Dick expostulated, almost to the extent of bluster, but quite in vain; Flint was already shaking hands with the ladies.

"My dear fellow," said he, "I leave these shores to-night; it's my annual holiday. I'm going to forget my peasants for a few weeks in Paris and Italy. If I lose this train I lose to-night's boat—I found out that before I came; so good-bye, my—"

"No, I'm coming to the station," said Dick; "at least I stickle for that last office."

Mrs. Edmonstone hoped that Mr. Flint—her boy's best friend, as she was assured—would see his way to calling on his way home and staying a day or two. Mr. Flint promised; then he and Dick left the house.

They were scarcely in the road before Flint stopped, turned, laid a hand on each of Dick's shoulders, and quickly delivered his mind:

"There's something wrong. I saw it at once. Tell me."

Dick lowered his eyes before his friend's searching gaze.

"Oh, Jack," he answered, sadly, "it is all wrong!"

And before they reached the station Flint knew all that there was to know—an abridged but unvarnished version—of the withering and dying of Dick's high hopes.

They talked softly together until the train steamed into the station; and then it was Dick who at the last moment returned to a matter just touched in passing:

"As to this dance to-night—you say I must go?"

"Of course you must go. It would never do to stay away. For one thing, your friend, the Colonel might be hurt and bothered, and he is now your best friend, mind. Then you must put a plucky face on it; she mustn't see you cave in after the first facer. I half think it isn't all up yet; you can't tell."

Dick shook his head.

"I would rather not go; it will be wormwood to me; you know what it will be: the two together. And I know it's all up. You don't understand women, Jack."

"Do you?" asked the other, keenly.

"She couldn't deny that—that—I can't say it, Jack."

"Ah, but you enraged her first! Anyway, you ought to go to-night for your people's sake. Your sister's looking forward to it tremendously; never been to a ball with you before; she told me so. By Jove! I wished I was going myself."

"I wish you were, instead of me."

"Nonsense! I say, stand clear. Good-bye!"

Away went the train and Jack Flint. And Dick stood alone on the platform—all the more alone because his hand still tingled from the pressure of that honest grip; because cheering tones still rang in his ears, while his heart turned sick, and very lonely.

CHAPTER XI

DRESSING, DANCING, LOOKING ON

The Bristos dined early that evening, and dressed afterwards; but only the Colonel and Miles sat down. Mrs. Parish was far too busy, adding everywhere finishing touches from her own deft hand; while as for Alice, she took tea only, in her room.

When Mr. Miles went up-stairs to dress, the red sunlight still streamed in slanting rays through the open window. His room was large and pleasant, and faced the drive.

Mr. Miles appeared to be in excellent spirits. He whistled softly to himself—one of Alice's songs; a quiet smile lurked about the corners of his mouth; but since his yellow moustache was long and heavy, this smile was more apparent in the expression of the eyes. He moved about very softly for such a heavy man—almost noiselessly, in fact; but this practice was habitual with him.

His dress-clothes were already laid out on the bed; they seemed never to have been worn. His portmanteau, which stood in one corner, also appeared to have seen little service: it would have been hard to find a scratch on the leather, and the glossy surface bore but one porter's label. But, naturally enough, Miles's belongings were new: a fresh outfit from head to heel is no slight temptation to the Australian in London.

The first step towards dressing for a ball is to undress; the first step towards undressing is to empty one's pockets. With Miles this evening this was rather an interesting operation. It necessitated several niceties of manipulation, and occupied some little time. Miles carefully drew down the blinds as a preliminary, and bolted the door.

He then crossed to the mantel-piece, lit the gas, and felt in his breast-pocket.

The first thing to be removed from this pocket was an envelope—an envelope considerably thickened by its contents, which crackled between the fingers. Miles dropped the envelope into the fender after withdrawing the contents. These he smoothed out upon the mantel-piece; he fairly beamed upon them; they were ten Bank of England ten-pound notes. Then he counted them, folded them into small compass, and transferred them to the trousers-pocket of his evening dress. In doing this his smile became so broad that his whistling ended rather abruptly. It was a pleasant smile.

The next incumbrance of which he relieved himself came from that same breast-pocket; but it was less easily placed elsewhere—so much less that the whistling was dropped altogether, and, instead of smiling, Mr. Miles frowned. Nay, a discovery that his dress-coat had no breast-pocket was followed by quite a volley of oaths. Swearing, however, is a common failing of the most estimable bushmen; so that, coming from a man like Miles, the words meant simply nothing. Miles then tried the trousers-pocket which did not contain the bank-notes; but though the article was—of its kind—remarkably small, it was obviously too large for such a pocket, and for the tail-pockets it was too heavy. Mr. Miles looked seriously put out. His face wore just that expression which might be produced by the rupture of a habit or rule of life that has become second nature. In despair and disgust he dropped the thing into his travelling bag, which he was careful to lock at once, and placed the key in the pocket with the notes: the thing was a small revolver.

There followed, from the waistcoat, penknife, pencilcase, watch and chain, and, lastly, something that created a strange and instant change in the expression of Mr. Miles; and this, though it was the veriest trifle, lying in a twisted scrap of printed paper. He spread and smoothed out the paper just as he had done with the notes, and something was displayed on its surface: something—to judge by the greedy gaze that devoured it—of greater value than the bank-notes, and to be parted with less willingly than the revolver. It was a lock of light-coloured hair.

Mr. Miles again unlocked his travelling bag, and took from it a packet of oiled-silk, a pair of scissors, tape, a needle and thread. It is a habit of many travellers to have such things always about them. Miles, for one, was very handy in the use of them, so that in about ten minutes he produced a very neat little bag, shaped like an arc, and hung upon a piece of tape with ends sewn to the ends of the chord. Holding this bag in his left hand, he now took very carefully, between the thumb and finger of his right hand, the lock of light-coloured hair. He let it roll in his palm, he placed his finger tips in the mouth of the little bag, then paused, as if unwilling to let the hair escape his hand, and, as he paused, his face bent down until his beard touched his wrist. Had not the notion been wildly absurd, one who witnessed the action might have expected Mr. Miles to press his lips to the soft tress that nestled in his palm; but, indeed, he did nothing of the kind. He jerked up his head suddenly, slipped the tress into its little case, and began at once to stitch up the opening. As he did this, however, he might have been closing the tomb upon all he loved—his face was so sad. When the thread was secured and broken, he loosed his collar and shirt-band and hung the oiled-silk bag around his neck.

At that moment a clock on the landing, chiming the three-quarters after eight, bade him make haste. There was good reason, it seemed, why he should be downstairs before the guests began to arrive.

In the drawing-room he found Colonel Bristo and Mrs. Parish. In face benevolent rather than strong, there was little in Colonel Bristo to suggest at any time the Crimean hero; he might have been mistaken for a prosperous stockbroker, but for a certain shyness of manner incompatible with the part. To-night, indeed, the military aspect belonged rather to the lady housekeeper; for rustling impatiently in her handsome black silk gown, springing up repeatedly at the sound of imaginary wheels, Mrs. Parish resembled nothing so much as an old war horse scenting battle. She welcomed the entrance of Miles with effusion, but Miles paid her little attention, and as little to his host. He glanced quickly round the room, and bit his lip with vexation; Miss Bristo was as yet invisible. He crossed the hall by a kind of instinct, and looked into the ballroom, and there he found her. She had flitted down that moment.

Her dress was partly like a crystal fall, and partly like its silver spray; it was all creamy satin and tulle. Or so, at least, it seemed to her partners whose knowledge, of course, was not technical. One of them, who did not catch her name on introduction—being a stranger, brought under the wing of a lady with many daughters—described her on his card simply as "elbow sleeves;" and this must have been a young gentleman of observation, since the sleeves—an artful compromise between long and short—were rather a striking feature to those who knew. Others remembered her by her fan; but the callow ones saw nothing but her face, and that haunted them—until the next ball.

Mr. Miles, however, was the favoured man who was granted the first glimpse of this lovely apparition. He also looked only at her face. Was she so very indignant with him? Would she speak to him? Would she refuse him the dances he had set his heart on? If these questions were decided against him he was prepared to humble himself at her feet; but he soon found there was no necessity for that.

For, though Alice was deeply angry with Mr. Miles, she was ten times angrier with herself, and ten times ten with Dick. Her manner was certainly cold, but she seemed to have forgotten the gross liberty Miles had taken in the afternoon; at any rate, she made no allusion to it. She gave him dances—then and there—since he brought her a programme, but in doing so her thoughts were not of Miles. She gave him literal carte blanche, but not to gratify herself or him. There were too few ways open to her to punish the insults she had received that day; but here was one way—unless the object of her thoughts stayed away.

She hurried from the ballroom at the sound of wheels. In a few minutes she was standing at her father's side shaking hands with the people. She seemed jubilant. She had a sunny smile and a word or two for all. She was like a tinkling brook at summer noon. Everyone spoke of her prettiness, and her dress (the ladies whispered of this), and above all, her splendid spirits. She found out, when it was over, that she had shaken hands with the Edmonstones among the rest. She had done so unconsciously, and Dick, like everybody else, had probably received a charming welcome from her lips.

If that was the case he must have taken the greeting for what it was worth, for he seized the first opportunity to escape from Fanny and Maurice, who were bent upon enjoying themselves thoroughly in unsentimental fashion. He saw one or two men whom he had known before he went to Australia, staring hard at him, but he avoided them; he shrank into a corner and called himself a fool for coming.

He wanted to be alone, yet was painfully conscious of the wretched figure cut by a companionless man in a room full of people. If he talked to nobody people would point at him. Thus perhaps: "The man who made a fool of himself about Miss Bristo, don't you know; went to Australia, made his fortune, and all the rest of it, and now she won't look at him, poor dog!" He was growing morbid. He made a pretence of studying the water-colours on the wall, and wished in his soul that he could make himself invisible.

A slight rustle behind him caused him to turn round. His heart rose in his throat; it was Alice.

"You must dance with me," she said coldly; and her voice was the voice of command.

Dick was electrified; he gazed at her without speaking. Then a scornful light waxed in his eyes, and his lips formed themselves into a sneer.

"You can hardly refuse," she continued cuttingly. "I do not wish to be questioned about you; there has been a little too much of that. Therefore, please to give me your arm. They have already begun."

That was so; the room in which they stood was almost empty. Without a word Dick gave her his arm.

The crowd about the doorway of the ballroom made way for them to pass, and a grim conceit which suggested itself to Dick nearly made him laugh aloud.

As they began to waltz Alice looked up at him with flashing eyes.

"If you hate this," she whispered between her teeth, "imagine my feelings!"

He knew that his touch must be like heated irons to her; he wanted her to stop, but she would not let him. As the couples thinned after the first few rounds she seemed the more eager to dance on. One moment, indeed, they had the floor entirely to themselves. Thus everyone in the room had an opportunity of noticing that Alice Bristo had given her first dance to Dick Edmonstone.

The Colonel saw it, and was glad; but he said to himself, "The boy doesn't look happy enough; and as for Alice—that's a strange expression of hers; I'll tell her I don't admire it. Well, well, if they only get their quarrels over first, it's all right, I suppose."

Fanny noted it with delight. The one bar to her complete happiness for the rest of the evening was now removed. The best of dancers herself, she was sought out by the best. To her a ball was a thing of intrinsic delight, in no way connected with sentiment or nonsense.

Mrs. Parish also saw it, but from a very different point of view. She bustled over to Mr. Miles, who was standing near the piano, and asked him confidentially if he had not secured some dances with Alice? He showed her his card, and the old schemer returned triumphant to her niche among the dowagers.

He followed her, and wrote his name on her empty card opposite the first square dance; a subtle man, this Mr. Miles.

At the end of the waltz Miss Bristo thanked her partner coldly, observed below her breath that she should not trouble him again, bowed—and left him.

Dick was done with dancing; he had not wished to dance at all; but this one waltz was more than enough for him—being with her. Love is responsible for strange paradoxes.

He found two men to talk to: men who gloried in dancing, without greater aptitude for the art (for it is one) than elephants shod with lead. Being notorious, these men never got partners, save occasional ladies from remote districts, spending seasons with suburban relatives. These men now greeted Dick more than civilly, though they were accustomed to cut his brother, the bank-clerk, every morning of their lives. They remembered him from his infancy; they heard he had done awfully well abroad, and congratulated him floridly. They were anxious to hear all about Australia. Dick corrected one or two notions entertained by them respecting that country. He assured them that the natives were frequently as white as they were. He informed them, in reply to a question, that lions and tigers did not prowl around people's premises in the majority of Australian towns; nor, indeed, were those animals to be found in the Colonies, except in cages. He set them right on the usual points of elementary geography. He explained the comprehensive meaning of the term, "the bush."

As Dick could at a pinch be fluent—when Australia was the subject—and as his mood to-night was sufficiently bitter, his intelligent questioners shortly sheered off. They left him at least better-informed men. Thereupon Dick returned to the ballroom with some slight access of briskness, and buried himself in a little knot of wall-flowers of both sexes.

A dance had just begun—scarcely necessary to add, a waltz. Every man blessed with a partner hastened to fling his unit and hers into the whirling throng. After a round or two, half the couples would pause, and probably look on for the rest of the time; but it seems to be a point of honour to begin with the music. As Dick stood watching, his sister passed quite close to him; she happened to be dancing with Maurice, her very creditable pupil, but neither of them saw Dick. Close behind them came a pair of even better dancers, who threaded the moving maze without a pause or a jar or a single false step; they steered so faultlessly that a little path seemed always to open before them; human teetotums, obstacles to every one else, seemed mysteriously to melt at the graceful approach of these two. But, in fact, it was impossible to follow any other pair at the same time, so great were the ease, and beauty, and harmony of this pair. They seemed to need no rest; they seemed to yield themselves completely—no, not to each other—but to the sweet influence of the dreamy waltz.

Dick watched the pair whose exquisite dancing attracted so much attention; his face was blank, but the iron was in his soul. The other wallflowers also watched them, and commented in whispers. Dick overheard part of a conversation between a young lady whose hair was red (but elaborately arranged), and a still younger lady with hair (of the same warm tint) hanging in a plait, who was presumably a sister, not yet thoroughly "out." Here is as much of it as he listened to:

"Oh, how beautifully they dance!"

"Nonsense, child! No better than many others."

"Well, of course, I don't know much about it. But I thought they danced better than anyone in the room. Who are they?"

"Don't speak so loud. You know very well that is Miss Bristo herself; the man is—must be—Mr. Edmonstone."

"Are they engaged?"

"Well, I believe they used to be. He went out to Australia because he couldn't afford to marry (his family were left as poor as mice!), but now he has come back with a fortune, and of course it will be on again now. I used to know him—to bow to—when they lived on the river; I never saw anyone so much altered, but still, that must be he."

"Oh, it must! See how sweet they—"

"Hush, child! You will be heard. But you are quite right; didn't you see how—"

That was as much as Dick could stand. He walked away with a pale face and twitching fingers. He escaped into the conservatory, and found a solitary chair in the darkest corner. In three minutes the waltz ended, and the move to the conservatory was so general that for some minutes the double doors were all too narrow. Before Dick could get away, a yellow-haired youth with a pretty partner, less young than himself, invaded the dark corner, and by their pretty arrangement of two chairs effectually blocked Dick's egress. They were somewhat breathless, having evidently outstripped competitors for this nook only after considerable exertion. The yellow-haired youth proceeded to enter into a desperate flirtation—according to his lights—with the pretty girl his senior: that is to say, he breathed hard, sought and received permission to manipulate the lady's fan, wielded it execrably, and uttered commonplaces in tones of ingenuous pathos. The conservatory, the plashing fountain, and the Chinese lantern are indeed the accepted concomitants of this kind of business, to judge by that class of modern drawing-room songs which is its expositor. At length, on being snubbed by the lady (he had hinted that she should cut her remaining partners in his favour), the young gentleman relapsed with many sighs into personal history, which may have been cunningly intended as an attack on her sympathy, but more probably arose from the egotism of eighteen. He inveighed against the barbarous system of superannuation that had removed him from his public school; inquired repeatedly, Wasn't it awfully hard lines? but finally extolled the freedom of his present asylum, a neighbouring Army crammer's, where (he declared) a fellow was treated like a gentleman, not like a baby. He was plainly in the confidential stage.

All this mildly amused Dick, if anything; but presently the victim of an evil system abruptly asked his partner if she knew Miss Bristo very well.

"Not so very well," was the reply; "but why do you ask?"

"Because—between you and me, you know—I don't like her. She doesn't treat a fellow half civilly. You ask for a waltz, and she gives you a square. Now I know she'd waltzes to spare, 'cause I heard her give one—"

"Oh, so she snubbed you, eh?"

"Well, I suppose it does almost amount to that. By the bye, is she engaged to that long chap who's been dancing with her all the evening?"

"I believe she is; but—"

It was a promising "but;" a "but" that would become entre nous with very little pressing.

"But what?"

"It is a strange affair."

"How?"

"Oh, I ought not to say; but of course you would never repeat—"

"Rather not; surely you can trust a fel—"

"Well, then, she used to be engaged—or perhaps it wasn't an absolute engagement—to someone else: he went out to Australia, and made money, and now that he has come back she's thrown him over for this Mr. Miles, who also comes from Australia. I know it for a fact, because Mrs. Parish told mamma as much."

"Poor chap! Who is he?"

"Mr. Edmonstone; one of the Edmonstones who lived in that big house across the river—surely you remember?"

"Oh, ah!"

"I believe he is here to-night—moping somewhere, I suppose."

"Poor chap! Hallo, there's the music! By Jove! I say, this is awful; we shall have to part!"

They went; and Dick rose up with a bitter smile. He would have given much, very much, for the privilege of wringing that young whippersnapper's neck. Yet it was not the boy's fault; some fate pursued him: there was no place for him—no peace for him—but in the open air.

A soft midsummer's night, and an evening breeze that cooled his heated temples with its first sweet breath. Oh, why had he not thought of coming out long ago! He walked up and down the drive, slowly at first, then at speed, as his misery grew upon him, and more times than he could count. The music stopped, began again, and again ceased; it came to him in gusts as he passed close to the front of the conservatory on his beat. At last, when near the house, he fancied he saw a dark motionless figure crouching in the shrubbery that edged the lawn at the eastern angle of the house.

Dick stopped short in his walk until fancy became certainty; then he crept cautiously towards the figure.

CHAPTER XII

"TO-MORROW, AND TO-MORROW, AND TO-MORROW"

Mr. Miles had written his name no fewer than six times on Alice's card. On finding this out Alice had resolved to recognise perhaps half these engagements—in any case, no more than should suit her convenience. After her dance with Dick she found it would suit her admirably to recognise them all.

For Dick had no word of apology or regret; in fact, he did not speak at all. He did not even look sorry; but only hard and cold and bitter. It was not in the power of woman to treat such a man too harshly.

Alice therefore threw herself into these dances with Miles with a zest which brought about one good result: the mere physical effort gradually allayed the fever of her spirit; with the even, rhythmical motion sufficient peace stole into the heart of the girl to subdue the passionate tumult of many hours. To this tranquillity there presently succeeded the animation inseparable from ardent exercise.

While the music lasted Alice could scarcely bring herself to pause; she seemed never to tire. Between the dances she spoke little to her partner, but filled her lungs with new breath, and waited impatiently for the striking of a new note; and when the new note sounded she turned to that partner with eyes that may have meant to fill with gratitude, yet seemed to him to glow with something else.

Once, when he led her from the heated room, she fancied many eyes were upon her. She heard whispers; a murmur scarcely audible; a hum of wonder, of admiration, perhaps of envy. Well, was she not to be admired and envied? Could she not at least compare with the fairest there in looks? Was there one with a foot more light and nimble? And was not this, her partner, the manliest yet most godlike man that ever stooped to grace a ballroom?—and the best dancer into the bargain?—and the most admirable altogether? These questions were asked and answered in one proud upward glance as she swept on his arm through the throng.

"She never looked so well before," exclaimed Mrs. Parish, in an ecstatic aside to Colonel Bristo; "so brilliant, so animated, so happy!"

"I don't agree with you," the Colonel answered shortly; and he added, with strange insight in one usually so unobservant: "Alice is not herself to-night."

That seemed absurd on the face of it. Who that watched her dancing could have admitted it for a moment? Well, last of all, probably her partner.

The music burst forth again. The dancers flocked back to the room, Alice and Mr. Miles among them. It was the sixth dance, and their third together.

Again they were dancing together, the glassy floor seeming to pass beneath their feet without effort of theirs, the music beating like a pulse in the brain. As for Alice, she forgot her partner, she forgot Dick, she forgot the faces that fled before her eyes as she glided, and turned, and skimmed, and circled; she only knew that she was whirling, whirling, and that for awhile her heart was at rest.

Before the dance was fairly over, Miles led his partner into the conservatory, but said to her: "We will go right through into the open air; it will be so much pleasanter." And he did not wait her consent either— which was characteristic.

The smooth lawn leading down to the river was illuminated, and now that it was quite dark it had a very effective appearance, and was a charming resort between the dances. The lawn was bounded on the right by the little inlet which has been mentioned. A rustic bridge crossed this inlet, leading into a meadow, where seven tall poplars, in rigid rank, fronted the river. Without a protest from the girl, Miles led her over the bridge, and across the meadow, and down to the river's brim, under the shadow of the stately poplars. Most likely she did not heed where they were going; at any rate, they had been there often enough together before—in daylight.

It was a heavenly night; the pale blue stars were reflected in the black still mirror of the Thames, the endless song of the weir was the only sound that broke the absolute stillness of the meadow. No voices reached them from the house, no strains of music. As though influenced by the night, the two were silent for some minutes; then Alice said lightly:

"I am glad you brought me out; I was beginning to stifle. What a lovely night! But I thought there would be a moon. When is there a moon, Mr. Miles?"

No answer but a deep breath, that was half a groan Alice thought. Perhaps she was mistaken. She could not see his face, unless she moved away from him, he was so tall. She repeated the question:

"I want to know when there will be a moon. It would be so delicious now, if it shot up right over there, to be reflected right down there—but why don't you speak, Mr. Miles?"

Still no answer. She drew back a step. He was standing like a monument, tall and rigid, with his hands clasped tightly in front of him and his face turned slightly upward. He seemed unconscious of her presence at his side. Something in his motionless attitude, and the ghastly pallor of his face in the starlight, sent a thrill of vague fear to the heart of Alice. She drew yet a little farther from him, and asked timidly if anything was the matter.

Slowly he turned and faced her. His head drooped, his shoulders sank forward. She could see little beads glistening on his forehead. His hands loosed each other, and his arms were lifted towards her, only to be snatched back, and folded with a thud upon the breast. There they seemed to sink and fall like logs upon a swollen sea.

"Matter?" he cried in a low, tremulous voice; then, pausing, "nothing is the matter!" Then in a whisper, "Nothing to tell you—now."

A strange coldness overcame Alice—the sense of an injury wrought in her carelessness on the man before her. She tried to speak to him, but could find no words. With a single glance of pity, she turned and fled to the house. He did not follow her.

So Mrs. Parish had been right, after all; and she, Alice—a dozen names occurred to her which she had heard fastened upon women who sport with men's hearts to while away an idle month.

She reached the conservatory, but paused on the stone steps, with a hand lightly laid on the iron balustrade—for the floor-level was some feet above that of the garden-path. The music was in full swing once more, but Alice's attention was directed to another sound—even, rapid, restless footsteps on the drive. She peered in that direction; for it was possible, from her position on these steps, to see both the river to the left and the lodge-gates far off on the right—in daylight. She had not long to wait. A figure crossed quickly before her, coming from the front of the house: a man—by his dress, one of the guests—and bare-headed. When he first appeared, his back was half-turned to her; as he followed the bend of the drive she saw nothing but his back! then she lost sight of him in the darkness and the shadows of the drive. Presently she heard his steps returning; he was perambulating a beat. Not to be seen by him as he neared the house, Alice softly opened the door and entered the conservatory. It was at that moment quite deserted. She moved noiselessly to the southern angle, hid herself among the plants, and peered through the glass. It was very dark in this corner, and the foliage so thick that there was small chance of her being seen from without. The solitary figure passed below her, on the other side of the glass; it was Dick: she had been sure of it.

She watched him cross and recross twice—thrice; then she trembled violently, and the next time she could not see him distinctly, because tears—tears of pity—had started to her eyes. If a face—haggard, drawn, white as death, hopeless as the grave—if such a face is a sight for tears, then no wonder Alice wept. Was it possible that this was he who landed in England less than a month ago—so gay, so successful, so boyish? He looked years older. The eager light had gone out of his eyes. His step, so buoyant then, was heavy now, though swift with the fever of unrest. He bent forward as he walked, as though under a burden: a month ago he had borne no burden. Was this the man she had loved so wildly long ago—this wreck? Was this the result of trying to rule her heart by her head? Was this, then, her handiwork?

Her cup to-night was to be filled to overflowing. Even now her heart had gone out in pity to another whom also she had wronged—in pity, but not in love. For here, at last—at this moment—she could see before her but one: the man who had loved her so long and so well; the man who had once held her perfect sun of love—Heaven help her, who held it still!

A faintness overcame this frail girl. Her frame shook with sobs. She could not see. She leant heavily against the framework of the glass. She must have fallen, but a gentle hand at that moment was thrust under her arm.

"Oh, fancy finding you here! Your father sent me—" the pleasant voice broke off suddenly, and Alice felt herself caught in strong and tender arms. She looked up and saw Dick's sister. Her poor beating heart gave one bound, and then her head sank on Fanny's shoulder.

Presently she was able to whisper:

"Take me up-stairs; I am ill. It has been a terrible day for me!"

Mr. Miles still stood by the river, erect, motionless; his powerful hands joined in front of him in an iron knot, his fine head thrown slightly backward, as though in defiance. At first the thoughts in his mind were vague. Then, very slowly, they began to take shape. A little later his expression was soft and full of hope, and his lips kept repeating inaudibly one word: the word "to-morrow."

Then in a moment his mind was chaos.

There is nothing more confusing to the brain than memory. Often there is nothing so agonising and unsparing in its torture, when memory preys upon the present, consuming all its peace and promise like some foul vampire. Miles was now in the clutch of memory in its form of monster. His teeth were clenched, his face livid, the veins on his forehead standing out like the spreading roots of an oak. Spots of blood stood under the nails of his clenched fingers.

The stars blinked high overhead, and the stars deep down in the tranquil water answered them. The voice of the weir seemed nearer and louder. A gentle breeze stirred the line of poplars by the river's brink in the meadow, and fanned the temples of the motionless man at their feet. A bat passed close over him, lightly touching his hair with its wing. Miles did not stir.

Slowly—as it were, limb by limb—he was freeing himself from the grip of the hideous past. At last, with a sudden gesture, he flung back his head, and his eyes gazed upward to the zenith. It was an awful gaze:

a vision of honour and happiness beyond a narrow neck of crime—a glimpse of heaven across the gulf of hell.

His tongue articulated the word that had trembled on his lips before: now it embodied a fixed resolve— "To-morrow! to-morrow!"

Mr. Miles became suddenly aware that his name was being spoken somewhere in the distance by a voice he knew—young Edmonstone's. A moment later the speaker was with him, and had added:

"There is someone who wants to speak to you, standing outside the gate."

There was a gleam of triumph in the younger man's eyes that shot out from the misery of his face like lightning from a cloud, throwing that misery into stronger relief. Miles noted this swift gleam, and it struck terror into his heart—at this moment, more than terror. He was as a general who, on the eve of the brilliant stroke that is to leave him conqueror, hears the alarm sounded in his own rearguard. He stared Dick up and down for some moments. When he spoke, it was—to the ear—with perfect coolness:

"Thanks. I half-expected something of the kind; but it is an infernal nuisance to-night. I must get a coat and hat, for I may have to go up to town at once." And he strode away.

Dick watched him out of sight, admiring more than anything he had seen in this man his readiness and resource at this moment. He would have liked to follow Miles, and keep him within reach or sight; but those were not his directions. Instead, he crossed the bridge, at once bore to the left, and crept into the shrubbery. Keeping close to the wall, without stirring a single leaf, he gained a spot within ten paces of the gate, whence he could command most of the drive and a fair slice of the road. In a minute Miles approached at a swinging walk. He passed close to Dick, and so through the gate. At that moment a man emerged from the shadows at the other side of the road; it was the man Dick had discovered in the shrubbery, though he had seen him before—in the Settler's Hut!

The two men were now but a few paces apart; with little more than a yard between them, they stopped. A low chuckle escaped one of them; but without another sound they turned—passed slowly down the road, side by side, and so out of sight.

Dick gasped: it was so very unlike his preconceived notions of arrest!

CHAPTER XIII

IN BUSHEY PARK

"So boss, you know me?"

"I have not forgotten you, you scoundrel!"

Such was the interchange of greetings between the man from the Exhibition and Mr. Miles, the Australian. They had halted at a lamp-post some distance down the road, and stood facing each other in the gaslight.

"That's right. I'm glad you don't forget old mates," said the stout, round-shouldered man. "That's one good thing, anyway; but it's a bad'un to go calling them names first set-off, especially when—"

"Look here," interrupted Miles, with an admirable imitation of his ordinary tone; "I haven't much time to give you, my man. How the deuce did you get here? And what the deuce do you want with me?"

"Oh, so you're in a hurry, are you?" sneered the man. "And you want to get back to the music, and the wine, and the women, do you?"

"Listen!" said Miles smoothly; "do you hear that step in the distance? It's coming nearer; it's the policeman, for certain; and if you don't get your business stated and done with before he reaches us, I'll give you in charge. Nothing simpler: I know the men on this beat, and they know me."

"Not so well as I do, I reckon!" returned the other dryly, and with the quiet insolence of confident security. "And so you're the fine gentleman now, are you?"

"If you like—and for all you can prove to the contrary."

"The Australian gentleman on a trip home, eh? Good; very good! And your name is Miles!"

"It's worth your neck to make it anything else?"

The other thrust forward his face, and the beady eyes glittered with a malignant fire. "You don't lose much time about coming to threats, mate," he snarled. "P'r'aps it'ud be better if you waited a bit; p'r'aps I'm harder to funk than you think! Because I dare prove to the contrary, and I dare give you your right name. Have you forgotten it? Then I'll remind you; and your friend the bobby shall hear too, now he's come so close. How's this, then?—Edward Ryan, otherwise Ned the Ranger; otherwise—and known all over the world, this is—otherwise—"

Miles stopped him with a rapid, fierce gesture, at the same time quietly sliding his left hand within his overcoat. He felt for his revolver. It was not there. He recalled the circumstance which had compelled him to lay it aside. It seemed like Fate: for months that weapon had never been beyond the reach of his hand; now, for the first time, he required it, and was crippled for want of it. He recovered his composure in a moment, but not before his discomfiture had been noticed, and its cause shrewdly guessed. Laying a heavy hand on the other's broad, rounded shoulder, he said simply and impressively:

"Hush!"

"Then let's move on."

"Where?"

"Where we can talk."

The man pointed across the road to a broad opening directly opposite the lamp-post. It was the beginning of another road; the spot where they stood was indeed the junction of the cross and down-stroke of a capital letter T, of which the cross was the road that ran parallel with the river.

"Very well," said Miles, with suspicious alacrity; "but I must go back first to make some excuse, or they will be sending after me."

"Then, while you are gone, I shall confide in your friend the policeman."

Miles uttered a curse, and led the way across the road and straight on. There were no lamps in the road they entered now—no houses, no lights of any kind—but on the right a tall hedge, and on the left trim posts and rails, with fields beyond. They walked on for some minutes in silence, which was at length broken by Miles's unwelcome visitor.

"It's no sort o' use you being in a hurry," said he. "I've found you out; why not make the best of it?"

"What am I to do for you?" asked Miles, as smoothly as though the man by his side were an ordinary highway beggar.

"You'll see in good time. Sorry I've put you to inconvenience, but if you weren't passing for what you ain't you wouldn't feel it so; so you see, Ned Ryan, playing the gent has its drawbacks. Now, after me having crossed the whole blessed world to speak to you, it would be roughish if you refused me your best ear; now wouldn't it?"

"You have just landed, then?" said Miles; and added, after a pause, "I hoped you were dead."

"Thanks," returned the other, in the tone of coarse irony that he had employed from the beginning. "Being one as returns good for evil, I don't mind saying I was never so glad as when I clapped eyes on you yesterday—alive and safe."

"Yesterday! Where?"

"Never mind where. But I ain't just landed—Oh, no!"

Suddenly Miles stopped short in his walk. They had entered again the region of lights and houses; the road was no longer dark and lonely; it had intersected the highroad that leads to Kingston, and afterwards bent in curves to the right; now its left boundary was the white picket-fence of the railway, and, a hundred yards beyond, a cluster of bright lights indicated Teddington station.

"Not a step further," said Miles.

"What! not to the station? How can we talk—"

"You are a greater fool than I took you for," said Miles scornfully.

"Yes? Well, anyway, I mean to say what I've got to say, wherever it is," was the dogged reply. "If you came to town to my lodging, not a soul could disturb us. We can't talk here."

Miles hesitated.

"There is a place, five minutes' walk from here, that I would trust before any room," he said presently. "Only be reasonable, my good fellow, and I'll hear what you have to say there."

The man turned his head and glanced sharply in the direction whence they had come. Then he assented.

Miles led the way over the wooden footbridge that spans the line a little way above the station. In three minutes they walked in the shadow of great trees. The high wall in front of them bent inwards, opening a wide mouth. Here were iron gates and lamps; and beyond, black forms and deep shadows, and the silence of sleeping trees. Without a word they passed through the gates into Bushey Park.

Miles chose the left side of the avenue, and led on under the spreading branches of the horse-chestnuts. Perhaps a furlong from the gates he stopped short, and confronted his companion.

"Here I will settle with you," he said, sternly. "Tell me what you want; or first, if you like, how you found me. For the last thing I remember of you, Jem Pound, is that I sacked you from our little concern—for murder."

The man took a short step forward, and hissed back his retort:

"And the last thing I heard of you—was your sticking up the Mount Clarence bank, and taking five hundred ounces of gold! You were taken; but escaped the same night—with the swag. That's the last I heard of you—Ned Ryan—Ned the Ranger—Sundown!"

"I can hang you for that murder," pursued Miles, as though he had not heard a word of this retort.

"Not without dragging yourself in after me, for life; which you'd find the worse half of the bargain! Now listen, Ned Ryan; I'll be plain with you. I can, and mean to, bleed you for that gold—for my fair share of it."

"And this is what you want with me?" asked Miles, in a tone so low and yet so fierce that the confidence of Jem Pound was for an instant shaken.

"I want money; I'm desperate—starving!" he answered, his tone sinking for once into a whine.

"Starvation doesn't carry a man half round the world."

"I was helped," said Pound darkly.

"Who helped you?"

"All in good time, Sundown, old mate! Come, show me the colour of it first."

Miles spread out his arms with a gesture that was candour itself.

"I have none to give you. I am cleaned out myself."

"That's a lie!" cried Pound, with a savage oath.

Miles answered with cool contempt:

"Do you think a man clears out with five hundred ounces in his pockets? Do you think he could carry it ten miles, let alone two hundred?"

Jem Pound looked hard at the man who had been his captain in a life of crime. A trace of the old admiration and crude respect for a brilliant fearless leader, succeeded though this had been by years of bitter hatred, crept into his voice as he replied:

"You could! No one else! No other man could have escaped at all as you did. I don't know the thing you couldn't do!"

"Fool!" muttered Miles, half to himself.

"That's fool number two," answered Pound angrily. "Well, maybe I am one, maybe I'm not; anyhow I've done what a dozen traps have tried and failed, and I'll go on failing—until I help them: I've run you to earth, Ned Ryan!"

"Ah! Well, tell me how."

"No, I heard a footstep just then; people are about."

"A chance passer," said Miles.

"You should have come with me. Walls are safe if you whisper; here there are no walls."

"You are right. We have stuck to the most public part, though; follow me through here."

They had been standing between two noble trees of the main avenue. This avenue, as all the world knows, is composed of nothing but horse chestnuts; but behind the front rank on either side are four lines of limes, forming to right and left of the great artery four minor parallel channels. Miles and his companion, turning inwards, crossed the soft sward of the minor avenues, and emerged on the more or less broken ground that expands southward to Hampton Wick. This tract is patched in places with low bracken, and dotted in others with young trees. It is streaked with converging paths—some worn by the heavy tread of men, others by the light feet of the deer, but all soft and grassy, and no more conspicuous than the delicate veins of a woman's hand.

They left the trees behind, and strode on heedlessly into the darkness. Their shins split the dew from the ferns; startled fawns rose in front of them and scampered swiftly out of sight, a momentary patch of grey upon the purple night.

"This will suit you," said Miles, still striding aimlessly on. "It is a good deal safer than houses here. Now for your story."

He was careful as they walked to keep a few inches in the rear of Pound, who, for his part, never let his right hand stray from a certain sheath that hung from the belt under his coat: the two men had preserved these counter-precautions from the moment they quitted the lighted roads.

"It is soon told, though it makes me sweat to think of it—all but the end, and that was so mighty neat the rest's of no account," Pound began, with a low laugh. "Well, you turned me adrift, and I lived like a hunted dingo for very near a year. If I'd dared to risk it, I'd have blabbed on you quick enough; but there was no bait about Queen's evidence, and I daren't let on a word else—you may thank the devil for that, not me! Well, I had no money, but I got some work at the stations, though in such mortal terror that I daren't stay long in one place, until at last I got a shepherd's billet, with a hut where no one saw me from week's end to week's end. There I was safe, but in hell! I daren't lay down o' nights; when I did I couldn't sleep. I looked out o' the door twenty times a night to see if they were coming for me. I saw frightful things, and heard hellish sounds; I got the horrors without a drop o' liquor! You did all this, Ned Ryan—you did it all!"

Inflamed by the memory of his torments, Pound raised his voice in rage and hate that a single day had exalted from impotency to might. But rage red-hot only aggravates the composure of a cool antagonist, and the reply was cold as death:

"Blame yourself. If you had kept clean hands, you might have stuck to us to the end; as it was, you would have swung the lot of us in a month. No man can accuse me of spilling blood—nor poor Hickey either, for that matter; but you—I could dangle you to-morrow! Remember that, Jem Pound; and go on."

"I'll remember a bit more—you'll see!" returned Pound with a stifled gasp. He was silent for the next minute; then added in the tone of one who bides his time to laugh last and loudest: "Go on? Right! Well, then, after a long time I showed my nose in a town, and no harm came of it."

"What town?"

"Townsville."

"Why Townsville?" Miles asked quickly.

"Your good lady was there; I knew she would give me—well, call it assistance."

"That was clever of you," said Miles after a moment's silence, but his calm utterance was less natural than before.

"I wanted a ship," Pound continued; "and could have got one too, through being at sea before at odd times, if I'd dared loaf about the quay by day. Well, one dark night I was casting my eyes over the Torres Straits mail boat, when a big man rushed by me and crept on board like a cat. I knew it was you that moment; I'd heard of your escape. You'd your swag with you; the gold was in it—I knew it! What's the use of shaking your head? Of course it was. Well, first I pushed forward to speak to you, then I drew back. Why? Because just then you'd have thought no more of knocking me on the head and watching me drown before your eyes than I'd think of—"

"Committing another murder! By heaven, I wish I had had the chance!" muttered Miles.

"Then, if I'd started the hue and cry, it would have meant killing the golden goose—and most likely me with it. I thought of something better: I saw you drop down into the hold—there was too much risk in showing your money for a passage or trying for a fo'c'stle berth; the boat was to sail at daylight. I rushed to your wife and told her; but her cottage was three miles out of the town, worse luck to it! and when I got her to the quay, you were under way and nearly out of sight—half-an-hour late in sailing, and you'd have had a friend among the passengers!"

"And what then?"

"Why, then your wife was mad! I soothed her: she told me that she had some money, and I told her if she gave me some of it I might still catch you for her. I showed her how the mail from Sydney, by changing at Brindisi, would land one in England before the Queensland boat. I knew it was an off-chance whether you ever meant to reach England at all, or whether you'd succeed if you tried; but," said Pound, lowering his voice unaccountably, "I was keen to be quit of the country myself. Here was my chance, and I took it; your wife shelled out, and I lost no time."

The man ceased speaking, and looked sharply about him. His eyes were become thoroughly used to the darkness, so that he could see some distance all round with accuracy and ease; but they were eyes no less keen than quick; and so sure-sighted that one glance was at all times enough for them, and corroboration by a second a thing unthought of.

They were walking, more slowly now, on a soft mossy path, and nearing a small plantation, chiefly of pines and firs, half-a-mile from the avenues. This path, as it approaches the trees, has beside it several saplings shielded by tall triangular fences, which even in daylight would afford very fair cover for a man's body. Miles and Pound had passed close to half-a-dozen or more of these triangles.

"Well?" said Miles; for Pound remained silent.

"I am looking to see where you have brought me."

"I have brought you to the best place of all, this plantation," Miles answered, leaving the path and picking his way over the uneven ground until there were trees all round them. "Here we should be neither seen nor heard if we stayed till daybreak. Are you going on?"

But Pound was not to be hurried until he had picked out a spot to his liking still deeper in the plantation; far from shaking his sense of security, the trees seemed to afford him unexpected satisfaction. The place was dark and silent as the tomb, though the eastern wall of the park was but three hundred yards distant. Looking towards this wall in winter, a long, unbroken row of gaslights marks the road beyond; but in summer the foliage of the lining trees only reveals a casual glimmer, which adds by contrast to the solitude of this sombre, isolated, apparently uncared-for coppice.

"I reached London just before you," resumed Pound, narrowly watching the effect of every word. "I waited for your boat at the docks. There were others waiting. I had to take care—they were detectives."

Miles uttered an ejaculation.

"I watched them go on board; I watched them come back—without you. They were white with disappointment. Ned Ryan, those men would sell their souls to lay hands on you now!"

"Go on!" said Miles between his teeth.

"Well, I got drinking with the crew, and found you'd fallen overboard coming up Channel—so they thought; it happened in the night. But you've swum swollen rivers, before my eyes, stronger than I ever see man swim before or since, and I was suspicious. Ships get so near the land coming up Channel. I went away and made sure you were alive, if I could find you. At last, by good luck, I did find you."

"Where?"

"At the Exhibition. I took to loafing about the places you were sure to go to, sooner or later, as a swell, thinking yourself safe as the Bank. And that's where I found you—the swell all over, sure enough. You stopped till the end, and that's how I lost you in the crowd going out; but before that I got so close I heard what you were saying to your swell friends: how you'd bring 'em again, if they liked; what you'd missed that day, but must see then. So I knew where to wait about for you. But you took your time about coming again. Every day I was waiting and watching—and starving. A shilling a day to let me into the place; a quid in reserve for when the time came; and pence for my meals. Do you think a trifle'll pay for all that? When you did turn up again yesterday, you may lay your life I never lost sight of you."

"I should have known you any time; why you went about in that rig—"

"I had no others. I heard fools whisper that I was a detective, moreover, and that made me feel safe."

"You followed me down here yesterday, did you? Then why do nothing till to-night?"

The fellow hesitated, and again peered rapidly into every corner of the night.

"Why did you wait?" repeated Miles impatiently.

An evil grin overspread the countenance of Jem Pound. He seemed to be dallying with his answer— rolling the sweet morsel on his tongue—as though loth to part with the source of so much private satisfaction. Miles perceived something of this, and, for the first time that night, felt powerless to measure the extent of his danger. Up to this point he had realised and calculated to a nicety the strength of the hold of this man over him, and he had flattered himself that it was weak in comparison with his own counter-grip; but now he suspected, nay felt, the nearness of another and a stronger hand.

"Answer, man," he cried, with a scarcely perceptible tremor in his voice, "before I force you! Why did you wait?"

"I went back," said Pound slowly, slipping his hand beneath his coat, and comfortably grasping the haft of his sheath-knife, "to report progress."

"To whom?"

"To—your wife!"

"What!"

"Your wife!"

"You are lying, my man," said Miles, with a forced laugh. "She never came to England."

"She didn't, didn't she? Why, of course you ought to know best, even if you don't; but if you asked me, I should say maybe she isn't a hundred miles from you at this very instant!"

"Speak that lie again," cried Miles, his low voice now fairly quivering with passion and terror, "and I strike you dead where you stand! She is in Australia, and you know it!"

Jem Pound stepped two paces backward, and answered in a loud, harsh tone:

"You fool! she is here!"

Miles stepped forward as if to carry out his threat; but even as he moved he heard a rustle at his side, and felt a light hand laid on his arm. He started, turned, and looked round. There, by his side—poverty-stricken almost to rags, yet dark and comely as the summer's night—stood the woman whom years ago he had made his wife!

A low voice full of tears whispered his name: "Ned, Ned!" and "Ned, Ned!" again and again.

He made no answer, but stood like a granite pillar, staring at her. She pressed his arm with one hand, and laid the other caressingly on his breast; and as she stood thus, gazing up through a mist into his stern, cold face, this topmost hand rested heavily upon him. To him it seemed like lead; until suddenly—did it press a bruise or a wound, that such a hideous spasm should cross his face? that he should shake off the woman so savagely?

By the merest accident, the touch of one woman had conjured the vision of another; he saw before him two, not one; two as opposite in their impressions on the senses as the flower and the weed; as separate in their associations as the angels of light and darkness.

Yet this poor woman, the wife, could only creep near him again—forgetting her repulse, since he was calm the next moment—and press his hand to her lips, so humbly that now he stood and bore it, and repeat brokenly:

"I have found him! Oh, thank God! Now at last I have found him!"

While husband and wife stood thus, silenced—one by love, the other by sensations of a very different kind—the third person watched them with an expression which slowly changed from blank surprise to mortification and dumb rage. At last he seemed unable to stand it any longer, for he sprang forward and whispered hoarsely in the woman's ear:

"What are you doing? Are you mad? What are we here for? What have we crossed the sea for? Get to work, you fool, or—"

"To work to bleed me, between you!" cried Ned Ryan, shaking himself again clear of the woman. "By heaven, you shall find me a stone!"

Elizabeth Ryan turned and faced her ally, and waved him back with a commanding gesture.

"No, Jem Pound," said she, in a voice as clear and true as a clarion, "it is time to tell the truth: I did not come to England for that! O Ned, Ned! I have used this man as my tool—can't you see?—to bring me to you. Ned, my husband, I am by your side; have you no word of welcome?"

She clung to him, with supplication in her white face and drooping, nerveless figure; and Pound looked on speechless. So he had been fooled by this smooth-tongued, fair-faced trash; and all his plans and schemes, and hungry longings and golden expectations, were to crumble into dust before treachery such as this! So, after all, he had been but a dupe—a ladder to be used and kicked aside! A burning desire came over him to plunge his knife into this false demon's heart, and end all.

But Ryan pushed back his wife a third time, gently but very firmly.

"Come, Liz," said he, coldly enough, yet with the edge off his voice and manner, "don't give us any of this. This was all over between us long ago. If it's money you want, name a sum; though I have little enough, you shall have what I can spare, for I swear to you I got away with my life and little else. But if it's sentiment, why, it's nonsense; and you know that well enough."

Elizabeth Ryan stood as one stabbed, who must fall the moment the blade is withdrawn from the wound; which office was promptly performed by one who missed few opportunities.

"Why, of course!" exclaimed Pound, with affected sympathy with the wife and indignation against the husband. "To be sure you see how the wind lies, missis?"

"What do you mean?" cried Elizabeth Ryan fiercely.

"Can't you see?" pursued Pound in the same tone, adding a strong dash of vulgar familiarity; "can't you see that you're out of the running, Liz, my lass? You may be Mrs. Ryan, but Mrs. Ryan is a widow; there's no Ned Ryan now. There's a Mr. Miles, an Australian gentleman, in his skin, and, mark me, there'll be a Mrs.—"

He stopped, for Liz Ryan turned on him so fiercely that it looked as though she was gathering herself to spring at his throat.

"You liar!" she shrieked. "Tell him, Ned! Give him the lie yourself! Quickly—speak, or I shall go mad!"

Her husband uttered no sound.

"He can't, you see," sneered Pound. "Why, if you'd only come in with me into the garden, you'd have seen the two together sweethearting in the starlight!"

"If I had," said Mrs. Ryan, trembling violently, "I pity both. But no, I don't believe it! O Ned! Ned! answer, unless you want to break my heart!"

"Well, well, what does it matter?" put in Pound hastily, speaking to her in a fatherly, protective tone, which hit the mark aimed at. "Liz, my dear, you and I have been good friends all this time; then why not let him go his ways?—after we've got our rights, I mean."

Ned Ryan glanced sharply from his wife to the man who had brought her from Australia; and then he spoke:

"My good woman, why not be frank? What's the use of acting a part to me? Anyway, it's a bit too thin this time. Only let me alone, and you two can go on—as you are. Come now, I don't think I'm hard on you; considering everything I might be a deal harder."

His wife sprang before him, her black eyes flashing, her whole frame quivering.

"Edward Ryan, you shall answer for these foul, cruel words before Him who knows them to be false. What do you think me, I wonder? That vile thing there—can't you see how I have used him?—he has been the bridge between me and you, yet you make him the barrier! Oh, you know me better than that, Ned Ryan! You know me for the woman who sacrificed all for you—who stood by you through thick and thin, and good and bad, while you would let her—who would not have forsaken you for twenty murders!—who loved you better than life—God help me!" cried the poor woman, wildly, "for I love you still!"

She rose the next moment, and continued in a low, hard, changed voice:

"But love and hate lie close together; take care, and do not make me hate you, for if you do I shall be pitiless as I have been pitiful, cruel as I have been fond. I, who have been ready all these years to shield you with my life—I shall be the first to betray you to the laws you have cheated, if you turn my love to hate. Ned! Ned! stop and think before it is too late!"

She pressed both hands upon her heart, as if to stay by main force its tumultuous beating. Her limbs tottered beneath her. Her face was like death. Her life's blood might have mingled with the torrent of her eloquence!

"You are beside yourself," said her husband, who had listened like a stone; "otherwise you would remember that tall talk never yet answered with me. And yet—yet I am sorry for you—so poor, so ragged, so thin—" His voice suddenly softened, and he felt with his hand in his pocket. "See here! take these twenty pounds. It's a big lump of all I have; but 'twill buy you a new dress and some good food, and make you decent for a bit, and if I had more to spare, upon my soul you should have it!"

Elizabeth Ryan snatched the notes from her husband's hand, crumpled them savagely, and flung them at his feet; with a wild sweep of her arm she tore off her bonnet, as though it nursed the fire within her brain, and coils of dark, disordered hair fell down about her shoulders. For one moment she stood glaring fixedly at her husband, and then fell heavily to the ground.

"She has fainted," said Miles, not without pity, and bending over her. "Bring her to, then lead her away. Take her back; she must not see me again."

Pound knelt down, and quietly pocketed the crumpled notes; then he raised the senseless head and fanned the ashy face, looking up meanwhile and saying:

"Meet me here to-morrow night at ten; I will come alone."

"For the last time, then."

"I am agreeable; but it will rest with you."

Miles drew away into the shadows. He waited, and presently he heard a faint, hollow, passionate voice calling his name:

"Ned Ryan! I will come back, Ned Ryan! Come back, never fear, and see you—see you alone! And if you are as hard then—as hard and cruel—Heaven help us both!—Heaven help us both!"

When Ned Ryan, alias Sundown, alias Miles, heard the footsteps fail in the distance and die on the still night air, a rapid change came over his face and bearing. Throughout the night he had lost his self-command seldom; his nerve never. But now the pallor of a corpse made his features ghastly, and a cold sweat burst forth in great beads upon his forehead. His limbs trembled, and he staggered.

By a violent effort he steadied his brain and straightened his body. In a few minutes he had well-nigh regained his normal calm. Then gradually his chest expanded, and his air became that of one who has climbed through desperate peril to the lofty heights and sweet breath of freedom. Nay, as he stood there, gazing hopefully skyward, with the dim light upon his strong handsome face, he might very well have been mistaken for a good man filled with dauntless ambition, borne aloft on the wings of noble yearning.

"After all, I am not lost!" The thoughts escaped in words from the fulness of his soul. "No, I am safe; he dares not betray me; she will not—because she loves me. Not another soul need ever know."

A new voice broke upon his ear:

"You are wrong; I know!"

His lowered gaze fell upon the motionless figure of Dick Edmonstone, who was standing quietly in front of him.

CHAPTER XIV

QUITS

For the second time that night Miles felt instinctively for his revolver, and for the second time in vain.

The younger man understood the movement.

"A shot would be heard in the road and at the lodge," said he quietly. "You'll only hasten matters by shooting me."

At once Miles perceived his advantage; his adversary believed him to be armed. Withdrawing his hand from the breast of his overcoat slowly, as though relinquishing a weapon in the act of drawing it, he answered:

"I believe you are right. But you are a cool hand!"

"Perhaps."

"I have only seen one other as cool—under fire."

"Indeed?"

"A fact. But I'll tell you where you come out even stronger."

"Do."

"In playing the spy. There you shine!"

"Hardly," said Dick dryly, and this time he added a word or two: "or I should have shown you up some time since."

The two men faced one another, fair and square, but their attitudes were not aggressive. Miles leant back against a tree with folded arms, and Dick stood with feet planted firmly and hands in his pockets. A combat of coolness was beginning. The combatants were a man in whom this quality was innate, and one who rose to it but rarely. In these circumstances it is strange that the self-possession of Dick was real to the core, whilst that of the imperturbable Miles was for once affected and skin-deep.

"Will you tell me," said Miles, "what you have heard? You may very possibly have drawn wrong inferences."

"I heard all," Dick answered.

"All is vague; why not be specific?"

"I heard that—well, that that woman was your wife."

Miles felt new hope within him. Suppose he had heard no more than that! And he had not heard anything more—the thing was self-evident—or he would not have spoken first of this—this circumstance which must be confessed "unpleasant," but should be explained away in five minutes; this—what more natural?—this consequence of an ancient peccadillo, this bagatelle in comparison with what he might have learned.

"My dear sir, it is nothing but an infernal lie!" he cried with eager confidence; "she never was anything of the kind. It is the old story: an anthill of boyish folly, a mountain of blackguardly extortion. Can't you see?"

"No, I can't," said Dick stolidly.

"Why, my good fellow, they have come over on purpose to bleed me—they said so. It's as plain as a pikestaff."

"That may be true, so far as the man is concerned."

"Don't you see that the woman is his accomplice? But now a word with you, my friend. These are my private affairs that you have had the impudence—"

"That was not all I heard," said Dick coldly.

Danger again—in the moment of apparent security.

"What else did you hear, then?" asked Miles, in a voice that was deep and faint at the same time.

"Who you are," replied Dick shortly. "Sundown the bushranger."

The words were pronounced with no particular emphasis; in fact, very much as though both sobriquet and calling were household words, and sufficiently familiar in all men's mouths. The bushranger heard them without sign or sound. Dick waited patiently for him to speak; but he waited long.

It was a strange interview between these two men, in the dead of this summer's night, in the heart of this public park. They were rivals in love; one had discovered the other to be not only an impostor, but a notorious felon; and they had met before under circumstances the most peculiar—a fact, however, of which only one of them was now aware. The night was at the zenith of its soft and delicate sweetness. A gentle breeze had arisen, and the tops of the slender firs were making circles against the sky, like the mastheads of a ship becalmed; and the stars were shining like a million pin-pricks in the purple cloak of light. At last Miles spoke, asking with assumed indifference what Dick intended to do.

"But let it pass; of course you will inform at once!"

"What else can I do?" demanded Dick, sternly.

Miles scrutinised his adversary attentively and speculated whether there was the least chance of frightening such a man. Then he again thrust his hand into the breast of his overcoat, and answered reflectively:

"You can die—this minute—if I choose."

Dick stood his ground without moving a muscle.

"Nonsense!" he said scornfully. "I have shown you that you can gain nothing by that."

Miles muttered a curse, and scowled at the ground, without, however, withdrawing his hand.

"The case stands thus," said Dick: "you have imposed on friends of mine, and I have found you—not a common humbug, as I thought all along—but quite a famous villain. Plainly speaking, a price is on your head."

Miles did not speak.

"And your life is in my hands."

Miles made no reply.

"The natural thing," Dick continued, "would have been to crawl away, when I heard who you were, and call the police. You see I have not done that."

Still not a word.

"Another, and perhaps fairer, way would be to give you a fair start from this spot and this minute, and not say a word for an hour or two, until people are about; the hare-and-hounds principle, in fact. But I don't mean to do that either."

Miles raised his eyes, and at last broke his silence.

"You are arbitrary," he sneered. "May I ask what is the special quality of torture you have reserved for me? I am interested to know."

"I shall name a condition," replied Dick firmly—"a single condition—on which, so far as I am concerned, you may impose on the public until some one else unmasks you."

"I don't believe you!"

"You have not heard my condition. I am in earnest."

"I wouldn't believe you on oath!"

"And why?"

"Because you owe me a grudge," said Miles, speaking rapidly—"because it is in your interest to see me go under."

"My condition provides for all that."

"Let me hear it, then."

"First tell me how you came to know the Bristos."

Miles gave Dick substantially the same story that he had already learned from Alice.

"Now listen to me," said Dick. "Instead of squatter you were bushranger. You had been in England a day or two instead of a month or two, and you had set foot in Sussex only; instead of masquerading as a fisherman you wore your own sailor's clothes, in which you swam ashore from your ship."

"Well guessed!" said Miles ironically.

"A cleverer thing was never done," Dick went on, his tone, for the moment, not wholly free from a trace of admiration. "Well, apart from that first set of lies, your first action in England was a good one. That is one claim on leniency. The account you have given me of it is quite true, for I heard the same thing from one whose lips, at least, are true!"

These last words forced their way out without his knowledge until he heard them.

"Ah!" said Miles.

An involuntary subdual of both voices might have been noticed here; it was but momentary, and it did not recur.

Dick Edmonstone took his hands from his pockets, drew nearer to Miles, slowly beat his left palm with his right fist, and said:

"My condition is simply this: you are to go near the Bristos no more."

If this touched any delicate springs in the heart of Miles, their workings did not appear in his face. He made no immediate reply; when it came, there was a half-amused ring in his speech:

"You mean to drive a hard bargain."

"I don't call it hard."

"All I possess is in that house. I cannot go far, as I stand; you might as well give me up at once."

"I see," said Dick musingly. "No; you are to have an excellent chance. I have no watch on me: have you? No? Well, it can't be more than one now, or two at the latest, and they keep up these dances till dawn— or they used to. Then perhaps you had better go back to the house now. Button-hole the Colonel; tell him you have had a messenger down from town—from your agent. You can surely add a London agent to your Queensland station and your house in Sydney! Well, affairs have gone wrong on this station of yours—drought, floods—anything you like; you have received an important wire; you are advised, in fact, to start back to Queensland at once. At any rate, you must pack up your traps and leave Graysbrooke first thing in the morning. You are very sorry to be called back so suddenly—they are sorrier still to lose you; but Australia and England are so close now, you are sure to be over again some day—and all the rest of it; but you are never to go near them again. Do you agree?"

"What is the alternative?"

"Escape from here dressed like that if you can! You will breakfast in gaol. At best you will be hunted for a week or two, and then taken miserably—there is no bush in England; whereas I offer you freedom with one restriction."

"I agree," said Miles, hoarsely.

"Very good. If you keep your word, Sundown the bushranger is at the bottom of the sea, for all I know; if you break it, Sundown the bushranger is a lost man. Now let us leave this place."

Dick led the way from the plantation, with his hands again deep in his pockets.

Miles followed, marvelling. Marvelling that he, who had terrorised half Australia, should be dictated to by this English whelp, and bear it meekly; wondering what it all meant. What, to begin with, was the meaning of this masterly plan for an honourable exit? which was, in fact, a continuation of his own falsehood. Why had not this young fellow—who had every reason to hate him, independently of to-night's discovery—quietly brought the police and watched him taken in cold blood? There would have been nothing underhand in that; it was, in fact, the only treatment that any criminal at large would expect at the hands of the average member of society—if he fell into those hands. Then why had not this been done? What tie or obligation could possibly exist between this young Edmonstone and Sundown the Australian bushranger?

The night was at its darkest when they reached the avenue; so dark that they crossed into the middle of the broad straight road, where the way was clearest. Straight in front of them burned the lamps of the gateway, like two yellow eyes staring through a monstrous crape mask. They seemed to be walking in a valley between two long, regular ranges of black mountains with curved and undulating tops—only that the mountains wavered in outline, and murmured from their midst under the light touch of the sweet mild breeze.

They walked on in silence, and watched the deep purple fading slowly but surely before their eyes, and the lights ahead growing pale and sickly.

Miles gave expression to the thought that puzzled him most:

"For the life of me, I can't make out why you are doing this" (he resented the bare notion of mercy, and showed it in his tone). "With you in my place and I in yours—"

Dick stopped in his walk, and stopped Miles also.

"Is it possible you do not know me?"

"I have known you nearly a month," Miles answered.

"Do you mean to say you don't remember seeing me before—before this last month?"

"Certainly, when first I met you, I seemed to remember your voice; but from what I was told about you I made sure I was mistaken."

"Didn't they tell you that at one time, out there I was hawking?"

"No. Why, now—"

"Stop a bit," said Dick, raising his hand. "Forget that you are here; forget you are in England. Instead of these chestnuts, you're in the mallee scrub. The night is far darker than this night has ever been: the place is a wilderness. You are lying in wait for a hawker's wagon. The hawkers drive up; you take them by surprise, and you're three to two. They are at your mercy. The younger one is a new chum from England—a mere boy. He has all the money of the concern in his pocket, and nothing to defend it with. He flings himself unarmed upon one of your gang, and, but for you, would be knifed for his pains. You save him by an inch; but you see what maddens him—you see he has the money. You take it from him. The money is all the world to him: he is mad: he wants to be killed outright. You only bind him to the wheel, taking from him all he has. So he thinks, and death is at his heart. But he finds that, instead of taking it all, you have left it all; you have been moved by compassion for the poor devil of a new chum! Well, first he cannot believe his eyes; then he is grateful; then senseless."

Miles scanned the young man's face in the breaking light. Yes, he remembered it now; it had worn this same passionate expression then. His own face reflected the aspect of the eastern sky; a ray was breaking in upon him, and shedding a new light on an old action, hidden away in a dark corner of his mind. A thing that had been a little thing until now seemed to expand in the sudden warmth of this new light. Miles felt an odd, unaccountable sensation, which, however, was not altogether outside his experience: he had felt it when he pulled Colonel Bristo from the sea, and in the moment of parting with his coat to a half-perishing tramp.

Dick continued:

"Stop a minute—hear the end. This new chum, fresh from 'home,' was successful. He made a fortune— of a sort. It might have been double what it is had he been in less of a hurry to get back to England." Dick sighed. "Whatever it is, it was built on that hundred which you took and restored: that was its nucleus. And therefore—as well as because you saved his life—this new chum, when no longer one, never forgot Sundown the bushranger; he nursed a feeling of gratitude towards him which was profound if, as he had been assured, illogical. Only a few hours ago he said, 'If he came within my power I should be inclined to give him a chance,' or something like that." Dick paused; then he added: "Now you know why you go free this morning."

Miles made no immediate remark. Bitter disappointment and hungry yearning were for the moment written clearly on his handsome, reckless face. At last he said:

"You may not believe me, but when you came to me—down there on the lawn—that's what I was swearing to myself; to begin afresh. And see what has come to me since then!" he added, with a harsh laugh.

"Just then," returned Dick, frankly, "I should have liked nothing better than to have seen you run in. I followed you out with as good a hate as one man can feel towards another. You never thought of my following you out here? Nor did I think of coming so far; by the bye, the—your wife made it difficult for me; she was following too. Yes, I hated you sufficiently; and I had suspected you from the first—but not for what you are; when I heard Jem Pound say your name I was staggered, my brain went reeling, I could scarcely keep from crying out."

"Did you recognise him?"

"Pound? No: I thought him a detective. He is a clever fellow."

"He is the devil incarnate!"

They had passed through the gates into the road.

"Here we separate," said Dick. "Go back to Graysbrooke the way you came, and pack your things. Is there any need to repeat—"

"None."

"You understand that if you break it, all's up with you?"

"I have accepted that."

"Then we are quits!"

"I like your pluck—I liked it long ago," said Miles, speaking suddenly, after staring at Dick for more than a minute in silence. "I was thinking of that new chum hawker awhile ago, before I knew you were he. You reminded me of him. And I ought to have known then; for I was never spoken to the same, before or since, except then and now. No one else ever bargained with Sundown! Well, a bargain it is. Here's my hand on it."

As he spoke, he shook Edmonstone by the hand with an air of good faith. Next moment, the two men were walking in opposite directions.

CHAPTER XV

THE MORNING AFTER

Dick reached Iris Lodge before the other two whom he had left at the ball. This was fortunate, not only because he had the latchkey in his pocket, but since it obviated crooked answers to awkward questions: they would, of course, suppose that he had gone straight home from the Bristos'.

He went quietly up to his room, changed his coat, and filled his pipe. In searching for matches on the dressing-table, however, he came across something which caused him to forget his pipe for the moment; a packet of letters in an elastic band, displaying immediately below the band a thin, folded collection of newspaper cuttings. They were the extracts Flint had given him, referring to the capture and subsequent escape of Sundown the bushranger. He had found no time to read them before going out, and now—well, now he would read them with added interest, that was all.

Yet he stood still with the papers in his hand, trying to realise all that he had seen, and heard, and said since midnight; trying not to separate in his mind the vaguely suspected rogue of yesterday and the notorious villain unmasked this morning; trying, on the other hand, to reconcile the Sundown of his remembrance—still more of his imagination—with the Miles of his acquaintance, to fuse two inconsistent ideas, to weld unsympathetic metals.

Standing thus, with all other sensations yielding to bewilderment, Dick was recalled to himself by hearing voices and footsteps below his window. Fanny and Maurice had returned; he must go down and let them in, and then—the cuttings!

"Why, how long have you been in?" was Fanny's first question; she had too much tact to ask him why he had left.

"Oh, a long time," Dick replied. "I didn't feel quite all right," he added, a shade nearer the truth; "but—but I thought it would only bother you."

"How could you think that? If you had only told me," said Fanny, with honest trouble in her voice, "you shouldn't have come alone."

"Then I'm glad I gave you the slip." Dick manufactured a laugh. "But, indeed, I'm all right now—right as the mail, honour bright!"

"But why didn't you go to bed when you got home?" his sister pursued.

"The key!" explained Maurice laconically, turning out the hall gas as he spoke.

They stole up-stairs in the pale chill light that fell in bars through the blind of the landing window.

Fanny laid her hand softly on Dick's shoulder.

"It was wretched after you went," she whispered sympathetically. "Do you know that—that—" timorously—"Alice went up-stairs and never came down again?"

"Did no one else disappear?" asked Dick, bending his head to read his sister's eyes.

Fanny hung her head. Mr. Miles had been missed by all; but no one—except the Colonel—had remarked Dick's absence in her hearing. When she had found Alice nearly fainting, and taken her to her maid, she had seen, indeed, that her friend was sorely distressed about something; but the friendship between them was not close enough for the seeking of confidences on either side; and, as the cause of so many sighs and tears, she had thought naturally, because she wished so to think, of her own brother. Now it seemed that perhaps, after all, Mr. Miles—whom she detested—had been the object of compassion. And Fanny had nothing to say.

"Good night," said Dick, quietly kissing her.

The next moment she heard the key turn in his door.

He sat down on the edge of the bed, lit his pipe, and withdrew the cuttings from the indiarubber band. There was not much to read, after all; only three paragraphs, of which two were telegraphic, and consequently brief. In no case was either name or date of the newspaper attached; but in the short paragraphs Dick seemed to recognise the type of the "Australasian," while there was internal evidence that the longer one emanated from a Queensland organ. After glancing rapidly at all three, he arranged them in an order that proved to be chronologically correct.

The first paragraph (telegraphic: headed "Brisbane, Friday,") stated that, on the afternoon of the day before, the branch of the Australian Joint-Stock Bank at Mount Clarence had been entered by two bushrangers, one of whom declared that he was Sundown, the New South Wales outlaw. That after "bailing up" everybody in the establishment, and shutting up the bank—which, as it was then closing-time, was effected without raising the suspicions of the township—the bushrangers had ridden away, taking with them about five hundred ounces of gold and a considerable sum in cheques and notes. That, at two o'clock the following morning, the bushrangers had been captured asleep under a gunyah, twelve miles from Mount Clarence, "through the rare sagacity of Sergeant Dogherty," and that Sundown's mate, a man named Benjamin Hickey, had been subsequently shot dead by the police on attempting to escape. "The redoubtable Ned Ryan, alias Sundown," the paragraph concluded, "gave no trouble on the way to Mount Clarence, whence he will be forwarded to Rockhampton without delay; but the gold has not yet been recovered, having evidently been 'planted' by the outlaws before camping for the night."

Dick believed that he had seen this identical paragraph in the "Argus" of February 13th, the day on which the Hesper sailed from Hobson's Bay.

The second cutting seemed to be part—perhaps the greater part—of an article from a Queensland pen, written in the first blush of triumph following the announcement of Sundown's capture. From it Dick learned so much concerning Ned Ryan that had never before come to his knowledge, that it is here reproduced word for word:

"Edward Ryan, or 'Sundown,' is declared by our informant to be a man of pleasing countenance, about six feet three inches high and thirty-seven years of age. He is a native of Victoria, where his parents resided for many years. Some six years ago—being then a horse-dealer of questionable repute—he married the daughter of a well-to-do farmer in the Ovens district (Vic.). But for some time past—since, indeed, a short time after his outlawry—he is said to have ceased all communication with his wife. About four years and a half ago, a warrant was taken out against Edward Ryan for some roguery connected with a horse. He, however, managed to escape across the Murray into New South Wales. A few weeks later his career of desperate crime—which has now happily ended as above detailed—was commenced in the partnership of two kindred spirits. One of these, Benjamin Hickey, has met with a summary fate, but one strictly in accordance with his deserts, as already described. The third of the band, however, who is believed by the police to be a Tasmanian 'old hand,' lost sight of for many years, was turned adrift some time ago by Sundown, on account, it is said, of his extreme bloodthirstiness. This statement receives colour from the fact that Sundown, since his capture, has declared that neither he nor Hickey ever spilt blood with their own hands; so that if this is true, not only the murder of Youl, the storekeeper near Menindie, on the Darling—which crime rendered the name of Sundown infamous at the commencement—but the grievous wounding of Constable O'Flynn, two years later, may be freely ascribed to the murderous hand of the miscreant that is still at large. However this may be, we have, in Sundown, succeeded in running to earth a freebooter equal in daring, impudence, and cunning generalship to the most formidable of the highwaymen who were the terror of the sister colonies in the early days. The credit of this brilliant capture, however, rests entirely with this colony. Indeed, it is to be hoped that we shall hereafter be able to boast that it was reserved to the youngest colony to add the finishing touch to the extermination of the Australian bandit. And as the bushrangers had been but a few months in Queensland, whereas their depredations in the neighbouring colony extended over as many years, it will be seen that on the whole the exploit of our police compares not unfavourably with the New South Wales method of doing business."

After this, the effect of the last extract was at least startling. The words in this case were few, and cruelly to the point. They simply told of the escape of the prisoner Ryan during a violent dust-storm that enveloped the township of Mount Clarence, and afterwards rendered tracking (when the bird was discovered to have flown) most difficult. No details of the escape were given, but the message ended with the confident assurance (which read humourously now) that the re-capture of Sundown, alive or dead, could be but a matter of hours.

There was a curious smile upon Dick's face as he folded up the cuttings. "I wonder how on earth he did it?" he asked himself as he slowly knocked the ashes from his pipe.

The sunlight was peeping in where it could through blind and curtains. Dick raised the first, drew back the second, and stood in the broad light of day. Then, throwing up the sash, he plunged head and shoulders into the fresh, fragrant morning air. The effect upon him was magical. His forehead seemed pressed by a cool, soothing hand; his throat drank down a deep draught of wizard's wine; he caught at his breath, as though actually splashing in the dewy air, and yet in a very little while the man's baser nature asserted itself. Dick yawned, not once or twice, but repeatedly; then he shivered and shut the window. Five minutes later the lively sparrows—if they took more than a passing interest in their early guest, as they should, since such very early guests were rare among them—the sprightly sparrows that visited the window-ledge might have seen for themselves that he was sound, sound asleep.

For some hours this sleep was profound, until, in fact, Dick began to dream. Then, indeed, he was soon awake, but not before his soul had been poisoned by a very vivid and full vision. This dream was not strange under the circumstances, but it was plausible, disturbing, and less bizarre than most—in fact, terribly realistic. He had gone to Graysbrooke and found Miles—Sundown the bushranger—still there. At once and openly he had denounced the villain, shown him in his true colours, and at once he had been disbelieved—laughed at by the enemy, pitied by his friends, treated as the victim of a delusion. With Miles's mocking defiant laugh in his ears, Dick awoke.

It was the dread, the chance of something like this actually happening, that hurried him to Graysbrooke with unbroken fast. He found Colonel Bristo plainly worried, yet glad to see him, eager to tell him what was the matter.

"We have lost our guest."

Dick felt the blood rushing back to his face at the words.

"Miles has gone," the Colonel pursued in a tone of annoyance; "gone this morning—a summons to Australia, he fears—a thing he had never dreamt of until last night."

"Dear me!" said Dick, with surprise that was partly genuine. For his plan had worked out better—he had been followed more strictly to the letter than he could have dared to hope; the misgivings of the last hour were turned to supreme satisfaction.

"Yes," sighed the soldier, "it was most unexpected. And I need not tell you how disappointed we all are."

Dick murmured that he was sure of it, with all the awkwardness of an honest tongue driven into hypocrisy.

"For my own part, I feel confoundedly put out about it. I shall be as dull as ditch-water for days. As for the ladies, they'll miss him horribly."

Dick's reply was monosyllabic, and its tone fell distinctly short of sympathy.

"He was such a good fellow!"

The Colonel said this regretfully, and waited for some echo. But Dick could have said nothing without the whole truth bursting out, so he merely asked:

"When did he go?"

"About nine—as soon as he could pack up his things, in fact. Alice was not down to say good-bye to him."

Dick's eyes glittered.

"He will be back to say it, though?" he asked suspiciously.

"No, I fear not; he will probably have to start at once; at least, so his agent told him—the fellow who came down last night, and robbed us of him for half the evening. By-the-bye, we missed you too; did you go home?"

"Yes." Dick faltered a little.

"Have you and Alice been quarrelling?" asked Alice's father abruptly.

Dick answered simply that they had. Colonel Bristo silently paced the carpet. When he spoke again it was to revert to the subject of Miles.

"Yes, I am sorry enough to lose him; for we had become great friends, intimate friends, and we understood one another thoroughly, he and I. But the worst of it is, we shan't have him with us in Yorkshire. What a man for the moors! And how he would have enjoyed it! But there; it's no use talking; we're all disappointed, and there's an end of it."

The Colonel laid his hand on Dick's shoulder, and added:

"You won't disappoint us, my boy?"

"For the moors, sir?"

"Why, of course."

"I cannot go—I am very sorry"—hastily—"but—"

"Nonsense, Dick!"

"I really cannot—I cannot, indeed," with lame repetition.

"And why?" asked Colonel Bristo, mildly. "Why—when you promised us weeks ago?"

Dick raised his eyes from the ground, and the answer was given and understood without words; yet he felt impelled to speak. He began in a low voice, nervously:

"Without disrespect, sir, I think I may beg of you not to insist on an explanation—either from me, or from—anyone else. It could do no good. It might do—I mean it might cause—additional pain. You have guessed the reason? Yes, you see it clearly—you understand. And—and you seem sorry. Don't let it trouble you, sir. There are lots better than I." He paused, then added uncertainly: "Colonel Bristo, you have been more, far more, than kind and good to me. If you treated me like a son before it was time—well—well, it will all be a pleasant memory to—to take away with me."

"Away?"

"Yes, away; back to Australia," said Dick, expressing his newest thought as though it were his oldest. "Before you get back from the north, I shall probably be on my way."

"Don't do that, Dick—don't do that," said Colonel Bristo, with some feeling.

Personal liking for Dick apart, it was not a pleasant reflection that his daughter had jilted the man who had come from Australia to marry her, and was sending him back there.

Dick answered him sadly.

"It can't be helped, sir. It is all over. It is decent that I should go."

"I don't understand 'em—never understood 'em," muttered the old man vaguely, and half to himself. "Still, there is no one but Dick, I dare swear; who should there be but Dick?"

Dick stepped forward, as though to push the scales from the eyes of this unseeing man; but he checked his impulse, and cried huskily, holding the thin hand in his own great strong one:

"Good-bye, Colonel Bristo. God bless you, sir! Good-bye!"

And the young man was gone.

CHAPTER XVI

MILITARY MANOEUVRES

"Well!" exclaimed Colonel Bristo, after some minutes. He leant back in his chair and stared sternly at his book-shelves. "It's a nice look-out for the moors; that's all."

His reflections were dispiriting. He was thinking that the only two men whom he had really wanted down in Yorkshire had this morning, almost in the same breath, declared that they could not go. They were, in fact, both going back to Australia—independently, from widely different reasons. With Miles the necessity was pressing enough, no doubt; and then he had only been visiting England, and never contemplated a long stay. But Dick's case was very different. He had come home for good, with his "pile" and his prospects. Could he possibly have been made so miserable during these few weeks that he would be glad to bury himself again in the bush? Could his case be really so hopeless as he himself believed it?

"If so," said Colonel Bristo with irritation, "then Alice has played the deuce with the best young fellow in England!"

But how could he tell? How was he, the father, to get at the facts of the case? Alice was all the world to him: but for all the world he would not have sought her confidence in such a matter. Then what was he to do?

He got up from his chair, and paced the floor with the stride of a skipper on his poop. He had liked young Edmonstone always—respected him as a mere stripling. Love-sick boys were, as a rule, selfish, if not sly, young fools—that was his experience; but this one had shown himself upright and fearless—had, in fact, behaved uncommonly well, once the mischief was done. But that liking had developed into affection since the night of Dick's arrival. Poor fellow! how grateful he had been! how hopeful! Who could have discouraged him? The Colonel, for his part, had no reason to do so now. What was there against him? what against "it"? In a word, he had soon—as he saw more of him—set his heart upon Dick for his son. Secretly, he had already formed certain projects of parental ingenuity. He had already, in his walks, held stealthy intercourse with house and estate agents, and otherwise dipped into the future of other people, further than he had any business. And here was the death-blow to it all! The pair had quarrelled so violently that the prospective son-in-law was on the point of taking himself back to Australia! One thing was certain: it could be no ordinary disagreement—she must have jilted him. But if so, for whom? She had seen nobody for months—nobody but Miles! And Miles—the Colonel smiled indulgently—with all his good points, with all his fine qualities, Miles was no marrying man. Then who could it be? Once more he, her father, was unable to tell, for the life of him.

He sat down, rose again in a moment, and rang the bell. Then he sent a polite message to Mrs. Parish, requesting her kind attendance, if not in any way inconvenient.

"She can at least put me right on one or two points. That is, if she doesn't go off at a tangent, down some blind-alley of a side issue!"

The lady appeared after the regulation delay, by which she was in the habit of italicising the dignity of her office.

By her greeting, one would have thought the appointment was of her making. She observed that she would have come before to inquire how the Colonel felt after it all, but understood that he was engaged.

The Colonel explained with a sigh.

"He is gone."

"Ah!" There was unprecedented sympathy in the lady's look and tone.

"You saw him go?" asked the Colonel, looking up in surprise.

"I did," sadly; "I did."

"He said good-bye to you, perhaps?"

"To be sure he did! He was hardly likely to—"

"He didn't ask to see Alice, I suppose?"

"Oh, yes, he did."

"Dear me!" said the Colonel to himself.

"But she could not see him, I grieve to say; it was a thousand pities, seeing that he's going straight back to Australia."

"Oh, he told you that too, did he?"

"Of course, Colonel Bristo, when he said good-bye."

"Dear me! But why wouldn't Alice see him?"

"It was too early."

"A mere excuse," exclaimed the Colonel angrily, looking at his watch. "Too early! It is plain that she has thrown him over. If so, then the best young fellow in England has been—But perhaps you can tell me whether it really is so?"

Mrs. Parish began to feel mystified.

"A young fellow?" she began doubtfully.

"Well, young in years; older than his age, I know. But that's not my point."

"Then I really don't know, Colonel Bristo. Alice seldom honors me with her confidence nowadays. Indeed, for the last year—"

"The point—my dear madam; the point!"

"Well, then," snapped Mrs. Parish, "to judge by their dances together, last night, I should say you are certainly wrong!"

"Ah, you thought that at the time, I know. Do you remember my disagreeing with you when you declared Alice had never been more brilliant, and so on? Why she only danced with the lad once!"

Only once! "The lad!" Colonel Bristo must certainly be joking; and jokes at the expense of the lady who had controlled his household for twenty years were not to be tolerated.

"Colonel Bristo, I fail to understand you. If it were not preposterous, I should imagine you had stooped to ridicule. Allow me, please, to state that your daughter danced three times, if not four, with Mr. Miles—I see nothing to smile at, Colonel Bristo!"

"My good—my dear Mrs. Parish," said he, correcting himself hastily, and rising urbanely from his chair, "we are at cross purposes. I mean young Edmonstone; you mean, I suppose, Mr. Miles. A thousand apologies."

Mrs. Parish was only partially appeased.

"Oh, if you mean that young gentleman, I can assure you he has absolutely no chance. Has he said good-bye, too, then?"

"Yes. He says he is going back to Australia."

"I said he would!" exclaimed Mrs. Parish with gusto.

"But—I say! You surely don't mean that it is Mr. Miles Alice cares for?"

Mrs. Parish smiled superior.

"Has it not been patent?"

"Not to me, madam!" said Colonel Bristo warmly.

"Love on both sides; I might say at first sight. I watched it dawn, and last night I thought it had reached high noon," the old lady declared with emotion. "But this unfortunate summons! Still, I think we shall see him again before he sails, and I think he will come back to England for good before long."

"You mean you hope so, Mrs. Parish," said the Colonel dryly. He seated himself at his desk with unmistakable meaning. "Confound her!" he muttered when the door closed; "the thing is plausible enough. Yet I don't believe it. What's more, much as I like Miles, I don't wish it! No. Now what am I to do about Dick?"

This question occupied his thoughts for the rest of the morning. He could not answer it to his satisfaction. In the afternoon he sent word to Iris Lodge, begging Dick to come over in the evening for an hour. The messenger brought back the news that Mr. Edmonstone was from home—had, in fact, left for abroad that afternoon.

"Abroad!" thought Colonel Bristo. "He has lost no time! But 'abroad' only means the Continent—it is 'out' when you go farther. And yet that is one way out—the quickest! Is he capable of such madness at a moment's notice? Never; impossible. But I had better look into the matter myself."

And this the Colonel did in the course of a few days, by himself calling at Iris Lodge. There was a little coldness, or it may have been merely self-consciousness, in his reception. But when, after a few preliminaries, the visitor began to speak of Dick, this soon wore off; for his regard was too warmly expressed, and his praise too obviously genuine, not to win and melt hearts half as loving as those of Mrs. Edmonstone and her daughter. The Colonel, for his part, was sufficiently rewarded when he learnt that Dick had merely joined an old Australian friend in Italy, and would be back at the beginning of August.

"I was half afraid," he observed tentatively, "that he was tired of England already, and was on his way out again."

The horror with which this notion was instantly demolished caused the old gentleman to smile with unconcealed satisfaction; for it assured him that Dick's intention (if it was an intention, and not merely the wild idea of a heated moment) had at least not yet been breathed to his family. He took up his hat and cane with a light heart. And he stopped to add a rider to his gracious adieu:

"We shall be tramping the moors when your son returns, Mrs. Edmonstone, so I beg you will forward him on to us. And pray, Miss Fanny, use your influence as well, for we have lost our other Australian, and I don't see how we can get on without Dick."

He went out in good spirits.

Thereafter, as far as the Colonel was concerned, young Edmonstone might bake himself to his heart's content—until the Twelfth—abroad. As it happened, Colonel Bristo found a far more immediate cause for anxiety at home. This was the appearance of Alice.

As July drew near its latter days, the change in her looks passed the perceptible stage to the noticeable. Her colouring had been called her best point by some, her only good one by others (possibly according to the sex of the critic); yet now her face was wholly void of colour. The flower-like complexion was, if possible, more delicate than before, but now it resembled the waxen lily instead of the glowing wild rose. Even the full, firm lips were pale and pinched. Her eyes were either dull or restless, and their dark setting seemed more prominent: shadows lay below them where no shadows should have been. For the rest, any real activity of mind or body seemed as impossible to her as any real repose; she appeared to have gained only in thoughtfulness—as indicated by silence. On fine days, though the river could not charm her, she would dress for walking, and come back tired out in twenty minutes. On wet ones she divided her time between the first few pages of a book, and the first few bars of a waltz; between the two she never got any farther in either. Perhaps experience had taught her that all the tune of a waltz is at the beginning; and I suppose she failed to "get into" her novels. Her ear was sensitive, attuned to her temper; common sounds startled her painfully; the unexpected opening or shutting of a door went far to unhinge both nerves and temper. The latter, indeed, was less sweet at this period than ever in her life before, and none knew it so well as she herself, who bore the brunt of it in her own heart.

None of these signs escaped the watchful eyes about her. But while, on the one hand, Mrs. Parish noted them with incomplete sympathy and impartial confidence in the justice of consequences (believing that Alice's indecision had brought this on her own head, and that a little uncertainty would do her no harm), the father's heart became more and more distressed as each new symptom was made plain to him. He was both worried and perplexed. He called in a local doctor. That move made her ill-health no better, and her ill-temper worse. What, then, could the father do? Always loving and indulgent—never intimate—with his child, it had been his practice, when serious matters arose, to employ the ambassador always at hand; thus there had never, during all the years, been a word of contention between father and daughter; and to this practice the father resorted now.

Late one afternoon they were all three sitting in the garden, when Alice rose, without breaking her long silence, and slowly walked towards the house. The Colonel followed her with his eyes; he held a glowing cigarette between his fingers; the distance was short enough, but before Alice reached the house the cigarette was out.

"Look at her now! Is that the step of a healthy girl? See her climb those six steps—they might be the top flight of St. Paul's! Mrs. Parish"—with sudden decision—"Mrs. Parish, you must see to the root of this matter before it gets any worse. I must know exactly what is at the bottom of it. I desire you to speak to Alice, for I cannot. You understand me, I think? Very well, then, pray watch your opportunity."

The very next morning the housekeeper came to the study. She had spoken to Alice. She did not require much questioning.

"Oh, as to young Mr. Richard. I could elicit nothing—nothing at all. He seemed quite outside her thoughts."

Mrs. Parish made this statement with a smack of satisfaction. Colonel Bristo, however, must have given it a construction of his own, for he did not look displeased. He simply said:

"Well?"

"Well, she was almost as reticent about Mr. Miles; though we know what that signifies!" (But here the Colonel shook his head.) "What she did say, however, is not worth repeating."

"Still, I should like to hear it."

"It does not affect matters in the least."

"Pray go on, Mrs. Parish."

"Of course, if you insist, Colonel Bristo! Well, then, Alice tells me that, two days after Mr. Miles went, a shabby kind of woman had the impudence to walk into the garden, accost her, and ask if Mr. Miles (how she had got his name, one cannot tell) was still here. Alice said 'No,' and was weak enough to give her money, because she seemed wretched, she says, and so got rid of her."

"One of the beggars he helped," said the Colonel. "He used to have long conversations with them, and tell them to emigrate."

"Why, to be sure!" cried Mrs. Parish, at once enlightened and relieved. And now she was as eager to tell the rest as before she had been slow to speak. "The very next day after that, Alice saw a man watching the house from the tow-path. He seemed to be there all day; so at last she rowed across and asked him if he wanted anyone. He said, 'Yes, the gentleman who's been staying there; where is he?' She told him he was on his way back to Australia. The man did not seem to believe it. In the end she gave money to him too, and soon she saw him go."

"Another of his beggars!" laughed Colonel Bristo. "Their name is legion, no doubt, and we shall see more of them yet. For the credit of the Mother Country, we can't shut the door in their faces after a Colonial has given them a taste of real downright generosity. Poor Miles!"

"Well, Alice, for her part, seems ready enough to carry on his works of charity," said Mrs. Parish, adroitly, with an emphasis ever so slight on the possessive pronoun.

The Colonel smiled. Then he thanked her graciously for the service.

"I am extremely obliged to you, Mrs. Parish, for the hundredth time. You have saved me yet another interview. That is, I should have made it awkward, but you, with your usual tact, have got at precisely what I wanted. I am perfectly satisfied."

Mrs. Parish bowed. She was not a little pleased with the compliment to her tact, on which she plumed herself above everything; but her pleasure was less than her surprise—that the Colonel should be so easily satisfied! She moved with dignity to the door. As she was shutting it, the Colonel rubbed his hands and exclaimed aloud:

"It is Dick!"

The door, which was at that moment swinging to, stopped, trembled, then shut with a vicious little bang. The Colonel could make a near enough guess at the expression of the face on the other side of it. He smiled benevolently.

"Silly lady! She thinks I have turned against my friend Miles—whom, by the way, she worships on her own account. Far from it, I miss him abominably. But when it comes to a choice between him and Dick—and where my girl is concerned—why, then, I confess, I'm all for the younger man and the older suitor."

CHAPTER XVII

"MILES'S BEGGARS"

Iris Lodge, during the first half of August, became for once gay, not to say festive—in a small way, as befitted a first experiment. Maurice managed to wrest his hard-earned annual holiday from the bank, and, on the very first day of the fourteen allotted him, back came Dick from abroad, bringing with him his friend Flint. After a remarkable display of obstinacy on this gentleman's part, Dick had at last prevailed upon him to leave his tenants to their own devices for one more week, and tarry by the Thames. But, though this was brought about by dint of hard persuading, in the end Mr. Flint somehow saw his way to doubling the week which at first he had grudgingly promised.

In his excuse it can only be urged that he enjoyed himself beyond expectation. The weather was very nearly faultless, the river at its best, formalities few, and the ladies—charming. The lawn-tennis court—though several inches short—was quite of the billiard-table order. The music in the evenings, though it did not run in a man's head, possessed a certain odd, mysterious, soothing, saddening, pleasing quality, that silenced one at the time, and left an impression that Miss Edmonstone could make her piano speak, if she tried. Perhaps it was classical music; very likely Chopin. Lastly—and last thing—the spirituous nightcap, though approached in a spirit of moderation, had a way of imparting the proper Eucalyptian flavour to all reminiscences of life among the gum-trees. Could there be better conditions for a pleasant visit? Flint asked himself. And if the house was the smallest he had ever stayed in, would not Castle Flint seem cheerless, vast, sepulchral, by comparison?

But indeed they were wonderfully bright and happy days: the ones on the river, when, in the bushmen's phrase, they all "camped," and Flint made tea in true bush fashion, and Dick a "damper" which no one but bushmen could eat; the afternoons at tennis, spent in wonderfully keen, if not deeply scientific, struggles; the morning at Hampton Court, when Flint owned himself completely "bushed" in the Maze, and when they were all photographed on the Green, bringing away with them the atrocious result in a gilt frame; and the day when Dick hired the four-in-hand (it created some sensation in the little road) and drove them all through Chertsey and Ascot, to Windsor, and back by Staines and Shepperton.

Certainly any outsider must have voted them a jovial, light-hearted party, without a serious care to divide among them; and even Flint, who had some power of observation, and also knew his friend thoroughly—even Flint told himself that old Dick had got back his good spirits, and was, in fact, "getting over it." But Flint did not know. Ever since their hurried interview on the 2nd of July, Dick had been as reticent as he had then been communicative of all that lay nearest his heart.

Yet never for one moment did Dick forget. He had no wish to forget. So long as he could keep his disappointment to himself, deep down within him, he would suffer and smile. For the sake of the others he could not rise in his place at the feast and declare himself the skeleton he felt. They must find it out sooner or later—then let it be later. Here his thoughts were all of his mother and Fanny; they would be heart-broken when he told them of his determination to go back to Australia. But a determination it was, growing more solid day by day, though as yet told only to Colonel Bristo, and that in the unguarded spontaneity of sudden emotion. But as for his people, better tell them just before he went—say the week before, or why not on the very day of sailing? Why make them unhappy before their time, when their happiness in having him back was still boundless?

After all, it would only be a temporary trouble; for Dick had evolved a great scheme for the future, which was this: He would go out and buy a small station in a first-rate district—at arm's length, indeed, from towns and railroads, but still just in touch with civilisation. Then he would send home for them all. Yes, all. For Maurice would make an ideal book-keeper. Fanny would revel in the life, and Mrs. Edmonstone would certainly prefer it to the small house at Teddington. This plan was conceived, matured, calculated out, and found feasible, during the many long summer nights wherein Dick never closed his eyes, when perhaps it was well that there was this object of focus for his mind.

As for his attitude towards Flint, Dick was well aware that his access of reserve, after the way in which he had unburdened his soul at their first meeting, must appear strangely inconsistent. He had rushed to join his friend on the Continent, travelled with him for nearly a month, and not told him another word of his affairs. It could not be helped; it would be impossible to tell Flint anything of what had followed their first talk at Teddington without making a clean breast of his discovery that Miles the Australian was no other than Sundown the bushranger, and this Dick would not tell a soul unless Miles broke faith with him. Least of all would he confide in Flint, for Flint would be the very first to turn round and call him madman.

Nevertheless the days seemed to chase each other pleasantly enough for one and all, actually doing so for all but one; and, as always happens in such cases, the fortnight drew far too quickly to its close.

"To-day is Thursday—the Twelfth, by-the-bye—and here we are within sight of Sunbury Lock; and on Monday, and ever afterwards, the bank; the blessed bank!"

This cheerful reminder proceeded (one day up the river) from the lips and soul of the man in the stern, who was steering. There was a sympathetic groan from the man in the bows, who was smoking. The working half of the crew received the observation, which was thrown out gratuitously to all, in business-like silence, broken only by the flash of four sculls as one, and the swish of the feather blades through the air. The groan in the bows was followed by a reflection of kindred pathos, delivered in a high key:

"We will call next Monday Black Monday; for to me it means Holyhead, Dublin, Kerry, and tenants! blessed tenants! But not for always," added Flint suddenly; "I don't say 'ever afterwards;' why should you? Why should I be a slave to my Castle and you to your City? Why shouldn't we emigrate together?"

No one in the boat could see the speaker's face; it was impossible to tell whether he was jesting or serious.

"Oh, I'm game!" cried Maurice, very much in earnest at once.

"Well, then, just hold on till I give Castle Flint the sack."

"Or until it is sacked about your ears," suggested stroke jerkily. "But what nonsense you two are talking!"

"Not at all, Miss Edmonstone—if you will allow me. You can't expect a man to live out his life in troubled Ireland when there's a happy Australia to go to: there, you know, you may combine the blessings of liberty, equality, and Home Rule of the most advanced kind, with the peculiar satisfaction of calling yourself a staunch Tory, and believing it! But as for our friend here, station life would add a year to his life for every year the City is capable of shortening it. He'd make a first-rate jackeroo."

"What is that?"

"What's a jackeroo? Oh, a young gentleman—for choice, the newest new chum to be found—who goes to a station to get Colonial experience. He has to work like a nigger, and revels in it, for a bit. If he is a black sheep, and has the antique ideas of the Colonies held by those who sent him out to whiten him, his illusions may last a couple of days; if he has read up Australia on the voyage, they will probably hold out a little longer, while he keeps looking for what his book told him he would find; the fact being that the modern bush life hasn't yet been done into English. Meanwhile he runs up the horses, rides round boundaries, mends fences, drives sheep to water—if it is a drought—and skins the dead ones, weighs out flour and sugar, cleans harness, camps anywhere, and lives on mutton and damper, and tea."

"But what does he get for all that?" asked Maurice, with visions of money-bags.

"Rations and experience," replied Flint promptly. "When he's admitted to be worth his salt he will be asked to make other arrangements. Then some still newer new chum will be selected for the post, through the introductions he has brought to the stock and station agents, and in his turn will drive his teeth into the dirty work of the station, which the ordinary pound-a-week hands refuse, and so get his Colonial experience!"

"Thanks; I'll stop where I am," said Maurice.

"He isn't fair," said Dick, speaking for the first time. "You know you aren't fair, old chap, raking up your own case as typical, when it was exceptional. Jackeroos are treated all right, and paid too, so long as they're smart and willing—the two things needful. Come, I've been a squatter myself, and can't hear my class run down."

"You won't hear me defend the landlords on that ground," remarked Flint, who had contracted eccentric politics.

"Well," said Dick, experimentally, "if I go back to it, Maurice shall be my jackeroo, and judge for himself whether you haven't painted us too black."

He shipped his oars. Flint was standing up with the boat-hook to pilot them through the open lock-gates.

"Then I'll ride the boundaries!" cried Fanny, who sat a horse like a leech, but had had no mount for years.

"In that case," added Flint quietly, "I'll apply for overseer's billet, with the right of sacking slack hands."

For a moment Dick looked really pleased: this jesting about a station in Australia was, so far, feeling the way, and might make matters a trifle easier when the time came. But the smile quickly faded from his face. In truth, on no day during these last weeks had he been so troubled in spirit, so tossed between the cross-currents of conflicting feelings.

That morning he had received two letters, apparently of contrary character: for while the perusal of one gratified him so intensely that he could not help handing it round for them all to see, the mere sight of the other was sufficient to make him thrust the unopened envelope hurriedly into his pocket.

The first letter was indeed a matter for congratulation, for it was the most completely satisfactory, though not the first, of several similar communications which Dick had received since his return from Australia. It was a short note from the editor of the "Illustrated British Monthly," accepting (for immediate use: a great point) a set of sketches entitled "Home from Australia," which set forth the humours and trials of a long sea voyage, and were, in fact, simply a finished reproduction of those sketches that had delighted the passengers on board the Hesper. But it was more than a mere formal acceptance: besides enclosing a cheque (in itself a charming feature) to meet the present case, the note contained a complimentary allusion to the quality of the "work," and a distinct hint for the future. This in a postscript—observing that as Australian subjects were somewhat in demand since the opening of the Colonial Exhibition—he (the editor) would be glad to see anything thoroughly Australian that Mr. Edmonstone might chance to have ready.

Of course the precious note was read aloud, and greeted with cries of delight. Fancy an opening with the "Illustrated British" at this stage! What could be better? And it did look like a real opening. The hero of the moment alone sat silent; the unread letter in his pocket checked his speech; it was from Yorkshire.

"Why did you ever leave us, when you can do so splendidly here at home?" Mrs. Edmonstone asked him, half in regret for the past, half in joy for the future.

Flint saw his friend's preoccupation, and answered for him.

"He didn't know it was in him till he got out there, I fancy. I remember him sending his first things to the Melbourne and Sydney papers; and before a year was out, his famous buck-jumping picture was stuck up in every shanty in New South Wales and Victoria."

"Eh?" said Dick, looking up abruptly. "Oh, they coloured it vilely! What do you say, mother? No, I say, don't jump to conclusions. How do you know I can do any real good? I've been lucky so far, but I'm only at the very, very beginning. I may fail miserably after all. And then where should I be without my little pile?"

After breakfast Dick read the letter from Yorkshire in his own room.

"At the risk of being unduly persistent," wrote Colonel Bristo, "I must ask you to reconsider your decision." (Dick had refused a short but pressing invitation the week before.) "I know something of your reasons for refusing, and I believe them to be mistaken reasons. If you have really settled to return to Australia, that is all the more reason why you should come. If you like, I will undertake not to press you to stay beyond one day; only do come to bid us good-bye. Do not, however, fear to offend me by a second refusal. I shall be grievously disappointed, but nothing more. We really want you, for we shall be short of guns; two of the men only stay till Monday, so come on that day. But apart from all this, I am very sure that your coming will make the days a little less dull and dreary for one of us. Everything else has failed."

The letter ended abruptly. Dick read it through twice, and put it back in his pocket with a full heart.

But what was he to do? Here was the good Colonel honestly trying, in his own way, to set matters right between him and Alice; but it was a childlike, if not a childish way—a way that ignored causes and refused to realise effects.

Dick trusted he was no such fool as to be affected by the hope that breathed in the Colonel's letter. The Colonel was confessedly unversed in women's ways—then why did he meddle? Surely it would have been more natural, more dignified, to send him, Dick, to the deuce, or to the Colonies—they were much the same thing in the Old Country—than to waste another thought on the man whom his own daughter (who could surely judge for herself) had chosen to jilt? Dick savagely wished that the former had been his treatment; and, rowing down from Sunbury that afternoon, he was so far decided that the phrases of his refusal were in his head. Call it rude, churlish, obstinate; he was obstinate, and was willing to own it; he had refused the Colonel once, and that refusal should be final.

Nevertheless, he was absent and distrait all day, whereas the others were in rather higher spirits than usual, and the contrast was uncomfortable. Dick therefore invented an excuse for running up to town, promising himself a quiet corner of his club, in which to write to the Colonel and pull himself together. He needed pulling together: he was yearning to see Alice again—perhaps only to ask her forgiveness and bid her good-bye—yet vowing between his teeth to see her no more; he would not be entirely himself until his refusal was penned and posted.

He walked absently to the station, forgot his change at the ticket-office, and jumped into the nearest compartment of the first train that came in. A man and a woman got into the same compartment. Dick did not see them, for he was attempting to interest himself in an evening paper; but he could not help hearing their voices as they sat opposite him in close conversation. And, hearing, Dick was startled. His pulse beat violently; his fingers tightened upon the edges of the newspaper.

"His fine friends," the man was saying, "are gone into the country somewhere. We must find out where."

The tones were Jem Pound's.

"Why?" asked the same woman's voice that Dick had heard in Bushey Park.

"Because if Ned Ryan hasn't fled the country, that's where he is!"

"But he has gone back to Australia."

"Not he! He daren't go out there again. He'd be a fool to do it if he dared. No, no. He cleared out o' this because of you and me. He cracked he was going out there again, because he knew we'd come asking after him and they'd tell us that yarn. But he's no more gone than I have. Mark me, missis, we'll find him at this here Colonel's country place! But we must find the place first."

Dick did not lower his paper until the train reached Waterloo. Long before that his mind was filled with one absorbing idea. A swift but complete reaction had taken place within him; he was charged with nervous energy and primed with impatience. Some of the impatience he worked off in a rapid walk to his club, where he answered Colonel Bristo's note in a dozen words; but one idea continued in fierce possession of his mind, to the exclusion of all others.

CHAPTER XVIII

ALICE SPEAKS FOR HERSELF

Monday, August 9th.—Here we are at last, at the shooting box on the Yorkshire moors; or rather in the Yorkshire dales. I mean, papa and I are here: our faithful Mrs. Parish follows to-morrow, and the "guns" are expected on Wednesday. We two have been staying at a little seaside place on the coast—quite a charming place, with not only broad sands, but very presentable cliffs, and other things worth looking at besides the sea; delightful gardens, for instance, where the inevitable band played, instead of on the everlasting pier. Of course, it was all rather tedious; but the North Sea breezes and the delicious air did one no harm, I felt, while they seemed to do papa visible good. Indeed, he declares he feels fit for anything now—meaning, of course, in the way of sport, which I only hope he won't overdo. So perhaps, after all, we did well to leave home a week earlier than we at first intended (much as I hated leaving home at all), for we have come to the moorland air with lungs full of sea-air, and papa says there couldn't be a finer mixture than that for me.

But it is difficult to think of the sea here in the dales, where we are so far from it. We are far from everything, as it seems to me. Yet I am told, and I suppose I must believe, that the great smoky town which we passed through the other day is within twenty miles of us, and we are assured that there is a very "canny" village—if not a small town—four or five miles from us. It is also true that it only took an hour and twenty minutes to drive from the railway station, but then there wasn't much of a village there. Now we expected to find one here, and papa even professed to point it out to me as we drove through; but as it was nearly dark, and I could only make out a short, huddled-up row of houses on one side of the road, I couldn't see where the village came in, and told him so. Still, it is down on the Ordnance map, Gateby by name; and, though it is too dark to see now, it can only be a few hundred yards from us.

As for this house—which, by-the-bye, is nameless—I am sure it has never been anything but a shooting box, for it has no pretence to a garden, but stands behind a hedge almost in a bare field—a plain, gaunt, two-storied, evenly-balanced stone building. In the three rooms down stairs there is very little furniture, except what we sent before us. In one of them, the smallest, a book-case with glass doors has been made into a gun-rack, and this may point to the fact that the place was not always what it is. This room we will call "the gun-room." Whether it was built for better things, I don't know; but for ages the house has been let year after year for the shooting alone.

At this moment an old man, with a pale blue eye and a bright red nose, who is apparently caretaker and general factotum of the establishment, is expatiating to papa on the birds: their probable quantity and unmistakable quality; but he has a barbarous tongue, and for my part I am too tired to listen to him any longer.

Yes, tired—and sleepy too. If writing a diary has always this effect upon me, it will more than fulfil its original mission—which was only to help me to pass the intolerable time!

Tuesday, 10th.—I was up and out quite early, long before breakfast, on a voyage of discovery. The first thing I had seen, on drawing up my blind, was red-tiled Gateby, straight in front of my window, across half-a-dozen fields. I could see a path winding through these fields, and coming out into the road just below our house; so on this pathway I settled for my first walk. I could see that it was the shortest way to Gateby. I would inspect Gateby.

It was a perfect morning, with plenty of sunshine and blue sky, and the last of a soft white mist just filling up the hollows of the meadows; so that I knew that it would be a hot day, as, in fact, it is.

When I had followed the path across the fields until I had only two left to cross (and these were a potato field and a meadow, from which a boy was driving in the cows), I stopped and perched myself on a stone gate-post, and surveyed Gateby. From there it looked like one long low irregular building, stone-built and red-tiled. Only one house, and that at the extreme left of the rest, was slated. More of Gateby I could not see from there, so I went on looking all round me. Over the village rose the hills, with bold but even outline. The hillsides are so evenly divided by the hedges into so many squares that they look as though great nets had been cast over them. The squares have all kinds of colours—greens, and yellows, and dirty browns (of ploughed fields). Following the bend of the valley, as the fields grew less in perspective, I noticed that they took a commoner tint, between pale green and dun, until the farthest range of all showed a uniform greyish-blue. I did not expect to be able to see half so far when deep down in a dale, and I thought the hills would be higher. In fact, with this particular dale of ours I am a little bit disappointed; for, instead of finding it a deep furrow in the face of Nature, as I had made up my mind it would be, it is, after all, the veriest dimple.

Well, Gateby is a quaint enough little place when you attack it fairly, from the front, as I presently did. It has about a dozen houses all told, and they are all on one side of the road, and hug each other as though space were an object of the first importance. Several of the houses are, at least, demi-semi-detached. The largest of them is the public-house; the best the schoolhouse, the front of which is simply one mass of pink roses—I never saw anything like it.

I walked back by the road. The pathway through the fields merely cuts off, I now found, the angle made by the two roads: the road in which we are, which leads over the moor, and the road in which Gateby is, which leads in one direction to the railway, six miles off, and in the other—I don't know where. These two roads join at right angles, and I believe they are the only roads in the dale.

Nearing home, I met the person with the gay-coloured nose and eyes, and he stopped to bid me good morning. I thought his complexion looked a little cooler, but then it was very early morning. He inquired, with some pride and expectancy, what I thought of the dale. I answered, rather unkindly I am afraid, that I thought it pretty, but a fraud: the hills were too low, the valleys were too shallow.

"Ah!" he observed compassionately, "waät till thoo's been ower t' mower, an' seen t' view from Melmerbridge Bank; an' waät till thoo sees Beckdaäl!"

He went on to tell me all about Melmerbridge. I almost think he offered to personally conduct me over to Melmerbridge, and to show me its church, and its beck, and the view from its bank. At any rate, before I could get away from him I had learnt that his name was Andy Garbutt, and that he had been eight and twenty years, man and boy, come next Michaelmas, in the service of the owner of our nameless shooting-box.

I found papa ready for breakfast, and delighted to find that I had been out and about so early; there was no need to tell him that it was simply because I could not sleep or rest. And of course we both duly voted the real Yorkshire bacon the very best we had ever tasted in our two lives; though, for my part, I must own I only swallowed it to please papa, whose eye was upon my plate.

In the afternoon we walked up to the moor together, and papa was charmed because we "put up" quite a number of birds. I could not stay long, however, as papa wished me to drive off to meet Mrs. Parish, and I am writing this while waiting for the trap, because, somehow, I cannot settle to reading—not even yellowbacks. A horrid nuisance, her coming! I do wish it had not been just yet. By-the-bye, papa tells me he has heard from Mr. Miles, who, after all, has not yet left England, his business having turned out different from what he expected. Then how strange that we have never heard from him all these weeks! I quite thought he would be out there by this time. However, he says he really does sail in a few days, and he only wishes he saw his way to running down to say good-bye to us—but that will be impossible. I believe papa has written to him, telling him all about the place, and the prospects, and who are coming. I am not sorry that he is not coming, I think. This reminds me that papa says that Dick Edmonstone has written saying that he cannot possibly come. I am not at all sorry to hear that. I think he shows his sense.

Thursday, 12th.—Everybody came yesterday; and now they are all on the moor, and we two women are to go and have lunch with them at one. There are five guns, and we hear them distinctly from time to time. Besides papa, there are Cousin Philip (who likes to be called Doctor Robson now), and Laurence Pinckney, and Captain Awdry, and Mr. Oliver.

Cousin Philip has been on a long voyage to New Zealand and back, as ship's surgeon, since we last saw him. It ought to have improved him, and perhaps it has; but to me he seems as dull and ponderous and undecided as ever. He tells me that he interested himself at sea by getting up prayer-meetings in the steerage, which, he says, had far more heart in them than the captain's perfunctory services on the quarter-deck; but it seems that his zeal got him disliked—most unrighteously—by the other officers. He is certainly a good young man. Captain Awdry I have met once or twice before; he is a great beauty, a great sportsman, and that's all; but Mr. Oliver is new to me. I fancy he is local—an ironmaster or something. He is old, and tall, and well set-up; very deferential to me, if you please, and tremendously keen about the grouse. As for Laurence Pinckney—one has to call him Mr. Pinckney now—he is nothing short of a revelation.

When I knew him before, he used to go to some public school—I forget which, but it can't be many years ago. And now he is a "writing man," fresh from Fleet-street, with all the jargon at his tongue's end—and, in short, quite the most amusing boy. In appearance he is just what he ought not to be. I have always pictured to myself the literary man—especially the literary young man—with long hair and eye-glasses, and the rest bizarre. Therefore Laurence Pinckney disappoints me; he is spruce, brisk, and sharp-eyed, short, dark, and unguarded.

He sat next me at dinner, and talked nothing but his "shop"—which, however, is a kind of "shop" that rather interests one; besides, the egotism of a raw recruit in the noble army of authors is really diverting. He talks fluently about all the new books, criticising most of them severely, and I should say that he has read and remembered at least two or three reviews of each. He has told me the different magazines he writes for, so that I shall know where to seek his name—if I don't forget. He "thinks nothing of bearding literary lions in their editorial dens;" and this, I shouldn't wonder, has something to do with that drawer full of rejected MSS. of which he has already been frank enough to whisper—in fact, he has quite taken me into his literary confidence. But indeed he is rather amusing.

Friday, 13th.—Mrs. Parish is really very agreeable, and easier to get on with than for a long while past. She tells me, among other things, that she saw more of Mr. Miles's beggars after we left home—caught them talking to the servants, and packed them off about their business. Poor things! From her account, I rather fancy they were the same I saw. She went with me to luncheon on the moor yesterday. It was really not bad fun. They were all in good spirits, because, on the whole, they had made a good start. Captain Awdry had done the most execution, and took it the most sadly. But old Mr. Oliver had drawn first blood, and, unlike the blasé Captain, was not above showing his delight. Papa and Cousin Philip were modest about their share: it was impossible to find out exactly what they had done. Poor Laurence Pinckney, however, had hit nothing at all; and, indeed, his shooting must be execrable, to judge by what one hears. I heard Mr. Oliver muttering that he would not get within range of him, not if he knew it; while Captain Awdry's contempt lies too deep for smiles or sneers. But Mr. Pinckney does not care; he carries a notebook with him, which he whips out whenever the view strikes him as worth remembering, or whenever something happy occurs to him. He says it is extraordinary what happy thoughts do come to a man who carries a gun. I tell him that to-morrow he must think of nothing but his next shot. He answers that to-morrow he must not shoot, as Saturday is always a busy day with him, wherever he is:— on it he writes for his weekly paper. He calls it "his," as though the paper belonged to him, and I tell him so. He explains that he is "on the staff—practically." He keeps to himself the name of the paper and the nature of his contributions: it is best to make no inquiries, I think.

Saturday, 14th.—Papa tells me that Dick has written to say he finds he can come after all, and is coming.

Somehow it has been a wretched day. I seem to have done absolutely nothing all day, and, now that it is evening, my head aches, and I have come upstairs quite early, though I know I shall never sleep. Poor papa has been saying he sees I find it dull, and blaming himself because I have no companion. As it happens, that is, in my eyes, the most joyful feature of the business, but I could not tell dear papa so; and he was full of regrets that Cousin Maggie was prevented from coming at the last moment—a circumstance for which I can never be too thankful. Poor Maggie would have been an infliction indeed. She has all the heavy virtues of her brother—and imagine a feminine Philip! That creature himself has annoyed me sufficiently this evening: tacked himself on to me, talked in a low voice, looked like a sheep, and would not be snubbed—he never would, and never will. To escape him, and for no other reason, I sang a song in response to Laurence Pinckney's absurd pleadings. But I hate singing! I hate the sound of my voice! I would give worlds to be away from here, and at home again and alone. I am tired of the place, and to be forever saying civil things to people is insupportable, and replying to their civility-speeches even worse. This minute I hate everything and everybody, and myself the worst of all!

Sunday, 15th.—I wrote some contemptible nonsense last night, when my head was splitting; but I will not score it out; if ever I go mad these gradations will be interesting, if not useful!...

It is, by-the-bye, to-morrow, papa tells me, that Dick is coming.

CHAPTER XIX

CONTERMINOUS COURSES

Between five and six o'clock in the afternoon of Monday, August 16th, when the last train but one steamed into the small station at Inglesby, six miles from Gateby, one passenger left it. He was a tall man in a light tweed suit. His luggage consisted of a portmanteau and a gun-case. After looking in vain for a conveyance outside the station, he found the station-master and asked where he could get one to take him to Gateby; the station-master directed him to the inn.

Between six and seven, but rather more than an hour later, the last train of the day came in. It also deposited a single passenger—another sportsman, for he too carried a gun-case; moreover, he went through the same performance as the last arrival: looked first for a conveyance and then for the station-master, to whom he put the same question about a trap and Gateby, and from whom he received the same direction. But the official was struck with the coincidence, and dropped a word or two about "the other gentleman;" at which this one, whose name was Edmonstone, started, though he walked off to the inn, a porter following with his baggage, without putting further questions.

The inn had a great square parlour, scrupulously clean and flagged with red tiles, where Dick entered, and clattered on the well-scoured table. The person of the landlady, who presently appeared, was in the nicest harmony with floor and furniture, so neat and spotless, and in hand and face so very red. Her speech, however, as she asked what was wanted, was by way of being rough.

"In the first place," said Edmonstone, "two glasses of beer"; and presently handed one to the porter, who tendered his respects, received sixpence, repeated his respects with emphasis, and withdrew. "In the next place a horse and trap."

"We've no hosses an' traps here, yooung man."

"Come now!" said Dick. "They told me at the station this was just the place where there was one."

"Mebbe it is, but it's out now. Where is't ye want to be?"

"Gateby."

"Gaätby! Why, that's where it's gone with t'other gentleman!"

"Indeed? To Colonel Bristo's, do you know?"

"That was it."

"It's a pity I didn't come by the other train!" His tone puzzled the woman. "We might have travelled together, by Jove! What was the gentleman like?"

"Very tall."

"Taller than I am, I suppose?"

"Yes—easy."

"A fair beard?"

"To be sure. You know him, then?"

"Very well indeed. We ought to have travelled together. Has the trap that took him come back yet?"

"Not it. It hasn't had time."

"It must go back with me when it does. Don't look like that, woman; here's a sovereign for the job!"

He flung the coin on the table. The woman stared at him and at it, seemed doubtful whether to take or leave the sovereign, but eventually overcame her scruples, honestly determining to throw in a good square meal for the money.

"The trap won't be back yet a bit, sir. You'll be wanting—"

"Nothing, except to be left alone," broke in the strange guest. "That's all the trouble I shall put you to—that, and to tell me when the trap's ready."

There was no use in saying more to the gentleman. He might not be quite right—he might fly at a body. The good woman left him gazing abstractedly out of the window; yet she had scarcely closed the door when she heard him clattering to and fro over the tiled floor like a caged beast.

His thoughts were in a tumult. He calmed them by a strenuous effort. He strove to look the matter in the face. What was the matter?

Ned Ryan, the Australian outlaw, who had been screened on condition that he came near the Bristos no more, had broken that condition; had somehow heard that Edmonstone was not to be one of the shooting-party in Yorkshire, and was even now the Colonel's newly-arrived guest.

After all, perhaps this was no more than Dick had been prepared for, since his journey from Teddington to Waterloo in the same compartment with Jem Pound and Elizabeth Ryan; he had listened to a villain's suspicions of a brother villain; from that moment he had shared those suspicions. Dick realised then, and only then, that while he was not near the Bristos they were not safe from the advances of "Mr. Miles," if he was bold enough to make them. But the sudden realisation of his fears took Dick's breath away; he had not bargained to find Miles already at Gateby—he had no definite plan for the defeat of

Miles, and he was certain that the man described to him by the mistress of the inn was Miles—as certain as if he had seen him himself.

Then how was he to act? Was he to show no quarter, since this villain had played false? That course presented difficulties—dangers as well; and at the least it involved a violent scene under Colonel Bristo's roof. Must he, then, parley a second time with the villain—let him off again, trust him again, go on shielding a known desperado? No. Ned Ryan could be trusted no further, shielded no more. There were more things than one to be considered—more people than one. The man must receive his deserts.

And to accomplish this—to deliver to justice a criminal of the first water—this young Edmonstone went blindly forward, with thoughts of doing it without fuss and all but single-handed.

There was little daylight left when Dick was driven out of Inglesby; night fell long before he saw the lights of Gateby; it was fully nine when they reached the little square stone house behind the hedge. The dogs in the kennel not far from the house barked an alarm. The front door opened, and Dick saw a well-known figure outlined against the light of the passage. It was the Colonel himself, and his greeting was most cordial. Yet how hard it was to put any heart into the answer! Dick tried, failed miserably, and knew it. Before there was time for many sentences, Dick found himself hustled into a room—a long, faded, unlovely room—in which sat two ladies, Miss Bristo and Mrs. Parish.

The meeting between Alice and Dick—who had not seen each other since that fateful second evening of July—was perfectly careless without being conspicuously cold. It may be assumed that neither was wholly free from some sort of agitation; but it is to be suspected that each had prepared for the same, and masked accordingly. The mummery on both sides was excellently well managed.

Observations the most natural in the world, as well as the most commonplace, were the order of the minute.

"How rude," said Alice, "you must have thought us not to send to meet you! But we have actually only one pony, and he had gone to Melmerbridge, which is in the opposite direction."

"We thought," said Mrs. Parish, "that as you had not telegraphed, and did not come by the usual train, you could not be coming to-night."

"Pray don't name it," Dick answered to the one lady; and to the other: "I really must apologise for forgetting to wire."

The window was wide open, for the night was warm: and through the window came the voices of men chatting, and the faint scent of cigars. Among the voices Dick immediately distinguished one that he was prepared for, and listened for—the soft, deep voice of Miles. Strangely enough, he only caught the well-known tones on the moment of entering the room; speaking himself, and being spoken to by those in the room, he could hear no more than a hum outside; and when he listened again, during the first pause, he could no longer hear Miles.

Very soon the conversation outside ceased altogether, and a moment later the men appeared in the room. There were but two of them, and Miles was not one. As for Mr. Oliver and Captain Awdry, they had only come for the first three days, and had both gone on the Saturday evening.

Dick remembered one of the two men; a heavy-jawed, squarely-built young man, whose eyes were of pale green, whose chin never by any chance appeared to have been shaved since the day before yesterday, whose expression in repose was too demure for a man. This was Philip Robson, and Dick shook hands with him. The dapper little dark man Dick had never seen before. Whoever he was, he seemed to know Alice pretty well, by the way he promptly pestered her for a song.

"So you have only recently returned from Australia, I understand," Robson said to Dick. "I, too, am fresh from those parts. And I am told you came by sailing-ship—so did I—as surgeon."

The dapper young gentleman at the other side of the room here made an inane remark in a loud tone about both being in the same boat, which was ignored by the worthy doctor and Dick, who stared. If they were listening they must have heard this wag informing Miss Bristo that she ought to laugh, and vowing that he would throw away no more good things in mere perishable words of mouth.

"No," said Alice, "write them. It is far the best. The point is so much more easily seen in print; and then, instead of pearls wasted on us poor things, the whole world roars at them."

"Sixty thousand people have the chance," Laurence Pinckney answered—in allusion, it was believed, to the circulation of "his" weekly paper.

But he seemed to have nothing smart ready just then, for he went back to begging for a song.

"Mr. Miles was somewhat tired, I presume, Dr. Robson?" Mrs. Parish was saying. "You see he had a great rush to come to-day. We only knew this morning, when we got his telegram—so thoughtful of him to send one!—that he had found it possible to come at all."

"Yes. He appeared to me to be considerably fatigued—indeed, when he left us I thought him looking pale. I offered to mix him a little something that would fit him for to-morrow. But he wouldn't let me."

Cousin Philip became professional on the slightest provocation.

Dick was asking the Colonel about the sport so far.

"Forty-eight brace the first day, forty-two the second; five guns; over dogs. But," added the Colonel, whispering, "my young friend over there hits nothing at all. Philip is fair; but as for me, I don't see as I used to. Awdry was the crack shot. But you and Miles will be a better pair than Awdry and Oliver."

Dick and Miles—coupled! That silenced Dick. He felt his very skin bristle at the thoughts that poured in upon his mind.

"Do you know Mr. Miles?"

The question was put in a solemn undertone by Cousin Philip. Considering Dick's thoughts at that moment, it was almost a startling question. He waited a moment before replying.

"Yes," he then said slowly, "I know him."

"An interesting man," said the doctor, "a profoundly interesting man; that I can see, and I congratulate myself on making his acquaintance. I shall enjoy his society, I know. And a Colonial, too."

"My dear fellow, Colonials are as good as any other people."

Dick had often to tell people that; but the words were scarcely spoken before it struck him that, in this connection, they were a little incongruous.

"They may be; they may be. But when I travelled for an insurance company in New Zealand, I know I didn't think so. We went round the stations—the agent and I—insuring people, you know."

Dick did know. He had himself met with many such professional Samaritans in Riverina. They were not popular there.

"Well," continued the young doctor, "I don't think we were always well treated. In some places they actually seemed to regard us with suspicion. We didn't meet with the least respect, I can assure you. Once or twice we were downright insulted. Now in England—"

"Let us listen to this song," said Dick. Robson was really too ponderous.

Alice had at last yielded to the importunities of Laurence Pinckney, and was singing something in French. That young gentleman turned over the leaves, but he did not look entirely appreciative. When the song was over, he complained of the French words. He wanted something in English; though he could not refrain from a trenchant and sweeping criticism of all the words of all the ballads and songs foisted on the musical world during this last decade of a degenerate age.

There was no more singing, however; and presently the small party broke up.

"Early hours for the moors," the Colonel said. "Philip, will you show Dick his room? I'm sorry we've had to put you outside, Dick; but there are more of us out than in, and there's really no choice. We all rough it when we go a-shooting."

Dick laughed, and mentioned that the last few years had not made him luxurious. The Colonel was on the stairs, candle in hand. Dick would have liked to speak to him then and there, and tell him everything—but Robson was there too: an inquisitive fellow, unless Dick's memory was at fault; a man who would prick up his ears if he heard a private interview asked for in his presence. So Dick merely said:

"I must be up early and look round. Shall I see you, sir, then?"

"See me? Why, you'll find I've been about for a good hour before you dream of awaking! Take it easy, boy; you've been travelling all day. I'm different. I never slept longer than six hours in my life. Good-night, Dick; good-night, Philip;" and Colonel Bristo went off to bed.

Edmonstone followed Robson out into the dark, comforting himself with the determination to tell Colonel Bristo everything before breakfast next morning. They walked for some moments, then stopped before a door that opened upon a flight of deal stairs. A candle and matches were on the bottom step. The good doctor discharged his duty to the full by lighting the candle and handing it to Dick.

"It is the room on the left," said Robson.

"Anyone in the room on the right?"

"No, I think not—I'm sure not. You are over the stable and that; Pinckney and I are a few yards away, over the laundry. Good-night."

"Good-night, Robson. I say, Robson!"

"Well?"

"Who is Pinckney?"

"Son of a brother officer of the Colonel's. Comes from town, I fancy."

"What does he do—besides making an ass of himself?"

"He writes, I think."

"I'm not surprised; he's got cheek enough for anything! Good-night, Robson."

CHAPTER XX

STRANGE HUMILITY

Dick found his room plainly and scantily furnished but delightfully fresh, clean, and comfortable. There was but one narrow strip of carpet by the bedside, but the boards were as snowy as an admiral's poop; the narrow bed stood out into the middle of the room, to the left as you came in at the door. The ceiling, and the walls, and the blind, and the bed, and the tall new candles, and the dressing-table on which they stood, were all very white indeed. At the foot of the bed Dick found his portmanteau and gun-case, and the first thing he did was to put together his gun, and stand it in one corner of the room, ready for next day. He happened to stand it in the corner nearest the bed head, and farthest from the door; but there was no design in that: the whole action was mechanical.

He undressed slowly, or rather he was long in beginning. He stood, resting his elbows on the chest of drawers, and his chin in his palms, and watched the candle burn half-way down before he so much as wound his watch. It was only the wick's last throes that reminded him to put an end to its flickering and get into bed. But by that time Dick's mind was made up. When he lay down to sleep he knew precisely what he was going to do first thing in the morning, and more or less what he meant to say. He fell quickly into a dreamless slumber.

After sleeping like an infant for two or three hours he experienced something very like a dream, and that about the very man of whom he would certainly have dreamt sooner or later. But this was no dream. Dick was awakened: he lay still for a moment, peering through the darkness, and listening with all his ears. Then he started up in his bed, and called sternly:

"Who is there? Who are you?"

At the foot of the bed a tall figure loomed through the darkness. The challenge was answered: first with a short, soft laugh, then in the mildest tones of the man who had passed himself off as Miles the squatter.

"Hush! I have come to explain."

"Oh, it is you!" though Dick had known who it was from the moment the light, stealthy step disturbed him.

"Yes; it isn't a burglar, so lie down again. I tell you I come with a frank explanation. I suppose you will listen to a man?"

"Why should I? You have broken faith with me!"

"It amounts to that, I own. It must seem to you that I deserve no further consideration at your hands. Very well; all I ask is a hearing."

The tones were so unlike anything that could have been expected from the lips of this man that Edmonstone was taken aback; they were so low as to be scarcely audible; they were humble, and they were sad. It was this very humility that at first excited Dick's suspicion.

"I will listen to you now," said he, after a moment's thought, "but it is the last thing I shall do for you. You might first strike a light. There are matches on the dressing-table behind you, and two candles, I think."

Miles complied unsuspectingly with this reasonable request. He was some time, however, in finding the matches. Yet he heard no sound (Dick's arm was so long, so lithe his movement) until the candles were alight; when two loud clicks caused him to wheel suddenly round, throwing one candlestick with a crash to the floor.

Dick was sitting up quietly in his bed, as he had been sitting a moment before; but in his hands was a double-barrelled gun—cocked—the butt not six inches from his shoulder, the muzzle not three feet from Miles's breast. It could be brought to the shoulder in a small fraction of a second. It could be fired with sufficient deadliness without being brought to the shoulder at all. A finger was upon each of the triggers. The light of the single candle glittered upon the barrels.

"Now, my friend," said Dick, "I am ready to listen to you as long as you like."

Miles stared fixedly at the hammers of the gun. He did not speak, he did not draw back. He stood there, in his shirt and trousers, motionless and silent. This was not, as we know, his first interview under arms, but it was the first in which the arms had been in the hands of the other side; moreover, he had once pressed a pistol to the head of this Edmonstone whose gun covered him now. The reversal of things was complete—the tables were turned to the last inch. The strange part of it was that the outwitted bushranger's face showed no trace of cunning baffled, or the fury of an animal at bay, which might have been expected of him. On the contrary, his countenance gradually filled with quite another expression—one of reproach.

"I am not a fool," he said, speaking at last. "I was never yet fool enough to tackle a forlorn hope. Therefore, even if I had come into this room armed to the teeth to offer you violence, I should not dream of competing against those double-barrels. But as I came empty-handed, and in peace, I, for my part, can say all I have to say comfortably into their muzzles—they can make no difference to me, unless you press too hard on those triggers in your anxiety; and if you did, perhaps it would be the best turn you or any man could do me! At the same time you are treating me like a dog. The only words that have left my lips were as submissive as any victor need want; I turned my back on you without the smallest suspicion, yet turn round again to find you pointing a gun at me!"

"You call that bad treatment!" Edmonstone sneered. "You forget, perhaps, that you have no business to be loose in the world; you forget that I found you out and shielded you, wrongly enough, on certain terms, which you have broken! Well, I am reminding you; but I am not likely to give you a second chance of playing me false. That is why I keep the sight of my gun in a line with your stud—so; that is why, if you come a step nearer, I won't answer for consequences."

"Considering," said Miles, "how I treated you a few years ago, and what you owe to that treatment, I should have thought you might behave rather differently to-night; you might have shown a little generosity, outlaw as I am."

"You remind me," said Dick, "that in '82, in the scrub near Balranald, you stuck up me and my mate, and took almost everything we had—except our money. I didn't require to be reminded of that forbearance of yours. I haven't forgotten it, and I know pretty well its worth by now, though hitherto I have overvalued it. But that old account—supposing it to be one, for argument's sake—was squared last month; you have been fool enough to open a new one."

"It is a pity," said Miles, bitterly, "that I didn't let Jem Pound knife you!"

"On the contrary, through saving me then you found one man in England actually ready to screen you from justice. If you had not broken faith with him that man would screen you still; but as it is—Steady! don't move! I am pressing the trigger."

"Do you mean that you are going to betray me after all?" cried Miles, in a quick gasp of dismay, yet drawing back—he had taken a step forward in his agitation.

"What else would you have me do? Give you another chance? Honestly," cried Dick, with honesty in his tone, "I wish that I could! But can you expect it?"

"Listen to me!" cried Miles, in a deep faltering voice. "Listen to me!"

"I am listening."

"The other day, then—I mean the night you found me out, you and those blood-suckers—I was on the brink of a new life! You smile—but before Heaven it is the truth! I had lived for weeks as I never lived before—among good people. Bad as I was, they influenced me, at first without my knowing it. It was a new side of life to me. I found it was the best side. I grew—well, call it happy. Then I looked back and loathed the old days. I began to map out a better life for myself. I was a new man, starting afresh. I thanked God for my escape, for it seemed like His act."

"If the fellow isn't in earnest," thought Dick, "this is the worst blasphemy I ever heard. I half think he means what he says, poor wretch."

"It was you that blotted out that new existence—just as it opened out before me! It was you that drove me from my haven! It was you that turned me adrift in a city full of foes! So much for your side of the balance between us!"

Dick was half-carried away by the man's rough eloquence, and the note of pathos in his deep tones. But he was only half-carried away; he was a man hard to shift when his stand was once taken. His answer was shrewd:

"That city is the safest place in the world for such as you—safer even than the bush. As to your friends, did you expect to live on them forever?"

The other's vehemence was checked.

"Perhaps you intended to become one of the family!" said Edmonstone scornfully, pursuing his advantage.

Miles pulled himself together, and dismissed this keen question with a smile and a wave of the hand; but the smile faded quickly; nor had it been anything better than a ghastly mockery.

"You do not appreciate my position," said Miles presently, fetching a deep sigh; "you cannot put yourself in my place. No honest man could, I suppose! And you shut me off from all decent living; you made me bid good-bye to the people who had befriended me, and somehow—well, made me wish I was a little less the ruffian! I became an outcast! I tried to make new friends, but failed. I had lost my nerve somehow—that was the worst of it! I resolved to throw it up, and quit England. I took my passage for New York, and—"

"Do you mean what you say? Have you actually done that?"

"Yes. The ticket is in my room, which is opposite this room." He pointed to the door. "I can bring it to show you."

"No; stay where you are; I believe you. When do you sail?"

"In a week—next Tuesday."

Dick breathed more freely. Here was an extenuating circumstance of the broken compact. On the whole, Dick was glad to find one.

"Go on," said Dick, in a slightly less hostile tone: "tell me the rest, and what it was that induced you to come up here."

"Surely you can see the rest for yourself? Surely you can put yourself in my place at this point? I own that hearing you were not to be of the party finally induced me to come—I thought you would not hear of it till afterwards; but I came to bid my friends good-bye! to get one more glimpse of a kind of life I had never seen before and shall never see again! for one more week in a pure atmosphere."

"Oh! not to make up to Miss Bristo, then?"

Blunt though the words were, each one was a self-inflicted stab to the heart of the man that spoke them.

"No!" cried Miles, and his voice was turned suddenly hoarse; "no, before Heaven!"

"If I believed it was that, I think I should pull this trigger on the spot."

"It is not," cried Miles; "I swear it is not," he whispered.

And Dick believed him then.

"Why, man," the bushranger went on, more steadily, "you have got me under the whip here. Down with the lash and cut me to ribbons the first time you see me playing false. Keep your eye on me; watch me all day; I can do nothing up here without your knowledge; I cannot speak but you will hear what it is I say. As to Miss Bristo, I will not go near her—but this is a small part of the whole. In my whole conduct you will find me behave like—like a changed man. Only let me stay this week out. But one other thing—a thing I would go down on my knees to you for, if that would do any good: don't open their eyes when I am gone. There will be no need to; they will forget me as Miles the squatter if you let them. Then let them. They think well of me because I saved the old man from drowning. Edmonstone, you can let me keep their good opinions if you will. God help me! they are the only good opinions I ever honestly earned, because I got them entirely through that simple, paltry affair at the seaside. Do not rob me of them, now or afterwards. That is all I ask."

Dick was beginning to waver.

There was an honest ring in Ned Ryan's asseverations; and after all it was just possible that a villain, who had shown a soft side at least once before, might be softened right through by the gracious influence of an English home. Then Sundown, the bushranger, desperado though he had been, had preserved hands unstained by blood; and Sundown the bushranger had saved him, Edmonstone, from death and ruin in the Australian wilds, and Colonel Bristo from drowning. Such acts could not be made light of or forgotten, no matter who was their author.

Dick was relenting, and the other saw it.

"Stay!" said Miles, suddenly. "You have my word only so far. I can show you a better pledge of good faith if you will let me."

"Where is it?"

"In my room."

Edmonstone nodded. Miles left the room, and returned immediately with a paper, which he handed to Edmonstone.

"Why, this is a receipt of passage-money for two!" said Edmonstone, looking up. "You are not going out alone, then?"

"No," said Miles. His voice was low. His back was to the window, through which grey dawn was now stealing. It was impossible to see the expression on his face—its outline was all that was visible.

"Who is going with you?"

"My wife!" whispered Miles.

Dick was taken aback, glad, incredulous.

"Your wife!" he said. "Then you admit that she is your wife? When did you see her?"

"Yesterday."

"But not until then!" Dick meant to put a question; he did not succeed in his excitement—his tone was affirmative.

"No, not until then," said Miles quietly; "because, though I have been watching her as closely as I dared, it was the first chance I got of seeing her without seeing Pound. He thinks she has not seen me since the night in Bushey Park. She must not escape him until the very day of joining me on board the steamer. If she did, he would find her sooner or later; and then he would find me, which is all he is living for. That man would murder me if he got the chance. Do you understand now?"

Dick made no reply, but it all seemed clear and intelligible to him; Pound's hold upon Mrs. Ryan, and the false position in which that fiend placed the woman at the meeting of husband and wife, which accounted for Ryan's misunderstanding and heartless treatment of his wife on that occasion; the reconciliation of husband and wife; their projected departure for America; the necessity of deceiving Pound meanwhile, and getting away without his knowledge. All these things seemed natural enough; and, told in the desperately earnest tones of a strong man humbled, they carried conviction with them. Nor were they pleaded in vain.

The way in which Dick finally put the matter was this:—

"Remember," he said, "that it is for my friends' sake as much as for yours; that this is our second treaty; and that if you break one particle of it there are always four men in the house here, and villagers in plenty within a cooee of us."

"I know all these things," said Miles, very humbly, "and will forget none of them."

And so the interview ended.

When Miles was gone, Dick lifted his gun, which had lain long upon the counterpane, pressed the lever, bent down the barrels, and aimed them at the glimmering window-blind. The early morning light shone right through the gleaming bores—the gun had been empty all the time! Dick felt ashamed of the part that it had played in the interview.

CHAPTER XXI

AN ALTERED MAN

Colonel Bristo was rambling about the place, according to habit, for a good hour the next morning before the early breakfast, but he saw nothing of Dick until the bell rang for that meal.

"I thought you meant turning out early?" said the old fellow to the young one, with a smile. "I've been looking for you in vain; but I'm glad you followed my advice and took it easy. Did you sleep well, though? That's the main thing; and 'pon my soul, you look as though you had been awake all night!"

"Oh, I was all right, thanks, sir; I slept pretty well," said Dick, with awkward haste.

The Colonel felt pretty sure that Dick had been all wrong, and slept not at all. There was a haggard look about him that put the fact beyond the contradiction of words.

"You didn't see Miles, I suppose?" said the Colonel after a moment's thought. "His room is close to yours, you know."

"I did see him. We—we exchanged a few words."

Dick's tone and manner were strange.

"Confound them both!" thought the Colonel. "They have clashed already. Yes, that is it. I wonder how it came about? I didn't think they were such implacable foes. Mrs. Parish hinted to me long ago that they were, and that it would be best not to have them here together. Is it all on Alice's account, I wonder? Anyway, it is by no scheme of mine that they are here together. Why, I wrote Miles a list of our little party without a word about Dick. I never thought Dick was coming. Yet I am glad now he is come."

"It was really kind of you," said Colonel Bristo aloud, "to give in and come after all."

"No," said Dick, with sudden fire. "I'm thankful I came! I am grateful to you for refusing to take my first refusal. Now that I am here, I would not be elsewhere at this moment for the whole world!"

The Colonel was pleased, if a little puzzled, by this vehement outburst.

"Are you really going out again—back to the bush?" he said presently.

"Yes," said Dick, the fire within him quickly quenched. "I have quite settled that point—though I have told no one but you, Colonel Bristo."

"Well, well—I think you are making a sad mistake; but of course every man decides for himself."

That was all Colonel Bristo said just then, for he knew that the young people had barely seen one another as yet. But up on the moor, an hour or two later, when the guns divided, he felt inclined to say something sharp, for the manner in which Dick avoided shooting with Miles was rather too pointed, and a good deal too ridiculous and childish for the Colonel's fancy.

That evening the conversation at the Colonel's dinner, and that around the beer-stained board—dedicated of an evening to the engrossing domino—in the inn at Gateby, were principally upon the selfsame topic—to wit, the excellence of Miles's shooting.

"I can't conceive," said the Colonel, "seeing that you have never shot grouse in your life before, how you do it."

"If I couldn't shoot straight," said the hero of the evening (for the bag that day was the biggest yet, thanks to Miles), "I ought to be shot myself. I was reared on gunpowder. In the bush—instead of the silver spoon in your mouth—you are born with a fire-arm in your hand!"

Dick smiled grimly to himself. And yet this was the longest speech the Australian had made all the evening. Miles was strangely subdued, compared with what he had been at Graysbrooke. The Colonel and his daughter had each noticed this already; and as for Mrs. Parish, she was resolved to "speak up" on the subject to Alice, whom she blamed for it entirely.

"Yon yoong man—him 't coomed las' night—t' long wan, I mean," declared Andy Garbutt in the pot-house, banging down his fourth glass (empty) upon the table, which upset several dominoes and led to "language"—"yon yoong man's t'bes' shot I iver seed. The way he picked off t'ould cocks, an' let be t'yoongsters an' all, was sumthink clever. I niver seed owt like it. They do say 'tis his first taast o' t'mowers—but we isn't the lads to swaller yon! Bob Rutter, y' ould divle—fill oop t' glasses."

And though perhaps, hyperbole ran riot upon the heels of intoxication, still in Robert Rutter's genial hostelry "t' long chap's" reputation was there and then established.

But the marked change in Miles's manner was, to those who had known him best before, inexplicable. Never had a shooting-party a more modest, mild, and unassuming member, even among the worst of shots; and Miles was, if anything, better than Captain Awdry. His quiet boastfulness was missing. He might have passed the weeks since the beginning of July in some school of manners, where the Colonial angles had been effectually rounded off, and the old free-and-easy habits toned down. Not that he was shy or awkward—Miles was not the man to become either the one or the other; but his manner had now—towards the Colonel, for instance, and Alice—a certain deference-with-dignity, the lack of which had been its worst fault before. Dick, who scarcely spoke three words to him in as many days, suddenly awoke to a sense of relief and security.

"Poor fellow!" he thought, "he is keeping his word this time, I must own. Well, I am glad I didn't make a scene; and the week is half over. When it is quite over, I shall be still more glad that I let him off. For, after all, I owe him my life. I am sorry I threatened him during our interview, and perhaps I need not have avoided him so studiously since. Yet I am watching him, and he knows it. I watch him sometimes when he cannot possibly know it, and for the life of me I can see nothing crooked. My belief is that he's only too thankful to get off on the terms, and that he wouldn't break them for as much as his life is worth; besides which, his remorse the other night was genuine."

Mrs. Parish, for her part, was quite sure that it was love unrequited with Mr. Miles, and nothing else. She fumed secretly for two days, and then "spoke up" according to her intention. What she said was not well received, and a little assault-at-words was the result.

Dr. Robson told Mr. Pinckney that he found Miles a less interesting man to talk to than he had been led to expect from his conversation the first evening. Mr. Pinckney replied that if all the Australians were as unsociable, he was glad he didn't live out there. Though Miles, he said, might be a fine sportsman and a devilish handsome dog, there was evidently "nothing in him;" by which it was meant that he was not intellectual and literary—like L. P.

Colonel Bristo was fairly puzzled, but, on the whole, he liked the new Miles rather less than the old.

As for Alice, though she did her best to exclude her personal feelings from the pages of her diary, she could not help just touching on this matter.

"I never," she wrote, "saw anybody so much changed as Mr. Miles, and in so short a time. Though he is certainly less amusing than we used to think him, I can't help admitting that the change is an improvement. His audacity, I remember, carried him a little too far once or twice before he left us. But he was a hero all the time, in spite of his faults, and now he is one all the more. Oh, I can never forget what we owe to him! To me he is most polite, and not in the least (as he sometimes used to be) familiar, I am thankful to say. The more I think of it the less I can account for his strange behaviour that night of our dance—because it was so unlike what he had been up till then, and what he is now."

Of Dick this diary contained no mention save the bald fact of his arrival. There was, indeed, a sentence later on that began with his name, but the few words that followed his name were scored out so carefully as to be illegible. The fact was that the estrangement between the pair was well-nigh hopeless. They conversed together, when they did converse, with mutual effort. Dick found himself longing to speak—to ask her forgiveness before he went—but without opportunity or encouragement. Alice, on the other hand, even if ready to meet an overture half-way, was the last person in the world to invite one. Under the conditions of the first few days, meeting only at breakfast and dinner, and for an hour or so in the drawing-room afterwards, these two might have been under one roof for weeks without understanding one another a whit the better.

But meanwhile, Alice seemed to benefit very little by her change from the relaxing Thames valley to the bracing Yorkshire moors; and as for Dick—except when the Colonel was present, for whose sake he did make an effort to be hearty—he was poor company, and desperately moody. He was also short-tempered, as Philip Robson found out one morning when they were tramping over the moor together. For Cousin Philip was sufficiently ill-advised to inform his companion that he, Dr. Robson, thought him looking far from well—at a moment when no good sportsman would have opened his mouth, unless in businesslike reference to the work in hand.

"I'm all right, thanks," Dick answered shortly, and with some contempt.

"Ah!" said Philip, compassionately, "perhaps you are not a very good judge of your own health; nor can you know how you look. Now, as a medical man—"

"Spare me, my dear fellow. Go and look at all the tongues of the village, if you must keep your eye in. They'll be charmed. As for me, I tell you I don't want—I mean, I'm all right."

"As a medical man," pursued Philip, "I beg to dif—"

"Hang it!" cried Dick, now fairly irritated. "We didn't come out for a consultation, did we? When I want your advice, Robson, you'll hear from me."

With such men as Robson, if they don't feel the first gentle snub (and the chances are all against it), anything short of an insult is waste of breath. Yet, having driven you into being downright offensive, they at once turn sensitive, and out with their indignation as though they had said nothing to provoke you. Witness the doctor:

"I thought," he cried, beginning to tremble violently, "I came out with a gentleman! I meant what I said for your good—it was pure kindness on my part, nothing else. I thought—I thought—"

At that point he was cut short; for Edmonstone had lost his temper, turned on his heel with a short, sharp oath, and made Philip Robson his enemy from that minute.

CHAPTER XXII

EXTREMITIES

That same evening (it was on the Thursday), on his return from shooting, Dick Edmonstone found, among the other letters on the table in the passage, one addressed to himself in a strange hand. The writing was bad, but characteristic in its way; Dick had certainly never seen it before. The envelope bore a London postmark. He took the letter into the little back room, the gunroom, and sat down to read it alone.

Twilight was deep in this room, for the window was in an angle of the house, facing eastward, and was overshadowed by the foliage of a fair-sized oak. Some out-lying small branches of this tree beat gently against the upper pane; the lower sash was thrown up. The window was several feet above the ground. The corner below was a delightful spot, shaded all day from the sun; a basket-work table and chair were always there, for the nook was much affected by Mrs. Parish, and even by Alice, in the hot, long, sleepy afternoons.

Edmonstone had read to the end of his letter, when the door opened and Miles entered the room. Dick looked up and greeted him: "This is lucky. I was just coming to look for you. I want to speak to you."

The other's astonishment was unconcealed. Since the small hours of Tuesday the two had not exchanged a dozen words. Edmonstone had avoided Miles on the moor, and elsewhere watched him as a terrier watches a rat in a trap. Miles could not guess what was coming.

"I have a letter here that will interest you," said Dick. "Listen to this:

"'Dear Edmonstone,—I thought I'd look you up yesterday, as I had nothing on, but, like my luck, I found you away. Your people, however, treated me handsomely, and I stayed all the afternoon. We talked Australia; and this brings me to the reason of my writing to you. Your people told me of a rather mysterious Australian who stayed some time with the people you are with now, and went out again very suddenly at the beginning of last month. His name was Miles; your sister described him to me, and the description struck me as uncommon like that of a well-known gentleman at present wanted by the police of the Colony. The fact is, I have stumbled across an old mate of mine (a sergeant in the mounted police), who is over here after this very gent, and who I am helping a bit in the ready-money line. As he is working on the strict q.t., I must not tell you whom he's after. In fact, it's all on my own account I am writing you. I haven't told him anything about it. It's my own idea entirely, and I want you to tell me just this: Have your friends heard anything of this Miles since he left them? because I've been making inquiries, and found that no such name as Miles has been booked for a passage out at any of the London offices during the past two months! Of course I may have got hold of a wild-goose notion; but Miss Edmonstone told me that your friends made this Miles's acquaintance in an offhand kind of a way, and nobody else knew anything about him. Anyway, I'll wait till I hear from you before telling Compton, who's down at the seaside on a fresh clue.—Yours faithfully, Stephen Biggs.'"

"What name was that?" asked Miles quickly. He had listened calmly to the end. But at the very end the colour had suddenly fled from his face.

"Biggs—the Hon. Stephen, M. L. C. A warm man for a campaign, rich as Croesus. If he's set his heart upon having you, he'll chase you round and round the world—"

"No. I mean the other man—the name of the sergeant."

Dick referred to the letter.

"Compton," he said.

"Compton!" repeated Miles in a whisper. "The only 'trap' in Australia I ever feared—the only man in the world, bar Pound, I have still to fear! Compton! my bitterest enemy!"

Edmonstone rose from the armchair in which he had been sitting, sat down at the table, opened a blotter, and found a sheet of notepaper.

"Must you answer now?" cried Miles.

"Yes; on the spot."

"What do you mean to say?"

"I have not decided. What would you say in my place? I am a poor liar."

"If we changed places, and I had treated you as you have treated me these two days—since our compact—I should write them the worst, and have done with it," said Miles, in a low tone of intense bitterness. "You professed to trust me. Yet you won't trust yourself near me on the moors; you fear foul play at my hands. You watch me like a lynx here at the house; yet I swear man never kept promise as I am keeping mine now! You do things by halves, Edmonstone. You had better end the farce, and wire the truth to your friend."

Reproach mingled with resignation in the last quiet words. Edmonstone experienced a twinge of compunction.

"Nonsense!" he said. "I should be a fool if I didn't watch you—worse than a fool to trust you. But betraying you is another matter. I don't think of doing that, unless—"

"I can keep my word, Edmonstone, bad as I may be! Besides, I am not a fool."

"And you are going on Monday?"

"Yes—to sail on Tuesday; you have seen my ticket."

"Then you shall see my answer to this letter."

Dick then dashed off a few lines. He handed the sheet, with the ink still wet, to Miles, who read these words:

"Dear Biggs,—A false scent, I am afraid. Ladies are never accurate; you have been misinformed about Miles. I knew him in Australia! He cannot be the man you want.—Yours sincerely, "R. Edmonstone."

The sheet of writing paper fluttered in Miles's hand. For one moment an emotion of gratitude as fierce as that which he himself had once inspired in the breast of Edmonstone, swelled within his own.

"You are a friend indeed," he murmured, handing back the letter. "And yet your friendship seems like madness!"

"My old mate swears that I am mad on the subject!"

Dick folded and enclosed his note in an envelope, directed it, and got up to go. Miles followed him to the door and wrung his hand in silence.

When the door was closed upon Edmonstone, Miles sank into the armchair, and closed his eyes.

His expression was human then; it quickly hardened, and his face underwent complete transformation. A moment later it was not a pleasant face to look upon. The ugliness of crime had disfigured it in a flash. The devils within him were unchained for once, and his looks were as ugly as his thoughts.

"Curse it!"—he was thinking—"I must be losing my nerve: I get heated and flurried as I never did before. Yet it was not altogether put on, my gratitude to this young fellow: I do feel some of it. Nor were they all lies that I told him the other night; I am altered in some ways. I believe it was that spice of truth that saved me—for saved I am so far as he is concerned. Anyway, I have fooled him rather successfully, and he'll know it before he has done with me! True, I did not bargain to meet him here, after what the Colonel wrote; but I flatter myself I made the best of it—I can congratulate myself upon every step. No; one was a false step: I was an idiot to show him the passage-money receipt; it was telling him the name and line of the steamer and opening up the track for pursuit when we are gone. And yet, and yet—I could not have laid a cleverer false scent if I had tried! Instead of money flung away, that passage-money will turn out a glorious investment; we'll show a clean pair of heels in the opposite direction, while our good friends here think of nothing but that one steamer! And so, once more, everything is turning out well, if only I can keep this up three days longer; if only Jem Pound and Frank Compton do not trouble me; if only—if only I am not mistaken and misled as to the ease with which I may carry off—my prize!"

And strange to say, as he thought of that final coup, the villainy faded out of his face—though the act contemplated was bad enough, in all conscience!

All at once a creaking noise startled Miles. He rose from his chair, and crossed with swift noiseless steps over to the window. A man was lifting himself gingerly from the basket-work chair—the man was Philip Robson.

Miles leant out of the window, seized him by the collar, and drew him backward with a thud against the wall below the window.

"Eavesdropper! listener!" hissed Miles; and quick as lightning he changed his hold from the doctor's collar to the doctor's wrists, which he grabbed with each iron hand and drew upward over the sill.

The sill was more than six feet from the ground. The doctor stood on tiptoe—helpless—in a trap. The doctor's face was white and guilty. The doctor's tongue was for the moment useless.

"What were you doing there?" Miles demanded quietly, but with a nasty look about the eyes.

"I—I had been asleep. I came back early from the moors because Edmonstone insulted me. I was just awake. Let go my hands, will you? I heard something—a very little—I could not help it. What do you mean by holding my wrists like this? Leave loose of them, I say!"

"Then tell me what you heard."

"Something that I could not understand. If you don't let me go this instant, I'll sing out!"

"Will you stand and talk sensibly, and listen to what I tell you?"

"Yes, I swear I will."

"There, then, you're free. Now I'll just tell you, in effect, what you did hear," said Miles, whose inventive brain had been busy from the moment he had discovered Robson. "You heard Edmonstone speak to me as though I was a villain: well, he firmly believes I am one. You heard him read me a letter from some one 'wanting' me: he has read me many such letters. I believe you heard me asking him in effect not to tell any one, and thanking him: this is what I make a point of doing. The fact is, Edmonstone is under the delusion that I am a man who robbed him in Australia. This is what's the matter!"

Miles tapped his forehead significantly.

"You don't mean it!" cried Robson, starting back.

"I do; but not so loud, man. His friends don't suspect anything; they needn't know; it's only on this one point. What, didn't you hear our last words? I said, 'It seems like madness.' He answered, 'My old mate'—meaning the man who was with him at the time of the robbery—'my old mate,' he says, 'swears that I am mad on that subject.'"

"Whew!" whistled the doctor. "Yes, I heard that."

"It speaks for itself, eh? But I put it to you as a medical man," said Miles, rising still more fully to the occasion, and remembering the doctor's weak point: "I put it to you as a medical man—has there not been something strange about his manner?"

Robson thought at once of the disagreeable incident of the morning.

"There has, indeed," he said, without hesitation; "I have noticed it myself!"

Even Miles marvelled at his own adroitness; he was elated, and showed it by fetching a deep sigh.

"Poor Edmonstone! he is quite touched on the point. Perhaps the affair brought on a fever at the time, for he is an excitable fellow, and that would account for it."

"But is he safe?" asked Robson, eagerly. "He can't be!"

"Oh, yes, he is; quite. I repeat, it is only on that one point, and nobody knows it here. And, mind, you are not to breathe a word of it to any single soul!"

Philip was entirely taken in for the time being; but his silence was another matter. That could only be pardoned, even on short lease, by an apology from the rude Colonial. The doctor's wrists smarted yet; his self-esteem was still more sore.

"I am so likely," said he, with fine irony, "to do your bidding after the manner in which you have treated me!"

"Call it taking my hint," said Miles, with a nasty expression in the eyes again. "You will find it a hint worth acting upon."

"You had no business to treat me as you did. It was a gross outrage!" said the doctor, haughtily.

"Come, now, I apologise. It arose from my irritation on Edmonstone's account, at the thing getting out. For his sake, you must indeed promise to hold your tongue."

"Very well," said Philip Robson, reluctantly; "I—I promise."

And he meant at the time to keep his promise, if he could. In fact, he did keep it. For a little calm reflection, away from the glamour thrown by Miles's plausibility, and in the sober light of Philip's own professional knowledge, served to weaken the case of insanity against Dick Edmonstone. At the same time, reflection strengthened Edmonstone's case against Miles, though Robson had only oblique information as to the specific nature of that case. But at any rate there was no harm in opening the letter-box (which was cleared in the morning) late at night, and sending just one anonymous line to the same name and address as those upon the envelope directed in Edmonstone's hand. If Miles was really a forger of some kind, and Edmonstone was really shielding him, then there was an excellent chance of scoring off them both at once. And Philip Robson had contracted a pretty strong grudge against both these men since morning.

Meanwhile Miles remained subdued and pensive, furtively attentive, but extremely humble, towards Miss Bristo, and talkative to one person only—Mrs. Parish. He was indeed, as he said, no fool. He was full of cunning and coolness, foresight and resource. He was biding his time—but for what?

CHAPTER XXIII

THE EFFECT OF A PHOTOGRAPH

Laurence Pinckney was a hopeless sportsman. When he realised this for himself he laid down his gun, and presently took up with Miss Bristo's camera as a weapon better suited to him.

Alice had made no use of the apparatus for weeks and weeks; it was sent down with other luggage without her knowledge, and she never thought of unpacking it until Mr. Pinckney pleaded for instruction; when—perhaps because Alice felt that without an occupation this visitor would be on her hands all day—he did not plead in vain. He did not, however, require many lessons. He knew something about it already, having given the subject some attention (in the reading room of the British Museum) before writing one of his rollicking articles. Nor were the lessons she did give him much of a nuisance to Alice, for when he forgot to talk about his work, and refrained from coruscation, there was no more sensible and polite companion than Laurence Pinckney.

When, therefore, he set out on that Friday's ramble, which produced one really good negative, and a number of quaint little Arcadian observations jotted down in his notebook, it was with the entire photographic impedimenta slung about his person, and some idea in his head of an article on "The North Yorkshire Dales," to be illustrated by the writer's own photographs.

His destination was a certain ancient abbey, set in gorgeous scenery, eight long miles from Gateby. But long before he got there a hollow of the plain country road tempted him, and he fell.

It was quite an ordinary bit of road; a tall hazel-hedge, and a pathway high above the road on the left; on the right, a fence with trees beyond it, one of them, an oak of perfect form, that stood in the foreground, being of far greater size than most of the trees in this district, and in strong contrast to its neighbours. That was really all. It never would have been picturesque, nor have taken our artist's fancy, but for the sunlight on the wet road and the fleecy pallor of the sky where it met the sharp line of distant dark blue hills far away over the hazel-hedge, to the left. But the sunlight was the thing. It came, as though expressly ordered, from, so to say, the left wing. It rested lightly on the hedge-tops. It fell in a million golden sparks on the shivering leaves of the old oak. But it cleared the deep-cut road at a bound, leaving it dark. Only a long way further on, where the bend to the right began, did his majesty deign to step down upon the road; and just there, because everything was wet from last night's rain, it was a road of silver.

No sooner, however, was the picture focussed than the sun, which made it what it was, disappeared behind a cloud—a favourite and mischievous dodge of his for the mortification of the amateur photographer.

Now, while Pinckney waited for the sun to come out again, which he saw was going to happen immediately, and while he held in his fingers the pneumatic ball connected with the instantaneous shutter, two figures appeared at the bend of the road that had been silver track a moment before. They were a man and a woman, trudging along with the width of the road between them. Pinckney watched them with painful interest. If the cloud cleared the sun at that moment they would be horribly in the way, for worse clouds were following on the heels of this one, and the opportunity must be seized. There was nothing, of course, to prevent his taking the tramps as they walked—no, it would spoil the picture. Stay, though; it would add human interest. But the cloud did not pass so rapidly after all, and the man and woman drew near the camera.

There was something peculiar in the appearance of the man that struck Pinckney at once as un-English. This peculiarity was difficult to localise. It was not in his clothes, which indeed looked new, but it was partly in his heavy face, smooth-shaven and suntanned, partly in his slow, slouching, methodical walk, and very much in his fashion of carrying his belongings. Instead of the pudding-like bundle of the English tramp he carried across his shoulders a long, neatly-strapped cylinder, the outer coating of which was a blanket. About the woman, on the other hand, there was nothing to strike the attention. Pinckney's first glance took in, perhaps, the fact that her black skirt was torn and draggled, and her black bodice in startling contrast to her white face; but that could have been all.

Back came the sun, in a hurry, to the hedge-top and the oak-tree, and the distant curve of the road. Pinckney had decided in favour of the tramps in his picture, but they were come too near. He requested them in his blandest tones to retrace a few steps. To his immense surprise he was interrupted by a sullen oath from the man, who at once quickened his steps forward, motioning to the woman to do the same.

"Thankee for nothing, and be hanged to you! Wait till we pass, will you?"

If Pinckney had wanted further assurance that the man was a foreign element, these sentences should have satisfied him; for your honest British rustic is not the man to reject the favours of the camera, be they never so promiscuous and his chance of beholding the result never so remote.

Pinckney's answer, however, was a prompt pressure of the pneumatic ball in his hand—a snap-shot at short range, the click of which did not escape the sharp ears of the strange-looking, heavily-built old man.

"Have you took us?" asked he fiercely.

"Oh no," replied the photographer, without a blush, "I'm waiting till you pass; look sharp, or I'll lose the sun again!"

The man scowled, but said no more. Next moment he passed by on one side of the camera, and the woman on the other. Pinckney looked swiftly from one to the other, and marked well the face of each. That of the man repelled him, as bull-dog jaws upon a thick, short neck and small, cruel-looking glittering eyes would repel most of us, even without this man's vile expression. The man was tall and broad, but bent, and he looked twenty years older at close quarters than at a distance. The woman, on the other hand, was young, but so worn, and pinched, and soured, and wearied that you had to look closely to find a trace of youth. She never raised her eyes from the ground as she walked; but Pinckney made sure they were dark eyes, for the well-formed eyebrows were blue-black, like a raven's feather. Her wrist-bone showed prominently—seeming to be covered by little more than skin—as she caught together the shawl at her bosom with her left hand; a plain gold hoop was on its third finger.

Pinckney watched the pair out of sight, still walking with the whole road between them.

"That brute," muttered Pinckney, "beats his wife!"

And then he exposed another plate from the same position, packed up the apparatus, and went his way.

Some hours later—towards evening, in fact—as Pinckney returned from his ruined abbey and came in sight of Gateby, the rain—which had gathered during the afternoon—came down from the leaden twilit sky in earnest. It rains violently in the dales; and the photographer, hungry though he was, and more than ready for dinner, saw no reason for getting wet to the skin when the village was within a stone's-throw, and the shooting-box half-a-mile further on. He burst into the inn for shelter; and honest Robert Rutter conducted him to the private parlour with peculiar satisfaction, having been intimate with Gateby rain many years, and knowing also a thing or two about the appetites of gentlemen from the south.

Pinckney, left alone, examined the room. It was gaudily carpeted, uncomfortably furnished, stuffy for want of use and air, and crowded with gimcracks. Foxes and birds, in huge cases, were perilously balanced on absurd little tables. The walls were covered with inflamed-looking prints, the place of honour being occupied by portraits of mine host and hostess unrecognisable. The large square centre-table was laid out in parterres of books never opened. In fact, the parlour was not what you would have expected of the remote dales. For this very reason, perhaps, that realist Pinckney took particular pains over the description which was promptly set down in his note-book. The landlord coming in during the writing, moreover, the poor man's words were taken out of his mouth and set down red-hot, and on the phonetic principle, in a parenthesis.

This visit of Rutter's resulted subsequently in a heavy supper of ham and eggs and beer, and a fire in the parlour, before which Pinckney contentedly smoked, listening to the rain, which was coming down indeed in torrents.

It was while this easy-going youth was in the most comfortable post-prandial condition that the voices in a room, separated from the parlour only by a narrow passage, grew loud enough to be distinctly audible in it. Up to this point the conversation had been low and indistinct, occasional laughter alone rising above an undertone; now the laughter was frequent and hearty. The reasons were that the room in question was the tap-room, and the fourth round of beer was already imbibed. One voice—in which the local accents were missed—led the talk; the rest interjaculated.

Mr. Pinckney pricked up his ears, and of course whipped out the insatiable note-book. Simultaneously, in the kitchen, connected with the tap-room on the opposite side, the landlord and his wife, with the schoolmaster and his, were bending forward, and solemnly listening to the stranger's wild stories, with the door ajar. Thus the glib-tongued personage had more listeners, and more sober listeners, than he was aware of.

"Sharks?" he was saying. "Seen sharks? You bet I have! Why, when I was or'nary seaman—betwixt Noocastle, Noo South Wales and 'Frisco it was; with coals—we counted twenty-seven of 'em around the ship the morning we was becalmed in three south. And that afternoon young Billy Bunting—the darling of our crew he was—he fell overboard, and was took. Took, my lads, I say! Nothin' left on'y a patch of red in the blue water and a whole set of metal buttons when we landed Mister John Shark next morning." (Sensation.) "And that's gospel. But the next shark as we got—and we was becalmed three weeks that go—the skipper he strung him up to the spanker-boom, an' shot his blessed eyes out with a revolver; 'cause little Billy had been pet of the ship, d'ye see? And then we let him back into the briny; and a young devil of an apprentice dived over and swam rings round him, 'cause he couldn't see; and it was the best game o' blindman's buff ever you seed in your born days." (Merriment.) "What! Have ye never heard tell o' the shark in Corio Bay, an' what he done? Oh, but I'll spin that yarn."

And spin it he did; though before he had got far the landlady exchanged glances with the schoolmaster's lady, and both good women evinced premonitory symptoms of sickness, so that the worthy schoolmaster hastily took "his missis" home, and hurried back himself to hear the end.

"A sailor," said Pinckney, listening in the parlour; "and even at that an admirable liar."

He went out into the passage, and peeped through the chink of the door into the tap-room. In the middle of the long and narrow table, on which the dominoes for once lay idle, stood one solitary tallow candle, and all around were the shadowy forms of rustics in various attitudes of breathless attention—it was a snake-story they were listening to now; and the face of the narrator, thrust forward close to the sputtering wick, was the smooth, heavy, flexible face of the man whom Pinckney had photographed unawares on the road.

Pinckney went softly back to the parlour, whistling a low note of surprise.

"No wonder I didn't recognise the voice! That voice is put on. The surly growl he gave me this morning in his natural tone. He's making up to the natives; or else the fellow's less of a brute when he's drunk, and if that's so, some philanthropist ought to keep him drunk for his natural life. The terms might be mutual. 'I keep you in drink, in return for which you conduct yourself like a Christian,—though an intoxicated one, to me and all men.'"

"Who is that customer?" Pinckney asked of Bob Rutter, as they settled up outside on the shining flags— shining in the starlight; for the heavy rain had suddenly stopped, and the sky as suddenly cleared, and the stars shone out, and a drip, drip, drip fell upon the ear from all around, and at each breath the nostril drew in a fragrance sweeter than flowers.

"He's a sailor," said honest Rutter; "that's all I know; I don't ask no questions. He says his last voyage was to—Australia, I think they call it—and back."

"I saw he was a sailor," said Pinckney.

"He asked," continued Rutter, "if there was anybody from them parts hereabout; and I said not as I knowed on, till I remembered waddycallum, your crack shot, up there, and tould him; and he seemed pleased."

"Has he nobody with him?" asked Pinckney, remembering the wan-faced woman.

"Yes—a wife or sumthink."

"Where is she?"

"In t'blacksmith's shed."

Rutter pointed to a low shed that might have been a cow-house, but in point of fact contained a forge and some broken ploughshares.

"Landlord," said Pinckney, severely, "you ought to turn that low blackguard out, and not take another farthing of his money until he finds the woman a fit place to sleep in!"

And with that young Pinckney splashed indignantly out into the darkness, and along the watery road to the shooting-box. There he found everyone on the point of going to bed. He was obliged, for that night, to keep to himself the details of his adventures; but, long after the rest of the premises were in darkness, a ruby-coloured light burned in Mr. Pinckney's room; he had actually the energy to turn his dry-plates into finished negatives before getting into bed, though he had tramped sixteen miles with accoutrements! Not only that, but he got up early, and had obtained a sun-print of each negative before going over to breakfast. His impatience came of his newness to photography; it has probably been experienced by every beginner in this most fascinating of crafts.

These prints he stowed carefully in his pocket, closely buttoning his coat to shield them from the light. At breakfast he produced them one by one, and handed them round the table on the strict understanding that each person should glance at each print for one second only. They were in their raw and perishable state; but a few seconds' exposure to the light of the room, said the perpetrator, would not affect them. In truth, no one wished to look at them longer; they were poor productions: the light had got in here, the focus was wrong in that one. But Mr. Pinckney knew their faults, and he produced the last print, and the best, with the more satisfaction.

"This one," said he, "will astonish you. It's a success, though I say it. Moreover, it's the one I most wanted to come out well—a couple of tramps taken unawares. This print you must look at only half-a-second each."

He handed it to Alice, who pronounced it a triumph—as it was—and glanced curiously at the downcast face of the woman in the foreground. She handed it to the doctor, sitting next her. The doctor put the print in his uncle's hand, at the head of the table. The Colonel's comment was good-natured. He held out the print to Miles, who took it carelessly from him, and leant back in his chair.

Now as Miles leant back, the sunlight fell full upon him. It streamed through a narrow slit of a window at the end of the room—the big windows faced southwest—and its rays just missed the curve of table-cloth between the Colonel and Miles. But on Miles the rays fell: on his curly light-brown hair, clear dark skin, blond beard and moustache; and his blue eyes twinkled pleasantly under their touch. As he idly raised the print, leaning back in the loose rough jacket that became him so well, the others there had never seen him more handsome, tranquil, and unconcerned.

Miles raised the print with slow indifference, glanced at it, jerked it suddenly upward, and held it with both hands close before his eyes. They could not see his face. But the sunlight fell upon the print, and Pinckney cried out an excited protest:

"Look out, I say! Hold it out of the sun, please! Give it here, you'll spoil the print!"

But Miles did not heed, even if he heard. The square of paper was quivering, though held by two great strong hands. All that they could see of Miles's face behind it was the brow: it was deeply scored across and across—it was pale as ashes.

A minute passed; then the print was slowly dropped upon the table. No print now: only a sheet of glossy reddish-brown paper.

Miles burst into a low, harsh laugh.

"A good likeness!" he said slowly. "But it has vanished, clean gone, and, I fear, through my fault. Forgive me, Pinckney, I didn't understand you. I thought the thing was finished. I know nothing about such things—I'm an ignorant bushman"—with a ghastly smile—"but I thought—I couldn't help thinking, when it vanished like that—that it was all a hoax!"

He pushed back his chair, and stalked to the door. No one spoke—no one knew what to say—one and all, they were mystified. On the threshold Miles turned, and looked pleadingly towards the Colonel and Alice.

"Pray forgive me, I am covered with shame; but—but it was strangely like some one—some one long dead," said Miles, hoarsely—and slowly, with the exception of the last four words, which were low and hurried. And with that he went from the room, and cannoned in the passage against Dick Edmonstone, who was late for breakfast.

That day, the champion from Australia shot execrably, which was inexplicable; and he kept for ever casting sudden glances over his shoulders, and on all sides of him, which was absurd.

CHAPTER XXIV

THE EFFECT OF A SONG

Late that afternoon, in Robert Rutter's meadow at the back of the inn, a man and a woman stood in close conversation. The man was Jem Pound, the woman Elizabeth Ryan.

"Then you have not seen him yet?"

"No, not yet; I have had no chance."

"You mean that you have been drunk, Jem Pound!"

"Not to say drunk, missis. But I've been over to a town called Melmerbridge, and I went a long way round so as not to cross the moor. They're shooting up there all day. It'd be no sort o' use tackling him there."

"But surely they are back by now?" exclaimed Mrs. Ryan, impatiently. "I tell you he must be seen to-day—this evening—now."

"Ay, ay; I'm just going. Straight along this path it is, across a few fields, and there you are—opposite the house; and you may trust me—"

"I know; I have seen it for myself. But I am going too."

This was precisely what Pound did not want. He was treating the woman with unwonted civility, not to say respect, with a view to the more easily dissuading her from dangerous projects. And this was a dangerous project from Pound's point of view; but Mrs. Ryan had set her soul upon it. Argue as Jem would, she was bent upon seeing her husband with her own eyes, and at once. And there, with that thin white face of hers she might go and get him actually to pity her, and spoil everything—for Jem Pound.

"After finding him again, do you think I will endure this a moment longer?" asked Elizabeth scornfully.

Pound's reply was in the reflective manner.

"Well," said he, with slow deliberation, "I'm not sure but what it mightn't, after all, do good for you to see him."

"Good—do good! To whom? What do you mean? What have you to do with it?"

Pound ground his teeth; he had everything to do with it. It was the old story over again: this woman was using him as the guide to her own ends, yet would cut him adrift the very moment those ends were in sight. How he hated her! With his lips he cringed to her, in his heart he ground her to powder; but if he was not in the position to bully her to-day, he had lost few opportunities when he was; and he was at least forearmed against her.

He affected a bluff kindliness of manner that would not have deceived her had Mrs. Ryan been a little more composed.

"Look here, missis, you and me, we've been bound up in a ticklish job together. I don't say as I've always done by you as I should, but there is allowances to be made for a man that carries, as they say, his life in his hand, and that's staked his life on this here job. I don't say, either, as we're both on the exact same tack, but one thing's certain; we must work together now, and if you can't work my way, why, I must work yours. Now, missis, you ain't fit for the strain of seeing him. If you could see your own face you'd know it, ma'am."

Her eyes had opened wide at his tone; she sighed deeply at his last words.

"No," she said sadly, "I know I'm not fit for much. But I must go—I must go."

"Then if you must, ma'am, take a teaspoonful of this first. It'll help you through, and anyway keep you from fainting, as you did last time. I got it in Melmerbridge this afternoon, after I see you look so sick."

He uncorked a small flask and held it to her lips.

"What is it?"

"Brandy—the best."

"And water?"

"Half and half. Remember that other night!"

"He is right," muttered the woman: "there must be no fainting this time."

She sipped from the bottle and felt revived.

"Now we will go," she said, sternly.

They crossed the meadow, and so over the stile into the potato-field that came next. Then Pound began to lag behind and watch his companion. When they reached the gate she was reeling; she clung to the gate-post, and waited for him to come up.

"You fiend!" she screamed, glaring impotently upon him. "Poisoner and fiend! You have—you—"

She fell senseless at his feet without finishing the sentence. Pound surveyed the helpless heap of clothes with complete satisfaction.

"Drugged you, eh? Is that what you'd say? Nay, hardly, my lass: p'r'aps the brandy was risky for a fool of a woman that won't eat—p'r'aps it was very near neat—p'r'aps there was more in it than that; anyway you took it beautiful—lovely, you devil in petticoats!"

He raised her easily enough in his strong arms, carried her through the gate into the next field, and dropped her upon a late heap of hay some distance from the track.

"Playing at triangles," said Pound, "it must be two to one, or all against all: one thing it sha'n't be—two to one, and Jem Pound the one! There you lie until you're wanted, my dear. So long to you!"

And with that this wretch strolled off.

The gap in the hedge dividing the last of these few fields from the road, and ending the path, occurred a few yards below the shooting-box. Pound crept along the ditch between hedge and field until he judged he was opposite the gate of the shooting-box. Then he stood up, parted the hedge where it was thinnest, and peered through. The room to the right of the porch was lit up within; though the blinds were drawn, the windows were wide open. Pound could hear a low continuous murmur of voices and other sounds, which informed him that the party were still dining. He waited patiently. At last he heard a pushing back of chairs: it must be over now, he thought; but no, the voices recommenced, pitched in a slightly louder key. The windows on the left of the porch shone out as brightly as their neighbours on the right of it. Light fingers ran nimbly over the keys of a piano—only once—no tune came of it.

Pound, too, had fingers that could not long be idle: thick, knotty, broad-nailed, supple-jointed; fingers that showed the working of the mind. They were busy now. In a little while all the hedge within their reach was stripped of its simple charms—its bluebells, its pink foxgloves, its very few wild roses. Even the little leaves of the hedge were plucked away by the handful; and on the grass, had it been lighter, you might have discovered in the torn and mutilated shreds of leaf and petal some index to the watcher's thoughts. At last there was a general movement inside. Dark forms appeared on the steps. Two or three came down the steps, and turned the corner of the house. One sauntered to the gate and peered up and down the road. There was no mistaking this figure.

Pound uttered in a low key a cry that is as common in the Australian bush as it is uncommon elsewhere. He expected his man to start as though shot, but he was disappointed. Ryan gave one sharp glance towards the hedge, then passed through the gate, and on to the gap.

"Lord! how he takes it!" murmured Pound. "Did he expect me? Has he been on the look-out night and day all this while?"

At the gap they met. Pound could restrain his exultation no longer.

"At last!"

"Yes," said the other, stepping quietly through the gap. He had given the whole day to preparation for this interview; but he had expected it to be an interview of three. Where was his wife? "Yes, and the fewer words the better. How you got here I neither know nor care; tell me what you want now that you are here."

"You know very well what I want."

"I may make a rough guess."

"I want money!"

"I thought so. It is a pity. You must go somewhere else for it: I have none."

"What!" cried Pound, savagely, "is it all gone? All that you landed with? Never! You have never got through all that!"

"'All that' is under a gum-tree somewhere in Queensland, unless some one has found it lately. I told you so before, didn't I? How could I clear out with the gold? How could I risk going back for it when once I got away? All I brought with me was what never left my body: the notes and some gold. It didn't come to much; the last of it went long since."

"Then how have you lived—what on?"

"My wits."

Jem Pound was in a towering passion.

"If I believed you," he hissed out, among his oaths, "I'd make a clean breast of everything—every blessed job—though I swung for it! No; I'd swing merrily, knowing they'd got you snug for the rest of your days, for you'd be worse off than me, Ned Ryan! But I don't believe a word of it; it's a lie—a lie—a lie!"

The utterance was that of a choking man. Miles wondered whether the man had the spirit to carry out what he threatened; he seemed desperate, and such confessions had been made before by desperate men. That the five hundred ounces of gold had been abandoned by Sundown in his flight was the simple truth. Yet if Pound realised this, he was capable of any lengths of vengeance—even to putting his own neck in the noose, as he said. Better, perhaps, leave him his delusion, and let him still think that the gold had been brought over; better give a sop to Cerberus—even though it were only a promise to-day and a few pounds to-morrow; for the next day—well, the next day Cerberus might growl in vain. But a fair round sum for Pound, if only it could be raised and handed over immediately, would raise high hopes of "the share" he coveted; would make him believe that the stronger man had given way at last; would pacify him for the time being—which was all that was necessary. For in two days Ned Ryan meant to fly from that place—in three, the shores of England should fade from his sight for ever. Pound must be put off his guard, like the rest; a fair round sum might do it—say fifty pounds. Fifty pounds, then, must be raised that night.

"Jem Pound," said Sundown, in tones of capitulation, "there is no getting over you! I throw up my hand, for the game's up. I thought I could get the best of you, Jem, but, Lord! I didn't know my man, and that's the fact. But listen to sense: you don't suppose I've got that money here, do you? It's in London; you shall have five hundred of it in hard cash, if you swear to stand by me, next week. I go up next week; you go before me and wait. You refuse? Stay, then; hear me out: you shall have fifty down, on this very spot, at this very hour, to-morrow night!"

"Do you mean it?" asked Pound, suspiciously, his breath coming quick and rapid with the excitement of the moment—his moment of victory.

"Every word of it."

"Fifty pounds—to-morrow night?"

"Every penny of it. Oh, there's no use in disguising it; you've got the better of me, Jem, and I must stump up."

Pound looked at him doubtfully, wishing to believe, yet finding it difficult.

"You gave us the slip before," he said; "how do we know you won't do it again?"

"Watch me—watch me," he said.

"Ay, we must and we will!"

"You need not remind me of—of her!" cried Ryan, fiercely, all in a moment.

"Ah, poor thing, poor thing!" said Pound.

"Why, has anything happened?"

"Poor soul!"

"Speak, man, for God's sake! Is she—is she—"

Ryan could not get out the word, trembling as he was with intense excitement. Pound broke into a brutal laugh.

"No, Ned Ryan, she isn't dead, if that's what you want. I am sorry for you. Now that you're going to behave handsome, I should have liked to bring you good news. Yet, though she hangs on still, she's going down the hill pretty quick—her own way. But she's waiting for us three fields off; we'd better go to her before she comes to us. Come this way."

Pound led the way to the hay-field. Miles followed him, filled with foreboding. What had happened to Elizabeth? Was the woman ill? Was she dying? Bad as he was—bad as she was—could he go coldly on his way and let her die? He thought of her as he had seen her last, two months ago; and then strangely enough, he figured her as he had first seen her, many, many years ago. Poor thing! poor Liz!

"She is not here," said Pound, when he came to the gate that Elizabeth Ryan had clung to. "Now I wonder—stay! what is that over there? Come, let's look. It may be—by Heaven, it is your wife!"

He had pointed to a dark object among the mounds of hay. Now the two men stood looking down on the insensible form of Elizabeth Ryan.

"No, not death," said Pound; "only brandy!"

The husband looked down upon his wretched wife without speaking or moving. Oh, that it were death! His muscles were rigid—repugnance and loathing froze him to the bone. How white her face was in the faint moonshine! how white that hand under the white cheek! and the other hand stretched helplessly out—good God! the wedding-ring he had placed there, she dared to wear it still! Oh, that this were death!

And a minute ago he had thought of her—for some seconds together—not unkindly!

At last Ryan spoke.

"I dare swear," he murmured, as though speaking to himself, "that she has not got our certificate! A ring is no proof."

Pound knelt down and shook some sense into the woman's head.

"Eh? What is it? Where am I?"

He whispered hurriedly in her ear: "He is here—your husband. He says something about your having no proof that you are his wife. Give me the certificate!"

Without grasping the meaning of any but the last word, Elizabeth Ryan mechanically drew forth from her bosom a folded square of paper. Pound took it from her, and unfolded it with his back to Ryan. When he faced about, Pound held the certificate in his left hand and a revolver in his right.

Ryan paid no heed to the pistol, beyond recognising it as one of his own—the fellow, in fact, to the one he at that moment carried in his own pocket; Pound's last transaction, as a member of Sundown's gang, having been to help himself to this and other trifles as keepsakes. The production of the weapon Ryan treated, or affected to treat, with contempt. The certificate took up his whole attention. Yet one glance, even in the moonlight, was sufficient to show him that the certificate was genuine.

"You may put them both away," was all he said. "But remember: to-morrow night, same spot and hour. Or let us say here, at this gate: it is farther from the house."

He turned to go, but suddenly recoiled, being face to face with his wife, who had struggled to her feet. With a strange wild cry the woman flung herself into his arms. Ryan caught her, held her one instant, then dashed her heavily to the ground, and fled like a murderer from the place.

The poor thing lay groaning, yet sobered.

"Ah, I remember," she moaned at last, gathering up her bruised and aching limbs. "I was drugged—by you!"

The look of terrible hatred which she darted at Jem Pound was ineffable but calm. He answered her with a stout denial:

"I gave you nothing but brandy, and that I gave you for the best. I didn't mean it to knock you over, but I'm not sorry it did. Bad as it was, it would have been worse if you had seen much more of him."

"Why? What did he say?"

"He said he wouldn't give us a farthing. No, not if you were starving. He said you were less than nothing to him now. He said we might do our worst, and the sooner hell swallowed both of us the better he'd like it."

Mrs. Ryan gave a little cry of pain and anger. She staggered across the dewy grass, and confronted Pound at arm's length. She was shaking and shivering like a withered leaf.

"Jem Pound," said she, "I will tell you what I have known for many weeks, but hidden from you. I will tell you where he has that money, or some of it."

"Where?" cried Pound.

She tapped him lightly on the chest.

"There!" said Mrs. Ryan.

"How the devil do you know?"

"By woman's wit. On that night, when my hand rested there on his breast for one moment, he pushed me from him. I remembered afterwards that he started from my hand as though I touched a wound. I did the same thing to-night, only on purpose, and you know how he took it: he flung me to the ground this time. Mark my words, there is that which he values more than anything else hung round his neck and resting there! Whatever it is, take it, Jem Pound! Do you hear? You are bad enough for anything: then take it—even if you have to take his life with it!"

Her voice was hoarse and horrible, yet so low that it could scarcely be heard. Without waiting for an answer, she turned swiftly away and disappeared in the darkness.

Jem Pound drew a long deep breath.

"This," said he, "is the best night's work I've done since I came back to the Old Country. This morning I didn't dream of anything so good. Now I see a better night's work not far ahead!"

He proceeded to carve a cake of black tobacco slowly and deliberately, then filled his pipe. As he did this, leaning with his broad back against the gate, a sound came to his ears across the silent sleeping meadows—a strange sound to him—the sound, in fact, of a woman's song. His pipe was by this time loaded, and the mouthpiece between his teeth. Moreover, the match-box was in his left hand and a match in his right. Yet Jem Pound actually did not strike that match until the strange sound had died away!

I know not what spirit was abroad that night to invest a simple, well-known drawing-room song with the sinews of Fate; yet not only in the fields, but far up the road, where Colonel Bristo was wandering alone in the faint light of the sickle moon, the low clear notes were borne out on the wings of the evening. The Colonel faced about at the first note, and walked back quite quickly. His solitary wanderings at all times of the day were a great weakness of the old fellow, but his daughter's singing was a greater; and she sang so seldom now. He walked on the wet grass at the roadside rather than lose a note through the noise of his own footsteps; and lo! when he came near the house, he descried a tall figure standing motionless in the very middle of the road.

Surely some spirit was abroad that night, that all the waking world drew near and listened to that song of Alice's! It should have been a greater song—noble poetry wedded to music such as the angels make in heaven and have sometimes—in golden ages gone by—breathed into the souls of men, who have found the secret too wondrous sweet and terrible to keep. To touch the sensibilities of the different unknown listeners, it should have been a mighty song indeed! But, you see, Alice herself knew nothing of what was happening; she was aware of only one listener, who was humbly standing by her side; and out of the pitiful fulness of her heart she sang the sad and simple words that you have heard often enough, no doubt:

Falling leaf and fading tree,
Lines of white in a sullen sea,
Shadows rising on you and me;
The swallows are making them ready to fly,
Wheeling out on a windy sky.
Good-bye, summer! good-bye, good-bye!

A thin film floated over the eyes of Colonel Bristo. The same thing had occasionally happened before when his daughter sang. But lately she had been singing so little, and the song was so sad, and the voice more plaintive than it had ever been formerly.

As for Miles, the other listener in the road, he stood like one entranced. Her singing had haunted his soul now many weeks; it was many weeks since he had heard it last—save in his dreams; besides, the words put the match to a desperate train of thought.

The last bars of the song, then, came as a shock to the audience of two outside in the road, who had not realised that the song would ever stop:

"What are we waiting for, you and I?"
A pleading look, a stifled cry;
"Good-bye for ever! good-bye, good-bye!"

The last notes of all were low, and the singer's best. They were charged with wild grief; they seemed to end in a half-sob of anguish. But the voice had caught all the passion of the words, and something more besides. For whom was this passion?

It all died away. The world outside was tamer than before; the sickle moon dipped down to rest below the hill beyond the village, and those lanes and meadows knew no such singing any more.

The tall listener in the road still gazed at the holland blind that flapped against the sash of the open window. It was all the sound that came from the room now. He was repeating the last words of the song, and weighing them.

"No, no," he was thinking, "if I may not live for her, what else is there to live for? God, let me die for her!"

A glowing red spot approached him through the darkness that had fallen upon the land; it was the Colonel's cigarette. It brought him back to the world as it was—his world, and a vile one.

"I was taking a little stroll," said Colonel Bristo. "Will you join me? I think Alice will sing no more to-night."

Meanwhile, in the room, the singer had risen. She meant to quietly put away the music, but it slipped from her fingers. She turned with wet gentle eyes to one who was speaking to her, then fled at his words from the room.

Yet Dick had only asked her: "Will you never, never forgive me?"

CHAPTER XXV

MELMERBRIDGE CHURCH

Dick was in the passage, brushing a week's dust from his hard felt hat; he was going to church this Sunday morning; half the party were going. From the gun-room came the sound of a pen gliding swiftly over foolscap, and the perfume of Mr. Pinckney's pipe; from the open air a low conversational murmur, kept up by Mrs. Parish and Mr. Miles on the steps. Dick, though not unconscious of these sounds, was listening for another—a certain footstep on the stairs. It came at last. Alice came slowly down; Alice, prayer-book in hand, in the daintiest of white dresses and the prettiest, simplest straw hat; Alice for whom Mrs. Parish and Miles and Dick were all three waiting.

Her step was less light than it should have been. The slim little figure positively drooped. Her eyes, too, seemed large and bright, and dark beyond nature, though that may have been partly from the contrast with a face so pale. The girl's altered looks had caused anxiety at Teddington, but the change to Yorkshire had not visibly improved them. This morning, after a night made even more restless than others by a sudden influx of hopes and fears, this was painfully apparent.

The Colonel, coming in from outside at this moment, gazed earnestly at his daughter. It was easily seen that he was already worried about something; but the annoyance in his expression changed quickly to pain.

"You are not going to walk to Melmerbridge Church?" he said to her.

"Oh, yes, I am," she answered.

Her tone and look were saucy, in spite of her pallor; one of the old smiles flickered for a moment upon her lips.

"My child," said her father, more in surprise than disapproval, "it is eight miles there and back!"

"With a nice long rest in between," Alice reminded him. "I thought it would do one good, the walk; otherwise, papa, I am not in the least eager; so if you think—"

"Go, my dear, of course—go, by all means," put in Colonel Bristo hastily; "unwonted energy like this must on no account be discouraged. Yes, yes, you are quite right; it will do you all the good in the world."

As he spoke, he caught sight of Miles in the strong light outside the door. The worried look returned to the Colonel's eyes. Anxiety for his daughter seemed to fade before a feeling that for the time was uppermost. He watched his daughter cross over to the door, and Dick put on his hat to follow her. Then the Colonel stepped forward and plucked the young man by the arm.

"Dick, I want you to stop at home with me. I want to speak with you particularly, about something very important indeed."

Dick experienced a slight shock of disappointment, succeeded by a sense of foreboding. He fell back at once, and replaced his hat on the stand.

As for Alice, she felt a sudden inclination to draw back, herself. But that was not to be thought of. Mrs. Parish and Mr. Miles were waiting now at the gate. Alice went out and told them that Dick was, after all, staying behind with the Colonel.

"Not coming?" cried Mrs. Parish. "Why, I had promised myself a long chat with him!" which, as it happened, though Dick was no favourite of hers, was strictly true. "Where is Mr. Pinckney?"

"Busy writing to catch the post."

"And Dr. Robson?"

"Cousin Philip has gone to read the lessons for the Gateby schoolmaster, his new friend. Had we not better start?"

The three set out, walking slowly up the road, for Mrs. Parish was a really old lady, and it was only the truly marvellous proportion of sinew and bone in her composition, combined with a romantic and well-nigh fanatical desire to serve the most charming of men, that fortified her to attempt so formidable a walk.

"You men are blind," she had told her idol, among other things on the steps. "Where a word would end all, you will not speak."

"You honestly think it would end it the right way?" Miles had asked her.

"I do not think, I know," the old woman had said for the fiftieth time.

She had undertaken to give him his opportunity that morning. With four in the party, that would have been easy enough; with three, it became a problem soluble only by great ingenuity.

For some distance beyond the shooting-box the road ascended gently, then dipped deep down into a hollow, with a beck at the bottom of it, and a bridge and a farmhouse on the other side. The hill beyond was really steep, and from its crest the shooting-box—with red-roofed Gateby beyond and to the left of it—could be seen for the last time. But when they had toiled to the top of this second hill, Mrs. Parish with the kindly assistance of the attentive Miles, it occurred to none of them to look round, or they might have made out the Colonel and Dick still standing on the steps, and the arm of the former raised and pointed towards them.

"It is about that man there," the Colonel was saying, "that I want to speak to you."

Dick could scarcely suppress an exclamation. He changed colour. His face filled with apprehension. What was coming next? What was suspected? What discovered? Until these words the Colonel had not spoken since the church-goers left, and his manner was strange.

The Colonel, however, was scrutinising the young man.

"What rivals they are!" he was thinking. "The one starts at the mere name of the other! The fact is, Dick," he said aloud, "Miles has dealt with me rather queerly in some money matters, and—What on earth's the matter?"

The strong young fellow at Colonel Bristo's side was trembling like a child; his face was livid, his words low and hurried.

"I will tell you in a moment, sir. Pray go on, Colonel Bristo."

"Well, the fact is I want you to tell me if you know anything—of your own knowledge, mind—of this station of Miles's in Queensland."

"Excuse me: I can only answer by another question. Has he been raising money on his station?"

"Do you mean by borrowing from me?"

"Yes, that is what I do mean."

"Well, then, he has. At Teddington—I don't mind telling you, between ourselves—I lent him a hundred pounds when a remittance he expected by the mail did not come. After that I found out that he had an agent in town all the while, and it then struck me as rather odd that he should have borrowed of me, though even then I did not think much of it. You see, the man did me the greatest service one man can render another, and I was only too glad of the opportunity to do him a good turn of any sort. I can assure you, Dick, at the time I would have made it a thousand—on the spot—had he asked it. Besides, I have always liked Miles, though a little less, I must confess, since he came up here. But last night, as we were strolling about together outside, he suddenly asked me for another hundred; and the story with which he supported his request was rambling, if not absurd. He said that his partner evidently believed him to be on his way out again, and therefore still omitted to send him a remittance; that he was thus once more 'stuck up' for cash; that he had quarrelled with his agent (whom I suggested as the most satisfactory person to apply to), and withdrawn the agency. Well, I have written out the cheque, and given it him this morning. His gratitude was profuse, and seemed genuine. All I want you to tell me is this: Do you know anything yourself of his station, his partner, or his agent?"

Dick made his answer with a pale, set face, but in a tone free alike from tremor or hesitancy:

"The man has no station, no agent, no partner!"

"What?" cried out the Colonel. "What are you saying? You must not make statements of this sort unless you are sure beyond the shadow of a doubt. I asked what you knew, not what you suspected."

"And I am telling you only what I know."

"That Miles is a common swindler?"

"That his name is not Miles, to begin with."

"Then do you mean to say," the Colonel almost shouted, "that you have known all this, and let me be duped by the fellow before your eyes?"

"I never suspected what you have told me now," said Dick warmly. "But it is true that I have known for some weeks who and what this man is. I found him out at Graysbrooke, and got rid of him for you within a few hours. I was at fault not to give him in charge. You have good cause to blame me—and I sha'n't want for blame by and by!—but if you will listen to me, I will tell you all—yes, all; for I have protected a worse scoundrel than I thought: I owe him not another moment's silence."

"Come in here, then," said Colonel Bristo, sternly; "for I confess that I cannot understand you."

Up hill and down dale was the walk to Melmerbridge; but the ascents really were a shade longer and steeper than the descents, and did not only seem so to the ladies. For when at last they reached the long grey stone wall at the edge of the moor, and passed through the gate into the midst of brown heather, dotted with heads of gay green bracken, they were greeted by a breeze—gentle and even fitful, but inexpressibly refreshing. Now below, in the deep lanes between the hedge-rows, there had been no breeze at all—for the morning was developing into hazy, sleepy, stifling heat, and the sun was dim—and the flies had been most pestilent. Accordingly they all drew breath on the moor. Mr. Miles uncovered his head, and let the feeble breeze make mild sport with his light brown locks. Then he lit a cigarette. As for the ladies, they sat down for a moment's rest; and, considering that one of them was well on in years, and the other combating with a sickness that was gradually tightening its hold upon her, they were walking uncommonly well. But conversation had flagged from the start, nor did the magic air of the moorland quicken it.

When they had threaded the soft, rutted track that girdled the heather with a reddish-brown belt, when they had climbed the very last knoll, they found themselves on the extreme edge of that range of hills. Far below them, to the right, stretched mile upon mile of table-land, studded with villages and woods, divided by the hedges into countless squares. No two neighbours, among these squares, were filled in with the same colour; some were brown, some yellow, and the rest all shades of green. Far ahead, where the squares were all lost and their colours merged in one dirty neutral tint—far ahead—at the horizon, in fact—hung a low, perpetual cloud, like a sombre pall of death. And death indeed lay under it: death to green fields, sweet flowers, and honest blue skies.

They viewed all this from a spot where the road had been carved round the rough brow of a russet cliff. This spot was the loftiest as well as the ruggedest of the whole walk. On the left the road was flanked by the ragged wall of the cliff; on the right it was provided with a low parapet, over which one might gaze forth upon the wide table-land, or drop stones upon the tops of the tallest fir-trees in the wood at the cliff's base.

Old Mrs. Parish pointed to the long black cloud on the horizon, and explained that it was formed almost entirely of the smoke of blast-furnaces, and was the constant canopy of a great town that they could not see, because the town was hidden in perennial smoke. More than this she might have said—about the mighty metals that were disgorged from under their very feet—about the rich men of yonder town (old Oliver, for one), not forgetting the poor men, beggar-men, and thieves—had the old lady not perceived that Miles was gazing furtively at Alice, and Alice gazing thoughtfully into space, and neither of them listening to a word.

They walked on, and the descending road became smoother, but tortuous; and trees arched over it, and the view was hidden until they stood at the top of straight, steep Melmerbridge Bank, and the good-sized prosperous village lay stretched at their feet.

One long row of houses and shops on the left; a long straight silvery stream for the right-hand side of the village street; a bridge across this stream, leading to a church and a public-house that stood side by side, on apparently the best of terms, and without another near neighbour on that side of the beck—such was Melmerbridge from its bank-top.

As they crossed a white wooden bridge at the foot of the bank (for the beck curved and twisted, like other becks, except where it did its duty by that straight village street), a simple, modest Sabbath peal rang out upon the sultry air.

The old church was roomy, twilit, and consequently cool. Strong light never found its way inside those old stone walls, for the narrow windows were pictorial, one and all. Dusk lingered in these aisles throughout the longest days; upon them day broke last of all; they met nightfall half-way.

After a long, hot, tiring walk there could have been no more grateful retreat than this church of All Saints at Melmerbridge. The senses were lulled in the very porch, nor were they rudely aroused when the quiet peal had ended and the quiet service began. Everything was subdued and inoffensive, even to the sermon: a vigorous discourse from the dark oak pulpit would have grated on the spirit, like loud voices in a death-chamber.

As for Mrs. Parish, she was soon sleeping as soundly and reverently as the oldest parishioner. Alice, on the other hand, gave her whole mind to the service, and her mind filled with peace. Her sweet clear voice chimed in with every response (at which the parish clerk, with the fine old crusted dialect, who enjoyed a monopoly in the responses, snorted angrily and raised his tones), while in the first hymn it rose so high and clear that the young curate peered over his book through the dusk, and afterwards lost his place in the Litany through peering again.

Miles, for his part, looked about him with a pardonable curiosity. He thought that he might have been christened in some church as an infant; he had certainly been married in one as a comparatively respectable blackleg—but that was not a pleasant thing to recall to-day. He had since been once in a little iron Bush chapel, on a professional visit with his merry men, the object of which visit was attained with such complete success that all Australia thrilled with indignation. In London, the Bristos had insisted on taking him to St. Paul's and the Abbey. This was the full extent of his previous church-going. He was interested for a little while in looking about him. His interest might have lasted to the Benediction had there been less subjective food for thought, or, perhaps, if he had been sitting there alone.

In the hush and the dusk of this strange place, and the monotonous declamation of phrases that conveyed no meaning to him, Miles set himself deliberately to think. Wild and precarious as his whole life had been, he felt its crisis to be within arm's length of him now at last—he joined hands with it here in this peaceful Yorkshire church. Even the past few years of infamy and hourly risk contained no situation so pregnant with fate as the present. He ran over in his mind the chain of circumstances that had led up to this crisis.

The train of thought took him back to Queensland, where, with Nemesis holding him by the throat at last, he had wrenched himself from her tightening grip, and escaped. He had tumbled upon English soil with a fair sum of money, a past dead and buried, a future of some sort before him; by chance he had tumbled upon his feet. Chance, and that genius in the water that had crowned his escape by drowning him in the eyes of the world, had combined at once, and helped him to save an unknown gentleman's life. Mother-wit and the laws of gratitude enabled him to dupe the man he had rescued, become his close friend, live upon him, draw upon him, extract with subtle cunning the last farthing of salvage, and all the while he guessed—pretty correctly—that his pursuers were arriving to learn his death and take ship back to Australia.

Thus far everything had worked out so prettily that it seemed worth while turning thoroughly honest and beginning this second life on entirely different lines from the old one. Then he fell in love and believed that his love was returned, a belief that was not fostered by his own fancy unaided; now more than ever he desired to improve on the past, and to forget all ties and obligations belonging to the past. Edward Ryan was dead; then Edward Ryan's wife was a widow; Miles the Australian was a new unit in humanity; then why should not Miles the Australian marry?

Up to this point he could look back on every step with intense satisfaction; but here his reflections took a bitter turn. To go on calmly recoiling step after step, beginning with the month of July, was impossible: he tried it; but to remember that night in the park—to remember subsequent weeks spent in scheming and plotting, in rejecting plot after plot and scheme after scheme, in slowly eating his heart out in the solitude of a London lodging, in gradually losing all taste for fresh enterprise and all nerve for carrying it out—to remember all this was to pour vitriol on the spirit. He would remember no more; he would shut the gate on memory; he would annihilate thought; he would make his mind a blank. Yet he was powerless to do any of these things.

In his helplessness he looked down on the white figure at his side. The second hymn was being sung. He had stood, and sat, and knelt or leant forward with the rest, by mere mechanical impulse. He was even holding the book which she held without knowing it. When he realised this, his hand shook so much that the hymn-book was almost jerked from his fingers. At this she looked up, and caught his eyes bent down upon her.

Now Miles was at the end of the pew, next the wall, and in shadow. Alice noticed nothing in his expression, and went on singing without pause or break. But either her face, as she raised it, came in direct line with the skirt of some saint, in the window above Miles, and the sun, or else the sun chose that moment for a farewell gleam; in any case, the girl's pale face was instantly flooded with a rich, warm, crimson glow. Miles looked down, and this warm glow caught in his heart like a tongue of live flame.

The hymn was over; they sank down side by side: she to listen to the sermon, no matter its calibre—he to his thoughts, no matter their madness.

What were his thoughts? Not reflections now. Not hesitancy, his new unaccountable failing; not nervous doubt, his new humiliating enemy. No, his thoughts were of the old kind, but worse. He was contemplating a crime. He was contemplating the worst crime of his whole career. The plain English of his thoughts was this:

"I believe that she likes me. I see that she is, in the catch phrase, 'pining.' I am told that it is for me. Very good. If that is the case she will believe what I tell her, and do what I ask her. I have some power of persuasion. I am not without invention. I shall represent to her all kinds of reasons for precipitancy and secrecy—temporary secrecy. In a word, she shall fly with me! Well, that is bad enough; but there my badness ends. I will live without crime for her sake; I will retrieve what I can of the past. Henceforth my life is of her, with her—above all, it is for her. She need never know how I have wronged her, therefore she will not be wronged."

He looked at the face beside him; it was white as alabaster. Alice was straining her eyes towards some object that filled them with sadness and sympathy. He followed the direction of her gaze; and he saw an old, old man—a man who would soon come to church for the last time, and remain outside the walls, under the grass—who was gazing with pathetic wistfulness at the preacher, and, with wrinkled hand raised to the ear, making the most and the best of every well-worn epithet and perfunctory stock phrase. That was all. Miles brought back his glance to the white profile at his side, and found it changed in this instant of time: the long eyelashes were studded with crystal tears!

How sad she looked—how thin and ill! Would she look like this afterwards? Would tears often fill her eyes in the time to come?

Miles shut his eyes, and again exerted might and main to blot out thought. But he could not do it; and half his confidence was gone at the moment when he most needed it all. He knew it, and shuddered. A thought that had haunted him of late crossed his mind for the hundredth time: he was an altered man not only in pretence but in reality; his nerve and coolness had deserted him!

The sermon was over, and the congregation awake. Miles stood up with the rest, and took between thumb and finger his side of the little hymn book held out to him. He heartily wished it all over. In his present unfortunate state of mind another hymn was another ordeal: her voice, when she sang, put such weak thoughts into his head. Was he not a fool and a madman to think at all of a woman who unmanned him so? Nay, hush! The hymn was begun. She was singing it with her whole heart, the little head thrown backward, the little white face turned upward. She was singing; he could hear nothing else. She was singing; would she sing afterwards? She was singing from the depths of her tired soul. Would she ever sing like this again? Would he ever hear her voice again. Hush! This might be the last time!

Colonel Bristo was back on the steps, gazing under his thin, hollowed hand up the road. He looked anxious, and indignant, and determined—but old and careworn.

"What a time they are!" said Dick, pointing to the crest of the second hill, where the brown road met the silver sky. Next moment he would have recalled his words, for two figures, not three, stood out black against the sky. They were only in sight for an instant, but during that instant they were hand in hand!

The two men on the steps waited without a word for many minutes. Neither could bring himself to speak—perhaps each hoped that the other had not seen everything. Besides, one was the father of the girl, and the other—her jilted lover. More than once the father shivered, and his fingers twitched the whole time. Simultaneously they both started in surprise; for all at once Alice appeared over the brow of the nearest hill, coming swiftly towards them—alone.

"Thank God!" murmured the Colonel, forgetting Dick's presence. "He has asked her to marry him, and she has refused. The villain!"

"Then, if you are right," cried Dick with sudden intensity, "a million times blacker villain he."

"What do you mean?"

"Mean? I mean—but there is no need to tell you now."

"You may as well tell me everything."

"Then I mean that he is married already."

CHAPTER XXVI

AT BAY

"Where is Mrs. Parish?" demanded Colonel Bristo, the moment his daughter reached the gate. In spite of a gallant effort to be calm before Alice, his voice quivered.

"The walk was too much for her." The girl's face was flushed, and her tones faint. "She said she couldn't walk back were it ever so. She spoke to Mrs. Commyns—who was called here, you know—and went to the Rectory. She wants us to send the pony-trap if—"

"Where is Mr. Miles?" Alice's father interrupted her.

"He is following."

She passed quickly by them into the house. Her face was full of trouble. Traces of tears were visible under her eyes. They heard her hurrying upstairs. Neither of them spoke a word. Dick had his back turned; he was watching the road.

The figure of Miles appeared on the nearest knoll. He walked slowly down the bank, his head bent, his eyes fixed upon the ground. Dick turned to Colonel Bristo.

"You had better leave me to speak to him," he said. "I will settle with him on the spot."

"It ought to come from me," said the Colonel doubtfully; "and yet—"

The old man paused. Dick looked at him with some anxiety.

"You had really better leave him to me, sir," he repeated. "I am sorry to say I am used to treating with him. There had better be no third party to our last parley. And the fewer words the better, on Alice's account; she need know nothing. Besides, I know your intentions—"

"Yes, yes; that for my part I will take no steps, not even to get back my money; that he may go to-day instead of to-morrow, and leave the country—we will not stop him. Of course, he will be only too glad to get off! Dick, I care nothing about the paltry pounds he has got out of me; he is welcome to them; I do not grudge him them, because of the service he did me—yet if I saw him now, I feel that I should forget to count that service. And you are right about Alice. Speak quietly, and get rid of him quickly. I will not see him unless I am obliged; at least, I will first hear from the dining-room what he has to say to you."

A moment later the Colonel was at his post in the dining-room. His retreat from the steps, which was really characteristic of the man, is open to misconstruction. He feared nothing worse than an unpleasantness—a disagreeable scene; and he avoided unpleasantnesses and disagreeables systematically through life. That was the man's weakness. Now if Dick had led him to suppose that Miles would do anything but take his congé philosophically and go, the Colonel would have filled the breach bristling with war. But from Dick's account of his previous relations with the impostor, he expected that Miles would be sent to the right-about with ease, and Colonel Bristo shrank from doing this personally.

The dining-room windows were wide open, but the brown holland blinds were drawn. Colonel Bristo did not raise them. He sat down to listen without looking. Almost immediately he heard a sharp click from the latch of the wicket-gate; then a louder click accompanied by a thud of timbers. Whoever had opened the gate had passed through and swung it to. The next sound that Colonel Bristo heard was the quiet, business-like voice of young Edmonstone:

"Stop! I have a word for you from the Colonel. Stop where you are! He does not want you to come in."

"What do you mean? What has happened?" The tones were apathetic—those of a man who has heard his doom already, to whom nothing else can matter much.

"He simply does not want you inside his house again. He is sending your things down to the inn, where he hopes you will stay until you leave the place according to your plans. Ryan," added Edmonstone in an altered manner, "you understand me by this time? Then you may take my word for it that you are as safe as you were yesterday; though you don't deserve it. Only go at once."

There was a pause. The Colonel fidgeted in his chair.

"So, my kind, generous, merciful friend could not keep his word one day longer!"

Miles's voice was so completely changed that the Colonel involuntarily grasped the blind-cord; for now it was the voice of an insolent, polished villain.

"If I had known before," Dick answered him coolly, "what I have found out this morning, you might have cried for quarter until you were hoarse."

"May I ask what you have learnt this morning?"

"Your frauds on the man who befriended you."

"My obligations to the man whose life I saved. Your way of putting it is prejudiced. Of course you gave him your version as to who I am?"

"My version!" exclaimed Edmonstone scornfully. "I told him that you and the bushranger Sundown are one."

Again Miles swiftly changed his key; but it was his words that were startling now.

"You are mad!" he said, pityingly—"you are mad; and I have known it for weeks. Your last words put your delusion in a nutshell. You have not a proof to bless yourself with. You are a madman on one point; and here comes the man that knows it as well as I do!"

In a whirl of surprise and amazement, not knowing for the moment whom or what to believe, the Colonel pulled up the blind and leant through the window. The Australian stood facing his accuser with an impudent smile of triumph. For once he stood revealed as he was—for once he looked every inch the finished scoundrel. If the Colonel had wavered for an instant before drawing up the blind, he wavered no more after the first glimpse of the Australian's face. He settled in his mind at that instant which was the liar of those two men. Yet something fascinated him. He was compelled to listen.

Robson was coming in at the gate.

"You are the very man we want," laughed Miles, turning towards him. "Now pull yourself together, Doctor. Do you call our friend, Mr. Edmonstone here, sane or not?"

"You said that he was not," said Robson, looking from Edmonstone to Miles.

"And you agreed with me?"

"I said I thought—"

"You said you thought! Well, never mind; I call him sane—practically; only under a delusion. But we will test him. You charge me with being a certain Australian bushranger, Mr. Edmonstone. Of course you have some evidence?"

An awkward sensation came over Dick: a consciousness that he had committed a mistake, and a mistake that was giving the enemy a momentary advantage. He choked with rage and indignation: but for the moment he could find no words. Evidence? He had the evidence of his senses; but it was true that he had no corroborative evidence at hand.

The bushranger's eyes glittered with a reckless light. He knew that the sides were too uneven to play this game long. He felt that he was a free man if he quietly accepted fate as he had accepted it before at this man's hands. The odds were overwhelming; but he was seized with a wild desire to turn and face them; to turn upon his contemptible foe and treat him as he should have treated him in the beginning. It might cost him his liberty—his life—but it was worth it! The old devilry had sprung back into being within him. He was desperate—more desperate, this half-hour, than ever in the whole course of his desperate existence. His life had seemed worth having during the past weeks of his cowardice; now it was valueless—more valueless than it had been before. He was at bay, and he realised it. His brain was ablaze. He had played the docile Miles too long. Wait a moment, and he would give them one taste of the old Sundown!

"At least," he sneered in a low, suppressed voice, "you have someone behind you with a warrant? No? Nothing but your bare word and the dim recollection of years ago? That, my friend, seems hardly enough. Ah, Colonel, I'm glad you are there. Is there any truth in this message that has been given me, that you have had enough of me?"

"I wish you to go," said Colonel Bristo, sternly. "I wash my hands of you. Why refuse a chance of escape?"

"What! Do you mean to say you believe this maniac's cock-and-bull yarn about me?" He pointed jauntily at Dick with his forefinger. But the hand lowered, until the forefinger covered the corner of white handkerchief peeping from Edmonstone's breast-pocket. For a moment Miles seemed to be making some mental calculation; then his hand dropped, and trifled with his watch-chain.

"I believe every word that he has told me," declared the Colonel solemnly. "As to warrants, they are not wanted where there is to be no arrest. We are not going to lay hands on you. Then go!"

"Go!" echoed Edmonstone hoarsely. "And I wish to God I had done my duty the night I found you out! You would have been in proper hands long before this."

"Suppose I refuse to go? Suppose I stay and insist on evidence being brought against me?" said Miles to the Colonel. Then turning to Dick with fiery, blood-shot eyes, he cried: "Suppose, since there is no evidence at all, I shoot the inventor of all these lies?"

The hand was raised sharply from the watch-chain and dived into an inner pocket. That moment might have been Dick Edmonstone's last on earth, had not a white fluttering skirt appeared in the passage behind him.

The hand of Miles dropped nervelessly.

Colonel Bristo heard in the passage the light quick steps and rustling dress, and ran to the door. At the same instant Pinckney jumped up from his writing to see what was the matter. They met in the passage, and followed Alice to the steps. Her father seized her hand, to draw her back, but she snatched it from his grasp. Her hand was icy cold. Her face was white as death—as immovable—as passionless. She stood on the steps, and glanced from Edmonstone at her side to Miles on the path below. On Miles her calm glance rested.

"You seem to forget!" she said in a hard voice that seemed to come from far away. "You are forgetting what you said to me a few minutes ago, on the road. I understand your meaning better now than I did then. Yes, it is true; you know it is true: you are what he says you are!"

Miles watched her like one petrified.

She turned to Dick at her side. And now a sudden flush suffused her pallid cheeks, and her eyes dilated.

"It is you," she cried impetuously, "you that we have to thank for this! You that have brought all this upon us, you that allowed us to be preyed upon by a villain—screened him, helped him in his deceit, plotted with him! Being what he was, it was in his nature to cheat us. I forgive him, and pity him. But you I shall never forgive! Go, Mr. Miles. Whatever and whoever you are, go as you are asked. And go you too—true friend—brave gentleman! Go, both of you. Let us never see you again. Yet no! Stay—stay, all of you" (her face was changing, her words were growing faint)—"and hear what it was—he said—to me—and my answer, which is my answer still! Stay—one moment—and hear—"

Her words ceased altogether. Without a cry or a moan she sank senseless in her father's arms.

Philip Robson rushed forward. They stretched her on the cold stone. They tore open the collar round her neck, breaking the pretty brooch. They put brandy to her lips, and salts to her nostrils, and water upon her brow. Minutes passed, and there was no sign, no glimmer of returning life.

When Alice fell, Miles took one step forward, but no more. He stood there, leaning forward, unable to remove his eyes from the white lifeless face, scarcely daring to breathe.

There was no noise, no single word! The doctor (to his credit be it remembered) was trying all that he knew, quickly and quietly. The Colonel said not a word, but silently obeyed his nephew, and chafed the chill hands. Edmonstone fanned her face gently. Pinckney had disappeared from the group.

Robson suddenly looked up and broke the silence.

"Where is the nearest doctor?"

"Melmerbridge," murmured someone.

"He should be fetched at once. We want experience here. This is no ordinary faint."

Before the doctor had finished speaking, Miles wheeled round and darted to the gate. And there he found himself confronted by a short, slight, resolute opponent.

"You sha'n't escape," said Pinckney through his teeth, "just because the others can't watch you! You villain!"

Pinckney had heard only the end of what had passed on the steps, but that was enough to assure him that Miles had been unmasked as a criminal. Of course he would take the opportunity of all being preoccupied to escape, and did; and David faced Goliath in the gateway.

In lesser circumstances Miles would have laughed, and perhaps tossed his little enemy into the ditch. But now he whipped out his revolver—quicker than thought—and presented it with such swift, practised precision that you would have thought there had been no hiatus in his career as bushranger. And he looked the part at that instant!

Pinckney quailed, and gave way.

The next moment, Miles was rushing headlong up the hill.

On the crest of the second hill, above the beck and the bridge, he stopped to look round. The people on the steps were moving. Their number had increased. He could distinguish a servant-maid holding her apron to her eyes. They were moving slowly; they were carrying something into the house—something in a white covering that hung heavily as a cerement in the heavy air.

CHAPTER XXVII

THE FATAL TRESS

Was she dead?

The question was thundered out in the sound of the runner's own steps on the flinty places, and echoed by the stones that rolled away from under his feet. The thought throbbed in his brain, the unspoken words sang in his ears: Was she dead?

The face of Alice was before Ryan as he ran: the pale, delicate face of this last week, not the face of old days. The early days of summer were old days, though it was summer still. June by the Thames was buried deeper in the past than last year in Australia, though it was but August now. What had come over the girl in these few weeks? What had changed and saddened her? What made her droop like a trampled flower? What was the matter—was it the heart?

The heart! Suppose it was the heart. Suppose the worst. Suppose this shock had killed her. Suppose he—the criminal, the outlaw, the wretch unfit to look upon good women—had murdered this sweet, cruel, wayward, winsome girl! Even so, he must still push on and bring her aid. If that aid came too late, then let his own black life come to a swift and miserable end. His life for hers; the scales of justice demanded it.

The afternoon was dull but not dusky. The clouds were so high and motionless that it seemed as if there were no clouds, but one wide vault of tarnished silver. To point to that part of this canopy that hid the sun would have been guesswork.

Between the tall hedges the air was heavier than in the morning; the flies and midges swarmed in myriads. Even on the moor there was now no breath of wind. The heather looked lifeless, colourless; the green fronds peeping between had lost their sparkle; the red-brown of the undulating belt of road was the brightest tint in the landscape up there.

When Ryan was half-way across the moor, rain began to fall. He threw back his head as he ran, and the raindrops cooled his heated face. His hat had long ago been jerked off, and his hair lay plastered by perspiration to the scalp. The man's whole frame was on fire from his exertions. The breath came hard through his clenched teeth. His blue eyes were filled with a wild despair. Since the last backward look, that showed him the solemn group on the steps, he had thundered on without an instant's pause; and the time lost in toiling up the banks was made up by dashing headlong down the other side.

Now he was climbing the steep ascent that culminated at the spot where the road was curved round the face of the cliff, and protected on the right by the low stone parapet. Once at the top, he would soon be in Melmerbridge, for the remainder of the road was down-hill.

The wall of cliff on the left was jagged and perpendicular, and of the same russet tint as the road. Detached fragments of the rock rested in the angle formed by its base and the rough-hewn road. Among these boulders was an object that attracted Ryan's curiosity as he climbed up from below: it was so like a boulder in rigidity and colour, and in outline so like a man. Ryan saw the outline alter: of course it was a man, and he was crouching with his back to the rock for shelter from the rain. Suddenly the man rose, and staggered into the middle of the pass, between rocky wall and stone parapet, while Ryan was still some yards below. It was Pound.

Ryan had seen him in the street at Melmerbridge, in coming from church. Pound had reeled out of a public-house and caught him by the arm. Ryan had shaken him off with a whispered promise to meet him in the evening as arranged; and had explained the occurrence to his companion by some ready lie.

So Pound was on his way back to Gateby, drunk. This was evident from his attitude as he stood barring the pass, and from the hoarse peal of laughter that echoed round the cliff, and from the tones of blusterous banter with which he greeted his quondam leader.

"Welcome! Glad to see ye! But who'd ha' thought you'd be better than your word? Better, I say—you're better than your blessed word!"

"Stand clear!" shouted Ryan, twenty paces below.

Pound leered down upon him like a satyr. His massive arms were tightly folded across his bulky chest. His smooth face became horrible as he stood looking down and leering. His answer to Ryan was hissed savagely through his teeth:

"Stand clear be—! I want my money. I'll have my whack o' the swag, and have it now! D'ye hear? Now!"

"I have nothing about me," Ryan answered. "You drunken fool, stand clear!"

The twenty paces between them were reduced to ten.

"Nothing about you!" jeered Pound, spitting upon the ground. "Ay, I know—you carry your nothing round your neck, old man! And I'll have my share of it now or never!"

They were almost at arm's length now.

"Never, then!" cried Ryan, half drawing his revolver.

In a flash Pound's arm unfolded, and his right arm shot out straight from the shoulder. There followed a streak of fire and a loud report. Thin clouds of white smoke hung in the motionless air. From their midst came a deep groan and the thud of a dead weight falling. And Pound was left standing alone, a smoking pistol in his hand. For a minute he stood as still as Ryan lay.

"A shake longer," he muttered at length, "and I'd have been there and you here. As it is—as it is, I think you're cooked at last, skipper!"

He put the revolver back in his pocket, and stood contemplating his work. The sight completely sobered him. To a certain degree it frightened him as well. Of the other sensations, such as might ensue upon a first murder, Jem Pound experienced simply none. Even his fear was not acute, for it was promptly swallowed by cupidity.

"Now for them notes!"

He knelt down beside his victim, eyeing him cautiously. The fallen man lay stretched across the road, on his back. He had torn open his coat and waistcoat while running, and the white shirt was darkened with a stain that increased in area every instant. Pound wondered whether he had hit the heart. The upturned face, with closed eyelids and mouth slightly open, was slimy and wet with perspiration and the soft August rain. By holding the back of his hand half-an-inch above the mouth, Pound satisfied himself that Ryan was still breathing—"his last," thought Jem Pound, without any extravagant regret. Blood was flowing from a scalp-wound at the back of the head, received in falling; but this escaped the murderer's notice. What he next observed was that the arms lay straight down the sides, and that the right hand grasped a revolver. At sight of this, Jem Pound leapt to his feet with an excited exclamation.

He drew forth again his own revolver, to assure himself that he was not mistaken. No, he was not. The pistols were an original brace, and alike in every particular. The smooth, heavy face of the murderer lit up with infernal exultation. He pointed with a finger that trembled now—from sheer excitement—to the pistol in the lifeless hand, then tapped the barrel of his own significantly.

"Suicide!" he whispered. "Suicide—suicide—suicide!" He reiterated the word until he thought that he appreciated its full import. Then he knelt down and leant over the prostrate Ryan, with the confident air of a lucky man on the point of crowning a very pyramid of good fortune.

Slowly and daintily he unfastened the studs in Ryan's shirt; he was playing with blood now, and must avoid unnecessary stains. He would just take what he wanted—take it cleverly, without leaving a trace behind—and satisfy himself that it was what he wanted, more or less. Then he would fire one chamber of Ryan's revolver, and make off. But first—those notes! The chest was already bathed in blood; but Pound saw at once the object of his search, the cause of his deed, and his black heart leapt within him.

Well, the little oiled-silk bag was small—unexpectedly small—incredibly small; but then there were bank notes for enormous sums; and one bank-note, or two, or three, would fold quite as small as this, and press as thin. To Pound's ignorant mind it seemed quite natural for Sundown, the incomparably clever Sundown, to have exchanged his ill-gotten gold for good, portable paper-money at some or other time and place. Dexterously, with the keen broad blade of his knife, he cut the suspending tapes and picked up the bag on its point. The oiled-silk bag was blood-stained; he wiped it gingerly on the flap of Ryan's coat, and then wiped the blood from his own fingers. He knew better than to allow bank-notes to become stained with blood.

Yet how light it was in his palm! It would not be lighter if the oiled-silk contained nothing at all. By its shape, however, it did contain something. Pound rose to his feet to see what. His confidence was ebbing. His knees shook under him with misgiving. He moved unsteadily to the low stone parapet, sat down, and ripped open the little bag with such clumsy haste that he cut his finger.

Jem Pound sat like a man turned to stone. The little bag was still in his left hand, and the knife; his right hand was empty the contents of the bag, a lock of light hair, had fallen from his right palm to the ground, where it lay all together, for there was no wind to scatter it.

Jem Pound's expression was one of blank, unspeakable, illimitable disappointment; suddenly he looked up, and it turned to a grimace of speechless terror.

The barrel of the other revolver covered him.

Bleeding terribly from the bullet in his lungs, but stunned by the fall on his head, Ned Ryan had recovered consciousness in time to see Pound rip open the oiled-silk bag, in time to smile faintly at what followed—and to square accounts.

Ryan did not speak. The faint smile had faded from his face. In the relentless glare that took its place the doomed wretch, sitting in a heap on the low parapet, read his death-warrant.

There was a pause, a hush, of very few moments. Pound tried to use his tongue, but, like his lips, it was paralysed. Then the echoes of the cliff resounded with a second, short, sharp pistol shot, and when the white smoke cleared away the parapet was bare; Jem Pound had vanished; the account was squared.

Ryan fell back. The pistol dropped from his hand. Again he became well-nigh senseless, but this time consciousness refused to forsake him utterly; he rallied. Presently he fell to piecing together, in jerky, delirious fashion, the events of the last few minutes—or hours, he did not know which—but it was all the same to him now. The circumstances came back to him vividly enough, if out of their proper sequence. That which had happened at the moment his senses fled from him was clearest and uppermost in his mind at first.

"The cur!" he feebly moaned. "He gave me no show. He has killed me—I am bleeding to death and not a soul to stop it or stand by me!"

Yet, very lately, he had decided that his life was valueless, and even thought of ending it by his own hand. Some dim reflection of this recent attitude of mind perhaps influenced him still, for, if an incoherent mind can be said to reason, his first reasoning was somewhat in this strain:

"Why should I mind? Who am I any good to, I should like to know? What right have I to live any more? None! I'm ready. I've faced it night and day these four years, and not for nothing—not to flinch now it's here!... And hasn't my life been gay enough, and wild enough, and long enough?... I said I'd die in the bush, and so I will—here, on these blessed old ranges. But stop! I didn't mean to be shot by a mate—I didn't mean that. A mate? A traitor! What shall we do with him?"

His mind had annihilated space: it had flown back to the bush.

A curious smile flickered over Ryan's face in answer to his own question.

"What have I done with him?" he muttered.

He raised himself on his elbows and looked towards the spot where he had seen Pound last. The formation of the parapet seemed to puzzle him. It was unlike the ranges.

"He was always the worst of us, that Jem Pound," he went rambling on; "the worst of a bad lot, I know. But those murders were his doing. So at last we chucked him overboard. And now he's come back and murdered me. As to that, I reckon we're about quits, with the bulge on my side. Never mind, Jem Pound"—with a sudden spice of grim humour—"we'll meet again directly. Your revenge'll keep till then, old son!"

All this time Ryan's brain was in a state of twilight. He now lay still and quiet, and began to forget again. But he could not keep his eyes long from the spot whence Pound had disappeared, and presently, after a fruitless effort to stand upright, he crawled to the parapet, slowly lifted himself, and hung over it, gazing down below.

Nothing to be seen; nothing but the tops of the fir-trees. Nothing to be heard; for the fir-trees were asleep in the still, heavy atmosphere, and the summer rain made no noise. He raised his head until his eyes fell upon the broad flat table-land. The air was not clear, as it had been in the morning. That pall of black smoke covering the distant town was invisible, for the horizon was far nearer, misty and indeterminate; and his eyes were dim as they never had been before. The line of white smoke left by an engine that crept lazily across the quiet country was what he saw clearest; the tinkling of a bell—for Sunday-school, most likely—down in one of the hamlets that he could not see, was the only sound that reached his ears.

Yet he was struggling to recognise as much as he could see, vaguely feeling that it was not altogether new to him. It was the struggle of complete consciousness returning.

He was exhausted again; he fell back into the road. Then it was that he noticed the parapet streaming with blood at the spot where he had hung over it. To think that the coward Pound should have bled so freely in so short a time! And how strange that he, Ned Ryan, should not have observed that blood before he had drenched himself in it! No! Stop! It was his own blood! He was shot; he was dying; he was bleeding to his death—alone—away from the world!

A low moan—a kind of sob—escaped him. He lay still for some minutes. Then, with another effort, he raised himself on his elbow and looked about him. The first thing that he saw—close to him, within his reach—was that fatal tress of light-coloured hair!

In a flash his mind was illumined to the innermost recesses, and clear from that moment.

Now he remembered everything: how he had come to his senses at the very moment that Pound was handling this cherished tress, which alone was sufficient reason and justification for shooting Jem Pound on the spot; how he had been on his way to fetch help—help for Alice Bristo!

He pressed the slender tress passionately to his lips, then twined it tightly in and out his fingers.

Faint and bleeding as he was, he started to his feet. New power was given him; new life entered the failing spirit: new blood filled the emptying vessels. For a whole minute Ned Ryan was a Titan. During that minute the road reeled out like a red-brown ribbon under his stride. The end of that minute saw him at the top of Melmerbridge Bank. There, with the village lying at his feet, and the goal all but won, he staggered, stumbled, and fell headlong to the ground.

CHAPTER XXVIII

THE EFFORT

Galloping over the moor, fresh from his corn, the pony suddenly swerved, and with such violence that the trap was all but overturned.

"What was that?" asked Edmonstone, who was driving.

"A hat," Pinckney answered.

These two men were alone together, on an errand of life or death.

Edmonstone glanced back over his shoulder.

"I'll swear," said he, "that hat is Miles's!"

"Good heavens! has he stuck to the road?"

"Looks like it."

"Then we're on his track?"

"Very likely."

"And will get him, eh?"

At this question Edmonstone brought down the lash heavily on the pony's flank.

"Who wants to get him? Who cares what becomes of him? The Melmerbridge doctor's the man we want to get!"

Pinckney relapsed into silence. It became plain to him that his companion was painfully excited. Otherwise there was no excuse for his irritability.

At the foot of the last steep ascent on the farther side of the moor, Pinckney had jumped out to walk. He was walking a few yards ahead of the pony. Suddenly he stopped, uttered a shrill exclamation, and picked up something he found lying in the road. He was then but a few feet from the top, and the low stone parapet was already on his right hand.

"What is it?" cried Dick, from the pony-trap below.

Pinckney threw his hand high over his head. The revolver was stamped black and sharp against the cold grey sky.

A cold shudder passed through Edmonstone's strong frame. The wings of death beat in his ears and fanned his cheek with icy breath. The dread angel was hovering hard by. Dick felt his presence, and turned cold and sick to the heart.

"Let me see it," cried Dick, urging on the pony.

Pinckney ran down to meet him with a pale, scared face.

"It was his," faltered Pinckney. "I ought to know it. He threatened me with it when I tried to stop him bolting."

The slightest examination was enough to bespeak the worst.

"One cartridge has been fired," said Dick, in a hushed voice. "God knows what we shall find next!"

What they found next was a patch of clotting blood upon the stones of the parapet.

They exchanged no more words, but Dick got down and ran on ahead, and Pinckney took the reins.

Dick's searching eyes descried nothing to check the speed of his running till he had threaded the narrow, winding lane that led to Melmerbridge Bank, and had come out at the top of that broad highway; and there, at the roadside, stretched face downward on the damp ground, lay the motionless form of Sundown, the Australian outlaw.

The fine rain was falling all the time. The tweed clothes of the prostrate man were soaked and dark with it. Here and there they bore a still darker, soaking stain; and a thin, thin stripe of dusky red, already two feet in length, was flowing slowly down the bank, as though in time to summon the people of Melmerbridge to the spot. Under the saturated clothes there was no movement that Dick could see; but neither was there, as yet, the rigidity of death in the long, muscular, outstretched limbs.

Dick stole forward and knelt down, and murmured the only name that rose to his lips:

"Miles! Miles! Miles!"

No answer—no stir. Dick lowered his lips to the ear that was uppermost, and spoke louder:

"Miles!"

This time a low, faint groan came in answer. He still lived!

Dick gently lifted the damp head between his two hands, and laid Ryan's cheek upon his knee.

Ryan opened his blue eyes wide.

"Where am I? Who are you? Ah!"

Consciousness returned to the wounded man, complete in a flash this time. At once he remembered all—tearing madly down from the top, in and out this winding track—and all that had gone before. He was perfectly lucid. He looked up in Edmonstone's face, pain giving way before fierce anxiety in his own, and put a burning question in one short, faint, pregnant word:

"Well?"

Had health and strength uttered this vague interrogative, Dick would have replied on the instant from the depths of his own anxiety by telling the little that he knew of Alice Bristo's condition. But here was a man struck down—dying, as it seemed. How could one think that on the brink of the grave a man should ask for news from another's sick bed? Edmonstone was puzzled by the little word, and showed it.

"You know what I mean?" exclaimed Ryan, with weary impatience. "Is she—is she—dead?"

"God forbid!" said Dick. "She is ill—she is insensible still. But man, man, what about you? What have you done?"

"What have I done?" cried Ryan, hoarsely. "I have come to bring help to her—and—I have failed her! I can get no further!"

His voice rose to a wail of impotent anguish. His face was livid and quivering. He fell back exhausted. Dick attempted to staunch the blood that still trickled from the wound in the chest. But what could he do? He was powerless. In his helplessness he gazed down the bank; not a soul was to be seen. He could not leave Ryan. He could hear the sure-footed steps of the pony slowly approaching from above. What was he to do? Was this man to die in his arms without an effort to save him? He gazed sorrowfully upon the handsome face, disfigured by blood, and pain, and mire. All his relations with this man recrossed his mind in a swift sweeping wave, and, strange to say, left only pity behind them. Could nothing be done to save him?

The pony-trap was coming nearer every instant. It was Dick's one hope and comfort, for Pinckney could leave the trap and rush down into the village for help. He hallooed with all his might, and there was an answering call from above.

"Make haste, make haste!" cried Dick at the top of his voice.

The shouting aroused Ryan. He opened his eyes, and suddenly started into a sitting posture.

"Haste?" he cried, with articulation weaker yet more distinct. "Yes, make haste to the township! To the township, do you hear? There it is!"

He pointed through the rain to the red roofs of Melmerbridge, on the edge of the tableland below. It was then that Dick noticed the lock of hair twisted about the fingers of Ryan's right hand.

"There it is, quite close—don't you see it? Go! go—I can't! Fly for your life to the township, and fetch him—not to me—to her! For God's sake, fetch him quick!"

For all the use of the word "township," his mind was not wandering in Australia now.

"Why don't you go? You may be too late! Why do you watch me like that? Ah, you won't go! You don't care for her as I did; you want her to die!"

Wildly he flung himself forward, and dug his fingers into the moist ground, and began feebly creeping down the bank on his hands and knees. Dick tried in vain to restrain him. The failing heart was set upon an object from which death alone could tear it. During this the last hour of his life this criminal, this common thief, had struggled strenuously towards an end unpretending enough, but one that was for once not selfish—had struggled and fought, and received his death-wound, and struggled on again. His life had been false and base. It cannot be expected to count for much that in his last moments he was faithful, and not ignoble. Yet so it was in the end. Edmonstone tried in vain to restrain him; but with a last extraordinary effort he flung himself clear, and half crawled, half rolled several yards.

Suddenly Ned Ryan quivered throughout his whole frame. Dick caught him in his arms, and held him back by main force.

The dying man's glassy gaze was fixed on the red roofs below. For an instant one long arm was pointed towards them, and a loud clear voice rang out upon the silent air:

"The township! The township—!"

The cry ended in a choking sob. The arm fell heavily. Edmonstone supported a dead weight on his breast.

"Pinckney!"

"Yes, yes?"

"God forgive him—it's all over!"

CHAPTER XXIX

ELIZABETH RYAN

Elizabeth Ryan did not return to Gateby after leaving Pound in the fields between the village and the shooting-box. All that night she roamed the lanes and meadows like a restless shade. Whither her footsteps led her she cared little, and considered less.

Though not unconscious of the mechanical act of walking, her sense of locomotion was practically suspended. A night on the treadmill would have left upon her an impression of environment no more monotonous than that which remained to her when this night was spent; and she never once halted the whole night through.

Her seeing mind held but one image—her husband. In her heart, darting its poison through every vein, quivered a single passion—violent, ungovernable anger. The full, undivided force of this fierce passion was directed against Edward Ryan.

Later—when the flame had gone out, and the sullen glow of stern resolve remained in its stead—the situation presented itself in the form of alternatives. Either she must betray her husband, or set him free by ending her own miserable life. One of these two things must be done, one left undone. There was no third way now. The third way had been tried; it should have led to compassion and justice; it had led only to further cruelty and wrong. One of the remaining ways must now be chosen; for the woman it little mattered which; they surely converged in death.

At daybreak Elizabeth Ryan found herself in flat, low-lying country. She looked for the hills, and saw them miles away. From among those hills she had come. She must have been walking right through the night, she thought.

She was by no means sure. She only knew that her brain had been terribly active all through the night—she could not answer for her body. Then, all at once, a deadly weariness overcame her, and a score of aches and pains declared themselves simultaneously. Prevented by sheer distraction from feeling fatigue as it came, by natural degrees, the moment the mental strain was interrupted the physical strain manifested its results in the aggregate; Mrs. Ryan in one moment became ready to drop.

She had drifted into a narrow green lane leading to a farmhouse. She followed up this lane till it ended before a substantial six-barred gate. She opened the gate and entered the farmyard. She tried the doors of the outbuildings. A cowhouse was open and empty; one of its stalls was stacked high with hay; to the top of this hay she climbed, and crept far back to the wall, and covered her dress with loose handfuls of the hay. And there Elizabeth Ryan went near to sleeping the clock round.

A hideous dream awoke her at last. She was trembling horribly. She had seen her husband dead at her feet—murdered at his wife's instigation!

The mental picture left by the dream was so vivid that the unhappy woman lay long in terror and trembling, not daring to move. Instead of paling before consciousness and reason, the ghastly picture gained in breadth, colour, and conviction with each waking minute. He was lying dead at her feet—her husband—her Ned—the man for love of whom she had crossed the wide world, and endured nameless hardships, unutterable humiliation. He was slain by the hand of the man who had led her to him—by the ruthless murderer, Jem Pound!

She remembered her words to Pound, and her teeth chattered: "Take it, even if you have to take his life with it!" Those were the very words she had used in her frenzy, meaning whatever it was that Ned wore upon his breast. He wore it, whatever it was, near to his heart; he must value it next to his life. What else could it be but money? Oh, why had she told Pound? How could passion carry her so far? If her dream was true—and she had heard of true dreams—then her husband was murdered, and the guilt was hers.

A low wail of agony escaped her, and for a moment drove her fears into a new channel. Suppose that cry were heard! She would be discovered immediately, perhaps imprisoned, and prevented from learning the worst or the best about her dream, which she must learn at any price and at once! Filled with this new and tangible dread she buried herself deeper in the hay and held her breath. No one came. There was no sound but her own heart's loud beating, and the dripping and splashing of the rain outside in the yard, and the rising of the wind. She breathed freely again; more freely than before her alarm. The minutes of veritable suspense had robbed the superstitious terror of half its power, but not of the motive half, she must go back and make sure about that dream before carrying out any previous resolution. Until this was done, indeed, all antecedent resolves were cancelled.

She crept down from the hay and peeped cautiously outside. She could see no one. It was raining in torrents and the wind was getting up. With a shudder she set her face to it, and crossed the yard. At the gate she stopped suddenly, for two unpleasant facts simultaneously revealed themselves: she had no idea of the way to Gateby, and she was famishing. Now to be clear on the first point was essential, and there was nothing for it but to apply boldly at the farmhouse for the information; as to the second, perhaps at the farmhouse she might also beg a crust.

"Dear heart!" cried the good wife, answering the timid knock at the door. "Hast sprung from t'grave, woman?"

"Nay," answered Elizabeth, sadly; "I am only on my way there."

The farmer's wife, a mountain of rosy kindliness, stared curiously at the pale frightened face before her, and up and down the draggled dress.

"Why, Lord, thou'rt wet and cold; an' I'll be bound thou's had nobbut hay for thy bed."

With a sudden flood of tears, Elizabeth Ryan confessed where she had been sleeping all day.

"Nay, nay, honey," said the good woman, a tear standing in her own eye, "it's nowt—it's nowt. Come in and get thysel' warmed an' dried. We're having our teas, an' you shall have some, an' all!"

Thus the poor vagrant fell among warm Yorkshire hearts and generous Yorkshire hands. They gave her food, warmth, and welcome, and pitied her more than they liked to say. And when, in spite of all protests, she would go on her way (though the risen wind was howling in the chimney, and driving the heavy rain against the diamond panes), honest William, son of the house and soil, brought a great sack and tied it about her shoulders, and himself set her on the high road for Melmerbridge.

"Ye'll 'ave te go there," said he, "to get te Gaatby. 'Tis six mile from this, an' Gaatby other fower."

Six miles? That was nothing. So said the strange woman, as she tramped off in the teeth of the storm; and William, hurrying homeward, wondered what had made her eyes so bright and her step so brisk all at once. He asked his parents what they thought, but they only shook their puzzled heads: they had done nothing out of the way that they knew of; how could they guess that it had been their lot to show the first human kindness to a poor forlorn pilgrim from over the seas—the first the poor woman had met with in all stony-hearted England?

Yet her treatment at the hands of these simple people had lightened the heart of Elizabeth Ryan, and the terror of her awful dream had softened it. Her burning rage against her husband was quenched; she thought of it with shuddering shame. Her wild resolves were thrown to the winds; she must have been mad when she entertained them. She must have been blind as well as mad; but now her sight was restored. Yes, now she could see things in their true light. Now she could see who had caused her husband's cruelty; who had poisoned him against her—subtly, swiftly, surely, at their first meeting; who had drugged her, and then shown Ned his drunken wife at their second meeting; whom she had to thank for all her misery: the fiend, Jem Pound.

It was true that Ned had treated her heartlessly; but, believing what he believed of her, could she blame him? She blamed him for listening to the first whisper against her, from the lips of a monster; but his fault ended there. He had never heard her in her own defence. He had not so much as seen her alone. There lay the root of it all: she had been allowed no chance of explaining, of throwing herself on his compassion.

But now she was going to put an end to all this. She was going to him at once, and alone. She was going to tell him all: how she had waited patiently for him at Townsville until the news of his capture drove her almost frantic; how, in the impulse and madness of the moment, she had trusted herself to Jem Pound, and followed him, her husband, to England; how she had followed him for his own sake, in the blindness of her love, which separation and his life of crime had been powerless to lessen; how, ever since, she had been in the power of a ruffianly bully, who had threatened and cajoled her by turns.

And then she would throw herself at Ned's feet, and implore his mercy. And he, too, would see clearly, and understand, and pity her, and take her back into his life. Whether that life was bad or good, it alone was her heart's desire.

A soft smile stole over the haggard face, upon which the wind and the rain were beating more fiercely every minute. Wind and rain were nothing to her now; she could not feel them; she was back in Victoria, and the sky above was dark blue, and the trees on either side the flint-strewn track were gaunt, grey, and sombre. The scent of the eucalyptus filled her nostrils. The strokes of two galloping horses rang out loud and clear on the rough hard road. She was mounted on one of these horses, Ned on the other. They were riding neck and neck, she and her handsome Ned—riding to the township where the little iron church was. It was their marriage morn. She had fled from home for ever.

Surely he loved her then—a little? Yet he had left her, very soon, without a word or a cause; for weeks she could gather no tidings of him, until one day news came that rang through the countryside, and was echoed throughout the colony—news that stamped her new name with infamy. But had she changed her name, or sunk her identity, or disowned her husband, as some women might have done? No. She had employed her woman's wit to hunt her husband down—to watch over him—to warn him where danger lurked. One night—it stood out vividly in her memory—she had burst breathlessly into his bivouac, and warned him in the nick of time: half-an-hour later the armed force found the fires still burning, but the bushrangers flown. And he had been good to her then; for it was then that he had given her the money to go to his only relative—a sister at Townsville; and he had promised in fun to "work up" through Queensland, some day, and meet her there. Yes, with the hounds of justice on his heels he had made time to be kind to her then, after a fashion. It was not much, that amount of kindness, but it would be enough for her now. After all that she had gone through, she would be content with something short of love, say even tolerance. She would try to win the rest, in after years—years when Ned settled down in some distant country—when Ned reformed. Could he refuse her now so small a measure of what she gave him without stint? Surely not. It was impossible. Unless—unless—unless—

What made Elizabeth Ryan clench her drenched cold fingers and draw her breath so hard? What blotted out the visionary blue skies, tore hope and fancy to shreds, and roused her to the bleak reality of wind and rain and the sickening memory of her husband's heartlessness? What, indeed, but the suggestions of Jem Pound?

She loathed herself for listening to a single word from that polluted source; yet, as Pound's words came back to her, she listened again to them all. She thought of the pretty, delicate, pink-and-white woman her own eyes had seen by the waters of the Thames, with whom she had spoken, who had dared to offer her money. The thought became a globe of fire in her brain; and soon the poor woman had worked herself back into a frame of mind bordering upon that frenzy which had driven her hither and thither, like a derelict ship at the wind's mercy, through the long hours of the previous night. The appearance of watery lights through the storm came not before it was time. Even to Elizabeth Ryan, with hope and passion wrestling in her breast, there was a certain faint excitement and satisfaction in reaching a village after a six-mile tramp through wind, rain, and dusk deepening into night. Besides, if this was Melmerbridge, she must ask and find out the road to Gateby.

Guided by the lights, she presently reached the north end of the long, one-sided village street; the long straight stream, now running turbulently, was on her left as she advanced, and Melmerbridge Bank straight ahead, at the southern end of the village. An irregular line of lights marked the houses on the right; to the left, across the beck, there were no such lights; but a set of church windows—the church being lit up for evening service—hung gaudily against the black screen of night; the outline of the church itself was invisible. The deep notes of an organ rose and fell in the distance, then died away; then suddenly, as the wayfarer gazed, the stained-glass window disappeared, and Mrs. Ryan found herself in the midst of a little stream of people who were coming from the bridge in front of the church to the cottages on the opposite side of the road.

From one of these people she received the directions she required, but she noticed that most of them were talking eagerly and excitedly, in a way not usual among folks fresh from worship, or indeed in a quiet country village at any time. Little groups formed in the doorways and kept up an animated conversation. Clearly there was something of uncommon interest astir. Mrs. Ryan passed on, mildly interested herself.

The last houses of the village were darker. Elizabeth touched their outer walls with her skirts as she trudged along the narrow uneven pavement. From one of them came a sound which struck her as an odd sound for a Sabbath evening—the long, steady sweep and swish of a plane. This house was a shop; for six parallel threads of light issued from the chinks of the tall shutters. Through one of these chinks a small boy was gazing with rapt attention and one eye closed. Mrs. Ryan stopped, and out of mere curiosity peered through another.

A burly old man was energetically planing a long, wide, roughly-shaped, hexagonal plank. The shape of the plank was startling.

"What is it he is making?" inquired Mrs. Ryan of the small boy. Perhaps she could see for herself, and put the question mechanically.

The answer was prompt and short:

"A coffin!"

Mrs. Ryan shuddered and stood still. The urchin volunteered a comment.

"My! ain't it a long 'un! Did ye iver see sich a long 'un, missis?"

He was little Tom Rowntree, the sexton's son and heir, this boy, so he knew what he was talking about; one day, all being well, he would dig graves and bury folks himself; he took a profound premature interest in all branches of the hereditary avocation.

"Who is dead?" asked Mrs. Ryan, in a hard metallic voice.

"Haven't heard tell his name, but 'tis a sooincide, missis—a sooincide! A gent's been and shot hisself upon the bank there, this afternoon. He's a-lyin' ower yonder at t' Blue Bell."

"Where is that?"

"Yonder, look—t' last house on this side. It's nigh all dark, it is, an' no one there 'cept my mother an' Mr. Robisson hisself, an' customers turned away an' all. That's 'cause Mrs. Robisson she's took the high-strikes—some people is that weak!"

But there was no listener to these final words of scorn. With a ghastly face and starting eyes, Elizabeth Ryan was staggering to the Blue Bell inn.

A square of pale light dimly illumined a window close to the ground to the left of the door, otherwise the inn was in darkness. Elizabeth Ryan crouched down, and never took her eyes from that window till the light was extinguished. Then she heard the door within open and shut, and the outer door open. A man and a woman stood conversing in low tones on the steps, the woman's voice broken by sobs.

"'Tisn't that I'm growing old and nervous, Mr. Robisson, and thinkin' that me own time'll come some day; no, it's not that. But all these years—and never such a thing to happen in the village before—little did I think to live to be called in to the likes o' this. And such a good face as I never seed in living man, poor fellow! You never know where madness comes in, and that's what it's been, Mr. Robisson. And now I'm out o' t' room I'm that faint I don't know how to get home."

"Come, come, I'll give you my arm and umbrella across, Mistress Rowntree."

"But ye've left t' key in t' door?"

"Oh, I'll be back quick enough; it's only a step."

He gave her his arm, and the pair came out together and went slowly up the village street. In less than five minutes the landlord of the Blue Bell returned, locked all the doors, and went to bed, leaving the inn in total darkness.

A quarter of an hour later this total darkness was interrupted; a pale light glimmered in the window close to the ground to the left of the door. This light burned some ten or twenty minutes. Just before it was put out, the window-sash was moved up slowly. Then, when all was once more in darkness, a figure stepped out upon the sill, leapt lightly to the ground, and cautiously drew down the sash.

CHAPTER XXX

SWEET REVENGE

Whistling over the hilltops and thundering through the valleys, down came the wind upon the little lonely house by the roadside; and with the wind, driving rain; and they beat together upon the walls of that corner room wherein Alice Bristo lay trembling between life and death.

The surgeon from Melmerbridge pronounced it to be brain fever. He had found the patient wildly delirious. The case was grave, very grave. Dangerous? There was always danger with an abnormal temperature and delirium. Dr. Mowbray stayed until evening and ultimately left his patient sleeping quietly. He promised to return in the early morning.

The doctor stopped, as he was driving off, to shriek something through the storm:

"Have you any one who can nurse—among the servants?"

Inquiries were immediately made.

"No," was the answer.

"I'll send over a handy woman from Melmerbridge," said Dr. Mowbray; crack went his whip, and the gig-wheels splashed away through the mud.

A young man standing at the other side of the road, bareheaded and soaked to the skin, wondered whether the nurse would be sent at once that night. Then this young man continued his wild rapid walk up and down the country road, glancing up every moment at the feeble light that shone from the casement of that corner room on the upper floor.

Up and down, never pausing nor slackening his speed, fifty paces above the house and fifty below it, this unquiet spirit strode to and fro in the wind and the rain, like Vanderdecken on his storm-proof poop.

Once, when opposite the house, he touched the skirts of a woman crouching under the hedge; but he was not aware of it—he was gazing up at the window—and, before he passed that spot again the woman was gone.

The woman had crept stealthily across the road and through the open wicket. She was crouching behind the opposite hedge, on the rough grass-plot in front of the house. Once more the swinging steps passed the house and grew faint in the distance. The crouching woman sprang erect, darted noiselessly up the steps, and grasped the door-handle. She turned the handle and pushed gently, the door was neither locked nor bolted; it opened. The woman entered, and closed the door softly behind her. She stooped, listening. The footsteps passed the house without a pause or a hitch, as before. She had been neither seen nor heard—from without. A horrid smile disfigured the woman's livid face. She stood upright for an instant, her hand raised to her forehead, pausing in thought.

A lamp was burning low on the table in the passage; its dull light flickered upon the dark, fierce, resolute face of Elizabeth Ryan.

The dark hair fell in sodden masses about a face livid and distorted with blind fury, the dark eyes burned like live coals in the dim light, the cast of the firm wide mouth was vindictive, pitiless; the fingers of the right hand twitched terribly; once they closed spasmodically upon a loose portion of the ragged dress, and wrung it so hard that the water trickled down in a stream upon the mat, and at that moment murder was written in the writhing face. The left hand was tightly clasped.

Elizabeth Ryan had crept into the chamber of death, in the Blue Bell at Melmerbridge, during the five minutes' absence of the innkeeper. It was she who had quitted that room by the window. She had fled wildly over the moor, maddened by a discovery that scorched up the grief in her heart, setting fire to her brain, changed in a flash from a bewildered, heartbroken, forlorn creature to a ruthless frantic vendetta. The substance of that discovery was hidden in her clasped left hand.

She stood for a brief interval on the mat, then stepped stealthily forward towards the stairs. A light issued from an open door on the left, near the foot of the stairs. She peeped in as she passed. Stretched on a couch lay an old white-haired man, dressed as though it were mid-day instead of mid-night, in a tweed suit. Though asleep, his face was full of trouble. Nothing in this circumstance, nor in the conduct of the man outside walking to and fro in the storm, nor in the dim lights all over the house at this hour, struck Elizabeth Ryan as extraordinary. Her power of perception was left her; her power of inference was gone, except in direct relation to the one hideous project that possessed her soul. She crept softly up the stairs. They did not creak. She appreciated their silence, since it furthered her design.

As below, a light issued from an open door. She approached this door on tip-toe. A pair of small light shoes, with the morning's dust still upon them, stood at one side of the mat; someone had mechanically placed them there. When Elizabeth Ryan saw them her burning eyes dilated, and her long nervous fingers closed with another convulsive grasp upon the folds of her skirt.

She crossed the threshold and entered the room. The first thing she saw, in the lowered light of a lamp, was an old, puckered, wrinkled face just appearing over a barrier of eiderdown and shawls, and deep-set in an easy-chair. The brown, wrinkled eyelids met the brown, furrowed cheeks. The watcher slumbered and slept.

As yet the room wore none of the common trappings of a sick-room: the illness was too young for that. The book the sick girl had been reading last night lay open, leaves downward, on the chest of drawers; the flowers that she had picked on the way to church, to fasten in her dress, had not yet lost their freshness; the very watch that she had wound with her own hand last night was still ticking noisily on the toilet-table. Thus, to one entering the room, there was no warning of sickness within, unless it was the sight of the queer old sleeping woman in the great chair by the fireside, where a small fire was burning.

The stealthy visitor took two soft, swift, bold steps forward—only to start back in awe and horror, and press her hand before her eyes. She, Elizabeth Ryan, might do her worst now. She could not undo what had been done before. She could not kill Death, and Death had forestalled her here.

A cold dew broke out upon the woman's forehead. She could not move. She could only stand still and stare. Her brain was dazed. She could not understand, though she saw plainly enough. After a few moments she did understand, and her heart sickened as it throbbed. Oh that it would beat its last beat there and then! Oh if only she too might die! Standing, as she thought, in the presence of death for the second time that night, Elizabeth Ryan lifted her two arms, and prayed that the gracious cold hand might be extended to her also. In the quenching of the fires that had raged in her brain, in the reawakening of her heart's anguish, this poor soul besought the Angel of Death not to pass her by, praying earnestly, pitifully, dumbly, with the gestures of a fanatic.

She lowered her eyes to face for the last time her whom death had snatched from vengeance. She started backwards, as she did so, in sudden terror. What was this? The dead girl moved—the dead girl breathed—the counterpane rose and fell evenly. Had she been mistaken in her first impression? Elizabeth Ryan asked herself with chattering teeth. No! More likely she was mistaken now. This must be an illusion, like the last; she had been terrified by a like movement in the room at the Blue Bell, and it had proved but a cruel trick of the sight and the imagination; and this was a repetition of the same cruel trick.

No, again! The longer she looked the more distinct grew this movement. It was regular, and it was gentle. Faint yet regular breathing became audible. The face on the pillows was flushed. Death had stopped short at Melmerbridge; Death had not travelled so far as this—at least, not yet: there was still a chance for vengeance!

But Elizabeth Ryan had undergone a swift psychological reaction. That minute in which she stood, as she believed, for the second time that night in the presence of Death—that minute in which her spirit yearned with a mighty longing to be stilled, too, for ever—that minute had done its work. In it the mists of passion had risen from the woman's mind; in it the venom had been extracted from her heart. Her eyes, now grown soft and dim, roved slowly round the room. They fell curiously upon something upon a chair on the far side of the bed—a heap of light hair; they glanced rapidly to the head on the pillows—it was all but shaved.

Elizabeth Ryan raised her clenched left hand; the hand trembled—the woman trembled from head to foot. She laid her arms upon the chest of drawers, and her face upon her arms, and stood there until her trembling ceased. When at last she raised her head, her eyes were swimming, but a bright determination shone out through the tears.

She moved cautiously round the foot of the bed and dipped her left hand into the heap of light hair, and for the first time unclasped her hand. The hand was lifted empty, but the heap of Alice's hair remained a heap of her hair still; it had but received its own again.

This strange yet simple act seemed to afford the performer the deepest relief; she gazed kindly, even tenderly, on the young wan face before her, and sighed deeply. Then hastily she retraced her steps to the door. At the door she stopped to throw back a glance of forgiveness and farewell.

Now it happened that the head of the sleeping girl had slipped upon the pillow, so that its present position made the breathing laboured.

Quick as thought, Mrs. Ryan recrossed the room from the door, and, with her woman's clever light hand, rearranged the pillows beneath the burning head, and smoothed them gently. But in doing this the silent tears fell one after the other upon the coverlet; and when it was done some sudden impulse brought Elizabeth upon her knees by the bedside, and from that bleeding heart there went up a short and humble prayer, of which we have no knowing—at which we can make no guess, since it flew upward without the weight of words.

How cold, how bitter, how piercing were the blast and the driving rain outside! In the earlier part of the night their edge had not been half so keen; at all events, it did not cut so deep. Where was a woman to turn on such a night? A woman who had no longer any object in life, nor a single friend, nor—if it came to that—a single coin: what was such an one to do on a night like this?

The picture of the warm, dry bedroom came vividly back to Elizabeth Ryan; she felt that she would rather lie sick unto death in that room than face the wild night without an ailment more serious than a broken, bleeding heart. She looked once back at the dim light in the upper window, and then she set her face to Gateby. Before, however, she was many paces on her way, quick footsteps approached her— footsteps that she seemed to know—and a man's voice hailed her in rapid, excited tones:

"Are you from Melmerbridge?"

"Yes," she faltered. What else dared she say. It was true, too.

"Then you are the nurse! you are the nurse! I have been waiting for you, looking out for you, all the night, and now you have come; you have walked through the storm; God bless you for it!"

His voice was tremulous with thanks and joy; yet trouble must have clouded his mind, too, or he never could have believed in his words.

"I do not understand—" Mrs. Ryan was beginning, but he checked her impatiently:

"You are the nurse, are you not?" he cried, with sudden fear in his voice. "Oh don't—don't tell me I'm mistaken! Speak—yes, speak—for here we are at the house."

The pause that followed well-nigh drove him frantic. Then came the answer in a low, clear voice:

"You are not mistaken. I am waiting to be shown into the house."

Dr. Mowbray, coming first thing in the morning, declared that the patient had passed a better night than he had hoped for; but he told Colonel Bristo privately that he must count on nothing as yet, and be prepared for anything.

To his surprise and delight, the physician found his patient in the hands of a gentle, intelligent nurse. This was the more fortunate since he had failed to find in Melmerbridge a capable woman who was able to come. Whoever the dark, shabbily-dressed woman was, she must not be allowed to leave the bedside for the present. "She is a godsend," said Dr. Mowbray on coming downstairs. Colonel Bristo, for his part, knew nothing of the woman; he supposed she was from Gateby. Mrs. Parish, no doubt, knew all about her; and after the doctor's account of her services, the Colonel made no inquiries.

Edmonstone and Pinckney were to drive back to Melmerbridge with the doctor to attend the inquest on the body of the suicide. Before they started the Colonel called the two young men aside, and a brief, earnest colloquy took place.

During the drive Dr. Mowbray mentioned a strange report that had reached him before leaving Melmerbridge; it was noised in the village, at that early hour, that the dead man had moved one of his hands during the night.

"It will show you," the doctor said, "the lengths to which the rustic imagination can stretch. The fact is, they are terribly excited and primed with superstition, for there hasn't been a suicide in the parish in the memory of this generation. What is more," added the old gentleman, suddenly, "I'm not sure that there's been one now!"

There was some excuse, perhaps, for the string of excited questions reeled off on the spur of the moment by young Pinckney: "Why? How could it be anything else but suicide? Had they not got the pistol—Miles's own pistol? Had not Dr. Mowbray himself said that the bullet extracted fitted the one empty cartridge found in the revolver? Besides, Miles had not denied shooting himself when asked by Edmonstone what he had done."

"But did he admit that he had shot himself?" asked Dr. Mowbray, turning to Edmonstone.

"No, he did not."

"Was his manner, up to the last, that of a man who had deliberately shot himself?"

"No, it was not. It might have been an accident."

"Neither the one nor the other," said the doctor. "Now I'll tell you two something that I shall make public presently: a man cannot point a pistol at himself from a greater distance than two feet at the outside; but this shot was fired at three times that range!"

"How can you tell, sir?" asked Pinckney, with added awe and subtracted vehemence.

"The clothes are not singed; the hole might have been made by a drill, it was so clean."

The young man sat in silent wonder. Then Dick put a last question:

"You think it has been—murder?"

"Personally, I am convinced of it. We shall say all we know, and get an adjournment. At the adjourned inquest Colonel Bristo will attend, and tell us his relations with the dead man, who, it appears, had no other friend in the country; but to-day that is not absolutely necessary, and I shall explain his absence myself. Meanwhile, detectives will be sent down, and will find out nothing at all, and the affair will end in a verdict against some person or persons unknown, at best."

Dr. Mowbray's first prediction was forthwith fulfilled: the inquest was adjourned. The doctor at once drove back to Gateby with the two young men. As they drove slowly down the last hill they descried two strangers, in overcoats and hard hats, conversing with Colonel Bristo in the road. Philip Robson was standing by, talking to no one, and looking uncomfortable.

When the shorter of the two strangers turned his face to the gig, Dick ejaculated his surprise—for it was the rough, red, good-humoured face of the Honourable Stephen Biggs.

"What has brought you here?" Dick asked in a low voice when he had greeted the legislator.

By way of reply, Biggs introduced him to the tall, grave, black-bearded, sharp-featured gentleman—Sergeant Compton, late of the Victorian Mounted Police.

There was an embarrassed silence; then Philip Robson stepped forward.

"It was my doing," he said, awkwardly enough; and he motioned Dick to follow him out of hearing of the others. "I listened," he then confessed, "to a conversation between you and Miles. I heard you read a letter aloud. From what passed between you, I gathered that Miles was a blackleg of some kind, whom you were screening from the police. Miles found that I had overheard you, and swore to me that you were the victim of a delusion. When I reflected, I disbelieved him utterly. I copied the address of the letter you had written, and the next day I wrote myself to Mr. Biggs, describing Miles as well as I could, and saying where he was. I did not dream that Miles was a bushranger, even then—I thought he was merely a common swindler. However, that's the whole truth. Edmonstone, I'm sorry!"

Dick's first expression of contempt had vanished. Frank admissions turn away wrath more surely than soft answers. Besides, Robson had behaved well yesterday: without him, what might not have happened before Dr. Mowbray arrived?

"I believe," said Dick, "that you were justified in what you did, only—I'm sorry you did it."

Mr. Biggs was in close conversation with Colonel Bristo. Sergeant Compton stood aloof, silent and brooding; in the hour of triumph Death had baulked him of his quarry; his dark face presented a study in fierce melancholy.

"If only," the Colonel was saying piteously, "the tragedy could stop at the name of Miles! The scandal that will attach to us when the whole sensation comes to light is difficult to face. For my part, I would face it cheerfully if it were not—if it were not for my daughter Alice. And, after all, it may not annoy her. She may not live to hear it."

The last words were broken and hardly intelligible.

The rugged face of Stephen Biggs showed honest concern, and honest sympathy too. It did not take him long to see the case from the Colonel's point of view, and he declared very bluntly that, for his part, he would be glad enough to hush the thing up, so far as the dead man's past life was concerned (and here Mr. Biggs jingled handfuls of coins in his pockets), but that, unfortunately, it did not rest with him.

"You see, Colonel," he explained, "my mate here he's been on Ned Ryan's trail, off and on, these four years. Look at him now. He's just mad at being cheated in the end. But he's one of the warmest traps in this Colony—I mean out in Vic.; and, mark me, he'll take care to let the whole Colony know that, if he warn't in at Sundown's death, he was nearer it than any other blessed 'trap.' There's some personal feeling in it, Colonel," said Biggs, lowering his voice. "Frank Compton has sworn some mighty oath or other to take Ned Ryan alive or dead."

"Suppose," said the Colonel, "we induce your friend here to hold his tongue, do you think it would be possible for us to let this poor fellow pass out of the world as Miles, a squatter, or, at worst, an unknown adventurer?"

"How many are there of you, Colonel, up here who know?"

"Four."

"And there are two of us. Total six men in the world who know that Ned Ryan, the bushranger, died yesterday. The rest of the world believes that he was drowned in the Channel three months ago. Yes, I think it would be quite possible. Moreover, I don't see that it would do the least good to any one to undeceive the rest of the world; but Frank Compton—"

"Is he the only detective after Miles in this country?"

"The only one left. The others went back to Australia, satisfied that their man was drowned."

"But our police—"

"Oh, your police are all right, Colonel. They've never so much as heard of Sundown. They're easily pleased, are your police!"

It was at this point that Dr. Mowbray reappeared on the steps. Colonel Bristo went at once to learn his report, which must have been no worse than that of the early morning, for it was to speak of the inquest that the Colonel hurried back the moment the doctor drove away.

"Dick," said he, in a voice that all could hear (Edmonstone was still talking to Robson—Compton still standing aloof), "you never told me the result. The inquest is adjourned; but there is a strong impression it seems that it is not a case of suicide after all, gentlemen—but one of wilful murder."

The personal bias mentioned by Biggs had not altogether extinguished ordinary professional instincts in the breast of Sergeant Compton; for, at this, his black eyes glittered, and he pulled his patron aside.

Biggs, in his turn, sought a private word with the Colonel.

"Compton," he said, "is bent on at once seeing the spot where Ryan was shot. Will you send some one with us? I'll bring my man back this evening, and we'll try to talk him over between us; but I fear it's hopeless."

Between three and four that afternoon the body of Jem Pound was found at the bottom of the cliff, a mile from Melmerbridge, among the fir-trees.

Between eight and nine that evening, in the little gun-room at the shooting-box, Biggs—in the presence of Colonel Bristo—made a last effort to induce Sergeant Compton to join the conspiracy of silence regarding the identity of Miles, the Australian adventurer, now lying dead at Melmerbridge, with Sundown, the Australian bushranger, supposed to have been drowned in the Channel in the previous April. All to no purpose. The Sergeant remained obdurate.

"Mr. Biggs," said he, "and you, sir, I must declare to you firmly and finally that it is impossible for me to hold my tongue in a case like this. I will not speak of fairness and justice, for I agree that no one will be a bit the better off for knowing that Ned Ryan died yesterday instead of last spring. I will be perfectly candid. I will ask you to think for a moment what this means to me. It means this: when I get back to Melbourne I will be worth twice what I was before I sailed. The fact of having been the only man to disbelieve in Ryan's drowning, and the fact of having as near as a touch taken both Ryan and Pound alive, will make my fortune for me out there."

Honest Biggs rattled the coins in his pockets, and seemed about to speak.

"No, sir," said Compton, turning to his patron. "My silence won't be given—it cannot be bought. I have another reason for telling everything: my hatred for Ned Ryan—that death cannot cool!"

These words Compton hissed out in a voice of low, concentrated passion.

"I have not dogged him all these years for mere love of the work. No! He brought disgrace upon me and mine, and I swore to take him alive or dead. I keep my oath—I take him dead! All who know me shall know that I have kept my oath! As for Jem Pound, his mate and his murderer—"

The door opened, and the nurse stood panting on the threshold. Even in her intense excitement she remembered that she had left her charge sleeping lightly, and her words were low:

"What is it you say? Do you say that Jem Pound murdered my husband?" Colonel Bristo and the Sergeant started simultaneously. "Well, I might have known that—I might have told you that. But upstairs—I have been forgetting! I have been forgetting—forgetting! Yet when I heard you gentlemen come in here I remembered, and it was to tell you what I knew about Jem Pound that I came down."

Sergeant Compton had turned an ashen grey; his eyes never moved from the face of the woman from the moment she entered the room. Elizabeth Ryan crossed the room and stood in front of him. His face was in shadow.

"You, sir—I heard your voice as my hand was on the door-handle; and I seemed to know your voice; and, while I stood trying to remember whose voice it was, I heard what you said. So you will not let the dead man rest! So, since he escaped you by his death, you would bring all the world to hoot over his grave! Oh, sir, if the prayers of his wife—his widow—"

She stopped. The man had risen unsteadily from his chair. His face was close to hers. She sprang back as though shot.

Sergeant Compton whispered one word: "Liz!"

Biggs and the Colonel watched the pale dark woman and the dark pale man in silent wonder. There was a likeness between man and woman.

"Liz!" repeated the Sergeant in a low, hoarse voice.

"Who—who are you? Are you—are you—"

"I am Frank!"

"Frank!" she whispered to herself, unable to realise all at once who Frank had been—it was so long since there had been a Frank in her life. "What!" she exclaimed in a whisper; "not my brother Frank?"

"Yes, your brother Frank. But—but I thought you were out there, Liz. I thought he had long ago deserted you; and that made me thirst all the more—"

His sister flung herself at his feet.

"Oh, Frank! Frank!" she wailed. "Since the day I married I have spoken to none of my own kith and kin until this night. And this is how we meet! Frank!—Frank!"—her voice fell to a tremulous whisper—"do one thing for me, and then, if you are still so bitter against me, go away again. Only one thing I ask—a promise. Promise, for your part, to keep silence! Let the dead man—let the dead man sleep peacefully. If the whole truth will come out, come out it must; but don't let it be through you, Frank—never let it be through you! Speak. Do you promise?"

The low, tearful, plaintive tones ceased, and there was silence in the room. Then Francis Compton bent down, and lifted his sister Elizabeth in his arms.

"I promise," he whispered in a broken voice. "God knows you have suffered enough!"

CHAPTER XXXII

SUSPENSE: REACTION

Days of suspense followed, while Alice's life trembled in the balance. In what way these days were passed the watchers themselves scarcely knew: for it is among the offices of suspense to make word and deed mechanical, and life a dream. The senses are dulled; nothing is realised—not even death itself, when death comes. Afterwards you remember with horror your callousness: when all the time your senses have been dulled by the most merciful of Nature's laws. Afterwards you find that you received many an impression without knowing it. Thus Dick Edmonstone, for one, recalled a few things that he had quite forgotten, on his way south in the train afterwards.

He could feel again the wind lifting the hair from his head on the dark hilltop. He saw the crescent moon racing through foamy billows of clouds, like a dismasted ship before the wind. He felt the rushing air as he sped back to the post in the lonely road from which he watched all night that square of yellow light— the light through her window-blind. This faint yellow light shot beams of hope into his heart through the long nights; he watched it till dawn, and then crept wearily to his bed in the inn. When he roamed away from it, a superstitious dread seized him that he would return to find the light gone out for ever. The pale, faint light became to him an emblem of the faint, flickering life that had burnt so low. He would wildly hurry back, with death at his heart. Thank God! the light still burned.

In memory he could hear his own voice treating with a carter for a load of straw. He was again laying down with his own hands the narrow road with this straw; he was sitting half the day at his post in the gap of the hedge, watching her window; he was tasting again of the delight with which he watched the first vehicle crawl noiselessly across that straw.

These were among his most vivid recollections; but voices came back to him plainest of all.

The voices of the professional nurses, whispering where they little dreamt there was a listener; foreboding the worst; comparing notes with their last fatal cases; throwing into their tones a kind of pity worse than open indifference—perfunctory and cold. Or, again, these same voices telling how a certain name was always on the feverish lips upstairs.

"Ah, poor soul!" said they; "she thinks of nothing but him!"

Of whom? Whose name was for ever on her lips? The name of him to whom she had breathed her last conscious words?

Even so; for another voice had echoed through the silent house more than once, and could never be forgotten by those who heard it; the piercing, heart-rending, delirious voice of Alice herself, reiterating those last conscious words of hers:

"Hear what it was he said to me, and my answer—which is my answer still!"

What had Miles said? What had been Alice's answer? Who would ever know? Not Dick; and these words came back to him more often than any others, and they tortured him.

But there were other words—words that had been spoken but yesterday, and as yet seemed too good to be true; the words of the kind old country doctor:

"She is out of danger!"

And now Dick Edmonstone was being whirled back to London. Alice was declared out of danger, so he had come away. Alice was not going to die. Her young life was spared. Then why was Dick's heart not filled with joy and thanksgiving? Perhaps it was; but why did he not show it? He who had been frenzied by her peril, should have leapt or wept for joy at her safety. He did neither. He could show no joy. Why not?

Edmonstone arrived in town, and broke his fast at an hotel—he had travelled all night. After breakfast he drove, with his luggage, first to the offices of the P. and O. Company in Leadenhall Street. He stepped from that office with a brisker air; something was off his mind; something was definitely settled. On his way thence to Waterloo he whistled lively tunes in the cab. By the time he reached Teddington and Iris Lodge, the jauntiness of his manner was complete. In fact, his manner was so entirely different from what his mother and Fanny had been prepared for, that the good ladies were relieved and delighted beyond measure for the first few minutes, until a something in his tone pained them both.

"Oh yes," he said, carelessly, in answer to their hushed inquiry, "she is out of danger now, safe enough. It has been touch and go, though."

He might have been speaking of a horse or dog, and yet have given people the impression that he was a young man without much feeling.

"But—my boy," cried Mrs. Edmonstone, "what has been the matter with you? We never heard that you were ill; and you look like a ghost, my poor Dick!"

Dick was standing in rather a swaggering attitude on the hearthrug. He wheeled round, and looked at himself in the large glass over the chimneypiece. His face was haggard and lined, and his expression just then was not a nice one.

"Why," he owned, with a grating laugh, "I certainly don't look very fit, now you mention it, do I? But it's all on the surface. I'm all right, bless you! I'm not on speaking terms with the sexton yet, anyway!"

A tear stood in each of Mrs. Edmonstone's dark eyes. Fanny frowned, and beat her foot impatiently upon the carpet. What had come over Dick?

He must have known perfectly well the utter falsity of the mask he was wearing; if not, self-deception was one of his accomplishments. Or perhaps those tears in his mother's eyes caused a pang of shame to shoot through him. In any case, he made a hasty effort to change his tone.

"How are you two? That is the main point with me. Bother my seediness!"

"We are always well," sighed Mrs. Edmonstone.

"And Maurice?"

"Maurice was never brisker."

"Lucky dog!" said Dick, involuntarily; and the bitterness was back in his tone before he knew it.

"Your friend Mr. Flint," said Mrs. Edmonstone, "is Maurice's friend now, and Mr. Flint finds all his friends in good spirits."

"Do you mean to say old Jack is doing the absentee landlord altogether? Did he never go back?"

"Yes. But he is over again—he is in town just now," said Mrs. Edmonstone.

"He's fast qualifying for buckshot, that fellow," said Dick, with light irony.

"I rather fancy," observed Fanny, with much indifference, "that you will see him this evening. I half think he is coming back with Maurice." And Miss Fanny became profoundly interested in the world out of the window.

"Good!" cried Dick; and there was a ring of sincerity in that monosyllable which ought to have made it appreciated—as much as a diamond in a dustheap!

In a little while Dick went up to his room. He had letters to write, he said; but he was heard whistling and singing as he unpacked his portmanteau. Neither of the ladies saw much more of him that day. They sat together in wretched silence; there was some constraint between them; they felt hurt, but were too proud to express the feeling even to each other. The fact was, they did not quite know why they felt hurt. Dick had greeted them kindly enough—it was only that there was a something in his manner which they didn't like and could not understand. And so both these women longed heartily for evening, and the coming of Maurice and merry Mr. Flint—Fanny, however, the more heartily of the two.

Maurice and Flint did come—in excellent time, too; and it so happened that when the little table-gong rang out its silvery call, Mr. Flint and Miss Edmonstone were still perambulating the dewy, twilit tennis-court. It further happened, in spite of the last-mentioned fact, that Miss Fanny contrived to reach the drawing-room before her mother was finally disentangled from the wools and needles that beset her at most hours of the day; that mother and daughter were the last to enter the little dining-room, hand in hand; that Miss Fanny looked uncommonly radiant, and that the usual stupid tears were standing in gentle Mrs. Edmonstone's soft, loving eyes.

Dick was unusually brilliant in his old place at the head of the table—so brilliant that his friend Flint was taken by surprise, and, for his own part, silenced; though it is true that the latter had something on his mind which would have made him, in any case, worse company than usual. Dick rattled on incessantly, about the dales, and the moors, and the grouse, as though his stay in Yorkshire was associated with no tragedy, and no sickness nigh unto death. His mood, indeed, was not taken up by the others, but he did not seem to notice or to mind that; only when he was quiet, all were quiet, and the sudden silences were embarrassing to all save their prime author.

The longest and most awkward of these pauses occurred while the crumbs were being removed. When the maid had withdrawn, Dick drank of his wine, refilled his glass, held it daintily by the stem between finger and thumb, leant back in his chair, and proceeded deliberately to break the spell.

"Ladies and gentlemen," he began, speaking the trite words in the same disagreeable tone that had pained the ladies that morning, "I am going to make you a little speech; a very little one, mind, so don't look uncomfortable—you needn't even feel it."

He glanced from one to another of them. They did look uncomfortable; they felt that somehow Dick was not himself; they heartily wished he would be quiet. His manner was not the manner to carry off a sneer as so much pleasantry.

Dick continued:

"All good things must come to an end, you know—and, in fact, that's my very original text. Now look at me, please—mother, look at your sheep that was lost: thanks. You will, perhaps, agree with me that I'm hardly the fellow I was when I landed; the fact being that this beautiful British climate is playing old Harry with me, and—all good things come to an end. If I may class myself among the good things for a moment—for argument's sake—it seems to me that one good thing will come to an end pretty soon. Look at me—don't you think so?"

The wretched smile that crossed his lean, pale face was not at variance with his words. He was much altered. His cheeks were sunken and bloodless, dark only under the eyes. His eyes to-night were unnaturally bright. His lips too were bloodless; to-night they were quivering incessantly. His question was left unanswered, as he meant that it should be. Flint was trying mentally to compute the quantity of wine his friend might possibly have taken; the others could not have spoken at that moment even if they would.

"Now," continued Dick, still toying with his wine, "the country I left a few months ago never allows a man to fall into my unhappy plight. It puts a man in good health at the beginning, and keeps him in it to the end, somewhere in the nineties. Why, Maurice, if he went out there, would find that he has never known what health is! Fanny, we know, is a hardy plant, and would thrive anywhere; yet she was made for the life out there, if girl ever was. As for you, mother, it would clap twenty years on to your dear old life—no, it would make you twenty years younger. No one who has once lived there will live anywhere else. Even old Flint here is dying to go back; he confessed as much last month. Now what I say is this: all good things, etcetera—England among them. Therefore let us all go out there together, and live happily ever afterwards! Stop; hear me out, all of you: it's arranged already—I go out first, to stock the station, and all the rest of it. The fact is, I booked my passage this morning! Come, you have had good patience; my speech, like better 'good things,' has come to an end!"

His tone had changed from half-jest to whole earnest—from earnestness to ardour—from ardour to something bordering on defiance. But, with the last word scarcely out of his mouth, he checked himself, and ejaculated below his breath: "Good heavens!"

Mrs. Edmonstone had rushed sobbing from the room.

No one followed her. The others stared blankly, then indignantly, at Dick, in whose face concern began to show itself. Then young Maurice spoke up.

"If I were you," he said hotly to his brother, "I'd go after her, and tell her you have taken too much wine, and beg her pardon for making a fool of yourself!"

Dick darted an angry glance at him, but rose and stalked from the room. In point of fact, the wine had not had much to do with it—no more and no less than it has to do with anybody's after-dinner speech. At the same time, Dick had not been altogether in his right senses, either then or any time that day. He found his mother weeping as though her heart would break; whereat his own heart smote him so that he came to his senses there and then, and knelt in humility and shame at her feet.

"Dearest mother, forgive me!" he murmured again and again, and took her hand in his and kissed it.

"But are you—are you really going back—back over the seas?" she sobbed.

"Yes. I can't help it, mother! No one knows how miserable I have been over here. Forgive me—forgive me—but I can't stay! I can't indeed! But—but you shall come out too, and the others; and your life will be happier than it has been for years, once you are used to it."

Mrs. Edmonstone shook her head.

"No; it is impossible," she said with sudden decision.

"How so? Both Fanny and Maurice, once when I sounded them—"

"Fanny will never go, and I cannot leave her."

"Why? Mother dear, what do you mean?"

"I mean that your sister is going to be married."

Married! The mere word ought not to have cut him to the heart; yet, in the state that he was in then, it did. He rose uncertainly to his feet.

"You take my breath away, mother! I know of nothing. Whom is it to?"

"Can you ask?"

"I cannot guess."

"Then it is to your friend, Mr.—no, Jack—Jack Flint."

"God bless old Jack!"

That was what Dick said upon the instant. Then he stood silent. And then—Dick sank into a chair, and laid his face upon his hands.

"I can go out alone," he whispered. "And—and I wish them joy; from my heart I do! I will go and tell them so."

CHAPTER XXXIII

The month was October; the day Dick's last in England. Both the day and the month were far spent: in an hour or two it would be dark, in a week or so it would be November. This time to-morrow the R.M.S. Rome, with Dick on board, would be just clear of the Thames; this time next month she would be ploughing through the Indian Ocean, with nothing but Australia to stop her.

"Last days," as a rule, are made bearable by that blessed atmosphere of excitement which accompanies them, and is deleterious to open sentiment. That excitement, however, is less due to the mere fact of impending departure than to the providential provision of things to be done and seen to at the last moment. An uncomfortable "rush" is the best of pain-killers when it comes to long farewells. The work, moreover, should be for all hands, and last to the very end; then there is no time for lamentation—no time until the boxes are out of the hall and the cab has turned the corner, and the empty, untidy room has to be set to rights. Then, if you like, is the time for tears.

Now Dick had made a great mistake. He had booked his passage too far in advance. For six weeks he had nothing to think of but his voyage; nothing to do but get ready. Everything was prearranged; nothing, in this exceptional case, was left to the last, the very luggage being sent to the boat before the day of sailing. If Dick had deliberately set himself to deepen the gloom that shadowed his departure, he could not have contrived things better. Maurice, for instance, with great difficulty obtained a holiday from the bank because it was Dick's last day. He might just as well have stopped in the City. There was nothing for him to do. The day wore on in dismal idleness.

About three in the afternoon Dick left the house. He was seen by the others from the front windows. The sight of him going out without a look or a word on his last day cut them to the heart, though Dick had been everything that was kind, and thoughtful, and affectionate since that evening after his return from Yorkshire. Besides, the little family was going to be broken up completely before long: Fanny was to be married in the spring. No wonder they were sad.

Dick turned to the right, walked towards the river, turned to the right again, and so along the London road towards the village.

"It is the right thing," he kept assuring himself, and with such frequency that one might have supposed it was the wrong thing; "it is the right thing, after all, to go and say good-bye. I should have done it before, and got it over. I was a fool to think of shirking it altogether; that would have been behaving like a boor. Well, I'll just go in naturally, say good-bye all round, stop a few minutes, and then hurry back home. A month ago I couldn't have trusted myself, but now—"

It was a joyless smile that ended the unspoken sentence. The last month had certainly strengthened his self-control; it had also hardened and lined his face in a way that did not improve his good looks. Yes, he was pretty safe in trusting himself now.

At the corner opposite the low-lying old churchyard he hesitated. He had hesitated at that corner once before. He remembered the other occasion with peculiar vividness to-day. Why should he not repeat the performance he had gone through then? Why should he not take a boat and row up to Graysbrooke? An admirable idea! It harmonised so completely with his humour. It was the one thing wanting to complete the satire of his home-coming. That satire had been so thoroughly bitter that it would be a pity to deny it a finishing touch or two. Besides, it was so fitting in every way: the then and the now offered a contrast that it would be a shame not to make the most of. Then, thought Dick, his foolish hopes had been as fresh and young and bright as the June leaves. Look at his bare heart now! look at the naked trees! Hopes and leaves had gone the same way—was it the way of all hopes as well as of all leaves? His mind, as well as his eye, saw everything in autumnal tints. Nor did he shirk the view. There is a stage of melancholy that rather encourages the cruel contrasts of memory.

"I'll row up," said Dick, "and go through it all again. Let it do its worst, it won't touch me now—therefore nothing will ever touch me as long as I live. A good test!"

He did row up, wearing the same joyless smile.

He stood the test to perfection.

He did not forget to remember anything. He gave sentimentality a princely chance to play the mischief with him. It was a rough and gusty day, but mild for the time of year; a day of neither sunshine nor rain, but plenty of wind and clouds; one of those blustering fellows, heralds of Winter, that come and abuse Autumn for neglecting her business, and tear off the last of the leaves for her with unseemly violence and haste. The current was swift and strong, and many a crisp leaf of crimson and amber and gold sailed down its broad fretted surface, to be dashed over the weir and ripped into fragments in the churning froth below.

Dick rowed into the little inlet with the white bridge across it, landed, and nodded, in the spirit, to a hundred spots marked in his mind by the associations of last June; those of an older day were not thought of. Here was the place where Alice's boat had been when he had found her reading a magazine—and interrupted her reading—on the day after his return. There were the seven poplars, in whose shadows he had found Miles on the night of the ball, when the miscreant Pound came inquiring for him. There was the window through which he, Dick, had leapt after that final scene—final in its results—with Alice in the empty ballroom. A full minute's contemplation and elaborate, cold-blooded recollection failed to awake one pang—it may be that, to a certain quality of pain, Dick's sense had long been deadened. Then he walked meditatively to the front of the house, and rang the bell—a thing he was not sure that he had ever done before at this house.

Colonel Bristo was out, but Mrs. Parish was in. Dick would see Mrs. Parish; he would be as civil to his old enemy as to the rest of them; why not?

But Mrs. Parish received him in a wondrous manner; remorse and apology—nothing less—were in the tones of her ricketty voice and the grasp of her skinny hand. The fact was, those weeks in Yorkshire had left their mark upon the old lady. They had left her older still, a little less worldly, a little more sensible, and humbler by the possession of a number of uncomfortable regrets. She had heard of Dick's probable return to Australia, long ago; but her information had been neither definite nor authentic. When he now told her that he was actually to sail the next day, the old woman was for the moment visibly affected. She felt that here there was a new and poignant regret in store for her—one that would probably haunt her for the rest of her days. At this rate life would soon become unbearable. It is a terrible thing to become suddenly soft-hearted in your old age!

"Colonel Bristo is out," said Mrs. Parish, with a vague feeling that made matters worse. "You will wait and see him, of course? I am sure he will not be long; and then, you know, you must say good-bye to Alice—she will be shocked when you tell her."

"Alice?" said Dick, unceremoniously, as became such a very old friend of the family. "I hope so—yes, of course. Where is she?"

"She is in the dining-room. She spends her days there."

"How is she?" Dick asked, with less indifference in his manner.

"Better; but not well enough to stand a long journey, or else her father would have taken her to the south of France before this. Come and see her. She will be so pleased—but so grieved when she hears you are going out again. I am sure she has no idea of such a thing. And to-morrow, too!"

Dick followed Mrs. Parish from the room, wishing in his heart that convalescence was a shorter business, or else that Alice might have the advantages of climate that in a few days, and for evermore, would be his; also speculating as to whether he would find her much changed, but wishing and wondering without the slightest ruffling emotion. He had some time ago pronounced himself a cure. Therefore, of course, he was cured.

There were two fireplaces in the dining-room, one on each side of the conservatory door. In the grate nearer the windows, which were all at one end, overlooking lawn and river, a fire of wood and coal was burning brightly. In a long low structure of basketwork—half-sofa, half-chair, such as one mostly sees on shipboard and in verandahs—propped up by cushions and wrapped in plaids and woollen clouds, lay Alice, the convalescent. There was no sign that she had been reading. She did not look as though she had been sleeping. If, then, it was her habit to encourage the exclusive company of her own thoughts, it is little wonder that she was so long in parting company with her weakness.

Dick stood humbly and gravely by the door; a thrill of sorrow shot through him on seeing her lying there like that; the sensation was only natural.

"Here is Mr. Richard come to—to—to ask you how you are," stammered poor Mrs. Parish.

Alice looked up sharply. Mr. Richard crossed the room and held out his hand with a smile.

"I hope from my heart that you are better—that you will very soon be quite better."

"Thank you. It was kind of you to come. Yes, indeed, I am almost well now. But it has been a long business."

Her voice was weak, and the hand she held out to him seemed so thin and wasted that he took it as one would handle a piece of dainty, delicate porcelain. Her hair, too, was cut short like a boy's. This was as much as he noticed at the moment. The firelight played so persistently upon her face that, for aught he could tell, she might be either pale as death or bathed in blushes. For the latter, however, he was not in the least on the look-out.

"Won't you sit down?" said Alice. "Papa will come in presently, and he will be so pleased to see you; and you will take tea with us. Have you been away?"

"No," said Dick, feeling awkward because he had made no inquiries personally since the return of the Bristos from Yorkshire, now some days back. "But I have been getting ready to go." He put down his hat on the red baize cover of the big table, and sat down a few chairs further from Alice than he need have done.

"What a capital time to go abroad," said Alice, "just when everything is becoming horrid in England! We, too, are waiting to go; it is I that am the stumbling-block."

So she took it that he was only going on the Continent. Better enlighten her at once, thought Dick. Mrs. Parish had disappeared mysteriously from the room.

"This time to-morrow," Dick accordingly said, "I shall be on board the Rome."

The effect of this statement upon Alice was startling.

"What!" cried she, raising herself a few inches in suddenly aroused interest. "Are you going to see them off?"

"See whom off?" Dick was mystified.

"My dear good nurse—the first and the best of my nurses—and her brother the Sergeant."

"Do you mean Compton?"

"Yes. They sail in the Rome to-morrow."

"So the brother," Dick thought to himself, "is taking the sister back to her own people, to be welcomed and forgiven, and to lead a better kind of life. Poor thing! poor thing! Perhaps her husband's death was the best thing that could have befallen her. She will be able to start afresh. She is a widow now."

Aloud, he only said: "I am glad—very glad to hear it."

"Did you know," said Alice, seeing that he was thinking more than he said, "that she was a widow?"

"Yes," said Dick.

It was plain to him that Alice did not know whose widow the poor woman was. She suspected no sort of bond between the woman who had nursed her and the man who had made love to her. She did not know the baseness of that love on his part. This was as it should be. She must never suspect; she must never, never know.

"Yes," said Dick slowly, "I knew that."

"Oh!" cried out Alice. "How dreadful it all was! How terrible!"

"Ay," said Dick, gravely; "it was that indeed."

There was a pause between them. It was Alice who broke it.

"Dick," she said frankly—and honest shame trembled through her utterance—"I want to ask your pardon for something—no, you shall not stop me! I want to tell you that I am sorry for having said something—something that I just dimly remember saying, but something that I know was monstrous and inexcusable. It was just before—but I was accountable enough to know better. Ah! I see you remember; indeed, you could never forget—please—please—try to forgive!"

Dick felt immensely uneasy.

"Say no more, Alice. I deserved it all, and more besides. I was fearfully at fault. I should never have approached you as I did, my discovery once made. I shall never forgive myself for all that has happened. But he took me in—he took me in, up there, playing the penitent thief, the—poor fellow!"

His voice dropped, his tone changed: many things came back to him in a rush.

"Papa has told me the whole history of the relations between you," Alice said quietly, "and we think you behaved nobly."

"There was precious little nobility in it," Dick said grimly. Nor was there any mock modesty in this. He knew too well that he had done nothing to be proud of.

There was another pause. Dick broke this one.

"Forgive me," he said, "if I refer to anything very painful, but I am going away to-morrow, and—there was something else you said, just after you administered that just rebuke to me. You said you would tell us what Miles had said to you. Now I do not mean it as presumption, but we are old friends"—she winced—"and I have rather suspected that he made some confession to you which he never made to anyone else. There was a lot of gold—"

Alice interrupted him in a low voice.

"I would rather not tell you what he said; it was nothing to do with anything of that kind."

Dick's question had not been unpremeditated. He had had his own conviction as to the "confession" Alice had listened to; he only wanted that conviction confirmed. Now, by her hesitation and her refusal to answer, it was confirmed. Miles had proposed marriage on the way from Melmerbridge Church, and been accepted! Well, it was a satisfaction to have that put beyond doubt. He had put his question in rather an underhand way, but how was he to do otherwise? He had got his answer; the end justified the means.

"Pray don't say another word," said Dick impulsively. "Forgive me for prying. Perhaps I can guess what he said."

Alice darted at him a swift glance, and saw his meaning in a flash.

"Do not get up," said she quietly, for Dick was rising to go. "Since it is possible that you may guess wrong, I will tell you all. I insist in telling you all! Here, then, are the facts: Mr. Miles scarcely spoke a word on the way from church, until suddenly, when we were almost in sight of home, he—he caught hold of my hand."

Dick knew that already. He was also quite sure that he knew what was coming. It was no use Alice going on; he could see that she was nervous and uncomfortable over it; he reproached himself furiously for making her so; he made a genuine effort to prevail upon her to say no more. In vain; for now Alice was determined. Seeing that it was so, he got up from his chair and walked over to the windows, and watched the brown leaves being whisked about the lawn and the sky overhead turning a deeper grey.

Alice continued in a voice that was firm for all its faintness:

"I suppose I looked surprised, and taken aback, and indignant, but he held my hand as if his was a vice, and still we walked on. Then I looked at him, and he was pale. Then he stared down upon me, closely and long, as if he meant to read my soul, and a great shudder seemed to pass through him. He almost flung my hand away from him, and faced me in the road. We were then on that little bridge between two hills, not far from the shooting-box: you will remember it. 'Miss Alice,' he said, 'I am a villain! a scoundrel! an impostor. I have never been fit to speak to you, and I have dared to take your hand. But I find I am a shade less black than I thought myself a minute ago; for what I meant to say to you I would not say now to save my soul, if I had one! Good-bye; you will see no more of me. Whatever you may one day hear of me—and you must believe it all, for it is every word true—remember this: that, bad as I still am, I am less bad than I was before I knew you, and I have found it out this instant. Go, leave me, run home; you shall never see me again. I shall go at once from this place, and I leave England in two days. Do you hear? Go, leave me alone—go! And God go with you!' His voice was breaking, his wild looks frightened me, but I answered him. I had my suspicions, as I told him, but I did not tell him that you put them into my head. What I did say to him was this: 'Whatever you have done, whatever you may do, you did one thing once that can never, never grow less in my eyes!' I meant his saving of my father's life; and with that I ran away from him and never looked round. That is every word that passed. I can never forget them. As to what happened afterwards, you know more than I."

Alice's own voice shook; it was hollow, and hoarse, and scarcely audible at the end. As for Dick, he stood looking out of the window at the whirling leaves, with not a word to say, until an involuntary murmur escaped him.

"Poor Miles!"

The girl's answer was a low sob.

Then here was the truth at last. The innocence and purity of the young English girl had awed and appalled that bold, desperate, unscrupulous man at the last moment. On the brink of the worst of all his crimes his nerve had failed him, or, to do him better justice, his heart had smitten him. Yes, it must have been this, for the poor fellow loved her well. His last thought was of her, his last, dying effort was for her, his life's blood ran out of him in her service!

But Alice! Had she not loved him when he spoke? Had she not given her heart to him in the beginning? Had she not tacitly admitted as much in this very room? Then her heart must be his still; her heart must be his for ever—dead or living, false or true, villain or hero. Poor Alice! What a terrible thing for a girl to have so misplaced her love. Dick felt his heart bleeding for her, but what could he do? He could do nothing but go back to Australia, and pray that some day she might get over it and be consoled. Now that he thought of it, he had not told her about Australia. He had tried twice, and each time been interrupted. It must be done now.

"By-the-bye," he began (it was after a long silence, and the room was filled with dusk, and the fire burning low), "I didn't tell you, after all, how it is that I shall be aboard the Rome this time to-morrow. It is not to see off Compton and his sister, because until you told me I didn't know they were going. Can't you guess the reason?"

"No!"

What could be the meaning of that quick gasp from the other side of the room that preceded the faint monosyllable?

"I will tell you: it is because I sail for Australia myself to-morrow! I am going back to the bush."

There was a slight shiver of the basketwork chair. Then all was still; and Dick watched evening gather over the flat Ham fields across the river. The next tones from near the fireplace had a steely ring about them.

"Why are you going back?"

"Because I have found England intolerable."

"I thought you were going to get on so well in England?"

"So did I."

Another silence. Dick drummed idly upon the pane with his fingers. There was certainly a degree of regret in Alice's tone—enough to afford him a vague sense of gratitude to her.

"Is it not a terrible disappointment to your family?"

"I suppose it is," said Dick uneasily.

"And can you lightly grieve those who love you?"

She spoke as earnestly as though she belonged to that number herself; but, thought Dick, that must be from the force of her woman's sympathy for women. There was a slight catch in her voice, doubtless from the same cause. Could it be from any other cause? Dick trembled in the dusk by the window at the thought. No; it could not be. No; he did not wish it. He would not have her relent now. It was too late. He had set his mind on going; his passage was booked, his luggage was on board; nothing could unsettle him now. Was it not admitted in the beginning that he was an obstinate fellow? Besides, hope had been out of the range of his vision these many weeks. When a faint spark of hope burned on the horizon, was it natural that he should detect it at once? Yet her tones made him tremble.

As for Alice, her heart was beating with wild, sickening thuds. She felt that she was receiving her just deserts. Dick was as cold to her now as she had been cold to Dick before; only far colder, for she had but been trying him. Ah! but Nemesis was cruel in her justice! And she, Alice, so faint, so weary, so heartsick, so loveless, so full of remorse, so ready to love! And this the last chance of all!

"Is there nothing that could stop you from going now?"

"Nothing."

"Nothing at all?"

"No consideration upon earth!"

"Ah, you have taken your passage!"

"That's not it!"

He was indignant. A paltry seventy guineas!

"Then what is? It must be that you've made up your mind, and would not unmake it—no matter who asked you."

The slightest stress imaginable was laid upon the relative.

Dick was leaning against the window-ledge for support. His brain was whirling. He could scarcely believe his ears. There was a tearful tenderness in her voice which he could not, which he dared not understand.

"What do you mean?" he asked hoarsely.

"I mean that—that you—that I—"

The words ended in inarticulate sobs.

"Do you mean that you ask me to stay in England?"

Dick put this question in a voice that was absolutely stern, though it quivered with suppressed agitation. There was no answer: sobs were no answer. He crossed the room unsteadily, fell on his knees at her side, and took both her hands in his. Then he repeated the same question—in the same words, in the same tones.

The answer came in a trembling whisper, with a fresh torrent of tears:

"What if I did?"

"The Rome might sail without me."

A tearful incredulous smile from Alice.

"Do you tell me to stay? I stay or go at your bidding. Darling! you know what that means to us two?"

No answer.

"Speak! Speak, Alice, for I cannot bear this! The Rome would sail without me!"

Alice did speak. The Rome did sail without him.

E. W. Hornung – A Short Biography

Ernest William Hornung was born on 7th June 1866 at Cleveland Villas, Marton, Middlesbrough. He was the third son, and youngest of eight children, to John Peter Hornung and his wife Harriet née Armstrong.

By the age of 13 Hornung had joined St Ninian's Preparatory School in Moffat, Dumfriesshire before enrolling at the exclusive Uppingham School, in Rutland, in 1880.

Hornung suffered from a general state of bad health, including asthma and poor eyesight but managed to be well-liked at school and to develop a life-long passion of cricket. He loved to play despite the obvious fact that his talents were rather limited.

At 17 his health worsened, and he left Uppingham to travel to Australia, where a sunnier climate was deemed to be better for his various ailments.

Upon arriving he worked as a tutor to the Parsons family in Mossgiel, in New South Wales. As well as teaching he spent time working in remote sheep stations in the outback and began to contribute materials to the weekly magazine; The Bulletin. It was also at this time that he began work on his first novel.

After two years of very valuable life experiences Hornung returned to England in February 1886, a few months before the death of his father, in November, whose deteriorating business interests had become a constant worry.

Hornung found work in London as a journalist and story writer. In 1887 he published his first story under his own name, 'Stroke of Five', which appeared in Belgravia magazine. His work as a journalist coincided with the reign of terror brought about by Jack the Ripper's grisly murders. From this Hornung developed an interest in criminal behaviour.

He had completed the manuscript of the novel he brought back from Australia and, between July and November 1890, the story, 'A Bride from the Bush', was published in five parts in the respected Cornhill Magazine. It was released later that year in book form. This, his first novel, was well received by critics.

Hoping to further his talents in cricket Hornung, in 1891, became a member of two cricket clubs: the Idlers, whose members included Arthur Conan Doyle and Jerome K. Jerome, and the Strand club.

Hornung knew Doyle's sister, Constance ('Connie') from when he had visited Portugal. Connie was described as attractive, "with pre-Raphaelite looks ... the most sought-after of the Doyle daughters".

They were married on 27th September 1893, although Doyle was not at the wedding and relations between the two writers were occasionally difficult. The Hornung's had their only child, a son, Arthur Oscar (but always called just Oscar), in 1895.

In 1894 Doyle and Hornung began work on a play for Henry Irving, on the subject of boxing; Doyle was, at first, eager to begin and paid Hornung a £50 advance but then withdrew before the first act had been completed: the play was never finished.

Like Hornung's first novel, 'Tiny Luttrell' had Australia as a backdrop and the device of an Australian woman in a culturally alien environment. This theme ran through his next four novels: 'The Boss of Taroomba' (1894), 'The Unbidden Guest' (1894), 'Irralie's Bushranger' (1896), in this Hornung introduced the character of Stingaree, an Oxford-educated, Australian gentleman thief. In 'The Rogue's March' (1896) Hornung began to show a growing fascination with the motivation behind criminal behaviour and was sympathetic to the criminal hero as a victim of events. It was different thinking but caused some consternation for others.

In 1898 Hornung's mother died and he dedicated his next book, a series of short stories; Some Persons Unknown, to her memory.

Later that year Hornung and Connie spent six months in Posillipo, Italy. An account of this trip was published in the May 1899 issue of the Cornhill Magazine.

The fictional character Stingaree was re-written to become his most famous creation; A. J. Raffles; the gentleman thief, first used in six short stories published in 1898 in Cassell's Magazine. Modelled on George Cecil Ives, a Cambridge-educated criminologist and talented cricketer who, like Raffles, lived in the Albany, a gentlemen's only residence in Mayfair. The first tale of the series 'In the Chains of Crime' was published in June that year, titled 'The Ides of March'.

Another account adds to the richness by asserting that Raffles and his sidekick, Bunny Manders, were based not only on Doyle's Holmes and Watson but also on his friends Oscar Wilde and his lover, Lord Alfred Douglas. Whatever the exact amalgam the characters were warmly embraced by the reading public who turned it into both a popular and financial success, although some critics echoed Doyle's own fears of the dubious nature of a criminal being used as a hero.

In early 1899, the Hornung's returned to London, and resided in Pitt Street, West Kensington, for the next six years.

After publishing two novels, 'Dead Men Tell No Tales' (1899) and 'Peccavi' (1900), Hornung published a second collection of Raffles stories, 'The Black Mask', in 1901. The critics again complained about the criminal aspect. The public who bought them had no such qualms.

In 1903 Hornung collaborated with Eugène Presbrey to write a four-act play, 'Raffles, The Amateur Cracksman', which was based on two previously published short stories, 'Gentlemen and Players' and 'The Return Match'. The play was first performed at the Princess Theatre, New York, on 27th October 1903 and ran for 168 performances.

In 1905, after publishing four other books in the interim, Hornung brought back the character Stingaree. Later that year, in response to public demand he published a third collection of Raffles stories in 'A Thief in the Night', in which Manders relates some of the earlier adventures he had had with Raffles.

In 1909 the final Raffles story was published, the full-length novel 'Mr. Justice Raffles'. It was poorly received. The Observer reviewer asking if "Hornung is perhaps a little tired of Raffles".

It seems not. That same year he partnered with Charles Sansom for the play 'A Visit From Raffles', which was performed in November that year at the Brixton Empress Theatre, London.

Hornung turned away from Raffles thereafter, and in February 1911 published 'The Camera Fiend', a thriller whose narrator is an asthmatic cricket enthusiast and his attempts to photograph the soul as it leaves the body. This was followed by 'Fathers of Men' (1912) and 'The Thousandth Woman' (1913) before 'Witching Hill' (1913), a collection of eight short stories in which he introduced the characters Uvo Delavoye and the narrator Gillon. In 1914 his fictional works ceased with 'The Crime Doctor'.

His son, Oscar, left Eton College in 1914, and was due to proceed to King's College, Cambridge later that year. However, the terrors of WWI were about to unleash themselves all over Europe. Oscar volunteered, and was commissioned into the Essex Regiment. He was killed, aged a mere 20, at the Second Battle of Ypres on 6th July 1915.

Although heartbroken Hornung edited and issued privately a collection of Oscar's letters home under the title 'Trusty and Well Beloved', in 1916.

Around this time Hornung himself joined an anti-aircraft unit. He also joined the YMCA and did volunteer work in England for soldiers on leave. In March 1917 he visited France, writing a poem about his experience afterwards—something he had been doing more frequently since Oscar's death—and a collection of his war poetry, 'Ballad of Ensign Joy', was published later that year.

In July 1917 Hornung's poem, 'Wooden Crosses', was published in The Times, and in September, 'Bond and Free' appeared. A few months later he was accepted as a volunteer in a YMCA canteen and library just a few miles behind the Front Line.

Hornung was concerned about support for pacifism among troops and wrote to Connie about it. She spoke to Doyle and, rather than discussing it with Hornung, he informed the military authorities. Hornung was naturally angered by Doyle's action and relations between the two men were further strained as a result. He continued to work at the library until a German offensive overran the British positions and he was forced to retreat, firstly to Amiens and then, in April, back to England. He stayed in England until November 1918, when he again took up his YMCA duties, establishing a rest hut and library in Cologne.

In 1919 Hornung's account of his time spent in France, 'Notes of a Camp-Follower on the Western Front', was published. Doyle later wrote of the book that "there are parts of it which are brilliant in their vivid portrayal". That year Hornung also published his third and final volume of poetry, 'The Young Guard'.

Hornung finished his YMCA work and returned to England in early 1919. He worked on a new novel but was hampered by poor health. But Connie's was of greater concern. In February 1921 they took a holiday in the south of France to recuperate. Whilst travelling there on the train Hornung fell ill with a chill that progressed to influenza and finally pneumonia.

Ernest William Hornung died on 22nd March 1921, aged 54.

He was buried in Saint-Jean-de-Luz, in the south of France, in a grave adjacent to that of George Gissing.

E. W. Hornung – A Concise Bibliography

Periodicals

Stroke of Five (1887, Belgravia)
Spoilt Negative (1887, Belgravia)
Nettleship's Score (January 1890, Cornhill Magazine)
A Bride From the Bush (5 Parts. July-Nov, Cornhill Magazine, 1890)
Thunderbolt's Mate (4 Parts. March 1892, Chambers's Journal)
Kenyon's Innings (April 1892, Longman's Magazine)
The Burrawurra Brand (November 1893, The Idler)
The Unbidden Guest (6 Parts. May-Oct 1894, Longman's Magazine)
The Governess at Greenbush (4 parts. February 1895, Chambers's Journal)
After the Fact (3 Parts. January 1896, Chambers's Journal)
The Ides of March (June 1898, Cassell's Magazine)
A Villa in a Vineyard (May 1899, Cornhill Magazine)
No Sinicure: More Adventures of the Amateur Cracksman (January 1901, Scribner's Magazine)
A Jubilee Present: More Adventures of the Amateur Cracksman (February 1901, Scribner's Magazine)
The Fate of Faustina: More Adventures of the Amateur Cracksman (March 1901, Scribner's Magazine)
The Last Laugh: More Adventures of the Amateur Cracksman (April 1901, Scribner's Magazine)
To Catch a Thief: More Adventures of the Amateur Cracksman (May 1901, Scribner's Magazine)
An Old Flame: More Adventures of the Amateur Cracksman (June 1901, Scribner's Magazine)
The Wrong House: More Adventures of the Amateur Cracksman (Sept 1901, Scribner's Magazine)
Chrystal's Century (June 1903, Atlantic Monthly)
Charles Reade (June 1921, London Mercury)

Novels and Short Story Collection

A Bride from the Bush (1890) Novel
Under Two Skies (1892) Short story collection
Tiny Luttrell (1893) Novel; two volumes
The Boss of Taroomba (1894) Novel
The Unbidden Guest (1894) Novel
Irralie's Bushranger (1896) Novel
The Rogue's March: A Romance (1896) Novel
My Lord Duke (1897) Novel
Some Persons Unknown (1898) Short story collection
Young Blood (1898) Novel

The Amateur Cracksman (1899) Short story collection
Dead Men Tell No Tales (1899) Novel
The Belle of Toorak (1900) Novel; published in the US as The Shadow of a Man
Peccavi (1900) Novel
The Black Mask (1901) Short story collection; republished as Raffles: Further Adventures of the Amateur Cracksman
At Large (1902) Novel
The Shadow of the Rope (1902) Novel
Denis Dent: A Novel (1903) Novel
No Hero (1903) Novel
Stingaree (1905) Novel
A Thief in the Night (1905) Short story collection; republished as A Thief in the Night: Further Adventures of A. J. Raffles, Cricketer and Cracksman
Raffles: The Amateur Cracksman (1906) Short story collection; stories taken from The Amateur Cracksman and The Black Mask
Mr. Justice Raffles (1909) Novel
The Camera Fiend (1911) Novel
Fathers of Men (1912) Novel
The Thousandth Woman (1913) Novel
Witching Hill (1913) Short story collection
The Crime Doctor (1914) Short story collection
Old Offenders and a Few Old Scores (Published posthumously) Short story collection

Plays
Raffles, The Amateur Cracksman (27th October 1903) By Hornung and Eugéne Presbrey; first performed at the Princess Theatre, New York
Stingaree, the Bushranger (1st February 1908) First performed at the Queen's Theatre, London
A Visit From Raffles (1st November 1909) By Hornung and Charles Sansom; first performed at the Brixton Empress Theatre, London

Non-Fiction
'Trusty and Well Beloved', The Little Record of Arthur Oscar Hornung (1915) Privately published
Notes of a Camp-Follower on the Western Front (1919)

Poetry
Ballad of Ensign Joy (1917)
Wooden Cross (1918)
The Young Guard (1919)